666
GABLE WAY

DANI LAMIA

WITH FREDERICK H. CROOK

Published by:
Level 4 Press, Inc.
13518 Jamul Drive
Jamul, CA 91935
www.level4press.com

Library of Congress Control Number: 2019943929

ISBN: 978-1-933769-62-2

Printed in USA

Other books by Dani Lamia

The Raven

Demonic

Younger

Hotel California

Scavenger Hunt

Prologue

The house on Gable Way was a lone one, built upon a gentle rise of land that could scarcely be referred to as a hill. The rise was a clearing within a forest, thick and green with great, tall white oak trees. In contrast, those nearest the Victorian residence, its carriage house, and outbuildings, were thin, weak, and pale with an illness unknown. Even in ideal conditions, they could only manage to cover their spindly branches with tiny leaves of ashen green. In winter, they appeared dead.

The lawns surrounding the mansion could yield nothing healthy in appearance, and nothing at all within a yard of the home. Groundskeeper after groundskeeper had come to the residence to take on the tasks of seeding, fertilizing, and watering, only to become perplexed over their ineffectiveness and subsequently get terminated by the landowners.

Some thirty yards away, the carriage house, which had capacity to grant shelter to four horses and two carriages, was embraced on three sides by a thick, lush lawn. It was here that gardeners concentrated their efforts. Nevertheless, even the annual flowers of the carriage house garden died well before their expected lifespan, and perennials never reappeared once winter melted into spring.

The house was built three levels high, not including the spacious attic, which drew to a long, peaked roof at the center with windows facing the east and west. Cupolas capped the corner rooms of the third floor, and the master bedroom sat overlooking the south-facing front porch. Each peak of the mansion, seven in all, was topped by a decorative gable, each ensconced with either griffins or gargoyles, except the largest set above the master bedroom. There, looking down on the cobblestone path, was the figure of a woman draped in robes and spreading her welcoming arms. Her hair fanned and arched behind her head, set to flight by unseen wind.

The lone residence of Gable Way, as the Pyncheons named their path upon the home's completion in the year 1887, had at first been regarded by the residents of White Lake, Michigan, as elegant, perhaps even decadent. The Pyncheons were well educated, successful, and well bred. However, in the short few years following their arrival, some of the people of White Lake incurred inexplicable tragedies, many in the form of family members gone missing or strange illnesses that doctors could not diagnose nor affect. Some of these sicknesses abated, while others ended tragically. There were accidents involving carriages, of which some were fatal. Homes or barns would spontaneously combust without apparent cause, and cases of accidental firearm discharge became common.

These seemingly unrelated incidents were cataloged by the local constabulary and spoken of by the victims' surviving family members. In some cases, members of the Pyncheon family were blamed outright, as whatever incident had befallen their loved ones had benefitted the Pyncheon family, either politically or financially.

Among these suffering families was one by the surname of Maule. Having emigrated from Great Britain before the colony declared its independence, the Maules were wealthy and owned much of the commerce and property in White Lake. Since the arrival of the Pyncheons, many tragedies befell the Maules, and many held a Pyncheon responsible.

However, no evidence could ever be found to tie any Pyncheon to any of the happenings, and never had any criminal charges been brought.

Despite this, rumors spread that the Pyncheons did indeed bring the bad tidings, and many residents of White Lake grew wary of those living in the House of the Seven Gables and remained aloof.

The Pyncheons were eventually forced to hire laborers from out of town, some out of state. One of which was a young woman named Alice Pyncheon, a distant cousin from an unfavored branch of the family from the East Coast. The Michigan Pyncheons took pity, so it seemed, when they hired Alice as a chambermaid. She was of a slight build, but mentally resilient and bright. She labored hard and efficiently for nearly two years until, by mid-September of 1895, she had witnessed many odd occurrences. Visitors would arrive at all hours of the night, their carriages and teams awaking her. Alice would watch from her bedroom window on the second floor of the southeastern turret as the passengers exited their luxurious vehicles and slipped out of sight under the porch roof on their way to the front door. The women always wore expensive black dresses with flouncy hoop skirts that skimmed the ground. When they weren't using umbrellas, the women wore hats with veils, so Alice never saw their faces, even in the daytime. Another visitor was a man of great height, but Alice never had a chance to see more than a glimpse of his face. His long gait spirited him along as quickly as some men ran. Alice asked the family's other servants about these visitors, but none knew of them—or at least would refuse to speak on the subject.

Clifford Pyncheon was a gruff, stern head-of-household who never smiled. His second wife, Alvaretta, was just as inanimate, and ordered Alice about like an untrained puppy. Her voice was sharp, her sentences short, and her glares hard. Clifford's daughter from his first marriage, Hepzibah, was the nastiest of the Pyncheons. Short, stout, and sporting an arched, bird like beak of a nose, she appeared at her most evil when she smiled. Her long black eyebrows arched high on her forehead and were steeped at a sharp angle, giving the impression that they would simply slide from her face. The servants avoided her whenever possible. Alice, too, vacated any room Hepzibah occupied, even if it meant leaving a task partially finished until Hepzibah moved on.

In the presence of Clifford, Alvaretta, and Hepzibah, Alice's skin would sprout goosebumps. Mealtimes were the worst, when the Pyncheons were together in the large dining room, sometimes with visiting relatives or business acquaintances. The vast mansion was quite capable of accommodating dozens of guests comfortably, though the Pyncheons had no friends, and never had the house been at capacity in the time Alice labored there.

Over time, with the snippets of information Alice's ears and eyes gleaned by her natural proximity to the family, it became obvious the family business affairs were not altogether legal, and she became uncomfortable in their employ.

Of late, Alice had her sleep interrupted by nightmares, almost none of the details of which made impressions on her memory. She became increasingly uneasy with each passing day, a feeling made worse by the strange late-night visitors. In her exhausted state, Alice's features became gaunt, her skin paled, and she developed shadowy pouches beneath her eyes.

Alice grew paranoid, convinced the family knew of her suspicions, though they had nothing to fear. A word overheard here and there, paperwork glimpsed but not understood, and the laughter she caught just before entering a room added up to nothing solid.

Finally, that September of 1895, Alice decided to leave without notice and under the cover of darkness, but on the night of her escape, a rainstorm covered White Lake. She retired to her room and fell asleep to the sound of it splattering against the windows.

A far-off crack of thunder startled her awake. The rain had slowed its assault, allowing her to hear the ticking of her nightstand clock. She looked to its face in time to see it set alight by a bolt of lightning, filtered as it was through her silk curtains. It was just after two in the morning.

Her sigh of melancholy was covered by the rumble of thunder some seconds after the flash. Exhausted, she let her head relax into the down pillow and closed her eyes. As she drifted back to sleep, the sound of hooves clip-clopping along the cobblestones of Gable Way brought her back to full consciousness. She yanked the sheets off and leaped from bed, her feet bare on the cool wood.

Looking down onto the street, she found a familiar carriage, the one with a deep cherry-lacquered finish, which was illuminated by its two large gas lamps. Its driver climbed down from his perch, lit a lantern, and opened the door for his employer, the taller of the female visitors. Her head was blocked from view by the familiar black and red umbrella. As she disappeared into the home, a second carriage turned onto Gable Way. Its mahogany finish appeared black, even with lamps and lightning glancing from it. The mysterious male disembarked and entered the home, appearing for perhaps a second. The third carriage soon arrived. This one was the most modest one, colored a natural light wood. The second female of the trio was certainly inside.

Alice jumped back from the window as the driver of the first carriage looked up. She crept to the far side of the window and moved the curtain away from the glass ever so gently. Alice found the driver again, his upturned face darkened and obscured by a rain-soaked, wide-brimmed hat. He was deadly still, as if staring into her window. She recognized him only by his build, as she had seen the drivers on many occasions in the light. All were grim, ugly men, tall and burly, hired for their imposing physicality as well as their driving skills.

Alice silently climbed back into bed, as she never knew when one of the Pyncheons was about, and the house had always filled her with disquiet, as if the walls had eyes. Irrational, she knew, but the feeling had always been there, unshakable. A chill ran through her, and she tugged the sheet and blanket over her face.

I should have left this Godforsaken house tonight, rain be damned, she thought and bit her lip. Another flash of lightning was screened by her sheets, and the explosive thunder that followed was startlingly close. She let slip a short cry into her blanket.

Alice had never been afraid of storms, but tonight was different. Her nerves had been worked raw with sleep so hard to attain. She took several deep breaths, attempting to calm herself. It was then she heard footsteps coming up the carpeted stairs near her door. One by one, the visitors reached the landing and continued onto the next flight, heading to the third floor.

She counted the footsteps. Each person was distinctive, having a different weight and gait. In her imagination, she could visualize each one of them. The tall man was leading. His walk was confident and slower due to his height. The next one was the shortest of the three. Her footfalls were the lightest, quickest, and quietest. The last was the woman whose carriage had arrived first. Tall with a solid build, her feet stomped along in an almost mechanical rhythm.

The visitors continued up, and from the soft thuds that emanated from the ceiling at which she blindly stared, it was obvious to Alice, who knew the layout of the house perfectly well, that the procession was not heading for any of the bedrooms or the master's den. Instead, as the footfalls faded to nothing, it was clear they were heading to the back of the house. There was a pair of sitting rooms there, the library, the dining room, and the stairwell leading to the attic.

Alice lay still in her bed, listening, but there was nothing beyond the ticking of her clock. Even the rain had stopped. Curiosity threatened to drive her mad, so she again tossed the sheets to one side and bounced onto her bare feet. Her restlessness escalated, and she silently paced the floor.

Their timing is almost too perfect. Could they suspect me of wanting to escape this place? In her sleep-deprived state, it seemed plausible. Though she had not spoken her intention to any of the other servants, she wondered if she had been conveying the message by her actions. *No*, she decided. *I've changed nothing of my behavior.*

Alice went to her door and gently gave the curved brass handle a turn. The latch clicked, and she pulled the door open partway. The amber light of kerosene lamps set upon wall sconces glowed against the burgundy and gold wallpaper.

A sudden urge to eavesdrop came to Alice. She absolutely had to see what the visitors were doing. She stepped to her closet, removed a shawl, and clumsily threw it over her shoulders. She thrust her feet into her slippers, picked up her candleholder with its single, half-consumed candle and her small box of matches, and ventured out of her room. Silently, she closed her door and lightly stepped to the staircase.

There she hesitated, thinking of things to say if she were discovered. She had taken the first few steps when another thought occurred. *What in God's name am I doing?* For this, she had no answer, but her feet kept moving, lightly and steadily, and continued the climb to the third floor.

Reaching it, she stopped. The lamps were lit here, too, creating a clear path to the north end of the house. The wallpaper in the third-floor hallway was a deep blue with an off-white flowery pattern, breaking for the entrances to the rooms beyond.

At the end of the hall, Alice turned and stepped to the door to the attic staircase. Usually, it was kept locked, but tonight, she grasped the handle and it turned freely. She looked up into the darkness, for there was no room here for wall-mounted lamps, nor shelving, nor tables on which to place them. Alice took a match from the box and lit her candle.

Maybe I'll overhear something useful enough to take to the sheriff, she convinced herself and took to the stairs. These were uncarpeted, so she took care not to slip on their lacquered wood finish. Near the top of the staircase, she began to hear voices. The attic was separated into two storage rooms, one on either side of the landing. Both doors were closed, but once Alice stepped high enough to become eye level with the landing, she found light coming from underneath the door on the left.

She arrived at the top and remained still for a moment. The voices were clearer now, but the subject of the conversation was lost to her.

This is a grave mistake, she thought. *I wish I'd not left my bed.*

The murmuring lured Alice in further. She pressed an ear against the wooden door, a far flimsier version of the portals hung throughout the lower floors. She caught a word here and there, but after a moment the gathering relaxed and their voices raised from hushed tones to that of regular volume.

A female voice, one that Alice thought sounded young and familiar, spoke out. Her tone was urgent, bordering on anxious. "But is there enough to split four ways?"

The male's penetratingly deep voice rumbled. "I never made promises. To any of you. Keep that in mind before questioning me."

"Yes, Panas," the same one replied.

Panas? What a strange name. Alice pressed her ear harder against the door, thinking she'd misheard.

The man continued. "With these in hand, it is we who have control of the Butterfield Overland Mail Company. The Maules are no longer a threat. The Pyncheons will keep this mansion in their possession indefinitely," he finished with a gravelly chuckle that chilled Alice's bones.

"Praise Ba'al," one of the women commented with satisfaction.

Ba'al? Alice had never heard the name, but she was instantly uncomfortable with the gathering's reverence. An unsettling whisper followed the mention of the strange moniker, one similar to those spoken in church, but different somehow.

"My thanks to High Priestess Ceridwen for her most masterful triumph," the male said. "I trust Maule was of no challenge."

Oh, my God! What have they done? Alice asked herself, feeling her heart quicken.

The woman, Ceridwen, laughed. It was airy and short. "He was not, Panas. He'll recover by morning."

Thank goodness, Alice thought and let out the breath she had been holding.

Suddenly, Alice smelled something burning. She opened her eyes and quickly found smoke rising from her person. She had brought her candle too close to herself. A fringe of her shawl had caught alight.

Alice let out a guttural call of alarm, a sound that never evolved into a scream. The noise that belted from her throat was a merging of a cry of surprise and a gurgle. She held the candle holder away and beat the quickly growing flame out.

An animal-like whimper sounded from the other side of the door halted all conversation in the attic chamber, and every eye of the coven fell upon it. Ceridwen turned and shot a commanding look at her subordinate wicca, Lornabeth, and pointed to the ceiling, holding it close to her own ear. Her other index finger covered her lips, the long, sharp fingernail clicking against the nose of her demonic mask.

With practiced precision, Lornabeth pulled a vial from her small waist satchel and uncorked it. She spilled its crystalline powder onto her palm, curled her fingers around it, then threw it into the air. With a subtle hiss, the colorful powder fought the force of gravity, not only well enough to slow its descent to the floor, but such that each minuscule crystal negated the fall and expanded in the blink of an eye to form a sphere, which hovered in the center of the foursome until it ignited with a muted report, not unlike that of a child's rubber balloon.

Lornabeth had cast the spell of silence, which was her specialty, a concoction she had taken a decade to perfect. No sound could travel into or out of the bubble, and no manmade material could impede its effect.

It was Panas himself that commanded the chamber latch to free without a touch and the door to swing inward, revealing the identity of their eavesdropper.

"Well, it's our sweet Alice," Hepzibah, the fourth occupant of the room, spoke in a singsong. "Come in, dear," she added and guided their bewildered visitor inside with a dual-handed gesture.

Wide-eyed and frightened, Alice felt a combination of compulsion and physical pressure work against her wish to flee. In her struggle, she let the candle holder slip from her hand. The brass instrument clattered against the wood floor and bounced down the steps in a succession of clangs. Droplets of hot wax splashed along them. The candle separated from it and was extinguished by wax landing on the wick.

Alice stammered into the room, fighting her mutinous legs at every step. She worked for breath as her eyes bounced from one outrageous face to the next, unable to comprehend what she was seeing. Her feet carried her to the closest of the women, the tall one. Never having been this close, she was getting closer, and soon the masked woman's breasts were eye level to Alice. The shiny green hoop skirt was impossibly wide, even wider when the stranger placed her gloved hands upon her shelf-like hips. She stared down upon Alice with a twisted smile showing from underneath the black and gold mask that covered every other facial feature.

Alice's legs came to a stop just before she would have collided, but she could do nothing to run in the other direction. She looked to her feet, willing them to move, but they were rooted. It was then she noticed the large round rug that the four visitors stood upon. It was black with a white pentagram woven into it. Alice knew the design by sight, only by what she had learned about witches from her mother.

"Oh. . ." Alice whispered. *Witches? Of course!*

"I've seen this one here," the tallest witch proclaimed. "Alice, is it?" she asked almost sweetly.

"She's the chambermaid, Priestess," the youngest witch said. "Alice *Pyncheon*. My cousin."

Alice thought the voice she had heard on the other side of the door familiar, but she would never have guessed that Hepzibah would be a witch.

Hepzibah continued, "She was going to sneak away in the night, but the rain stopped her."

Alice gasped. She had told no one of her plan. No one at all. She would have stepped to the side to gaze upon Hepzibah, but her feet were planted.

"Leaving? Is that so?" the tall witch they called the high priestess said through a smile that was not quite pleasant. "Why sneak? Why don't you tender your resignation in the proper fashion? Feel the need to escape something?"

Alice couldn't speak as she tried to hold back sobs of fear and panic. Her eyes bulged and tears ran down her cheeks.

The witches tittered behind their high priestess. Alice's body grew hot with anger, but she was powerless to do anything.

"It matters not a bit, young thing," Ceridwen cooed. The tall witch turned to the priest and looked into his eyes. His mask, resembling that of a goat, concealed much of his face. Ceridwen turned her head to the side but kept her icy blue eyes on Alice. "Hepzibah, is Alice the chambermaid a virgin?"

"She is, Ceridwen," Hepzibah answered with much glee.

Alice became incensed at this declaration, no matter how accurate. "Hepzibah! How dare you? I may be a lowly chambermaid in this house, but I'll not take—"

A great hand struck Alice's face, probably that of Ceridwen's, but she never saw it coming. Her sentence was aborted, and the blow would have sent her sprawling onto the floor if her legs had not been bound to the spot on which she stood. Her world was dark for several seconds but returned little by little. Ceridwen remained in her view, but there were two of her and all was fuzzy.

"Panas, tie this sweet thing up and suspend her from the hook," Ceridwen commanded.

Alice said nothing as the immensely strong man manipulated her, binding her wrists behind her, her ankles together, and then a tight wrapping around her chest that constricted her breathing. She looked up as the rope went over the hook that had been mounted in the roof beam above her. As Panas drew the rope, she felt it constrict her chest, tighter, ever tighter, until her feet left the floor.

Alice tried to scream. The pain in her chest grew intense, and she looked to Hepzibah pleadingly. She drew in as much air as she could and spoke in spurts. "Please . . . stop. I don't . . . know what . . . you want!"

To the young woman's horror, the four of them simply looked up at her in amusement. Hepzibah gave a pitiless laugh and came closer. She stared into Alice's face, her little dark eyes barely visible through the black cat mask.

Alice closed her eyes and just kept breathing. Her involuntary movements had started her body slowly swinging.

Ceridwen stepped to a tall cabinet set against the inner wall, opened it, and retrieved an elegant box of cherry wood. Setting it on a shelf, she swung the lid upward. With both hands, she reached inside and, as she picked the object out of the box, she looked to the bound chambermaid's face for a reaction.

Alice screamed. The coven surrounding her laughed heartily.

The blade seemed to be so long that Alice thought it was a short sword. As Ceridwen turned it in her hands, the yellow lamplight reflected in her eyes. The knife was curved like a scimitar, but it had a hilt too small to be a sword.

"The coven could always use a fresh supply of virgin blood. Wouldn't you say, Panas?" Ceridwen asked in a husky, creamy voice. Her eyes drilled into Alice's face as she moved toward their captive. With her great, emerald green hoop skirt skimming the floor, she appeared to float.

"Always, Ceridwen," Panas answered and grabbed the suspended chambermaid at the hips, ceasing her swinging. He lifted Alice's hair from around her neck. "Especially a Pyncheon woman bearing the mark. It is as you said, Hepzibah."

Mark? What's he mean? Alice's eyes darted from the knife to the masked eyes of the three witches standing before her. She was crying uncontrollably now, panicking and short of breath, she could form no words at all.

"Lornabeth, darling, would you mind?" Ceridwen cooed, nodding to a brass bowl on the mantel behind her.

Lornabeth turned and reached for the copper-colored vessel, decorated with a pentagram and slivers of moons. Lornabeth came forward with it held up in both hands.

Ceridwen nodded in Alice's direction and Lornabeth took her place at Alice's right, holding the bowl near her chest.

"I think it may be time for you, Hepzibah," Ceridwen said. She lay the blade over her palms and looked to the youngest witch expectantly.

Without hesitation, Hepzibah came forward and took the blade from her high priestess's hands. A wicked smile spread across her thick lips as she gripped the handle tightly, relishing the weight of the ceremonial device.

"You've seen us perform the ritual," Ceridwen stated.

"I have," Hepzibah agreed.

"Then you know what is expected."

Hepzibah nodded. Quite aware of her short stature, she retrieved a step stool from the corner of the room and placed it in front of Alice. Hepzibah stepped upon it, fully enjoying the expression of horror on Alice's face.

Alice was beyond panic. She had no control of her breathing, and her vision was growing dark at the edges. With the rope around her chest and Panas's powerful arms constricting her further, she could make no sounds beyond the rasping cries of her labored breathing.

Hepzibah, now eye-to-eye with her cousin, brought her masked face close to Alice's ear. "I've read your mind, little chamber-pot girl. You arrogant little bitch. How dare you have such mean thoughts about your master's daughter. It's time to silence you."

Alice inhaled with great burning effort. "Please—"

Quickly and perfectly, Hepzibah touched the blade against Alice's throat, pressed into her flesh, and drew it swiftly downward. A torrent of blood appeared, missing much of the bowl until Lornabeth corrected, lifting it higher and closer.

"Very well done, Hepzibah!" Ceridwen praised.

Hepzibah backed away and stepped from the stool as Alice choked and spat. In her throes of death, Panas struggled to keep her still.

The bowl filled quickly, and Lornabeth withdrew. The flow was ebbing in strength as Alice Pyncheon died. The rest ran down her body and dripped to the floor.

1

Phoebe

Phoebe sat at her desk, one of three remaining pieces of furniture in her tiny first-floor apartment. Once she was done packing her clothes, which were always few, she opened one of the windows in her living room and tossed out every remaining possession she could fit through it. That left the bed, the desk, the round kitchen table, and her tired old office chair. She had never been a fan of couches, so she didn't own one.

Phoebe's landlord, Travis Beldnar, was an ugly, balding, obese man in his sixties and was not one that appreciated the younger generation. He often referred to Phoebe as "a damned millennial" to her face and, no matter how legitimate the reason for her having to speak to him in person, always looked her up and down with a sneer on his lips and a hunger in his muddy brown eyes. In her proximity, his thoughts would not only wander to visions of basic lust, which repulsed her, but he broadcast to her, without conscious effort, imagined scenes of brutality with himself in a starring role and her as the object of his angst.

Recognizing the dangerous duality of the man, Phoebe remained aloof, calling him on the phone if she had anything to say to him, rather than cross the hall and knock on his door. He had come to her door last month and promised her, with feigned regret, that she would be evicted by noon on the first of May. Having been fired from her job with the newspaper, and buried in student loans, she had not been able to pay her rent since January. She understood and didn't argue. The man was an ass, but he was still entitled to the rent.

Phoebe Pyncheon had been working for the suburban Detroit newspaper for just over two years when she was officially laid off by the editor in chief. Deanna Engles, a dark-haired, severe-looking woman with beady eyes and glasses too small for her head, had called Phoebe into her office and informed her of the layoff. Phoebe had immediately sensed the truth rolling from the boss's psyche like a cold, ocean-born fog oozes its way onto a beach. No matter how much Phoebe had tried to suppress her unnatural, invasive ability, she couldn't help but read the message plainly when the editor in chief thought, *No one in the office likes you . . . you're too edgy . . . you awkward liberal twit.*

Phoebe had left the office in tears, but not until she had backhanded Engles's coffee cup, knocking over the hot beverage, and told her what she thought of the paper and the job. These last things were lies, of course, as Phoebe had truly loved the job.

The editor in chief had called security, and Phoebe had been escorted from the building.

Even with her bachelor's degree in journalism, Phoebe had been unable to find another job in her field. She'd found a part-time job in the local library and another as a part-time waitress at the family restaurant just a few blocks away, but it was not enough to cover everything. In fact, after paying her student loan each month, she would be left with less than a hundred dollars to her name.

Her mother had instilled in her the concept of personal responsibility, so Phoebe always strived for that, but lately, things rarely worked out in her favor. Her boyfriend, Thomas, another journalist from the paper, had broken up with her a short time after Phoebe was fired, so she could not count on him. Her mother had passed away long before, and she never knew who her father was. Having nowhere else to go, Phoebe clung to the apartment for every last minute.

The only thing that brought solace to Phoebe was writing fiction. She enjoyed meeting people, interviewing them, and writing articles for the paper, but it wasn't the same as writing something that was completely her own. With the newspaper, everything was in management's control. She wrote what they needed her to write. With her novels, however, it was different. That world was hers and no one else's.

In between her part-time shifts, Phoebe would sit and stare at her laptop screen, tapping away at the keys like her life depended on it. Her mind would run a mile a minute as she typed out the adventures of her made-up biker-chick heroine in *Judy, the Midnight Rider*. The first novel had been finished quickly after Phoebe was laid off, and now with so much time on her hands, she was well into the sequel.

Phoebe didn't know if the books would fit into any particular genre, or if any publisher would ever touch them, but she knew one thing. They were good.

She ceased her typing, sat back in the chair, and read the paragraph she'd just written. The breeze from the open window landed on her face, and she took a deep breath.

"It's perfect," she whispered. The prose flowed, the sentences linked together well, and the picture she was trying to paint came across clearly. "Of course, I'm biased."

When she wrote, reality was forced out of her mind. There was no concern over where she was going to sleep that night, where she was going to go, or from where her next meal would come. The only things that existed for Phoebe Pyncheon in that moment were biker-chick Judy, the road Judy traveled on, the story's studly love interest, and, at that moment, the random stranger that Phoebe sensed coming up to her window.

"Fuck," she grunted and gave a sigh. She sat back, annoyed to be pulled away from her creation for an apparent pervert that liked to peek into women's apartment windows. She crossed her arms, swiveled the chair so she could face the window, and crossed her legs.

She waited. He was close. *Shut up!* she thought in a shout and repeated her mantra: *I don't believe in psychic powers. Obviously, I heard him coming.*

A moment later, as she bounced her left foot in anticipation, the stranger's shadow fell across the windowpane. After that, a big hand landed on the sill, and the rest of his body filled the opening. A silvery badge was pinned to a dark brown shirt buttoned onto a large chest.

Not the UPS guy, Phoebe thought ruefully.

The clean-shaven face of a Wayne County sheriff's deputy appeared next, trooper hat and all.

Phoebe stopped bouncing her foot. His eyes landed on her immediately and, finding that the young woman was apparently expecting him, he gave the small apartment a scrutinous eye.

"Ma'am," he greeted. "Are you Miss Phoebe Pyncheon?"

Phoebe breathed a sigh of relief and, suddenly self-conscious of her appearance, snatched a rubber band from her desk and put her platinum blonde and blue hair into a ponytail.

"Yes, officer, that is I."

The trooper nodded to his right while keeping his eyes on her. "Are these your belongings on the front yard, ma'am?"

She sighed and dropped her hands dejectedly onto her lap, making a muted clap against her sweatpants. "They are." She tilted her head to one side and planted a faint smile on her lips. "I'd offer you some coffee, but the machine's out there."

The trooper smiled. "You did receive an order of eviction from Travis Beldnar, did you not?" His tone was neither accusatory nor demeaning. The trooper had somehow inserted a note of pleasantness in the question.

"I have, sir."

"Miss Pyncheon, I have a summons for you to appear—"

"Officer, I'm leaving today," Phoebe blurted. "I'm waiting for

Goodwill to come pick up that stuff. As you can see, I'm mostly moved out."

"I'll say," the deputy agreed and gave the pile on the lawn another glance.

"I didn't mean to cause Mr. Beldnar any trouble," Phoebe volunteered. "I was laid off, and I just can't do anything about it." She adjusted her rectangular-lensed glasses, trying to look as cute and innocent as possible. "I tossed everything. It's just stuff, and sometimes it's healthy to start over with a clean slate."

The trooper nodded and thought for a moment. "Tell you what . . . when's the truck gettin' here?"

"They said between ten and one," she lied. There was no truck, and she had not called Goodwill. The guilt of lying to someone, especially a policeman, felt immediately heavy and debilitating.

"Okay, Miss Pyncheon. I didn't see you," he stated flatly and checked his watch. "But my partner and I'll be circlin' back here at . . . shall we say . . . two?"

Having no clock, cellphone, or even a watch, she checked the display on her computer. It was almost eleven. "Two. Got it."

"And if you and your pile are still here . . ." he trailed to let his meaning stand.

"If I'm still here at two, I'm screwed, blued, and tattooed," she finished for him and put on her best smile.

The cute deputy laughed.

Yes! Winning!

"That's exactly right, miss," he said and retreated from the window.

Phoebe turned back to the laptop, saved her work, backed it up on two thumb drives, and shut it down. She popped up from the chair, taking the laptop from the desk and slipping it into her backpack. She hurriedly went about the three-room apartment, tossing items into the pack. When she came across the framed photograph of her mother, Phoebe sat down hard in the chair one last time.

The picture was the oldest one she had, taken when her mother was younger than Phoebe herself was at that moment. Some people had said that they looked exactly alike, but Phoebe was never sure about that. Perhaps it was all in the eyes.

"I know what you'd have said, but I've got no choice," she whispered and shoved the photo into her backpack. The threat of tears spurred her on, so she rose and picked up a box of belongings. Not knowing if the creepy Mr. Beldnar was home or not, Phoebe climbed through the window.

She cast glances back to the apartment building as she walked around her pile of belongings: her coffeemaker, tiny television, the small circular table she had it standing on, a folding chair, a mismatched pair of tall three-way lamps, and other miscellaneous bric-a-brac. She searched her hoodie's pockets and pulled out the old Chevy's keys. The trunk lid opened with a creak. She set the box inside and put the lid down without latching it.

Reentering the apartment through the window, she retrieved her two garbage bags of clothes and sundries. She took them to the car and came back for the pack.

Phoebe looked about one last time to make sure she had everything. She pulled her hood over her head and left. Walking one last time past the pile, a glint of something gold caught her peripheral vision. She stopped and scrutinized it.

Oh, it's just the potpourri bowl, she thought and gazed at it for a moment. It still had an unopened bag of potpourri and a few wildflowers she had picked on a hike the other day. *That was Mom's, I shouldn't leave that.*

She bent and picked up the heavy copper bowl. It was ugly and a bit tarnished, but it had belonged to someone in her family before her mother, though she couldn't remember just who. She reopened the trunk and set the bowl inside, pinning it between her bags of clothes to keep it stationary. The old Caprice rattled enough without the help of luggage.

Once behind the wheel of the thirty-year-old car, Phoebe thought over her next move. She had a half tank of gas and just over fifty dollars. She wasn't scheduled to work at either job until the next day, but the time had come to leave, to start completely over. She hated to abandon any job without notice, and now she was about to do it to two at the same time. It was not like her.

She placed the key in the ignition and turned it. The starter motor whined as it spun freely. Phoebe let the key go and tried it again. Eventually, the engine started and settled into its uneven idle. She knew better than to throw the transmission in gear and leave right away. The engine would stall, and if Beldnar was home, perhaps he'd hear the rumbling of her holey mufflers and come running after her.

Awkward, she thought, visualizing the scene of the old creep running outside in his undershirt and shorts to catch her while she frantically tried to restart the big beast.

Phoebe watched the front door of the apartment building as she gave the car a moment of mechanical contemplation. She looked into the rearview mirror and focused on her deep brown eyes. There were lines on her forehead, dark patches under her eyes, and her lids were droopy.

I'll get some rest at Aunt Hester's if she lets me in. She might . . . I think.

Her memory flashed the image of her destination and, at that moment, a strong wave of nausea and dizziness hit her. She sat back into the cloth bench and groaned. She gripped the door handle and was ready to throw it open, convinced that she was about to vomit. The feeling passed after a long moment, and she relaxed.

Too much coffee . . . not enough food, she decided and shook the light-headedness away and cleared her throat. The wait was long enough. She put the car in reverse, aimed for the street, and drove.

It was under fifty miles to her destination, but traffic was heavy, and the Chevy's old radiator couldn't handle it. The temperature light came on just in time for an exit, so she got off and pulled into a gas station conveniently located at the first intersection.

After waiting a half an hour to let the engine cool, Phoebe topped off the radiator with water. She went inside the gas station, gambled on a ninety-nine-cent hot dog, and purchased a can of soda and a paper map. The clerk teased her a bit about why she didn't just use her cellphone for the GPS. She just glared at him with her head cocked to one side to show she was in no mood. The willingness to jump the counter and throttle his bony throat with her bare hands was evident. He shut up and gave over her change.

She returned to the car and opened the map. While she was almost certain she would remember where the old Victorian house was located, it had been over a decade since she'd been at the strange old abode and hadn't spoken to her great-aunt Hester since her mother's funeral nearly seven years prior. Hester had started an argument with Phoebe at the wake, making a stink over some of her mother's belongings, which left her losing all respect for the old bird.

Phoebe had let Hester have whatever she wanted, which amounted to a closet of clothes, a few pieces of furniture, some books, and personal items. Phoebe had no room for anything in her dorm room at the University of Michigan, the institution she would be repaying for the rest of her life.

She found White Lake on the map right away, but the street the House of the Seven Gables was on, Gable Way, wasn't there. It was more of a cul-de-sac, as she recalled. There were only a few roads running through the northern part of White Lake, so she was pretty sure she could find it.

Phoebe wished there had been someone else, anyone else, to turn to, but there was no one. She felt a failure, and Great-Aunt Hester was sure to augment that emotion.

Maybe in her old age, she's mellowed, she told herself.

With the Chevy cooled and watered, herself fed and refreshed, she set off again.

2

The Arrival

It was nearly five o'clock when Phoebe drove past the three-way intersection for Gable Way. The turn lay just past a gentle bend to the left, obscured by trees. The road was too narrow for her to turn around. Instead, she stomped the brake pedal with both feet, sending the Caprice's rear end up and the nose down. The hot, worn brakes were just effective enough to lock up the rear wheels, leaving two streaks of rubber on the road. The old Chevy came to a stop, though the body wobbled and rocked on its weak and creaky suspension.

"Oh, gawd," Phoebe uttered and shut her eyes. The undulations of the car had rekindled the nausea. She covered her mouth and waited for the car to still and her stomach to settle. "Whoa, Nellie."

Fortunately, no one else was on the road. Phoebe rolled down the window, put the car in reverse, and stuck her head out as she let the car creep back to her missed turn.

When she finally turned onto Gable Way, she didn't recognize it. She checked the sign twice, coming nearly to a stop to do so, as many of the rusted sign's letters were covered in vines. It had been shot several times as well, further distorting the readability. The forest on either side of this narrow pathway had once been lush, thick, and green. Now, however, it appeared that the trees had contracted some horrible disease that browned the leaves and gnarled the branches. Phoebe goosed the accelerator then let the car settle to its idle speed. The street had once been made of cobblestones, but now, the tires rolled over dirt and gravel. Bits of the original stone roadway lay in the middle.

"What the *shit?*" Phoebe muttered and came to a stop again. A yellow sign with a black arrow, warning drivers of the bend to the left, was covered with a purple banner with turquoise cursive letters announcing, "Madam Hester's Just Ahead!"

"Madam Hester's *what* is just ahead?" she wondered aloud and urged the car forward once more. "What have you done, Auntie Hester?"

As she continued on at a crawl, she began to wonder what she was about to find. She hadn't so much as called Aunt Hester since their last high-spirited meeting, and the possibilities that the old woman had either died, moved, or both, dawned on her.

A mild panic began to brew within her chest and rounding the last curve did nothing to alleviate it. The House of the Seven Gables appeared ahead.

Feathering the brake, Phoebe rolled up to the house and breathed through her nose, forcing the anxiety away. She could see the house had seen much better days well before she parked on the brown grass across from it. She turned off the car and remained seated, being in no hurry to go ring the bell. The three-story structure stretched skyward, making Phoebe stick her head out of the open window to take it all in.

The old stone Victorian was in need of a new roof, not just in one place, but in every section Phoebe could see. The slate gray shingles were in terrible shape, with many missing. Above most windows of clear glass were decorative stained-glass panels. The colors of some appeared to be faded, and some were cracked.

The welcoming woman etched into the gable above the master bedroom had not aged well. The chipped and blackened figure glared down at Phoebe, not appearing to welcome her at all. The outstretched arms promised harm, not home.

To her memory, the stone walls had never been perfect, with many of their bricks chipped and the mortar in between receded. The structure seemed to have settled since then, making the rows of stone crooked throughout. Some sections appeared to be missing mortar altogether, filling Phoebe with the perverse need to walk up to one of the bricks and give it a tug.

The open stone porch was still the same, though it suffered from weather and neglect like the rest of the house. The pillars looked wet and green with moss. The curve of the arches seemed imperfect. She recalled spending time on that porch as a child, feeling the wind accelerate as it was pressed through the arched openings, disturbing the pages of her coloring books and putting a chill in her bones. Frustrated, young Phoebe would pick up her books and crayons and sit in the sunny yard.

A window in the first-floor parlor held something that she had never seen before, but considering the signs on the road, she wasn't surprised. A neon sign took up the window, shouting at the dead forest in red and green light that a psychic resided within. A small sticker placed in the corner next to it had a white pentagram on a black background.

From the several cars that were parked on either side of the house, one of which was a brand new and expensive European sedan, Phoebe figured that the psychic business must be booming.

Phoebe sighed and rolled her eyes. Great-Aunt Hester had always been on the lookout for the quick buck and had claimed that she was a gifted wiccan. She adopted affectations to support this, wearing dresses with long, wispy skirts and sleeves, oversized costume jewelry, and even, on a few occasions, a black cape, complete with hood.

Everything but the stupid pointed hat, Phoebe recalled. She suddenly felt tired and let her head relax into the headrest. Her droopy eyes settled on the old carriage house, just ahead. The structure was stone, matching the house in color and architecture. It, too, was in obvious need of care. It seemed crooked, as if the front had been settling one way and the rear the other. The big wooden double doors were askew, and Phoebe could see the grille, bumper, and driver's side headlights of Hester's car, a sixties-era Cadillac that had been in the family since it was new.

Scratch the psychic reading business, Phoebe thought and gave a weak giggle. *I can't believe she still has that piece of crap. It's older than mine.*

Phoebe's eyes closed, and she breathed deeply. The air, while mostly fresh, had a scent behind it, like a pile of grass clippings from a weeks-old mowing job, rich with rotting fallen branches mixed with wet, dead leaves. The odor triggered a memory of her childhood days, where she spent many an after school hour waiting for her mother to pick her up.

As Phoebe began to doze, the silence of the semi-dead forest occurred to her and struck her as odd. Not a bird chirped, nor an insect buzzed. She decided there was a good reason for it, and let it be.

The temperature dropped and the wind rose, making the vehicle wiggle and bob. Phoebe let this be, too, finding the conditions soothing.

A long belt of thunder came to her. It was far away, and being so sleepy, she didn't find it worth opening her eyes to crank the windows up. She shifted in her seat, stretching out her legs.

Rustling in the dirt outside her driver's door disturbed her slumbery mood. The skittering of what sounded like claws startled her, and she opened her eyes. Anxiety froze her in place, for what felt like a few moments had apparently been long enough for the sun to go down. The wind outside began to carry uncomfortably cold raindrops, but the noises from whatever was coming closer to her car frightened her away from even closing her window.

Then, a thump on the other side of the door startled Phoebe. A clipped cry left her mouth and her eyes widened. She pressed her palms into the seat, preparing herself to launch, but what direction she'd go was left undecided.

Another strike to the door sent her sliding across the bench seat. Her breaths sped up and little cries accentuated each one. She slammed her back against the passenger door and, while her eyes were locked on the opposite door, something cold took her by the throat, silencing her and cutting off her breath.

Phoebe clawed at the constriction. Her fingertips tried to dig in, but there was nothing to dig in to. Whatever it was felt like a tree branch, but it was strong, and it was squeezing. She followed the branch with her right hand, as it was curled around her from that side. Unable to put eyes on it, Phoebe let her fingers work over whatever was strangling her.

She wrapped her hands around the object, but somehow, it had more strength than she. Her left hand tried picking the thinner bits away from her throat, but they were locked in place.

As Phoebe tried to get free, she kicked and bucked. Her body was plucked from the old car, dragged through the open window. She was picked up, spun around, and slammed against the side of her Caprice.

There was no air to scream with, her ears pulsed, and her eyes bulged as she stared into the eyeless, skinless face of her attacker. The lack of lips left the face to express horrific contempt for her, and a black hood cast darkness over empty eye sockets.

"Leave," said the skeleton standing over her in a long, raspy screech.

Phoebe's first thought was that this apparition was Death himself, but she noted he was without his sickle. The skeleton was draped with a tattered and torn black garment. The bony hand around her throat tightened even more, somehow not crushing her esophagus. Then, her feet were off the ground, her spine pressed painfully against her car.

The entity repeated his demand.

Phoebe tried nodding. Anything to get out of the grip. She was beginning to doubt that he had noticed the small motion of her head when the skeletal hand left her neck.

She did not hit the ground, nor was she freed. The hands went to her hoodie, and he yanked her toward him, bringing her inches from his face. This time, the hood slipped back partway, bringing the skull into the starlight. There were dry wisps of hair fluttering about the head, sprouting from what was left of the dead man's paper-thin flesh.

"Leave. If you look back, you'll find me behind you."

Phoebe, lungs recharged with oxygen, screamed. She screamed loudly and strongly with her eyes closed. When her feet hit the ground, she tried to kick, then curled her right hand's fingers and swung on the toothy skull.

Pain enshrouded her hand and an unearthly voice cried out in what she took as surprise. Confused but inspired, Phoebe swung again, and the sound repeated. In a third attempt to get him away from her, Phoebe pressed both hands into his face, careful to avoid the teeth that she felt certain could bite off her fingers.

The wraith cried out again, the sound eerily unrestrained, like a shout from a child, or a wounded animal, or a car horn.

Phoebe awakened with her hands pressed into the center of the Caprice's steering wheel. Realizing that she was reacting to a nightmare, she pulled her hands away, ceasing the call of the car horn. Beyond her windshield was fading daylight and the carriage house. She blinked and sank into the car seat, catching her breath and whimpering in relief.

"What in hell's going on out there?" an old woman called from Phoebe's left.

Phoebe sat straight up, recognizing the voice as Aunt Hester's. She looked to the house's windows but only caught a glimpse of a curtain dropping back into place. The window with the pentagram sticker had been opened, apparently in response to Phoebe's inadvertent sounding of her car's horn.

"Shit," Phoebe muttered. She checked her hair in the rearview mirror out of habit, pocketed her car keys, and jumped out. *So much for a smooth announcement of my arrival.*

Phoebe walked toward the house and saw Hester through the screen door. The old woman pushed it open and stepped onto the porch. In the shade provided by the deep structure and the fact that Hester was wearing black, Phoebe at first saw only Hester's frowning white face and two disembodied hands.

Phoebe squinted and shaded her eyes from the cloud-scattered sunlight. In a moment, Aunt Hester became visible. Phoebe stopped walking toward her, remaining in the dirt street so her relative could recognize her.

"Who are you?" said Hester in her aged but smooth voice. She continued forward out of the shade and down the first step. Her eyes searched Phoebe's face, showing no recognition.

Phoebe waved with embarrassment on her face. "Aunt Hester, it's me, Phoebe. Your grandniece."

Hester was imposingly tall in comparison to Phoebe, who stood at five and a half feet to Hester's five foot eleven, but as her aunt was standing on the fourth step, Phoebe had to tilt her chin up to meet Hester's pale blue eyes, which, in the sunlight, appeared almost as light as the whites. Her white hair was drawn up in a bun, her forehead covered with bangs. The dress Great-Aunt Hester wore was typical of the woman. It was black, high-collared, frilly at the ends of her wrist-length sleeves, with a skirt that nearly covered her feet. The material was light and airy, easily pushed by the gentle breeze. A necklace with a pentagram charm hung around her neck, and her fingers held several large rings with faux stones.

Aunt Hester had apparently not forgotten their last encounter. She raised her nose and looked at her grandniece down its angles. "What have you done to your hair?" she asked with obvious distaste.

Phoebe had also not forgotten the last time she had spoken, or rather shouted, with her great-aunt. The pointless fight had ended with Phoebe's acquiescence, which she had yet to get over. "I dyed it. You should give it a shot."

Hester ignored the insult. "We have a client in my parlor," she said. "Did you come to my home just to blast your horn and disrupt my peace, or is there something you want?"

Phoebe blushed. She hated groveling, but she didn't have a choice. Thinking quickly, she said, "Sorry about the horn. There's a loose wire or something. Happens sometimes when I put it in park."

A wave of energy washed over Phoebe at that moment. Her nausea struck again, and her temples began to pound sharply. She blinked and received the notion that the woman had not just cast doubt upon her words but was reading her innermost thoughts.

Ridiculous, Phoebe thought.

Before her great-aunt could say anything, Phoebe quickly pressed on, explaining about her losing her job, the eviction, and having only a quarter of a tank of gas left.

"Please, Aunt Hester," Phoebe pleaded, which turned her stomach more. "I've got nowhere else—"

"Please, child! Shush," Hester admonished and lifted her index finger to the air. She had grown her fingernails so long they looked like claws. Hester placed her hands on her hips and sighed. "Very well. You may come in. Be quiet until my client leaves and we'll discuss it." She turned and went back inside, not waiting for Phoebe to follow. The screen door screeched and slammed the second Hester's long skirt fluttered past it, narrowly escaping being caught in it.

"Well, gee, Phoebe," Phoebe mocked. "Nice to see you. Fuck you very much for stopping by, Phoebe." Shaking her head in disgust over her own obsequious behavior and Hester's arrogance, Phoebe stepped onto the porch, feeling its cool, damp air bring out the goosebumps on her skin. The feeling brought back memories.

There was something new here, however. Three sixes on a black plaque were screwed into the stone wall next to the front door. It was the address, if it was to be believed, though arbitrary, as the old Victorian had always been the only residence there.

"Six-six-six Gable Way, huh? Oh, that's just *perfect*," Phoebe muttered and rolled her eyes.

"Rawk!"

"Shit!" Phoebe cried and jumped to the right, turning midair to face the noise. One hand covered her heart, the other her mouth.

The source of the call was a raven in a wrought-iron birdcage suspended from a hook in the porch's ceiling. The black bird regarded her with one eye, then the other. It shifted its weight from one claw to the other, giving motion to the perch on which it clung.

"Holy shit. Big bird," she whispered hoarsely. She hated birds, and getting out of the creature's line of sight became paramount. Quickly, she opened the screen and stepped inside the House of the Seven Gables for the first time in nearly fifteen years. She made sure the screen door latched securely once she was inside.

At first, Phoebe saw no changes to the home. She could see the kitchen door down the long hallway ahead. The tall double doors to the parlor on her right, where Aunt Hester had returned, were the same carved mahogany she remembered. She ran her hand along the cool, smooth surface. The wood felt dry, coarser than she remembered but otherwise the same.

She took further steps inside and left the foyer to look into the living room. It seemed the same there, too, from the giant brown leather Barcalounger, the cream-colored chaise lounge, the obscenely large, marble-topped coffee table, the ugly yellow couch that she remembered was so uncomfortable, and the Price & Teeple upright piano near the window next to the vast credenza. Everything, it seemed, right down to the four-legged television near the door and the tube-amplified radio on the bookshelf. Most of the books even sparked familiarity.

"No way," Phoebe whispered. She walked up to the television and opened its cherry wood cabinet. The small screen was there, just as she remembered. The rabbit ears antenna still sat on top. "There's no way this still works."

Sure enough, looking at the back of the device, the wires from the antenna were still attached to the back of the unit. *No digital signal converter thingy. Why is it still in here?*

Phoebe stepped back after closing the cabinet doors and let her eyes wander over the room. It was silent aside from the ticking of the mantle clock on the fireplace. Her eyes went to the great big credenza still under the window, wondering if it was still stocked with liquor. The doors were colorfully hand-painted with life-like tulips, honeysuckle, and zinnia flowers, all gathered together in a scene of arrangements. When she was small it had been locked to keep her from its contents.

The woodwork around the room's windows and doors was just as she recalled. The rug under her feet was even still the same. The maroon-bordered, rectangular floor covering featured more flowers and elaborate designs and ran the length of the walking area, from the door to the credenza. The huge coffee table was the only piece of furniture that sat upon it.

Phoebe turned around, and her eyes found two things that weren't familiar. Two paintings hung on the wall above the world's most un-comfortable yellow couch. She took a step forward for a better look and immediately regretted it.

The paintings were horrifying, grotesque scenes of disfigurement, torture, and murder. The one on the left featured three men bound to posts, a fire set at their feet. The men appeared to have been whipped as well, and their mouths were open, depicting screams of unimag-inable pain. There was blood and blackness caked to their flesh. To the left of the burning men were spectators, and upon their faces were expressions of amusement.

Phoebe turned away from that one and bypassed much of the sec-ond, though it seemed to share a similar motif. "Gross," she mumbled and crossed her arms.

She realized that, up until she'd discovered the ridiculous paintings, she had been enjoying being in that room. This she thought odd, as the memories she had of her mother and Great-Aunt Hester were scarcely of good times. Hester had been a mostly absent babysitter, placing Phoebe in that very room for hours, alone and unsupervised, with nothing but her homework, some coloring books, and the tiny-screened black-and-white television.

Phoebe stood for a moment near the window, letting the weak sunlight wash over her. She crossed one arm under her breasts and propped the other's elbow on it, letting her hand cover her lips. The sky was still overcast, and the dead or dying trees at the periphery of the property cast morbid shadows on black earth below. Looking right, Phoebe found the eyes of the raven upon her.

Phoebe closed her eyes and let her mind drift to a time when she stood in this oddly unchanged room, when she was small, in school, and waiting for her mother to pick her up after work. She had come to hate the House of the Seven Gables. She dreaded having to walk to it after school. She remembered the times when she'd be in a room, doing homework, here or in the kitchen, and she'd get that feeling of being watched. She'd become nervous—so distracted that little of her work would be done.

Phoebe recalled the noises that accompanied that feeling. She listened, but none were present at that moment. The strange human-like humming or breathing sounds that she dismissed as shifting breezes were common occurrences that she attributed to the oddities of an old structure. Sometimes there would be a far-off groan or the sound of footsteps with no one there.

It certainly didn't help young Phoebe when Great-Aunt Hester addressed her fears by telling her it was all due to the spirits dwelling within the House of the Seven Gables.

Phoebe thought through her mantra. *I don't believe in haunted houses.* She breathed deeply, picturing herself sitting in the ugly couch behind her, watching afterschool cartoons. *I don't believe in ghosts. I just don't . . .*

"Hello."

Phoebe screamed and jumped at the strange male voice. She spun around, and though her body never contacted the credenza, a framed photograph of the house set upon its top fell on its face with a bang. The sound gave her a second start. She covered her mouth with both hands and looked back and forth between the man who had entered and the fallen picture.

"Terribly sorry," the man offered and took a step forward.

Phoebe moved her hands away from her mouth. "What the *fuck*, dude."

The man, a tall one, too, taller than Hester, was blocking her exit. He appeared to be in his thirties, with dark hair and a perfectly trimmed beard that framed his face. His eyes were dark brown, almost black, and the eyebrows, high on his forehead, were angular and perfect.

"I didn't mean to frighten you, miss," the man insisted and took another step forward.

That accent. British? Here? Phoebe shook her head clear of the thought and focused on him. She put on her best frowny face, the one she practiced in the mirror whenever she felt the need to convince herself that she was, indeed, Queen of the Badasses. *Fierce, Phoebe. Fierce!*

"That's close enough!" she warned, pointing at his chest.

His eyebrows went further up his skull, and he halted. "Of course." He clasped his hands together, as if he were a haberdasher waiting on a customer, and pulled his bottom lip into his teeth.

Phoebe drew a deep breath and leaned back on the credenza. She tried to look nonchalant in front of the stranger and realized he was rather handsome. He wore a black pullover sweater with a dark blue shirt's collar protruding over the top and black pants. She closed her eyes again and exhaled through her pressed lips, trying to stave off an anxiety attack.

"I do humbly apologize," the man whispered.

Phoebe kept her eyes closed, nodded at his words, and just kept breathing. In through nose, out through mouth. *He doesn't look like an axe murderer. I think.*

"I didn't know anyone was in here," he tried to explain.

Definitely British, Phoebe decided. She opened her eyes and kept her breathing rhythm. She relaxed her frown, shook her head, and waved him off with the hand she wasn't leaning on.

"Dude—" she started.

"I know."

"—you scared the shit out of me."

"I noticed."

"Don't *ever*—"

"Won't happen again."

Phoebe cut herself off from finishing the sentence. The Brit did look contrite as he released his lip to reveal a smile, which, while cartoon-like, seemed sincere.

"I didn't know Miss Pyncheon had accepted another boarder," he said.

"I'm not a boarder," Phoebe began, then added haltingly, "Well, maybe I am. I mean I don't know if she'll let me stay. I'm more of a guest. I think. But not yet."

"Oh," he said, though he clearly didn't follow.

"I'm her niece."

"Oh?" This time he was taken aback, and his eyebrows dropped.

"Well, grandniece."

"Ah." The Brit scrutinized her face, adopting a curious expression as his hands disappeared behind his back.

Phoebe shook her head once again and smiled. "I'm Phoebe Pyncheon," she introduced and stepped toward him, offering her hand.

The stranger tipped his head back apprehensively. Like Aunt Hester had done just a few minutes before, he looked down his perfectly straight nose at her. Slowly, he took his right hand and shook hers briefly.

"Pyncheon," he said as if he had never heard the name. "You're *Phoebe* Pyncheon."

Puzzled by his change of demeanor, Phoebe just nodded and smiled up at him.

"You're Miss Pyncheon's grandniece."

"Yup," she answered brightly. "And you are . . . ?"

"Oh," he uttered and blinked. "Beg your pardon. My name is Holgrave. Alec Holgrave." His eyes shifted ever so slightly from left to right. "Everyone refers to me as Mr. Holgrave—or simply Holgrave."

"Okay," she replied. He was hiding something but she didn't feel threatened by him. She looked past him, noticing something on the mantle above the fireplace. "What is *that?*"

Holgrave watched the youngest Pyncheon as she stepped past him. She was attractive, he thought, though the blonde and blue hair seemed out of place for someone of her family line. He followed where her attention was focused.

The statue upon the mantle was shy of a foot tall. It appeared to be a man wearing a pointed hat, sitting upon a plain high-backed chair. His hands lay upon the straight armrests. Looking closely, the figure wore a neutral expression on his face and featured a chin beard. At first, he appeared naked, but there was some type of wrap around his lower half. There were candles on either side of the statue, many halfway consumed.

"Ah. That is Ba'al, a god of all seasons," Holgrave explained. "He appears in many religions and mythology."

"He looks Egyptian."

"The figurine is styled in that fashion, yes."

Phoebe turned to face him. "Weird, huh?" she said, not knowing what else to say.

"Indeed."

At that moment, the doors to the parlor opened and Aunt Hester's voice and that of another woman could be heard. Phoebe held up her finger to silence Holgrave.

Phoebe, overcome by curiosity, unashamedly tiptoed to the open living room door and arched her neck to listen.

"By Friday morning, things will look differently, I assure you," Aunt Hester said in a strangely melodic tone that Phoebe had never heard from the woman. It was calming and soothing, two things that Hester was not.

"Thank you, Lady Hester," the unseen visitor replied.

To Phoebe, the woman sounded unsettled. Perhaps she had been crying some moments before.

"Take care and get some rest, Mrs. Carp," Hester wished her client.

"Good afternoon, Lady Hester," bid Mrs. Carp, and the screen door's springs announced their movement.

"Good afternoon," Hester returned.

Phoebe sensed that her great-aunt was not to wait for the closing of the door and dashed on tiptoes to the cushioned red chair next to the credenza. Holgrave watched with amusement, only to be caught with the goofy grin by the lady of the house.

"Mr. Holgrave," Hester addressed with surprise. "I didn't hear you come down."

Holgrave wondered how she could have but let it pass. "Good day, Ms. Pyncheon. I have indeed."

Hester arched an eyebrow as she looked into his face. Holgrave simply glanced in Phoebe's direction. Hester followed his eyes and found her grandniece sitting by the window.

Phoebe tried to look as innocent as possible, still hoping her aunt would grant her a bedroom and a place to write her novel.

Outside, a car drove past. Phoebe turned to look as the expensive imported sedan headed up Gable Way. The caged raven caught Phoebe's eye and squawked.

"Phoebe," Hester called. "Come." With that, the old woman turned on her heel and left the room.

Phoebe looked to Holgrave, who widened his eyes comically and mocked Hester's arched eyebrow. Phoebe uttered a giggle as she left the chair, walking after her great-aunt.

Holgrave watched her as she went past. "Welcome to the House of the Seven Gables, Miss—" he began but paused awkwardly, "—Pyncheon. Welcome, indeed."

Phoebe hesitated at the door, and turned, noting his sudden uncomfortableness. "Thank you, Mr. Holgrave," she replied and strode out, following her aunt.

3

The Room

Hester's long skirt flowed behind her as she walked up the hallway, her figure appearing to float as she went. Hester was wearing shoes with a substantial heel, and they reported loudly against the floorboards with every step, the sound echoing from the closely placed walls.

Approaching a door on the left, Hester halted, turned to her grand-niece, and opened it. She gestured for Phoebe to enter, which she did.

Phoebe recognized the sewing room from her childhood. In it was the same ancient Singer pedal-driven machine, the same chair, rug, elaborate curtains, everything. Even the pillows on the small rosewood-carved twin-backed couch had not been replaced. More of the same books were on the shelves here, too. Like the living room, the items were the same, just older, more worn, dustier.

Phoebe resisted the urge to comment on the sameness of the house, leaving that topic for another time, if it were ever to come up. Somehow, small talk seemed out of the question, despite the huge favor she was asking of her relation.

"So, after all these years, you come to me needing a place to stay," Hester flatly stated.

Phoebe faced her great-aunt and swallowed. She knew she was not the one to apologize for that, considering their last encounter. Realizing the greater need, she said, "If I'm imposing, Aunt Hester, I'll leave."

"Nonsense. Of course, you'll stay." She gazed fixedly on Phoebe. "I will ask only that you help out around the place. Laundry, washing dishes, helping the cook, that sort of thing. I'm not a young woman and there are boarders here."

"Oh, I understand. I'm writing a novel and just need a quiet place—"

"You'll have it. There are four guests here, not including yourself. You'll meet them at dinner."

Phoebe nodded and let her great-aunt do the talking.

"The rules are simple. No late-night guests. Write your name on your food items when you put them in the kitchen. No noise, especially when clients come in. Clean up after yourself."

"Got it," Phoebe inserted, thinking the list would go on. It didn't.

Hester seemed to lighten a little, though she didn't smile. Her pale blue eyes searched Phoebe's face for an elongated moment. "Come. Let me show you the available rooms."

Phoebe followed again, this time up the narrow staircase. The railings were unchanged from her youth, though as she took them in hand, she could feel a looseness in the mountings. The steps creaked loudly beneath their feet, and when Hester reached the second floor, Phoebe noted that the light switches were still the push-button type. The one on top was "on," the one below was "off."

The wall-mounted, low-watt bulbs in the twin faux candle sconces lit weakly, yellowing the burgundy and gold wallpaper in the hall.

The same lights, the same damn paper, Phoebe marveled. It's older, it's fading, it's peeling, but all the same.

"You have your choice of two rooms on this floor," Hester said. "The southeast corner in the turret has windows, but it's smaller. The other up the hallway has the one window facing west."

"Oh, the corner one would be wonderful," Phoebe proclaimed with excitement. She remembered it well, though she had only been inside it a few times as a girl.

"So be it," Hester said and led Phoebe that way.

So be it? Who talks like that?

Hester opened the door to the corner room. It was musty and dusty inside, and boxes of books and odds and ends cramped the floor. "You'll have to move these. The small room up the hallway has been used for storage."

"Okay."

"Do you have many things to move in?"

"No, Aunt Hester. Just a couple bags of clothes, my laptop, and a bowl."

"A bowl?"

"Yes," Phoebe said and looked at Hester's face for a reaction. "It was my mother's."

That arched eyebrow appeared again. "I see. I'll leave you to it, then. When you're finished, clean yourself up and pay the cook a visit. She'll be down in the kitchen now, preparing tonight's supper, which is served promptly at seven every evening. Introduce yourself, help out wherever you can."

"I will," Phoebe agreed. "Thank you so much, Aunt Hester."

"Of course," Hester replied. She looked to Phoebe like she was about to say something else but didn't. Instead, she retreated from the room, closing the door behind her.

Phoebe turned to the window, relieved but bewildered at the same moment. As she looked about the room, it, too, was the same as she remembered. Multicolored throw pillows lay on the deep blue cushions on the benches beneath the windows, which were on three sides of the room. The mahogany dresser was a giant, with large, decorative handles that had lost the shine from their brass and gone black. On top of it sat the old fan, an Air Castle, with its two wooden blades carved in the shape of airplane propellers.

The bed looked like the same one that she remembered. Patting her hand on the comforter, a cloud of dust rose up and made her sneeze. When the air cleared, she gasped, having found a painting above the bed.

"Oh, hell no," she almost shouted.

Her eyes couldn't leave it. The work was masterfully done, but like the paintings in the living room on the first floor, the scenes were horrific. This one was of a battlefield somewhere, of soldiers that were perhaps French, from the days of Napoleon. The men wore off-white, ruffled shirts with two- or three-cornered hats, long blue coats, and blood. Blood was prevalent. There were muskets, pistols, swords, and pikes, and blades running through everything.

"Augh, for fuck's sake," Phoebe uttered. She put her knees on the bed and sank into it, making it tricky to keep her balance as she took the painting down. Gently, she set it on the floor behind the tall dresser, out of sight.

Phoebe tried to think of something else, anything else, but the distorted faces of the dead and the dying, tortured souls in the painting were too well etched in her mind. She changed tack, concentrating on pulling up the blankets and shaking out the dust. She opened the windows, their frames' paint peeling. One wouldn't stay up, another would barely go up, the third, like the little bear's porridge, was just right.

Phoebe went about moving the boxes out of the room. As Hester described, that one was loaded with boxes and its bed removed. She returned to the corner bedroom, feeling drained and warm. She found the switch on the fan and it whirred to life. She watched it for a moment and listened to the noise it made. The soothing murmur relaxed her, so she stretched out on the bed. The frame and springs creaked with every muscle she moved, and she sank deeply into the mattress. The pillows were so thin, they needed to be stacked.

With her hood pulled up over her eyes, she passed out almost immediately.

Hester left her grandniece to her room and ascended the stairs. Once on the landing, she slipped out of the heavy shoes and continued up. The floorboards still creaked, but the clopping stopped.

She floated from the top of the stairs to the room above Phoebe's and tapped upon it with her claws. It opened without a delay and without physical interference.

Hester went in and it swung quietly shut behind her.

"It *is* her," the woman inside said. She sat in a rocking chair by the windows, not rocking, not content.

"It is," Hester replied in contrast, almost gleeful.

"She's dangerous. She shouldn't stay." At this statement, the woman rose. Shorter than Hester, the younger woman's yellow and white hair flowed freely over her shoulders in ringlets and waves that ran nearly to her tailbone. Her frilly dress was similar to Hester's, being that it was black with a skirt that went to her feet, but the high collar which encircled her neck was a deep purple on the inside. A woman just beyond what was considered middle age, she was handsome, with high, prominent cheekbones.

"Glendarah, she's my niece's daughter," Hester reminded her sister wiccan.

"Yes, High Priestess," the other answered. "And as such, is powerful." Glendarah moved about the small room, gazing at the world below. "She just doesn't know it."

"She is desperate, alone. We can turn her to our way of thinking," Hester said lowly, moving closer to her longtime companion

Glendarah moved to her vanity and sat. She stared into her mirror for a moment in thought, then began touching up her eye makeup. As she did, the years melted away from her flesh. She smiled when Hester placed her hands on her shoulders and leaned low so Glendarah could see her face in the reflection. As she watched, Hester transformed with her, morphing into the image that Glendarah adored.

Hester's long hair was black again, her lines and wrinkles gone, her neck taught and porcelain. She smiled into the mirror, displaying her perfectly white and straight teeth, and began caressing Glendarah's cheek.

"I do so love being young for you, Glendarah dearest."

"I know," Glendarah replied and turned to kiss Hester's offered palm. "And I for you."

"Do you trust me?" Hester asked.

"You know I do," Glendarah answered and pushed a brush through her golden hair. "I worry." Her deep blue eyes searched the pale ones of Hester's reflection.

"We will be careful," Hester assured her.

"What will Dzolali think?"

"She will think as I do. As *we* do," Hester assured her as she massaged Glendarah's shoulders.

"I feared she'd never turn to you, Hester," said Glendarah, searching her lover's reflection. "She's like her mother. Independent and stubborn."

"The Coven will go on and the house will flourish."

Phoebe snapped awake, her mouth wide open and her lungs nearly depleted of oxygen. She saw only darkness when she opened her eyes and soon realized that she had rolled onto her stomach. She turned her head, finding muted sunlight spilling through the windows, but she couldn't move. Another bad dream had taken over her thoughts in her brief slumber, and she was grateful that her memory of it faded quickly along with its horrors.

Phoebe worked to catch her breath and discovered that she was lying on her arms and they had fallen asleep. There was no tingling, they just felt dead and useless. Slowly, feeling returned, starting with her upper arms and moving down. The tingling did happen and became intense. She flexed her fingers to regain feeling.

Phoebe sat up, realizing that stiffness had settled into her body.

The mattress was soft, perhaps too soft. She stood and stretched. As she did, she heard something close to her.

Breathing. Slow and deep. She spun around, convinced that someone was standing right behind her. There was no one. She yanked down her hood and listened.

Her eyes went to the open windows and the swaying curtains.

"Wind," she whispered and wiped her forehead. *What is going on? Two nightmares in the same day and I'm freaking out.*

She shook her head, annoyed. The stress she had built up over the past few months was certainly getting to her. The eviction and moving into Hester's creepy house were the cherries on top.

Phoebe noticed that the skies had darkened, both due to time passing and the thickening, graying clouds. She closed the windows, opened the door, and listened for a moment before leaving.

The faintest of sounds could be heard at the stairwell. Voices, some footsteps, activity from the first floor. She walked up the hall to the large bathroom and went in. Everything here was just like the rest of the house. All the same, just older.

The toilet was just as icy cold as she remembered, and when finished, she washed her hands and looked at herself in the mirror. She thought she still looked tired, and her nap had pressed her hair in every direction.

Phoebe brushed it out and went downstairs. She encountered no one, but she heard voices from the direction of the kitchen, muffled by the door. She cautiously pushed it inward and went in.

Hester and a short, roundish woman looked up. They had been discussing something while preparing dinner.

"You're late," Hester said.

"Am I?" Phoebe returned. "Sorry, I don't have a clock." Looking to the one on the wall above the sink, she saw it was nearly 6:00.

Hester bypassed the excuse by way of introduction. "This is Alva. Alva, this is my grandniece, Phoebe."

Alva smiled and gave a nod in greeting. Her hands were covered in flour and dough. She was a woman slightly beyond her middle years, with gray splattered throughout her black hair, which was trapped under a net for kitchen duty. Her eyes were dark and friendly.

"Hi," Phoebe offered.

"Alva, don't let Phoebe get away with anything just because she's relation," Hester said without humor. "She's to help you in any way you see fit."

"Yes, ma'am," Alva said. She looked to Phoebe and gave a wink that Hester didn't see.

Alva had Phoebe wash her hands and stir a pot of gravy for the chicken fried steak, and then wash the pans and utensils that had been used in the preparation for that night's meal.

Hester remained to watch for a time, perhaps to make sure Phoebe would keep up her end of the bargain. Phoebe did as Alva directed and was beginning to enjoy herself for the first time that day when the kitchen door was flung open inward. The sound gave Phoebe and Alva both a start. Phoebe cursed under her breath, drawing an unpleasant gaze from Aunt Hester.

Into the kitchen walked a wild-haired, thin man with a couple of days' scruff on his face. He was not as tall as Mr. Holgrave, but with his highly piled, curly brown hair, he was close. The man's dark brown eyes darted from Alva to Hester, then to Phoebe, at which point he went still and looked her up and down slowly.

Oh, what in the ever-lovin' hell is wrong with this creep? Unconsciously, she had drawn back her lips and scrunched her nose in disgust.

The creep had a large, angled beak of a nose and a prominent chin with a dimple. He wore what used to be a plain beige t-shirt with a pocket, but it was dotted with multiple shades of paint, as were his pale blue jeans. There were even a couple dabs of white and red on his sandal-clad feet. The sandals themselves had been through a lot worse, bearing more shades than even the shirt.

"Hell-oooo," the paint-streaked weirdo greeted as he moved his hands to his back pockets.

"Mr. Onenspek," Hester uttered and slapped the great wooden countertop of the island in the center of the kitchen. "You cannot burst into the kitchen like that, especially so close to suppertime."

Onenspek blinked, and his smarmy smile slipped away as he looked to Hester. "Oh, uh, yeah. Sorry."

"And please tell me that you will clean up and change before seven," Hester added.

Onenspek nodded madly, long after the lady of the house had finished speaking. He stammered but formed no words.

Hester came closer to the nervous, disheveled, and hungry-looking man. Stopping within a few inches of him, the two locked eyes. Hester reached to a cabinet door on her right and opened it. She then lifted the lid on a cookie tin and picked one out.

Onenspek passed the tip of his tongue over his lips, and his eyes went wide. He brought his hands up and rubbed his fingers over his thumbs in anticipation.

What the fuck? Phoebe wondered. She looked at Alva, who had turned her back and busied herself at the stove.

Then, to top off the odd scene, Hester smiled while looking down her nose at him. Her lips curled upward at an angle that was usually reserved for people that were happy.

Hester smiling? Now I've seen flippin' everything.

The cookie was a dark brown gingerbread man with white and red frosting. Hester held it up for Onenspek, whose eyes nearly bulged from their sockets. Her claw-like nails alone gripped the morsel. The paint-spattered man reached for it.

Hester moved it away. "Is it nearly done?" she asked.

"Oh, yeah. Yeah, almost," he agreed quickly, nodding.

"When?"

"Uh, day after tomorrow."

Hester seemed to consider his answer. She looked at the gingerbread man, as did he. "Promise. Day after tomorrow."

Onenspek's head went up and down as if hinged and motorized. "Yup. Promise. No problem. Absolutely no problem."

Hester's smile turned almost gleeful, a sight that made Phoebe's chin drop. Then, her great-aunt gave the cookie to Onenspek, which he gratefully accepted and immediately bit into. His eyes closed in delightful bliss, and he uttered a small groan of satisfaction.

"Very well," Hester granted, then turned to look at Phoebe. The smile disappeared only slightly faster than the cookie. "Ned Onenspek, this is my grandniece, Phoebe Pyncheon," she said, indicating Phoebe with her left hand.

Ned, with crumbs still sticking to his pink lips, reached out with both hands, and before Phoebe thought it over, she struck out her own right hand. Ned grasped it tightly and pumped it up and down like a man dying of thirst would to a water pump.

"Aaaahhh, aahhh, okay. Hi. Yes, okay," Phoebe blurted as her arm was yanked up and down.

"Nice to meet you," Onenspek said as he continued shaking it. "Ned Onenspek," he repeated and searched her face for a reaction.

Mercifully, his handshake stopped, though her hand remained a hostage in his grip. "Right. That's what she said, too," Phoebe said and jerked her head in her great-aunt's direction.

"That's Ned Onenspek the artist," Ned added.

"That explains the paint," Phoebe said.

Alva, without turning from the stove, giggled again.

Phoebe looked to her great-aunt for help and shrugged. There was none to be found. The man was simply never going to let go, Phoebe felt certain.

"Ned is our resident artist," Hester explained. "He's responsible for the paintings in the house."

"Ah," Phoebe allowed. Her hand was starting to hurt.

"No doubt you've seen them," Hester went on.

"Oh, they're absolutely unforgettable," Phoebe promised.

Onenspek smiled widely. He let her hand go and said, "Grazie, bella!" Then, with a flourish and a dramatic nod to Hester, he gave the kitchen door a shove and followed it out of the room. The spring-hinged door returned and flitted back and forth until it settled down.

Hester turned to Phoebe and said sincerely, "A very talented man."

"Uh-huh," Phoebe replied and wiped her hand with a towel.

"In case you weren't sure, Phoebe, you are welcome to join us in the dining room at seven. There are other guests that I'm sure would love to get to know you."

Phoebe agreed and thanked her great-aunt, who then left the kitchen. Phoebe stared at the swinging door a long moment after Hester left and shook her head.

"That Ned is a wack-a-doo," Alva said.

Phoebe laughed, but when she looked over at Alva, her big eyes were set on Phoebe's face. She was making light of the man but warning the youngest Pyncheon woman at the same time.

"Just be careful around him," Alva said with sincerity.

"I will."

Alva smiled. "Help me get the tray out of the oven, huh?"

"Sure thing," Phoebe said and went to her aid.

4

Hester and Her Boarders

Phoebe stuck to Alva's side, watching the experienced cook and lending her hands with whatever the woman needed. Then it became time to serve, which meant that Phoebe had to head up to the third floor to accept the covered dishes from the dumbwaiter.

She remembered playing with the dumbwaiter as a child, placing toys or dolls upon it and sending it down and bringing it up. To a child, it was an extraordinary device, with no discoverable bottom.

Phoebe arrived upstairs and found no one in the dining room. The double sliding doors were already open, and the table had been set for six, most likely by Hester herself.

Phoebe went to the dumbwaiter and slid the doors open. There was the chicken fried steak within a domed, silver tray. It was hot, and steam seeped into the air. Carefully, she removed it and placed it onto the center of the table. Then, she returned to the dumbwaiter and sent the car down, all the while trying to recall the day she'd given her doll a ride in it. She'd sent her doll down, down, past where it could not even be found at the portal in the basement.

But where had it gone? Phoebe asked herself as she placed another covered tray of food on the table. She recalled cranking the little elevator cable for so long that she was sure she had sent her doll to China. That's what the grown-ups had always told her when she was little. You could dig your way to China, they said.

So she had sent her doll down the shaft. Then, becoming confused over the ceaseless descent and wanting her doll back, young Phoebe had cranked the wheel the other way. She'd pulled and pulled, this direction a little harder for her short arms to reach. Until, finally, the dumbwaiter had come up.

Her doll was there, but it was very warm, hot in fact, around the fringes of its little red dress. It was at that moment that Aunt Hester had found her and punished her for her game, locking her in the living room to either do homework or watch cartoons. A week later, she had done it again and gotten the same result. A hot doll and confinement to the locked living room.

Now, with the last dish placed on the table, Phoebe decided to make herself more presentable. She went to the second floor and made her way to the bathroom nearest her corner room and washed up. Her clothes and sundries were still in the car, but she was famished, and the mantle clock in the dining room had said it was nine minutes to 7:00.

When she returned, she could hear the murmuring of conversation. As she entered, it was clear she was horribly underdressed in her t-shirt and sweatpants. She halted at the doorway, nearly overcome with the urge to run.

Great-Aunt Hester was not the first to notice her approach. A woman that she guessed was close to her age, with curly, perfectly drawn-up and piled hair of black cherry had spotted her and looked into her eyes with an expression Phoebe could not define, though it made her nervous. Her skin was a lovely shade of mocha, and her eyes a hypnotizing coppery brown, giving her away as a Latina, possibly something even more exotic. The woman wore an elaborate gold chain around her neck, anchored to her heavy chest by a goat's-head charm. Her dress's high collar was lined with emerald green, while the rest of the dress was black.

Once Phoebe could break the redhead's warm gaze, she noticed that everyone was wearing black. Hester, seated at the head of the table to Phoebe's left, had remained in the same outfit from earlier.

An older blonde-haired woman sat on the opposite end from Hester. Phoebe guessed from the graying wisps at her temples and the tiny wrinkles that accentuated her features that she was perhaps in her late forties. Her eyes were deep blue and as penetrating as the Latina's, and her straight, prominent nose and cheekbones made her stunningly attractive.

Ned Onenspek sat next to the redhead and had changed into a black suit with a black ascot upon a deep gray dress shirt. There was no trace of paint on him, and his hair, while still almost comically large, was perfectly arranged. His eyes appeared dazed and sleepy. His eyelids blinked slowly, and he seemed to have barely noticed Phoebe's arrival.

Alec Holgrave was not present, though there was a place set for him.

Hester gave Phoebe a head-to-toe glance and rolled her eyes. Saying nothing, she gestured to the seat on her right. Phoebe sat with her hands in her lap. The redhead was right across from her and eyeing her so intently, she felt her cheeks redden.

"Phoebe," Hester began in a regal tone, "this is Dzolali Alameda." She gestured to the curvaceous redhead with her hand palm up.

Phoebe was obligated to look up and meet the stare. "Hello," she said and nodded with a smile.

"Hello indeed," Dzolali answered smoothly. She smiled, revealing brilliantly white teeth. Her canines appeared to be on the large side, hinting at fangs.

Hester continued, shifting her hand to indicate the woman on Phoebe's far right. "This is Glendarah D'Amitri."

Phoebe acknowledged D'Amitri in the same manner.

"It's a pleasure to make your acquaintance, Phoebe," Glendarah said in a wonderfully husky voice that sent goosebumps sprouting along Phoebe's spine.

"You met Mr. Onenspek earlier," Hester said.

"Huh?" muttered Ned. He had been looking into the chandelier above the table. His eyebrows bounced as he concentrated on Phoebe's face. "Ah."

"I did, yes," Phoebe said.

"I suppose Mr. Holgrave is on his way," Hester said with mild annoyance. "Alva, if you would."

The cook approached the table and removed the lids to every dish, setting them on a side table. Hester bid Phoebe to serve herself, so she did, following the examples set by the other table guests.

A few moments later, Alva served the wine, a hearty-looking red.

"Pardon my tardiness, everyone," Holgrave greeted them and took his seat next to Phoebe.

Phoebe brightened when she saw him. Holgrave had changed into a magnificent-looking black suit, featuring a gray hounds tooth vest, a black and silver tie, and a white dress shirt.

Dzolali and Glendarah greeted him brightly as well. Phoebe was relieved to have the attention shifted from her, but slightly unnerved when she noticed Dzolali and Glendarah stared at him with the same intensity. Phoebe shivered when she realized that she felt a mixture of relief and jealousy.

Phoebe ate in silence as the others shared small talk. Hester was silent as well, though Phoebe noticed her give Glendarah many long, knowing gazes, which were returned in kind. Dzolali, too, exchanged such looks with Hester and Glendarah. Phoebe couldn't help but think that it looked like the three women were communicating without talking.

Don't be stupid, Phoebe, she thought to herself and smiled.

"So, Phoebe," Glendarah piped up. Her voice was strong and clear, with commanding enunciation. "Hester mentioned that you were let go from your last place of employment."

"Um, yes," Phoebe admitted, blushing.

"And you just . . . left?" Glendarah added, blinking her deep blue eyes.

Phoebe was aware that all eyes were on her and her blush deepened, warming not only her face, but her entire body. "Well, they did have to call security," she said brightly.

"Then you were okay with it?" Dzolali put in.

"No, of course not. What should I have done?"

"Did you not try to influence your superior to alter the decision?" asked Glendarah. Her tone was of surprise dipped lightly in disgust.

Hester chimed in, cutting off the question Phoebe was formulating. "I'm afraid my grandniece has not embraced her true heritage, my dear Glendarah."

Dzolali gasped. Ned gazed into Phoebe's face, blinking as if fighting sleep. Holgrave's eyes bounced from one person to the other, an eyebrow arched.

"Um, if it helps, I got mad and knocked over her coffee," said Phoebe.

The admission drew silent, confused stares from all but Holgrave.

"Bravo," he said, smiling.

Several long, uncomfortable seconds passed before Dzolali posed a question. "Did you at least put a hex on her?"

Phoebe chuckled, a sound cut short by a sudden change in Dzolali's expression. Her smile left her lips and, while she didn't exactly frown, the flattening of her brow portrayed a perturbance. Nervously, Phoebe turned to Glendarah and saw the same.

Holy shit. These bitches are serious. She tried to think of something to say to dig herself out of the conversational hole, but her mind went blank.

"Well, then," piped up Hester. "Mr. Holgrave, I do believe you were telling us something of an archeological site?"

Holgrave blinked and turned to Hester Pyncheon. "Ah, yes. I was considering a drive up to Michilimackinac sometime soon. There are digs going on there quite often and I'm reading a book about what's been found. Everything from petroglyphs to Native American and early colonial settlement artifacts."

"How interesting," said Hester.

Phoebe had turned to look at Holgrave as he spoke, though only for something to concentrate on other than the obviously disappointed Dzolali and Glendarah.

"It's really quite fascinating," he added, then noticed Phoebe's stare. "I could lend you the book when I'm finished."

"Sure," she replied automatically.

Ned suddenly jerked and burst into laughter, his strange dark eyes bouncing from one person to the next. His cheeks turned pink and he grinned madly before turning his attention back to the wineglass in his grip. Dzolali brought her hands above the table and put on a grin, looking like a woman that had just gotten away with a prank. Hester and Glendarah appeared not to have noticed.

Did she just . . . grope the weird guy? Phoebe thought and glanced at Holgrave, who met it and arched an eyebrow. Phoebe let a giggle slip, while Holgrave suppressed his own.

A few minutes later, when Alva poured more wine for all, Dzolali addressed Phoebe. "I just *adore* your hair."

Phoebe blushed. "Oh! Thank you. Yours is beautiful," she replied.

"Very kind," Dzolali said. "What did you do, dear?"

"Well—"

Hester interrupted. "She was a reporter for a newspaper."

"Fascinating!" Dzolali complimented. "So sorry it ended badly."

Annoyed at the interruption, Phoebe hid it well. "Thank you. I'm writing a book."

"Wonderful," commented Glendarah.

"Just a little fiction series. Maybe it'll blossom into something else."

"I'm sure it will," Dzolali encouraged.

The meal ended shortly after eight, and Phoebe remained with Alva when the others left. She helped clear the dishes, piling them into the dumbwaiter. She couldn't get the whole dinner scene out of her head. The archaic manner of dress, as beautiful as it was, seemed to have an ulterior purpose.

Alva left for home just before ten that night, leaving Phoebe to finish washing and drying the dishes. Once finished, she dried her hands and stretched. Her feet hurt, her back ached, and her fingers looked like pale raisins.

Leaving the kitchen with the intent of heading to bed, Phoebe heard something from the front of the house and walked toward it. The lights were on, though due to their low wattage the place maintained a dim, dreary aura. When she was near the living room, she realized that the sounds were coming from the old television.

Phoebe looked inside the living room and found Holgrave sitting on the yellow couch. When she filled the doorway, he looked up.

"Oh, hello," he greeted her, brightening.

"Hi," she returned and went in. She sat on the recliner and found an episode of *Perry Mason* was playing.

"How was your dishwashing?" Holgrave asked, not knowing what else to say.

Phoebe shrugged, not looking away from the little screen. "All done," she said distractedly. "Just how the hell is this thing working?"

Holgrave chuckled. "Damned if I know. Bloody thing's ancient."

"I know, but it shouldn't be getting a signal."

"It shouldn't," he agreed, unconcerned.

"No one broadcasts analog signals anymore," she added, not sure he was getting her meaning.

"Very true."

"But yet . . ." she trailed and pointed to the screen. She spread her arms, the upturned palms questioning the seemingly impossible.

"I *know*," said Holgrave with a grin.

On the screen was Mason, arguing his case in a court, wrapping up the plot with the inevitable witness confessing guilt and exonerating the accused.

"I don't get it," she said.

"Of course you don't you've just arrived."

"I mean the TV."

"Oh, yes."

She turned to him, slightly annoyed at his nonchalant attitude. "Doesn't it bother you?"

"It did," Holgrave conceded. "Then I learned to stop worrying and enjoy it." He finished with a crooked grin.

Phoebe put a hand to her forehead and sighed. "Whatever."

"You must be knackered."

She had seen enough British television to know that meant 'tired.' "Yeah. I'm heading up. Good night." With that, she stood and turned to leave.

"Just a moment," Holgrave said. He got to his feet, turned off the lamp and the television, and followed. "It is late. I'm turning in as well."

Phoebe took a step toward the door but stopped abruptly. "Oh, shit!"

"What is it?" Holgrave asked. He had almost run into her and was quite close.

"I forgot to bring in my stuff from the car," she said.

"Allow me to assist you," he said and followed her outside.

Phoebe was pleased to find that the raven was no longer on the porch. The cage had been taken from the hook. *Ack, that means it's inside the house. Ew.*

They walked to the Chevy, and she popped the trunk. The car's trunk light had quit working long before her ownership, so Phoebe reached in, feeling for the plastic bags. She held one out to Holgrave, who took it in hand.

"Is this . . . your luggage?" he asked.

She turned to his figure, silhouetted by the yellow-green glow of the porch lights mixed with red from the 'Psychic' neon sign. "I'm not exactly a world traveler, you know. I used what I had."

"Oh, I didn't intend to be critical. Just an observation."

"Uh-huh." She shut the trunk and stood a moment, taking a deep breath. She frowned and tilted her head to one side.

"What is it?"

"I don't hear any crickets. No birds either."

"Yes. I've noticed the same," Holgrave said. "It probably has something to do with the dying trees."

"Yeah, what's with that?"

"I don't know," he answered. "Some sort of disease, I suppose."

She trudged toward the house, wanting nothing more than to get her feet out of her sneakers, to change her clothes, and to slip into bed. "Does she ever turn that off?" she asked him, gesturing with her head toward the neon sign as they walked past.

"Not as long as I've been here," he answered.

She opened the screen door, allowing him ahead. "How long is that?"

"This is my second week."

"How long have you been in the States?" she asked when they got to the stairs.

"Just a couple of months," Holgrave answered over his shoulder.

They reached the second floor and the door of her room. She opened it, tossed one bag onto the bed, and took the second from Holgrave. "What do you do?"

Holgrave hesitated for the briefest of moments. "I'm an archaeologist. I'm a researcher, thus the book I mentioned at supper. I'm also an amateur photographer."

"Ah," she said. "Do I have to call you, like, doctor or something?"

Holgrave chuckled. "Not at all."

"Cool. Well, thank you for lending a hand," Phoebe said and backed into the room. Her hand was on the door. "Good night."

"Good night, Ms. Pyncheon," he bid and walked away.

Phoebe closed the door, searched through the bag for a change of clothes, and took them to the bathroom up the hall to clean herself up and put them on.

She returned to the room, dumped her laundry on the floor and turned off the light before collapsing onto the noisy but soft bed.

5

Deeds in the Night

Dzolali stood next to the bed, staring down upon the snoring, slumbering Phoebe Pyncheon. She had tugged the blankets up to her neck, enjoying the conflict of cool air slipping under the partly open windows and her own trapped body heat.

"Goddess Aphrodite, I pray to you. Hear me," Dzolali uttered in a shaky whisper. From a velvet sack, she removed a small glass vial and beheld it in the faint moonlight. The liquid within glinted metallically as Dzolali tilted the container back and forth.

Dzolali repeated her pleas to Aphrodite as she uncorked her vial and set its powers free upon the sleeping Pyncheon.

In the depths of a dream state, Phoebe felt someone get in bed with her, but she was calm. An arm draped over her midsection, and a warm hand caressed her. Her eyes opened and she saw Dzolali's face turned to hers. Phoebe's corner bedroom was gone, replaced by a brilliantly lit room of white. The bed was vast and round, and her nostrils filled with the scent of water lily.

Under the powerful gaze of Dzolali's bronze eyes, Phoebe succumbed to her kiss.

Hester and Glendarah prepared the charm bag, adding the hair and fingernails that their client, Darla Carp, had brought for the concoction.

Hester unrolled the pentagram rug and set it down in the middle of the master bedroom's floor. With a kick of her bare foot, it unrolled.

It was then Dzolali returned to the room.

"Ah, Dzolali," Hester conceded. "It's getting close to the witching hour. Let's proceed. Glendarah, are you ready?"

"I am, High Priestess," she replied and stepped to the corner of the room. There was kept a brass statue of Hecate, the goddess of witchcraft. Glendarah moved it to border the round rug, and Dzolali placed candles on either side.

"Cast the spell of silence, Dzolali," Hester commanded.

Dzolali bowed her head and threw a palmful of powder into the air, forming a cloud. A white flash erupted at the center and expanded with a pop.

Hester widened her arms, inviting her sisters to take their places round the circle. She retrieved the picture of Darla Carp's son-in-law from her dresser and placed it on the altar of Hecate, then stepped to the glass double doors that led to the balcony. She opened them and the night air washed inside, setting the candles' flames flickering.

Hester returned to her place at the edge of the pentagram and watched her companions relax their arms and close their eyes. All was ready.

"Goddess Hecate, hear us," the High Priestess began.

Glendarah and Dzolali repeated it.

"We pray for your favor and blessings," Hester continued with her sisters chanting her words just after, their task for the entire ritual. "We beseech you for the power of your daughter, Circe." The coven repeated the mantra.

"Grant us your favor, Circe!" Hester called and raised both hands, palms forward, in the direction of Glendarah, who went silent, her head tilting up to the ceiling.

Dzolali seconded the chant, and the hand gesture toward Glendarah.

"I call upon the High Priest Panas, spirit of this house!" Hester went on. "Grant us the power to be heard by Circe! Transform our sister into the creature she desires!" Hester and Dzolali said in unison. The demand was said twice more.

The wind rose suddenly and powerfully, threatening to tip the smallest candles or at least blow them out, but they remained upright, burning. The electric lights of not only the master bedroom, but that of the entire House of the Seven Gables went out, and the sky above the property flickered, then glowed with lightning. A bolt of electricity struck the house upon the iron spire on the southwest corner turret, and another set the opposite one aglow. Both strikes sent vibrations throughout the structure and would have awakened the lone, unbewitched figure in the home, had not Dzolali's spell of silence been cast.

The form of Glendarah turned dark, as if she had been subjected to a blast furnace's heat. Her blonde hair disintegrated to nothingness, as did her lavish dress. From her back, two small limbs appeared. Her arms and hands elongated and thickened, as did her legs. The relatively short, attractive human female's body bulged with suddenly added girth, and the new limbs stretched and grew.

The distorted form of Glendarah collapsed to the pentagram on all fours. A shrill cry of pain and fury erupted from her inhuman mouth, and from the new limbs spread a sheet of black flesh.

Dzolali took a step back, in tears as she watched her sister transform. She knew from experience that the wishes of the goddess Circe resulted in great pain once granted.

Hester knew this, too, but smiled at the sacrifice. It would be well worth it.

Glendarah rose to her new height, easily beyond seven feet. She stretched the wings to their full reach, even wider than she was tall. Miraculously, in the movement, not a candle was tipped.

Hester bent at the gargoyle's feet, retrieved the photograph from Hecate's altar, and showed it to Glendarah. "Do you know him? Do you remember?" she asked, for sometimes the freshly transmogrified lose their human memory.

Glendarah nodded. Her naked form flexed as muscles relearned their duties and limitations.

"And you know what to do? Where you can find him?" Hester followed.

Glendarah answered with a short, ear-piercing shriek and flexed her new upper body.

"Then go, Glendarah, darling," Hester bid and pointed to the open balcony doors. "Do what need be done and return."

Glendarah moved to the open balcony doors, awkwardly at first, as the strange muscular legs bent to her will. She flapped her wings, making the edges of the fresh black flesh snap like whips. Retracting herself into a crouch, and combining it with another flap, she launched into the air.

Hester rushed onto the balcony, grasping the rail as she tried to follow Glendarah's flight. The magnificent gargoyle's wings pumped furiously with a fleshy report, keeping the body aloft. Barely visible, Glendarah the gargoyle rose above the tree line, a jet-black figure against the night sky.

Hester noticed Dzolali at her side and placed her arm around her. "Look at our sister go."

"Beautiful," Dzolali whispered.

"With Carp's son-in-law out of our way," Hester said, "the house will be saved."

"I've been considering that, High Priestess."

Hester turned to Dzolali, eyeing her steadily in the starlight. "What troubles you?"

"Won't someone replace Hillsborough as village president, and may they not pursue his plan?" Dzolali asked.

Hester turned to look at the night's sky. "Then we will deal with that in like fashion. And if another, the same fate. We must not allow anyone to harm our house."

Kenneth Hillsborough had been asleep just moments ago, but a sound had awakened him. At first, he thought it was a branch scraping on the porch screen door. It was subtle, but repetitive. As it continued, he grew restless and looked at the clock. It was three thirty in the morning.

"Shit," he muttered. It was too late, there was no getting back to sleep, even after removing the pesky branch. He might as well get up and watch television. There was not much else to do in his girlfriend's apartment, where he was now living since his wife kicked him out of his house.

Kenneth got out of bed and dressed from the pile of clothes he had shed on the floor. He left the lights off and wandered through the ground-floor apartment, heading toward the kitchen. He paused at the glass patio doors and looked outside. In the dim light provided by the streetlamp, he could see the tree had no branches near the glass.

Kenneth checked the lock out of habit. It was secure. He checked the front door, thinking that perhaps someone was trying to pick the lock, for there was no window. That door, too, was secure. He turned from it, determined to check the back door, but when he was halfway up the hall, the sound resumed. It had definitely come from behind him.

Puzzled, he returned to the patio doors and stood still, listening and looking out onto the patio and the street beyond.

A rustling came from the bushes just beyond the end of the patio bricks. He saw the bush at the end move.

"Damn it," Kenneth mumbled. "Raccoon in the garbage again."

He flipped the patio light on, unlocked and slid the glass door to the side, and closed it behind him. Stepping onto the sharp edges of the bricks in bare feet made him cringe, but he knew the creature would run as soon as they saw him, if it or they had not fled already.

He was near the end of the row of bushes when he spoke, "All right, shoo, you motherfuckers!" he called.

There was nothing there. The garbage cans were apparently untouched, their lids were still shut tight.

"What the . . . shit?"

A long, low growl came to his ears and froze him in place. Whatever the creature was, it was something taller than himself. The growl grew to a sudden ear-ringing snarl, and Kenneth felt the hot breath on his neck.

"Oh, pl . . . please, God . . . nooo," he whispered.

Another snarl spurred his wobbly legs moving, but he only made it two steps before a great clawed limb seized him by the shoulder and spun him to the ground. Kenneth began screaming. Flat on his back, he saw the great black creature looming above him. His mind couldn't comprehend the sight of the monster's muscular frame and great span of wings.

Kenneth's bowels and bladder released as teeth and claws ripped into his prone body. His screams reached higher volume and pitch, waking not only his girlfriend inside the apartment but several neighbors. Lights soon began to appear in many windows of the homes and apartments on both sides of the street.

The gargoyle dug its claws into him and lifted his limp body from the bloody lawn. Its wings pumped up and down, lifting itself and its prey off the ground, flying straight up. Then, with a bite to Kenneth's throat, the gargoyle shook its head back and forth until the body separated from the head, which toppled to the patio brick with a hollow crack.

The rest of Kenneth followed shortly, landing in the grass a few feet away.

Hester and Dzolali lounged in the master bedroom, though they were not relaxed. Hester waited from her bed while she tried to read a book, though many minutes passed before a page was turned. Dzolali would sit for a time, then rise to pace, casting glances through the rain-streaked glass.

Another storm had come to White Lake, and they had closed

the balcony doors. The wind and rain pelted the glass, and lightning flashed through the room.

The time on the mantle clock oozed by, agonizingly slowly, until, at nearly four thirty, the gargoyle landed on the balcony with a floor-quivering thud. Dzolali was the first to reach the doors. She pulled them open and backed away, letting them swing wide for their sister. When Glendarah was inside, Dzolali quickly shut the doors to the weather.

Hester came near but stayed to one side as Glendarah brought in her wings and went to the middle of the pentagram rug.

"Glendarah, are you all right?"

The gargoyle shrugged and nodded. Mute, Glendarah's black eyes conveyed exhaustion.

"Quickly, Dzolali, we must release the spell."

The ritual was reversed and Glendarah's human form was restored, dress and all, though it reformed soaked. Dzolali, in her haste to help, forgot to recast the spell of silence. Hester did not notice.

Glendarah crumpled to the floor. She panted for breath but otherwise did not move.

"Glendarah!" Dzolali cried and kneeled next to her.

Hester said nothing but kneeled on the other side of Glendarah, searching the fallen witch's face.

"I'm all right," Glendarah answered weakly.

Hester gave an approving nod. "Is it done?"

"It is," Glendarah replied and sat up.

"Bright girl," Hester praised and helped Glendarah to her feet.

"Let's get you to your room and out of those clothes."

A flash of lightning cascaded through the room, and the power to the house went out, leaving them in candlelight.

Glendarah nodded and let her sisters take an arm each. Together, they left the master bedroom and took the slow but short walk to the southeastern turret, Glendarah's bedroom.

Holgrave heard the lightning strike from the basement, and it knocked the lights out. He cut his nocturnal activities short and made his way to the stairs with the help of his flashlight. He walked up to the first floor as stealthily as he could, but the creaking steps threatened to give him away. It was the same problem throughout the house. The very structure of the ancient abode broadcast the presence of its occupants.

He reached the first floor and stepped into the hall. The raven squawked from its cage in Hester's closed parlor. Without hesitating, Holgrave went to the staircase and began his ascent, cringing at every pop and creak of the wood beneath his feet.

Holgrave, having dirtied his jeans and t-shirt during his excursion, sifted through the possible excuses he would give if he were caught. As he reached the second floor's landing, the lights came back on.

Just as he set foot on the third floor, the master bedroom door opened. Being in plain view, Holgrave backed down a few steps and crouched. The sound of conversation covered the creaks.

Peering through the railing, he watched as Hester and Dzolali helped Glendarah walk, each with one of her arms around their necks. She looked as if she had been saved from drowning in a pool. Her hair was dark and plastered against her skull, and her dress badly wrinkled and drooping.

What in the world have they been up to?

The three women were taking Glendarah to her bedroom, heading in his direction. Quickly but lightly, Holgrave retreated in a backward crawl until he was lying prone along the steps beneath the third-floor landing. He watched the women go past above him, seeing only their heads and shoulders from his vantage point. He heard them enter the room and close the door behind them.

Immediately, he got to his feet and ascended to the third floor. Pausing for a second to listen. He could hear the women speaking but could make out none of the words. He then made his move.

He felt ridiculous, a grown man tiptoeing through a hall in the wee hours of the morning, but there was much at stake. It was not at all like the times he had done the same at his family home in Hull, England, after a night out with his mates. He was sure to get more than a grounding if he were caught.

Holgrave stopped just outside Hester's large, chamber-like bedroom. The door had been left open, and light, both of lamp and candle, spilled out into the hall. The little statue of Hecate, the pentagram rug, and the mass of burning candles were enough clues to lead him to the obvious. The witches had been up late, working on their dark magic.

Holgrave stealthily made his way up the hall in the direction of his room, trying but failing to keep the floorboards silent. He kept looking over his shoulder, expecting to be discovered at any moment. His face was etched with a perpetual cringe, as almost every step he took announced his position.

Finally, he went around the last corner and stood a moment with his back and head pressed against the wall, catching his breath and letting his heart slow down.

Holgrave checked his watch. It was twenty to five in the morning. *Damn*, he thought, knowing that he would be a zombie long into the morning. Fortunately, the occupants of the house were routinely slow to meet the day.

He moved to the door leading to his attic room, went inside, and escaped up the steps. Moments later, having undressed, he was in bed. He wondered for a time what had gone on that night in the master bedroom, but as exhausted as he was, he didn't wonder long. He fell asleep.

Phoebe awakened shivering and found herself covered in half-dried sweat and nothing else.

"What the . . . *fuck*?" She felt about the mattress but could locate nothing, not even the pillows. She recalled many details of the dream but had the sense that it had ended some time ago.

Groggily, she rolled off the soft and giving mattress, turned on the lamp, and located her three discarded garments. They were on the floor, next to the bed. Quickly, she dressed. Looking around, she found the top sheet and comforter at the foot of the bed. The two skinny pillows were found on the floor on the other side of the bed by the open windows, which she closed. The rain had soaked the bench cushions.

Her body was ice cold, even when she returned to bed, complete with blankets. She shivered in a fetal position as the memory of the dream replayed. She had never had a dream so intense that she'd undressed, but then again, she had never experienced one so vivid or long lasting.

Phoebe was aware of a deep thirst but had no energy to do anything about it. Her body ached. She smelled the sheets, then the pillows, then her armpit. She reeked with sweat and groaned in disgust. She pressed her nose into the thick comforter and inhaled again, noting some other odor behind her own.

It wasn't a masculine scent, so she ruled out aftershave or men's cologne. It was earthy, with notes of water lilies, one of her favorite flowers. Along with that was a hint of vanilla. *Had that scent been in the sheets before? What detergent uses water lily?*

Phoebe's exhaustion overrode any concern over the undressing incident. She had no idea what time it was, but she knew the coming day was going to be rough. Eventually, she fell asleep.

6

A Dark Day for White Lake

"Phoebe!" a female voice called sharply.

Phoebe stirred awake, feeling that she had only been asleep for a few minutes. The memory of the previous night touched on her mind, and she popped her eyes open and checked about herself. The blankets were still on, and she found her clothes in the right places.

The sun poured into the room through the windows, bringing some of its warmth with it. Phoebe saw this through heavy eyelids.

"Phoebe," Aunt Hester called again, perturbed. "I don't know what you got away with in your previous life as a journalist, but here, we rise before ten in the morning."

"Uh-huh."

"If you are going to live up to your agreement, you need to do some chores around here," Hester added.

"Oh," Phoebe mumbled. "What time is it?"

"It's *after* ten."

Phoebe whispered profanely. She had hoped she wouldn't be bothered until much later, perhaps close to dinner time.

"I need your help cleaning some rooms today," Hester persisted.

"Okay." She pressed her head into the pillows, taking in that sweet scent that she was sure hadn't been there before her mad dream. Unconsciously, she smiled. Then the memory of the rest of the sexy dream recurred at the same time as her own foul scent, trapped as it had been under the bedsheets.

"*Now*, Phoebe."

"Yes, Aunt Hester," she slurred and sat up. Seeing her relation standing in the doorway, concealed from the sunlight by the door, Phoebe gave her a sarcastic salute. "I'm up."

Hester shook her head, making sure her display of disappointment was witnessed. "It's no wonder you were laid off with this work ethic," she judged. "Come down to the kitchen as soon as you clean yourself up. I'll describe in detail just what needs to be done."

"Yes, Aunt Hester," Phoebe droned.

The door closed before she had her aunt's name off her tongue. Eyes tearing with exhaustion, Phoebe searched through her garbage bags for a fresh t-shirt and sweatpants. What she had put on to go to sleep had been fresh when she'd put them on, but they had been ruined.

She shuffled to the bathroom with her change of clothing and took a shower. The tiredness insisted on staying in her head and, if Phoebe didn't know better, she would have thought she was hungover. She'd had only the two glasses of wine at dinner, so that ruled out the hangover.

Throughout her task of washing up, the memories of the seemingly days-long dream starring Dzolali remained in her head. Phoebe visualized the voluptuous redhead and felt her heartbeat quicken. Phoebe began to form many questions about herself as she dressed and went downstairs.

Am I attracted to a woman? I didn't even know that about myself, but what triggered this dream? More than just stress, Phoebe discussed with herself.

Over coffee and breakfast cereal, Hester instructed Phoebe to strip the beds of the master bedroom and those of Dzolali, Mr. Onenspek, and Mr. Holgrave. Glendarah, she was told, was not feeling well and was still in bed. She was not to be disturbed.

"Oh, before I forget," Hester said as she moved to leave the kitchen. "Please remove that *thing* you have parked in front of this house."

Oh, fuck right the hell off, Phoebe thought, but said, "No problem."

"I don't want clients seeing it and thinking we're the auto wrecker's yard," Hester added, quite unnecessarily. "Park it around the side if you can get it running." With that last spoken over her shoulder, she left Phoebe to her coffee.

Phoebe mocked her aunt's words and mannerisms in exaggerated but accurate aplomb. "Get *this* running, bitch," she said lowly and displayed her middle finger to the still flapping kitchen door.

Phoebe finished breakfast and headed for the staircase, intending to get started right away. She stopped at the foot, however, hearing not a soul in the house. The entire place, at that very instant, felt empty. Breaking the silence was the sound of a car starting and the motor humming awake. Phoebe casually walked to the front door and opened the inner one. She stood behind the screen door and watched Hester's antique Cadillac drive past, heading for the main road. Phoebe was surprised it ran, given the age of the deep red beast. The tinted windows kept her from seeing who was inside, though she simply assumed it was Hester and that she was alone.

As was her habit, Phoebe kept her keys in the pocket of whatever she was wearing, so she decided to take the time to move her Caprice right then. Despite Hester's crude hint, it did start, and she pulled it around to the side of the house, parking it alongside one that had been in the same place since her arrival. Phoebe didn't know her cars, but she was sure it was old, though not nearly as old as Hester's Coupe De Ville and likely newer than her Caprice. It was a deep blue sedan—and an attractive one at that. Walking past it, she recognized the emblem of Mercedes in the center of the trunk lid.

Phoebe returned to the porch and was greeted by the abrupt call of the raven again. She hadn't realized the cage was there, as the bird had been quiet when Phoebe had gone out. Cussing through clenched teeth and fists, Phoebe pushed on, swinging the screen door out of her way.

She closed the inner door as Hester had done and stood still for a moment, listening. There was nothing. The living room was empty, and she reminded herself that a good dusting was in order.

Phoebe turned and looked at the closed parlor doors, and when she tried the knob, it was unlocked. This struck Phoebe as odd, but her curiosity crushed her caution. She pushed the door in and went inside. The room was sunlit, so she left the lights off and looked around. The neon 'Psychic' sign was lit, though in the day, it was hardly noticeable from outside. Phoebe was tempted to turn it off but decided it wasn't her place.

In the middle of the room was, as she'd expected, a round, wooden table with a pentagram-splattered tablecloth. A crystal ball was set in the center.

"Oh, boy," Phoebe groaned, shaking her head at the cliché.

A large chair facing the doors, clearly meant for Hester, was of finely carved dark wood with a high back. It was thickly cushioned and covered with red velvet. The rest of the chairs were comfortable-looking, wood-framed ones with thick, yellow cushions.

Behind the big chair was what appeared to be an antique liquor cabinet. It was lacquered in black, and yet another pentagram was on the front, crudely spray-painted in white.

There were candles aplenty, both on the cabinet, a side table, the desk by the window, and the shelf beneath the wall-mounted mirror. Beneath the shelf was set an old couch of red upholstery. The walls were made of a gorgeous wood paneling that went halfway up the walls. The upper half was done in red wallpaper, featuring a repeating pattern of gold flowers.

She was about to leave when she noticed something on the floor on Hester's side of the round table. A black line stood out from the maroon carpet. At first, Phoebe simply thought that it was a split, but when she looked more closely, she discovered that it was a wire.

Phoebe bent and tugged the tablecloth up and found a small, loose plank of wood, lying in between the feet of the round table. On the plank were wide plastic buttons, each shaped differently. She could see more wires coming from the plank. Some went up the table, others passed out of sight through a slit in the carpet.

Never fearful of buttons, Phoebe pressed one, then another, and another. Nothing happened. She looked up at the chandelier-styled light fixture. It was off, but the neon sign was on. She went to the button and pressed it. The little electric faux candles came on. She went back to the table to try the other buttons again, but there was still nothing.

With the room illuminated to its fullest, she looked again at the wall to her right, the same one sharing the mirror and the couch. There she found a line running the length of the wood paneling, invisible to anyone on the client's side of the room.

"Oh, Great-Auntie Hester," Phoebe said to herself, "you're such a phony!"

Giggling with a sleuth's delight, Phoebe dashed to the line in the wall and passed her hands up and down, all over the wallpapered section, then down to the wood paneling. She expected to find a handle or something, but when she pressed both hands against the wall, it swung inward. It was heavy enough that she needed to put her weight into it.

Phoebe's heart pounded, not necessarily in fear, but in excitement. Her exhaustion forgotten, she boldly entered the hidden room. A dim glow was centered on the wall at her left, leading her to the discovery that the mirror was a one-way deal. She could see the parlor on the other side.

She let go of the secret door and it swung shut, its hinges were spring-loaded. Under the phony mirror was a desk, and behind the desk, a simple, inexpensive office chair. On the desk was a rectangular box with an angled top, upon which were set buttons and slide controls. It looked to Phoebe like some sort of tiny broadcaster's controls, the ones used to set the levels on microphones and tape players.

Phoebe looked all over for a light switch but found none. She supposed it didn't do for the person in the little side room to be backlit. She inspected the little control box and flipped the toggle switch labeled "Master Power." A low hum began, and tiny red lights appeared at her right. Looking closer, she found another box, this one black with the name of a manufacturer of home electronics ensconced on the upper left.

Phoebe looked at the first box again and found that one of the slide controls had been labeled "Ball." She slid it halfway up. The crystal ball glowed white. Phoebe laughed and clapped her hands like a child on Christmas morning.

Daringly, she tried out some of the other switches and controls, but she could manipulate nothing beyond the light levels of the crystal ball and the chandelier. There was obviously a sound system, from the presence of the amplifier on the right, she had found a small microphone, but she could discern the functionality of nothing else.

Phoebe decided that enough was enough. She had pressed her luck plenty that morning. She set the slide controls to where they'd been when she'd come in and turned off the box. The hum quieted, so she pulled the door handle and reentered the psychic reading room. On her way out, she turned off the chandelier.

Feeling empowered and reenergized by her discoveries, Phoebe bounded up the noisy stairs to get to her chores. She started with Hester's big room. She removed the pillowcases and bedsheets, leaving the great comforter curled up at the foot. She gave the place a long look while she worked, curious to see if there were any surprises here. Like the parlor, candles were everywhere, on the fireplace mantel, the floor around it, and the furniture, and the air was thick with their mixed scents. Phoebe walked on the black pentagram rug as she moved to the other side of the bed and heard the squish beneath her pull-on sneakers. Checking the rug with her palm, she found it soaked.

The wet rug and the thick air were all the excuses she needed to open the double doors to the balcony. The sun shone through the sparse white clouds, bathing her light skin. The breeze was cool, almost enough to make her shiver.

Phoebe draped the goofy rug over the railing to dry in the sun and was just turning away when she saw movement along the dirt road below. It was a car.

A red and blue light bar tucked inside at the top of the windshield, the driver's side spotlight, and the antennae on the trunk gave the vehicle away. Phoebe assumed that the officer had come for her about the state of her old apartment.

Oh, shit. It was just some old furniture and junk for fuck's sake!

Her eyes followed the unmarked cruiser, which parked in front of the house in the very spot Phoebe had parked her Caprice the previous day. It was then that Phoebe looked down at her feet and was startled enough by what she saw on the stone tile that she took a short hop backward.

Footprints. Two together, then staggered as they led through the balcony doors. *Feet? No, not feet.* Four toed and gigantic, whatever had planted them must have been big. Now receiving direct sunlight, they were drying and soon would be gone.

Some kind of gag, like the crap in the reading room downstairs, Phoebe assumed. Though why Hester would bother, she didn't know.

Phoebe went down to meet the police. There was no point in running away from her old life any longer. It was most likely going to end in a charge for littering, or illegal dumping, or something like that.

"Community service," Phoebe said aloud as she strode to the front door. The silhouette of two figures could be seen through the front door glass. "Six months. I'll get six months' community service. At the most."

Phoebe pasted on a pleasant smile and opened the door. She was assailed with a woman's high-pitched whine before the door had traveled halfway.

"Hester Pyncheon?!" the as-yet-unseen woman cried. "Where is she?!"

Phoebe's smile disappeared, replaced by a grimace. The woman's vocal range and power were incredible, but her wavering pitch guaranteed she'd never have a singing career. With the door wide open, Phoebe set eyes on the auditory offender, standing next to a towering man in a blue suit.

It was the woman that Phoebe had seen leaving the parlor the previous day, Mrs. Carp. Without waiting for the blonde and blue-haired young lady to respond, Mrs. Carp repeated her demand in like tones but at a higher volume.

This time, the raven responded with a powerful squawk.

"She's not here," Phoebe said.

The policeman calmed Mrs. Carp. "Now, Darla, just hold it down a moment, okay?"

Darla Carp, her hair in misdirected black strands and runny make-up about her eyes, burst out in tears for what was obviously not the first time that day. She impatiently nodded at the policeman's request and pulled a handkerchief from her purse, using it to dab her nose and eyes.

"You say Hester isn't here?" the detective asked.

"I'm pretty sure she isn't," Phoebe restated. "I saw her car pull out of here a while ago. I honestly can't say for certain she was driving it."

"I know the car," the detective said and showed his badge and identification. His name was Clive Backstrom and his rank, lieutenant. "I understand. When do you think you saw it leave?"

Phoebe thought about the time she spent in the reading room, discovering the hoaxy toys inside, and then the time spent stripping Aunt Hester's bed. "Not even an hour," Phoebe decided.

"I don't believe you!" Darla Carp howled, making both people wince and the bird squawk again. The frantic woman stepped into the doorway and pushed against Phoebe. The detective restrained her. "Get her out here! Hester!"

"Mrs. Carp," Backstrom said warningly, "this isn't helping."

"What's happened?" Phoebe asked sympathetically.

"We're not entirely—" he started.

"That witch killed my son-in-law!" Carp screamed.

Oh, my God, Phoebe thought and placed a hand on her heart. She watched helplessly as the pro-wrestler-sized detective guided Carp away from the door and into the back seat of his cruiser. A moment later, he returned to Phoebe.

"Here's my card," he said and retrieved one from his jacket pocket.

Phoebe accepted the card and was about to say that she'd have Hester call him immediately, when the rumbling of a V-8 engine came to them on the stiff breeze.

"You know, I think—" Phoebe began and pointed up the dirt road.

"Yeah, I'd know that sound anywhere. I've pulled Ms. Pyncheon over a few times when I was working patrol."

Phoebe gave the detective a smile and pocketed the card. She watched as the Coupe De Ville pulled up and parked behind the police vehicle. The engine quieted and Hester got out, greeting Backstrom with a puzzled expression.

As the two shook hands, Dzolali appeared, having come out of the car from the passenger side. Phoebe felt her heart flutter slightly, and she blushed when she realized she was staring at the woman. Dzolali's hair was done in a fishtail-style ponytail, and she wore a black, off-the-shoulder, short-sleeved dress that came down to just above her knees. Her legs looked bare, but Phoebe couldn't be sure. She looked at them long and hard.

Dzolali noticed Phoebe standing at the screen, smiled, and waved. Phoebe returned it without a thought, then forced herself to stop when she realized Dzolali had turned her attention back to the detective and whatever was being said.

Phoebe felt like slapping herself in the face from embarrassment. *What is going on with me?*

Phoebe caught Mrs. Carp thrashing about in the back of the unmarked squad. Her mouth was moving like she was screaming. Backstrom approached the car and talked to the woman through the closed window.

Hester and Dzolali looked at each other and, to Phoebe's utter confusion, they actually shared smiles of intense enjoyment, though they turned them off the second Backstrom returned.

There was something very wrong with that reaction to Carp's tragedy. The two of them sharing joy at such a time bothered Phoebe immensely, so she decided she would find out more about what had happened to Darla Carp's son-in-law another time, perhaps at dinner that night.

Disappointed in her great-aunt Hester and in Dzolali, though she was yet a stranger, Phoebe returned to the third floor and continued her chores.

Hester and Dzolali waited by the Coupe De Ville as Backstrom spoke through his police car's window, trying to calm Darla Carp. The woman was hysterical, calling Hester a murderer, a witch, a charlatan—only the last of which did Hester Pyncheon take offense to.

"Hey!" Hester called out in the direction of the police car, feigning a wound by insult.

Dzolali giggled and watched Mrs. Carp's breakdown. It was by no means a small entertainment for the two witches, who stood with arms crossed as they tried to look bored.

Backstrom returned to the two women, leaving his complainant in the car to scream insults. The icing on the cake for Hester was that Lt. Backstrom appeared apologetic over the outburst. He was taller than she, one of the few in town that required Hester to crank her neck upward to keep eye contact.

"Just what in the *world* is wrong with Darla?" Hester asked, dripping on the extra notes of concern.

"Ms. Pyncheon," Clive Backstrom began, locking eyes with the old woman, "May I ask where you two are returning from?"

"We had paintings to take to the gallery and get them on display," Hester informed him. "Our resident, Ned Onenspek, is a fastidious artist and a genius." This she declared and punctuated by pointing her index finger skyward.

"Okay," Backstrom said with mild distaste, familiar as he was with the man's work. "Mrs. Carp's son-in-law was attacked and killed just before sunup this morning."

Dzolali gasped and slapped her hands over her mouth, displaying a passable expression of shock.

"That's terrible!" the eldest Pyncheon exclaimed. "Attacked? Attacked by whom, Clive?" She had known the policeman for over a decade, and she always made a point of ignoring his police rank and title. It promoted familiarity while belittling his role in the community.

"Well, ma'am, there's conversation about that at the station," Backstrom said, looking into Hester's eyes steadily. "Are you keeping any wild animals—"

"Squawk!" protested the raven from his cage on the porch.

"—other than that?" the detective conceded.

"It's a him," Dzolali corrected.

"*Him*, then," Backstrom finished with a quick eye roll.

Hester smiled. She loved it when she noted frustration in others. "We only have the bird, Clive. Why do you ask?"

"Mr. Hillsborough seems to have been attacked by a wolf, or a large feral dog, perhaps a pack. We're not sure," Backstrom explained.

Hester Pyncheon, ever the expert actress, cleared her throat and put on her best mask of confusion. She narrowed her eyelids and shifted her eyes left and right quickly as she tilted her head to one side. "And . . . you think that we have this—or rather—*these* animals, Clive?"

"Well, Ms. Pyncheon—"

"And what is Darla accusing me of? Is she telling you I have a zoo here?"

"Um, well, she says that you put a hex on her son-in-law, and she paid you to do that yesterday," Clive finally got out.

"Yes? And?" Hester said but held her stance.

"So you admit that?"

"Certainly. Why not? What does that have to do with an animal attack?"

Backstrom shifted his weight from one foot to the other and glanced back at Carp, quiet now but still staring at the two witches with unveiled anger.

"She says your hex killed her son-in-law," Backstrom said.

Hester dramatically dropped her head down, her chin resting on her chest. Her fists slipped from her hips and dangled at her sides, dragging down her shoulders. "You simply *must* be joking."

"Nope," the detective said.

Hester brought her head up and glanced at Dzolali, who played dumb. Her expression was one of concern, with her lavish eyebrows drawn low in thoughtfulness.

"Can you believe this?" Hester asked her fellow coven member.

Dzolali shrugged and shook her head.

Hester turned her attention to Backstrom. "Look, Clive. I provide a means for distraction. It is entertainment. And, yes, Darla Carp was here yesterday afternoon, quite upset, I might add, and said her son-in-law . . . what was his name?"

"Kenneth Hillsborough, White Lake's town president, Ms. Pyncheon," Backstrom provided. "It was Hillsborough that proposed the appropriation of your land for that expansion. You two had words, as everyone knows."

"Oh, of course! I thought the name was familiar when Darla mentioned it," Hester said and waved it off. "Anyway, Mrs. Carp said this Hillsborough fellow is married to her daughter and was cheating on her and all that, and she wanted a spell put on him."

"What kind of spell, Ms. Pyncheon?"

"A simple revenge spell," Hester answered, adding the element of boredom to her façade. "I told her it would make him a failure in his business and repulsive to women."

"And Darla paid you for that?" Clive asked with an edge of incredulity.

"Yes, one hundred."

"A *hundred dollars?*" he exclaimed.

"I have overhead," Hester shouted indignantly, sweeping her left arm to include the house. "Clive, people come to me with problems, and I listen. I take their hands in mine and supply them with a fancy explanation of the meaningless lines on their hands or read their fortunes from cards. Sometimes I give them a little light show on the crystal ball, and when they have a special issue, whether it is a séance to communicate with their departed loved ones or they have a wish, I cast a spell. They get a little solace from thinking that a witch is on their side and has a solution. They leave here feeling a little better for a while, and I am compensated for my time."

"Okay, okay," the detective muttered. He cast a look over his shoulder at Mrs. Carp, still agitated but quiet.

"If you honestly think I have the magical ability to conjure up a sort of killer wolf from thin air, slap the cuffs on!" Pyncheon threw her hands out in front of her, crossing the wrists in surrender. She stared at him defiantly.

"Now, Hester," Backstrom said soothingly, holding up a hand, "you know I have to check these things out. This woman's son-in-law was mutilated."

"Ew," put in Dzolali.

He looked to the redhead and smiled but said to Hester, "And I just have to put a report together is all."

"Yeah, okay," Hester said. "I'm sorry for her loss, but I don't know what to tell you."

Backstrom took a deep breath and let it out slowly as he regarded the two women for a moment. "Hester, you have to understand, it just comes across as odd that just last week, you and Hillsborough had that shouting match—"

"*Heated* discussion," Hester interrupted.

"—in the middle of the village hall meeting over the proposition—"

"Ridiculous notion, you mean."

"—that threatened to knock this . . . this . . . pile of village ordinance citations you call home—"

"Clive Backstrom!" Hester exclaimed indignantly and folded her arms.

"—to the ground in exchange for a *generous* sum."

"Pittance!"

"And then, combined with Mrs. Carp's visit to you just yesterday, makes more than one factor in Hillsborough's death point in your direction."

"This has been my home since I was born, young man," Hester Pyncheon said in a scolding tone. "And no one shall remove me from it while I live. If you think I've spent all that money on electronic gizmos in my parlor because I'm some evil magical being capable of conjuring a murder, then haul me away!" She finished with a dramatic thrusting of her wrists toward Backstrom.

7

Onenspek

It was Mr. Onenspek's turn to have his bed sheets changed, so Phoebe knocked on the door. She heard nothing in response, so she tried the knob. The door was unlocked and swung freely inward. The room was one of the smaller bedrooms of the House of the Seven Gables, being only larger than Phoebe's quarters due to its rectangular shape.

Phoebe stepped inside warily and called out to announce her presence. It was a gloomy room with the curtains drawn over the west-facing windows, darkened further by the navy blue wallpaper that featured stretches of strange, bronze-colored designs resembling garlic cloves that repeated vertically.

She stepped to the bed, one that was identical to hers in size, only to stop short in a moment of indecision. The bed appeared to have not been slept in. The colorful and new-looking comforter was perfectly tucked about the pillows, which, she noted with a downturned lip, were much fluffier than those in her room.

Mercifully, the walls were bereft of the dark works of the man who was supposed to sleep here. Phoebe became aware that someone was behind her, watching.

"Good morning, Mr. Onenspek," she said without turning around. "You don't have to make your bed yourself. Would you like new sheets anyway?" With that, she turned and was startled by the man's appearance.

Ned Onenspek appeared gaunt, with sunken cheeks that Phoebe swore had not been in such a condition the previous evening. His eyes were sunken as well, with the flesh darkened around them. His forehead, cheeks, and chin were smeared with a multitude of colors, primarily based in reds, fooling Phoebe into thinking for a heart-fluttering moment that he had been injured. His stare was hard, and the pupils appeared unreal, bead like and fixed like a doll's. Ned's tall hair was pressed into a rough pompadour, as if his hands had been run through it repeatedly throughout the night. Flecks of paint were present throughout his thatchy mane, so Phoebe thought this was likely. Over his thin body he wore an artist's smock that had once been perfectly white. It was now a masterpiece on its own, and due for proper framing.

Ned watched Phoebe and deeply inhaled through his nose, which, by the sound of it, was quite congested. He wiped at his nose with the back of his right hand, blinked, and looked about the room as if just realizing he had entered it.

In this moment, Phoebe was blanketed with emotions of despair, broadcast from him with such power that she was sure she could have felt it a mile or more away. Her maternal instincts arose in response, and only the unfamiliarity with the man, and the fact that he was covered in paint that may or may not have been dry, kept her from embracing him immediately. Instead, her eyes watered with sympathy.

"My God," she whispered shakily, "are you all right, Mr. Onenspek?"

In her eyes, Ned found her soul, and it brightened him instantly. A great smile beamed, displaying his fortunate, paint-free white teeth. "Perfectly!" he called out, nearly in a shout. Softness dawned on his facial features, and his body relaxed. He put forward his left foot and adopted a casual stance. "I heard someone over here, so I thought I'd take a break and see."

"Ah," Phoebe said. "So, is there anything you need in here? Clean sheets or whatever?"

"Umm," Ned pondered. He sucked his bottom lip into his mouth and cast his eyes over the room as if he had never seen it. He looked at Phoebe with a kind glance, noting her tired appearance as well. "Nah, it's fine. All good, you know," he waved her off. "I'm sure everyone else's rooms are much more in need."

Still thick with concern for the man, despite the nature of his horrific artwork, she pressed him. "Are you sure you're okay? Is there something I can get for you?"

Ned considered this gesture for a long moment. Finally, he said, "Thank you, Phoebe. I'll let you know. Quite busy painting in the next room." He indicated the room to her left, one nearly identical to this one.

"Need anything cleaned over there?"

"No!" he protested almost before she was done with the question. "No, not at all. That room's not to be disturbed." He looked into her eyes with an expression that would have been intensely grave had it not been for his arched right eyebrow and the leftward tilt of his head.

She gave him an amused smile. "No problem. I will not be doing *that* then."

They left the mostly unused room together, and Phoebe closed the door behind her.

"Have a good day painting, Mr. Onenspek," Phoebe called after him.

Onenspek turned to her with his hand on the studio's doorknob, "I do thank you for that, Phoebe." He said this with heartfelt appreciation and went inside. She heard the lock click.

Phoebe walked toward the front of the house, looking ahead to the next room on her list, the corner bedroom in the southwest turret. Dzolali's room. She sighed heavily and knocked, though she was almost certain that Dzolali was still with Hester downstairs.

There was no answer, so Phoebe entered. The room was much like hers, though the windows were much taller, topped with a stained-glass decoration shaped in a half-circle. These third-floor corner bedrooms featured walls done with a dark wood paneling that ran from the floor to the arched ceiling of the cupola, and it was from these beams that the ceiling light and fan were mounted.

The sunlight washed over the room through the parted drapes, and the upper part of the wall to Phoebe's right was tattooed with the colors from the stained glass, haloed by a rainbow.

The bed had been slept in and was not made, so Phoebe went about her task of stripping it. As soon as she touched the sheets, the scent that was in Phoebe's own bedsheets filled her nose. Her body instantly reacted to the water lily and vanilla and exploited her memory of the previous night's dreams.

Phoebe was surprised by a sudden lightheadedness. She backed away from the bed and steadied herself by leaning against the dresser for a moment, drawing air through her nose and exhaling it with a puff of her cheeks. Once recovered, she went back to work, piled the sheets and pillowcases on the floor, and took fresh ones out of the corner dresser's bottom drawer. Curious, she put them close to her nose and inhaled.

Fresh, clean, but no water lily and vanilla. She went about dressing the bed in the fresh linens, her mind distracted by the possible reasons for her own sheets exuding the scent that Phoebe had come to associate with Dzolali Alameda.

As Phoebe slipped the pillowcases onto the pillows, she recalled waking several times out of the ongoing dream, enough to realize that she was alone in the bedroom before rolling over and going back to sleep and the dream resumed.

She replaced the top sheet and finished tucking the pillows into the comforter and thought of the obvious answer. The sheets had been transferred to her room, unwashed from Dzolali's use.

Of course! How else? She smiled to herself, convinced that she had solved the mystery. *You're such an idiot, sometimes, Phoebes.*

"Well, hello there."

Phoebe cried out, startled, and spun around. There was Dzolali, just feet away and blocking the door.

Dzolali looked surprised at Phoebe's reaction and placed a hand over her bosom. "I'm so sorry!"

Flustered, Phoebe waved it off. "It's okay. Didn't hear you come in." *Or feel you near, either*, she thought. Phoebe looked to the pile of laundry and bent to gather it up. She regretted it immediately, for the scent invaded her again. She stood, involuntarily looked upon the redhead, and felt near to a swoon. Dzolali's lips were covered in a delicious red that nearly matched her hair, and her eyes were decorated with a black eyeliner. Catlike in an upward sweep, it set her coppery eyes aflame. Her jawline glowed in a shade of almond.

"Thank you so much for doing all that." She indicated the bed and stepped forward, remaining in the path of Phoebe's escape.

The closeness set Phoebe's heart racing. Worse, her knees began trembling. "Oh, it's um . . . no problem. No problem whatsoever." *Damn it, shut up! And stop staring at her!*

Dzolali knew well her effect and took another step closer. She relished in Phoebe's expression and the fact that her eyes kept wandering over her face, down to her vast cleavage, and back up. In that moment, Dzolali's attraction to Phoebe deepened.

"Um, what did the cop want?" Phoebe asked.

"Oh, there was a man killed by wolves or dogs or something," Dzolali answered and dismissed it with a brief wave of her hand.

"That's awful!" Though she truly felt that it was a terrible tragedy, Phoebe did feel a relief knowing that the detective had not come for her.

"So, you mentioned something about writing a book," Dzolali said as she clasped her hands together. "What's it about? I'm *dying* to know."

"Well, um," Phoebe stammered, unable to cease her stare into the other woman's face. "It's uh, about a woman who . . . rides this motorcycle—"

"Oh, I *love* motorcycles!"

"—and she rides all over the country, just having little adventures and stuff," Phoebe fumbled. "There's, like, this murder that happens in South Dakota at this bar one night—"

"Uh-huh," Dzolali interjected and stepped to Phoebe's right side.

Phoebe followed her movement and swallowed hard when she realized she was getting a double-dose of the water lily and vanilla, one live, one recorded on fabric. At some point, Phoebe realized she had stopped talking and, bringing her eyes up, found that Dzolali had followed Phoebe's gaze to her own fleshy chest, which was now almost grazing Phoebe's shoulder. Dzolali's eyes flicked back up to Phoebe's.

Busted, Phoebe admonished herself. *Busted checking out another woman's tits! Damn it, Phoebes!* She turned to face Dzolali and took a step back but smacked into the vanity against the wall behind her.

"Careful," Dzolali cooed and reclosed the gap.

"Um yeah, so this woman in the story sort of, you know, solves the murder," Phoebe finished.

"Sounds great," Dzolali said. "Can I read it?"

"It's not done," Phoebe blurted too forcefully. "I mean it *is* done, but it's not edited or anything. I just went right on into part two."

"Fascinating."

Lightheaded, weak in the knees, and filled with the want to drop the linens to her feet and plant a deep, meaningful, and hours-long kiss on the red lips of the vixen in front of her, Phoebe's fight-or-flight response saved her.

"I gotta get done. See you at dinner. Bye!"

Phoebe glided out of the room and, with the intent of dropping the laundry down the chute, realized she had gone the wrong way. She whispered a profane word and spun around. Dzolali was standing in her doorway, one fist on a cocked hip, and the other palming the doorjamb. The expression on Dzolali's face was terribly inviting.

Phoebe uttered a small laugh as she forced herself to again pass the opportunity by. "It's this way silly me."

"See you later," Dzolali sang out.

Phoebe didn't dare cast another glance behind her. She dumped the sheets down the chute and headed to her next chore. Holgrave's room.

She went around the corner and put her palms and forehead against the wall, opposite the closed dining room doors. Frustrated with her suddenly supercharged libido and its symptoms, she bit her lip and berated herself internally, willing herself back to some sense of normalcy. Almost in tears, Phoebe pushed herself from the wall and approached the attic door. She yanked it open and slammed it when she entered the stairwell and bounded up, not caring how loud they creaked or thumped when she stomped on them.

She knocked on the door to Holgrave's suite but was so off kilter, she didn't wait for a reply. She pushed the door open and went in.

Holgrave was standing just inside the door with something in his palm. He was wide-eyed in surprise at her appearance and, when she took a step back from him, ended up slamming his door with her back to it.

The contraption in Holgrave's hand exploded into activity with a metallic snap that made the tall man flinch severely. The little item flipped into the air between himself and Phoebe and clattered to the floor.

Phoebe looked up at Holgrave's twisted face, then to the floor. It was a mousetrap. She raised her gaze to him again and, to Holgrave, she appeared frazzled, but not from something he had done or his touchy mousetrap. Something else had gone wrong, he felt certain, to drive her inside his room in such a flurry.

Rendered curious at this, he softened his expression and greeted her mildly. "Hello."

"Hi," she replied, though somewhat gruffly. Her back remained plastered against the door, as were her palms. She felt herself blush, but the overwhelming need that Dzolali had instilled within her just by her very presence was fading.

Holgrave was dressed in black trousers and black sweater over a white linen shirt complete with collar.

"That's a mousetrap," she muttered, not looking at it. Her eyes were locked on his.

"Indeed, it is."

"You have mice?"

"Indeed, I do." He thought about his answer. "Well, one. *A* mouse."

Phoebe gathered herself and stepped from the door. She took a deep breath and let it out before continuing. "Well, I am here to take care of your bed."

"Pardon?"

"The sheets. I have to change the sheets," she retried.

"Ah. Thank you," he said and gestured unnecessarily toward it.

As she carried out the chore, her eyes scanned the room. Unlike the rest of the house, this attic suite could be considered cozy. There were no odd talismans, no altars, no pentagrams, and, most mercifully, she noted, not a single Onenspek work on the walls. The bookshelves along the south wall were mostly full. The books within were almost all ancient, finely bound in leather. On top of the black-lacquered mantle was an elegant clock, which softly and pleasantly ticked along.

In the fireplace, the wood had been burned, and the room was still saturated with the aroma of it. A fresh stack of logs lay alongside in a wrought-iron basket. There were two cozy chairs in the room, one of which was a rocker. The other, a light-brown, low-backed, thickly cushioned armchair, looked well used. Its ottoman matched. It was upon this that Phoebe stacked the used bed linen.

On his small table sat three cameras of different sizes, the largest of which was equipped with a wide, padded neck strap. Next to them were two bags, one a carrying case, presumably for the cameras, the other was a large square black one with zippers.

"Why so many cameras?" was the only thing she could think to ask him.

"Ah, well, each one has a different nuance," Holgrave explained. "This one is a thirty-five millimeter," he said, pointing to the largest one. "I use traditional film in that one, both color and black and white. And these two are digital."

"So, why mess with the film?" Phoebe asked, intrigued.

"The pictures come out differently. Softer, I guess you'd say," Holgrave said. "I do enjoy developing the film, despite the odiferous chemicals. Your aunt allows me to use the utility sink in the basement."

Phoebe had something more pressing on her mind. "Mr. Holgrave, did you hear what happened in town last night?"

"I haven't." He studied Phoebe's face with keen interest, resuming his task of spreading peanut butter on the mousetrap's activator plate.

"A man was killed by wolves or dogs," she explained darkly. "They can't even tell which for sure."

"At what time?" he asked, seemingly unsurprised.

Phoebe frowned in wonder. "I don't know. Is that important?"

Holgrave shrugged. "Probably not. Poor devil."

"I thought the cop was here for me," Phoebe let slip. She regretted it immediately.

"Oh? Do tell, Ms. Pyncheon," Holgrave bid her with a crooked grin.

"I'm sorry. I didn't mean to bring it up," she said, annoyed with herself. "I didn't sleep well at all last night."

"Is the bed uncomfortable?"

"Well, it's way too soft, but I had a dream that wouldn't quit," she explained.

"I see," Holgrave commented. His face remained neutral as he concentrated on the trap.

"Don't you have to set that?" Phoebe asked and walked up to him.

"Hmm?"

"The trap. Don't you have to set it first?"

"Oh, not just yet. You have to get the mouse interested in the bait.

Accustomed to the trap. Then you set it," he said and set it on the floor, near a small hole in the wall.

"Have to get it comfortable," she concluded. "Then, wham!"

Holgrave blinked at the ferocity of the young woman's exclamation, but her smile elicited his own. "Exactly."

Phoebe retrieved the clean set of sheets and dressed the bed.

Thinking back on Phoebe's news, Holgrave frowned. "Why did the police come *here*?"

"Excuse me?"

Holgrave repeated the query. "Hester owns no such ferocious creatures. What was their interest in Hester?"

Phoebe thought of the wet footprints on Hester's balcony but decided to keep it to herself. "Mrs. Carp came to the door along with Detective—" she paused to remove the card from her pocket. "—Backstrom. Carp says Hester killed him. The dead guy was her son-in-law."

"Oh, my."

"*Indeed*," she said, mocking Holgrave's manner of speech playfully. "She seemed to think whatever Hester did caused it."

"Intriguing."

"I know, *right?*" Phoebe agreed. She turned contemplative and her voice lowered to a near whisper. "Do you believe in this witchcraft stuff?"

"Oh, certainly not," Holgrave answered instantly. "It has no more substance than astrology. Merely an entertainment taken far too seriously."

"So, just a coincidence, then."

"Surely."

Phoebe gathered the used pile of linen. "Well, see you at dinner?"

"Most definitely," Holgrave said as he moved to the door and opened it.

"Thank you," she said and left his pleasant quarters.

8

The Second Dinner

Phoebe retrieved the soiled bedding from the hamper in the basement and started the first load in the large, industrial-sized washing machine. The old thing squeaked, thumped, rocked, and groaned loudly, and she was grateful to get some distance from it when she returned to the first floor.

Realizing she had some time before she needed to help Alva cook, Phoebe went to her room and retrieved her laptop and eyeglasses from her backpack. Anxious to return to her second novel, she swiped the dust from the small writing desk and sat. Opening the computer, she turned it on.

It booted to the home screen, and she noticed the available battery life. It read "10%."

"Augh," she uttered and reached into the bag for the power cord. She picked it out and unraveled it as she looked for an outlet. She checked the one her bedside lamp was plugged into.

"Two-prong! Shit!"

She looked for another and saw none. Then her eyes settled on the Air Castle fan. She followed the cord behind the tall dresser, where she could not reach it. Putting her weight into it, she managed to scoot it forward a little. There on the wall was another two-pronged outlet.

Phoebe dropped onto the chair and cussed her luck. She had so looked forward to some writing time. She wondered if there was an adapter somewhere in the house.

She looked out her window and noted a strange car parked in front of the house. A client, she assumed. She set off downstairs, considering the places where such an item might be found.

Phoebe searched through a closet here, a cabinet there, and found herself with only the kitchen left. Walking past the parlor, she could hear the voices of Hester and Glendarah, apparently with a client.

Thinking better of it, Phoebe went to the kitchen and was startled by movement on her left. It was Mr. Onenspek with his hand on a cabinet doorknob. He eyed her cautiously, then seemed to relax when he recognized who it was.

"Hi," Phoebe said, her hand on her chest. *This house is putting me on my last nerve*, she thought.

"Hello again," Ned said and brought his hand away from the cabinet. He turned his back on it and leaned against the counter, trying to appear casual. It failed miserably, since he looked as disheveled as when he'd found her in his room earlier.

Phoebe smiled. "Are you after one of those little gingerbread dudes?"

Ned's head swiveled toward her like it was on a ball bearing. His eyes widened in a flash and, for just a second, Phoebe was convinced the man was going to lunge at her.

"How do you know about those?" he asked, becoming deadly still except for his eyes, which bounced from wall to wall like ping pong balls.

"I met you yesterday," Phoebe said. "Right in here. I saw Aunt Hester giving you one. She introduced us, remember?"

Onenspek's eyes settled on her face, and he blinked madly for a passel of seconds. "Yup!" he exclaimed. "She did. We did. Yup."

Phoebe looked at the clock. It was almost two in the afternoon.

"There's plenty of time until dinner. Need a snack?" The man was too thin, way too thin. His eyes were glassy, a little red, too.

Onenspek brightened like she had just offered him a thousand dollars, tax-free.

"I think they were up here, right?" Phoebe moved next to Onenspek and opened the cabinet behind his head. Recognizing the cookie tin from the previous day, she pulled it down and opened it. Inside, carefully laid upon wax paper, were three gingerbread men, nearly identical to one another. Deeply brown in body, their 'hair' was white frosting, as were the dashes they wore for eyebrows, and their beards. Their eyes were red frosting crosses and their lips a flat red line.

They were not the cheeriest of gingerbread men.

She picked one up, gave it a curious sniff and, finding nothing unusual beyond the scent of molasses, handed it to Onenspek.

"You're an angel," Ned said and promptly decapitated the cookie with his mouth. The satisfaction on his face was ethereal, as if he had just been granted manna from heaven. Ned finished off the cookie in two more bites, moaned as if he had just been relieved of an immense pain, and took a seat upon the cook's stool. He closed his eyes, set one elbow on the counter, and rested his chin on his hand.

Phoebe looked upon the other cookies doubtfully. "Say, Mr. Onenspek?"

"Uh-huh," he answered dreamily.

"Does my Aunt Hester make these?"

"Uh-huh."

"Does anyone else eat them?"

"I don't know," Ned said and shrugged. "Have one if you want."

I think not. She quickly replaced the tin to the cabinet, suddenly feeling like she had done something quite wrong.

Phoebe watched Ned as she went about searching drawers for an adapter to solve her original problem. At least one of the drawers in the big kitchen was used for miscellaneous knickknacks.

After a few minutes of fishing around in one of them, Phoebe found what she was looking for among a scattering of spare light bulbs, pens, and rubber bands.

When she looked up, Ned Onenspek was gone. The swinging kitchen door was not yet settled from his passage.

Phoebe went to the creepy basement once again and moved the finished load from the great washer into its mate, a matching dryer. She put in the next load to be washed and set both machines in motion.

Phoebe fled from the symphony of mechanical discord she had let loose and went back to her room. She connected the power to her computer and resumed writing her book. After a few moments, she realized she had to look up something on the internet, but when she launched her browser, it flagged her, indicating that she was not connected to wi-fi.

"Augh! Of course," Phoebe grumbled. She clicked on the wi-fi search, wondering if Hester's network required a password.

No Networks Detected.

"You have *got* to be fuckin' kiddin' me!"

The list of networks in range of the laptop's transceiver was empty. Phoebe had never seen it empty. She sat back hard and shook her head in dismay. She was utterly cut off from civilization. *How can I still be within the borders of the United States of Mother-Flippin' America and be so completely isolated? I'm in hell and hell is a third-world country.*

"You know what? Never mind!" she called out to no one and went back to work. Whatever details she needed to research she could fill in later. For now, she needed to write—and write she would.

Time flew by when Phoebe Pyncheon was writing, and this afternoon was no exception. She sat back after a particularly exciting chapter, in her opinion, and adjusted her glasses to read it back. She glanced at the time in the bottom right corner of her screen. Even though she was not connected to the internet, the clock would continue, left to its own devices, to mark the passing of time as long as it received power.

It was after four and she knew she should have checked in with Alva by now. She saved her work, backed it up on a thumb drive, and shut the computer down. She washed herself up and changed clothes in the bathroom. Wishing to look a little more presentable than she had yesterday, she chose her best jeans and a black-and-white floral-patterned tunic top.

Entering the kitchen, Phoebe found her tasks were the same as those of the day before. Only the menu had changed. Alva directed the action, prepared everything in trays, and when the time came, just ten minutes before serving, Phoebe rushed up to the dining room, removed the food from the dumbwaiter, and set the table.

Phoebe sent the dumbwaiter down once more, waiting for the last of the meal to be sent up. She looked at the table, making sure she had forgotten nothing.

A hum and a rush of air grabbed her attention. Turning to it, she found that the sound was coming from the dumbwaiter. She opened the door but found it empty. The little car was still somewhere below. Phoebe put her ear closer. The hum continued, or what she thought was a hum. The sound was not consistent, varying in pitch slightly and silencing altogether every few seconds. A delicate breeze washed over her face, then ended. The hum resumed.

Phoebe wondered what Alva could be doing in the kitchen to make that happen and recalled that the washer and dryer could be heard running from the dumbwaiter shaft. It had been a couple of hours since she had set them running, so they should be silent. The hum was nothing she had heard coming from the two behemoths. It didn't even sound mechanical.

At that moment, the cable came alive. The car was on its way up. Phoebe resumed her duties and the dinner commenced.

Aunt Hester, Dzolali, and Glendarah had arrived in their decorative, black, and heavy-looking apparel once again. Phoebe noticed that Glendarah looked a bit tired, but otherwise fine.

"Glad to see you're up and about," Phoebe greeted her.

Glendarah smiled. "Why thank you, dear. A bit of a headache," she said and winked.

Dzolali and Hester, who were standing behind Phoebe, giggled. Phoebe's heart raced the moment she heard Dzolali, and in that same moment, water lily and vanilla came to her nose. Without a conscious decision, Phoebe turned and saw Dzolali, just inches from her, smiling seductively and locking eyes with hers.

"Hi, Phoebe," she purred and winked.

Phoebe felt weak all over. "Hi," she managed in a whisper. She watched Dzolali walk away from her, making her way around the table to her place.

Dzolali had let her hair down, and it flowed down her back in hypnotizing waves. Her black dress did not have a hoop skirt. Instead, it followed her swaying form snugly, finishing near the floor, where only her high-heeled shoes could be seen.

Dizzy, Phoebe looked away, again admonishing herself for being so taken with a woman. She took her seat at the table, giving her trembling knees a rest.

Nervously, she glanced at Glendarah. The blonde wore a smirk as she met her eyes. Certainly, she had witnessed Phoebe gawking at Dzolali. Phoebe's face reddened.

"Everything all right, Phoebe?" Hester asked as she took her seat at the head of the table.

Phoebe uttered an unintelligible but affirmative grunt. She focused on the food on the table to keep from looking at Dzolali, whose eyes Phoebe felt upon her face like a heat ray.

Onenspek and Holgrave joined them a moment later. Phoebe was grateful to have Alec sitting next to her for a distraction. The artist, however, still looked awful. His eyes were watery and red, his cheeks more sunken than they had been just hours before. His ascot was askew, and his hair a disaster. It was a wonder that he had managed to remove the paint from his features. His hands shook so that he put them on his lap when he took his seat.

Holgrave noticed, too, and leaned into Phoebe's ear. "I don't think Ned is altogether here," he whispered.

Phoebe flashed her eyes at him in agreement.

The meal commenced, and small talk ensued. Though Phoebe tried to avoid it, she couldn't help keeping her eyes from sneaking glances at Dzolali. Her dress was very low cut in comparison to the others she had worn, and her choice of necklace was, no doubt, strategically chosen. The round pendant, featuring three topless women, or perhaps goddesses, with hair that stretched above them and filling the circle like thick tree branches, lay perfectly above her cleavage, glinting in the chandelier light and drawing Phoebe's eyes.

Even Dzolali's hands gathered attention whenever she moved to take a bite of food or pass a plate. The long nails were luxuriously painted deep red and black, and her rings were large and ornate, encrusted with ruby-colored gemstones. Her wrists bore matching spider web bracelets that stretched up the brown skin of her forearm.

Phoebe found herself wishing to own such clothing, such accoutrements, and to possess such allure. For long moments, as she ate her dinner among the finely dressed people, she envisioned herself wearing finely made dresses, shoes, and jewelry. She knew she would never be so bold, however, and let out a sigh.

"Are you all right, Phoebe?" asked Great-Aunt Hester once more.

Phoebe blinked and, for what seemed like the first time that day, looked upon her great-aunt. Her hair was done up as it had been the day before, and the dress she wore, while a slightly different style, was still magnificent in its shiny black fabric.

Phoebe stammered for a moment, trying to sift through her muddled mind for something to say other than what she had been pondering. Accidentally, her eyes went to Dzolali, and her thoughts stalled.

Finally, with all eyes on her, except those of Ned, who seemed fascinated with unseen intricacies on his fork, she spoke. "I was just thinking about my novel. I was working on it today."

"Phoebe told me about it earlier," Dzolali volunteered. "I can't wait to read it."

Phoebe smiled and gave a modest shrug.

"Have you finished the laundry?" Hester asked, staring at her grandniece coldly.

"It's halfway there."

"Well, be sure to get it completely done before everyone retires," Hester commanded. "Those machines are not to run into the night. Understood?"

"No problem."

Phoebe continued eating, famished as she was from all she had done that day. Catching movement across the table, she looked up to see that Dzolali had turned to Ned Onenspek and had taken his chin in her left hand. She was studying his face, especially his teary, unfocused eyes. An expression of concern came over Dzolali, and she turned to Hester, keeping Ned's chin in her fingers.

Phoebe kept her head down, pretending to be devoted to the potato on her fork. In her peripheral vision, she saw Hester lean forward, taking notice of what Dzolali was wordlessly bringing to her attention.

Hester exhaled harshly and cleared her throat. Dzolali released Ned's chin, but a long moment passed before he turned his gaze from Dzolali. He resumed his meal, though he proceeded exceedingly slowly, taking a great amount of time in between his samples of food.

Phoebe felt a restrained rage from her great-aunt Hester but rejected the notion. Despite this, Phoebe downed the glass of wine in front of her, certain that Hester was about to voice her angst.

Hester remained silent.

Phoebe turned her head to see if Holgrave had noticed the exchange between Dzolali and Ned. He had. He watched them both as he ate, his brow knit low in thought.

Looking past him at Glendarah, Phoebe saw that she, too, had taken notice. Glendarah studied Onenspek gravely, giving glances to Hester.

What in the world is in those gingerbread men? What have I done?

"I heard there were some grim tidings in town last night," Holgrave said, shattering the silence.

"Tragic, yes," Hester said without emotion after a moment.

"Have the police found the animal, or animals?" he asked.

"They have not," Hester answered.

"Poor Mrs. Carp is so distraught," Dzolali said. "She even blamed Hester for the attack."

"Really?" Holgrave feigned surprise. "Interesting. Grief can certainly muddle a person's mind."

"Tragic, indeed," Glendarah put in. Her voice was sanitized of emotion, but a twinkle in her deep blues hinted at something Phoebe could not begin to guess.

"You should have been there, Glendarah, dear," Hester said. "Clive all but accused me of murder."

Glendarah gasped. "No!"

Dzolali nodded with widened eyes. "Truth."

Phoebe frowned, remembering how Hester and Dzolali had grinned at each other when the Carp woman had ranted in the detective's car. She got the feeling the women were putting on a show.

"Are you a suspect, then, Hester?" Glendarah inquired, almost gleefully.

"I do believe I am," she answered with equal delight. "On a positive note, however, I have to say that his demise puts an end to that awful plan of his."

"Oh!" said Glendarah. "Is he the same man? The . . . what was it? Village president?"

"The very same," confirmed Hester.

"I'll be damned," Glendarah said with an evil-looking grin, and the three of them laughed loud and long.

Phoebe, with a chill washing over her body, looked at Holgrave, who shared her expression of guarded shock. Ned, seeming not to comprehend the conversation, smiled toothily as he passed his eyes over each of them.

The meal finally and mercifully came to an end, and Phoebe managed to refrain from watching Dzolali exit. With a solemn promise to

Great-Aunt Hester that she would get the next load of bedlinen finished shortly, Phoebe went about clearing the dishes and sending them
down to Alva in the kitchen.

It was nearly eight thirty when Phoebe was able to get into the
kitchen to do the dishes. Alva had begun the project but had left for
the night.

Well into the task, Holgrave entered. Phoebe did not hear him
approach over the running water.

"Hello."

Phoebe screamed, dropping the handful of silverware loudly into
the sink. She turned on him, eyes full of riled spite. "*Dude!*"

"Sorry!" he said, surrendering with his hands raised.

Startling them both, a wine glass tipped from the kitchen island
next to them and shattered against the stone-tiled floor. Both stared
at the sparkling wreckage. Neither had been near the glass to send it
tumbling to its demise.

"Interesting," Holgrave said, and he lowered his hands.

Phoebe huffed in frustration, shut her eyes, and turned her head
ceiling ward. "Fuck." She knew she had done it. Like the picture on
the credenza the previous day, and so many of her own household
items of the past, her so-called gift had struck again.

Holgrave looked at the smattering of glass shards. "Don't move.
Your feet are surrounded."

"*Dude,*" she said warningly. She felt her patience was on its last
nerve. Her fists clenched and she wanted to swing at something or,
perhaps, the someone next to her.

"I apologize. It's my fault," Holgrave said soothingly. "Let me help."

Phoebe resignedly crossed her arms and leaned against the counter. She reached for the faucet and slammed it, cutting off the flow of
hot water.

Holgrave bent to open a cabinet door and retrieved a dustpan
and brush. Without a word, he meticulously swept up the mess. He

dumped the pieces in the trashcan, put away the pan and brush, and removed his suit jacket.

"What are you doing?" Phoebe asked glumly.

"As I said, helping." He moved to the sink and turned the water back on. He paused to roll up his sleeves, then began washing a plate.

"You don't have to do that."

"I know," he answered while he rinsed.

Phoebe sighed loudly and thought it best to change the subject. "Ned is on something."

"I know."

"I think whatever it is, is in the gingerbread guys that Hester makes."

"I know."

She was shocked by his admission. "You know?"

"Indeed." He pointed to the plates he had just washed and placed in the rack to dry.

His hint taken, Phoebe grabbed a towel and began drying. "Okay, so how do you know?"

Holgrave stopped washing the bowl in his hand and looked at her with a suppressed grin and laughing eyes. "Have you *seen* his paintings?"

Phoebe giggled, her annoyance with him disarmed. "Yes, well—"

"Well, there you are." He continued scrubbing.

"Seriously, though," Phoebe said lowly, "I don't think he's well, and don't say you know."

Holgrave flashed a smile. "He was an utter mess this evening."

Phoebe swallowed and made her confession. "It's my fault."

"What? How?" Holgrave asked with genuine surprise.

"I found him in here a few hours ago and gave him one."

"Oh, *God*. You didn't!" He stared at her in shock.

Phoebe could only nod in response. Her guilt was real.

"I've noticed that Hester gives him one. One a day," Holgrave said.

"I didn't know that," she said as she put away the cleaned and dried plates. "I mean, I suspected there was something weird about him and those cookies, but I didn't know the dosage, I guess you'd say."

"Understandable," he conceded. "I do have to admit, I'm only guessing about it being only one per day. I can't say I've ever seen him down here in the evening. Perhaps it's more."

Phoebe thought about her question before she asked it. "Do you think it's witchcraft or some kind of drug?"

"You kid me."

"No. Really."

"Phoebe. Witchcraft is nonsense. I've told you this." The washing done, he shut off the water and began drying his hands.

"I wonder," she said, drying a bowl. "I mean, what Hester's got going in the parlor are, literally, parlor tricks."

Holgrave rolled his sleeves back down. "They have a client in there now," he said and shook his head.

"I went in there today," she whispered.

"Oh?" His expression was knowing but guarded.

"I found wires leading from the table to a hidden room," she said and gave a short laugh.

"Well, there you are," Holgrave concluded, feeling his point made. "How adventurous of you."

"You haven't been in there?"

"I have, actually," he admitted. "Your great-aunt Hester was kind enough to offer to read my palm, so I humored her."

"And?"

"And what?" A frown of confusion slowly descended on his brow.

Phoebe matched his expression. "She didn't show you any of the toys? The lights in the crystal ball? No sound effects, nothing?"

"No," he said. "Perhaps she held back, knowing I'm a skeptic."

"I guess," Phoebe said and shrugged. "Say, you've been here a couple of weeks, right?"

"Sixteen days, to be exact, but yes."

Phoebe cleared her throat, unsure of just how to ask the next question. "How *well* are you sleeping?"

"Pretty well," Holgrave said at first. He noted something else in Phoebe's eyes. "How do you mean?"

Phoebe blushed. "Well, I had one of those recurring dreams," she said. "I mentioned it earlier."

Holgrave turned and looked at her sidelong.

"Well, it was bizarre, kinda nice, and it was like I was in a movie."

"I see."

"And it was really intense and . . . well—"

"I think the word you're searching for is 'vivid.'"

"Exactly," Phoebe agreed. "So, you have had that happen here."

Holgrave seemed reluctant to answer. "Yes."

Phoebe was about to go on and mention Dzolali's leftover scent, her nakedness upon waking, but Holgrave explained further.

"On both occasions I awakened before hitting the ground outside."

"Oh? In the dream, you what, jumped out the window?" she asked, grateful that she need not describe the scene further.

"Actually, no," he went on, "a gargoyle threw me through it."

"Yikes. Yours sounds more like a nightmare."

"Quite."

"That's the whole dream?" she pressed.

"No, but after a prolonged, somewhat one-sided struggle, that's how they ended."

With the dishes done, Holgrave excused himself to watch the television in the sitting room for a short while before turning in. They wished each other a good night and left the kitchen at the same moment.

Depleted beyond the ability to think straight enough to do any writing, as she had thought she might, Phoebe went up to her second-floor room, cleaned herself up, made some preparations, and went to bed. Just before drifting off, she thought to bury her nose in the sheets. Only the comforter bore the scent of water lily and vanilla, and it was faint. She had left the windows opened, which had aired out the room.

Exhaustion overcame Phoebe's worries, and she fell asleep.

9

Nighttime Seduction

Dzolali, having taken some time to change into her nightclothes, casually and silently stepped along the hall in bare feet. As she had the night before, she willed the key to turn and unlock the door. This time, however, the door didn't budge. Projecting her consciousness into the room, the redheaded witch quickly discovered the problem.

Phoebe had braced the door with the wooden chair.

Dzolali laughed and flipped her long wavy mane from her shoulders. "Oh, darling girl," she called in a singsong that carried her will and her magic.

"Hmmm?" Phoebe answered with her mouth half-buried into the pillow. She did not awaken, but the dream had begun.

"Come open the door for me," Dzolali called sweetly.

Phoebe raised her eyelids sleepily, tossed the covers to the side, and shuffled to the door. Clumsily, she swiped an arm at the chair, knocking it to the side. She turned about and reclaimed her bed, burying herself under the comforter up to her nose. She snored lightly as the door swung open.

Dzolali stepped inside and closed the door behind her. "Good girl."

"Mmhm," Phoebe hummed.

"Look at me," Dzolali gently commanded.

Phoebe did so, opening her eyes fully, though they were without focus. Next to her bed was Dzolali, dressed in a black kimono with large red carnations patterned throughout and a sheer nylon negligee that clung to her form and hid nothing. She took off the robe, let it slide to the floor, and joined Phoebe in her bed.

Dzolali embraced Phoebe fully, trapping Phoebe's legs with her own and pressing her upper body against hers. She followed it with a kiss. By the light of the stars and a partial moon, they stared at each other. With the youngest Pyncheon's mouth open and eyes dreamily closed, Dzolali raised her hand over her victim's face. Uncurling her fingers, a glowing pink powder took a gentle flight, descended to Phoebe's face, and was absorbed into her skin.

Phoebe moaned, smiled, and her eyes focused. Caution was replaced by hunger. Pleased, Dzolali smiled, and another kiss followed.

Though Phoebe met the dream with a curiosity not born entirely of innocence, she took Dzolali's advances for what they were: intoxicating and thrilling. She was aware, however, that her own movements were restrained.

The pleasure dealt by the redhaired Latina was unrelenting, tender, and loving. Still, as time passed and Phoebe's delight reached new levels, her inability to reciprocate led her to frustration, then rose to near rage.

Phoebe became determined to continue her struggles against the unseen bonds about her wrists and ankles. In her delirium, she did not correlate the restraints with the presence of Dzolali, simply an obstacle that Phoebe wished to remove.

Phoebe fought willfully, and over the course of the dream, she felt she was beginning to have an effect over her imprisonment. While Dzolali enjoyed Phoebe, Phoebe worked her wrists apart, then after what seemed to be an immense, exhausting struggle, she was able to move her legs.

"Don't fight me, Phoebe," Dzolali warned.

Regardless, Phoebe demanded to be free, to be allowed to pleasure Dzolali, who had done so much for her. With a great effort, Phoebe willed her arms apart completely and embraced Dzolali.

Just as she began to repay Dzolali's favors, a great thunder crashed around her bed. In a flash, Dzolali was gone, and Phoebe was left utterly alone. Her corner room glowed intensely, as if the moon had grown full and had focused its light through her windows.

Glendarah then appeared next to Phoebe's bed, wearing her usual high-collared, hoop-skirted attire. She appeared to have lost twenty years from her appearance, but her cobalt eyes were hard and dark.

"There is a price," Glendarah whispered and was gone.

Something powerful yanked Phoebe's right arm, and she screamed in pain. Her body was launched from the bed, and it felt like her arm was going to be pulled free from her shoulder.

Phoebe was flung to the wood floor, and she felt bones break, heard them snap. Reduced to tears, Phoebe tried to gather herself up but was torn into again. There were claws in the grip, and she was tossed into the air. Her room's ceiling, normally just a few feet above her five-and-a-half-foot frame, had become vaulted, arching away into darkness, and into this darkness she was hurled.

Broken, bleeding, and feeling tremendous pain, in such contrast to the ecstasy Dzolali had entreated her to, Phoebe wept freely. She missed her bed and the redhead's sweet company, thinking of her image as she tumbled upward.

The claws again ripped into her, and Phoebe howled. She was spun to face her attacker and screamed doubly when she set eyes on it. The beast was massive, with a skin of burnt charcoal and burning, golden eyes. It was winged, and the span was so great that Phoebe would have had to turn her head to view them whole. She could not, however, so hypnotized with fright had she become.

In the tight, torturous grip of the gargoyle, Phoebe did not feel the fall until she and the monster met the floor. She was jarred harshly, and she felt a shooting pain in her neck and back. Then, with a snarl that threatened to destroy her eardrums, the gargoyle pushed her away, and Phoebe sailed across the small room and burst through the windows back first.

She screamed as the turret of the House of the Seven Gables receded from her. She hit the ground and the world went black.

Phoebe awoke on the floor of her room, staring through tears at the ceiling, now back to its original height. It was dark again, at least to the point where it was lit only by the stars. She was cold, covered in sweat, and again, naked.

"Fuck," she groaned and tried to get up. Her back ached and her head throbbed. She rolled over, onto her knees and elbows, then leveraged herself up. She was spent, dizzy, and bruised from the fall.

Phoebe looked about the room. All was as it had been when she'd gone to sleep, except for her condition and the chair, which was on its back, lying on the floor a few feet away from the door.

She clearly remembered knocking it away in her dream. That, and everything she and Dzolali had enjoyed all ran through her aching mind. She gathered her clothes, dressed, and retrieved the blankets, reeking as they did with water lily, vanilla, and her own sweat.

Phoebe sobbed, realizing at that moment she had fallen in love with Dzolali Alameda, and over nothing, it seemed, more substantial than an intense dream. She cried herself to sleep, thinking that she had gone insane, confused at having developed feelings for someone she had spoken to only a handful of times and who was so closely linked to her great-aunt Hester.

Sunlight penetrated Phoebe's eyelids, and in time, the red glow grew uncomfortable enough to awaken her. She covered her head with the sheets and, taking the scent of Dzolali into her nostrils, instantly remembered the dream. From the pleasurable time in the beginning, all the way to the nightmarish end, it played in her mind like a movie in fast forward.

Phoebe held the sheets to her nose and wandered blissfully in and out of sleep for a while, thinking of Dzolali. The intensifying brightness of her little room marked time and reminded her that she needed to get out of bed.

"Ow!" she cried when she tried to move. Her spine felt like it was on fire, and her stiffness made it a chore to leave the bed. She sucked air through her teeth when she finally reached her modest height. "Ow," she repeated when she felt the bump on the back of her head.

Phoebe pulled some clean clothes from a garbage bag and waddled to the bathroom for a shower. Her pains made the process take much longer. The warm water helped loosen her muscles, though hot water would have been better. The water heater seemed to be incapable of that, however.

Phoebe stared into her eyes in the mirror as she dried her hair with the towel. She became painfully aware of two things in that moment. These two things outstripped her desires to write her book.

Firstly, she needed to know what was in the gingerbread men that was keeping Ned Onenspek in such a horrific state. Since the realization of her error in giving the man an extra cookie, she felt duty-bound to do something. Onenspek's very life may be in danger.

Secondly, she was in love with Dzolali. If it was not love that she was feeling for this person, it felt strong enough to be confused for love. She had felt similarly for the two men she had brought into her life. Jeremy, who she had met in college, had gone his separate way after graduating, and it had broken Phoebe's heart. It had been broken again when Thomas had left after she'd been laid off, but those relationships had taken time to cultivate. Dzolali was, in every way imaginable, a completely different experience.

Phoebe sighed and shook her head. "Un-fuckin'-believable, Phoebes."

Phoebe walked back to her room to make her bed, this time making it her first maid's stop for the day and stripping it completely. She dumped the sheets down the chute and, once they were gone, found herself shamelessly inhaling the lingering water lily and vanilla that lingered in the hall.

Phoebe took her time descending the stairs to the first floor. Going quickly seemed impossible, so stiff and achy her back remained, from neck to tailbone. She headed to the kitchen, hoping for coffee and painkillers if she could find any.

Pushing past the kitchen door, she found a woman standing near the window overlooking the vast back yard and sipping coffee. Phoebe froze and blinked, trying to focus her eyes. The woman was tall, straight-backed, with hair so black it was blue in the morning light. Her cheeks were smooth and pink.

Phoebe blinked and the vision was gone, replaced by her great-aunt Hester. Silver haired, slightly hunched at the neck, with wrinkles at her eyes and those that carved far into her cheeks.

Hester turned at the sound of the door. Her clear blue eyes turned hard and piercing. "It's about time you got up. It's past ten again."

Phoebe, thinking that she had gone insane in the night, now stood, staring.

Hester noticed Phoebe's odd stance. "What's the matter with you?" she asked in a dull tone.

"I fell out of bed," Phoebe answered with one hand on her back, the other on the island.

"Why?"

Phoebe chuckled harshly. "It seemed a great idea at the time, Auntie Hester. Thanks."

Hester clucked her tongue and stepped toward her grandniece. Her stare was not harsh, but it was stern. She set her coffee cup down on the wooden surface of the island.

"Stand up straight and turn around," she directed.

Phoebe looked at Hester for a moment, unsure. Sighing, she did as her great-aunt told her.

"I can't have you going about your work in this condition," Hester said with the slightest hint of kindness. She placed her wrinkled hands on Phoebe's shoulders, thumbs pressing into the base of her neck. She whispered words so quietly, Phoebe turned her head to hear. Hester interrupted herself. "Face forward, child."

Phoebe was uncomfortable with the touch for a few seconds, but Hester's hands were strong and soothingly warm. In her great-aunt's chant, she caught only the words, "Great Goddess Hecate," and two others: "grant" and "healing."

Phoebe closed her eyes and lifted her head. Whatever Hester was doing was working on the place of her neck that hurt the most. Only the bump on her head was more intense.

Great-Aunt Hester moved her hands down Phoebe's back, pressing her fingers and whispering the chant. Her right thumb found a sore spot under her right shoulder blade.

"Ow," Phoebe uttered.

"Shh!" Hester said in the middle of her whispers.

Phoebe quieted. Surprisingly, Hester's warm hands were doing wonders. Phoebe's bound-up muscles loosened, and the horrible aching lessened. Overall, she felt relaxed, relieved. She sensed not so much a kindness in Hester, but a purpose, as if her acts constituted a step in a process.

A moment later, Hester's hands left Phoebe's spine. She opened her eyes to find Hester standing in front of her with the cup of coffee in her hand, watching Phoebe's face with a faint air of impatience.

Phoebe foolishly checked behind her, as she had not noted her aunt's movement. The hands had just left her being a second before.

"Better?"

"Um, yeah," Phoebe answered gratefully.

"Good," Hester said and turned to the kitchen door. "Can you clean the microwave for Alva? Today or tomorrow is fine, depending on how things go for you."

"Oh, sure," Phoebe said, after considering her aunt's choice of words for a heartbeat.

"Excellent," Hester said and exited the kitchen.

Phoebe stared at the empty space for a moment, shocked that Hester had such a magic touch. She tilted her head, bent at the waist, and straightened. Only a faint trace of the pains remained.

"Well, I'll be cheese in a pretzel," she said to the empty kitchen.

Phoebe poured a cup of coffee and made some toast. She leaned against the counter, enjoying her quick breakfast. Her eyes fell on the cabinet next to the door, the cabinet where the gingerbread men dwelled.

She set her coffee down and went to the cabinet, opened it, and retrieved the tin. She set it on the counter and removed the lid. There was a new batch below the two that had remained from yesterday, when she had handed one to Ned. The new ones were separated from the old by wax paper.

Phoebe contemplated the idea and took stock of her feelings. Her yearning for Dzolali was real, it was intense, but whether it was love or extreme lust was in question. The image of the redhead appeared in her mind, and her hands shook with want.

Suddenly irritated by her situation, Phoebe knew she had to have answers. She dropped the aluminum lid onto the granite counter with a clatter and began searching the kitchen. She found a box of sandwich bags, took one, and tossed a gingerbread man into it. She replaced the tin back into the cabinet.

Phoebe bounded upstairs to her room and retrieved her car keys and her black hoodie. She went to the front door and pushed the screen door out of her way. The springs sang and the raven called as she exited.

"Shut it, bird," Phoebe grunted and headed for her Chevy.

She strode along, hoping that Hester and the others in the parlor would not observe her leaving. She tried to mingle her pace with an air of casualness, turning her face to the sky and planting a smile on her lips, just in case.

Phoebe dropped into the driver's seat and shut the door, trying not to make it slam. She turned the key, and the starter, as it was apt to do on occasion, just whirred. Its brushes failed to contact the flywheel and didn't turn the engine over. She let go of the key and tried again with the same result.

"Damn you!" she shouted and hit the steering wheel with the back of her fist. Furious, she turned the key once more.

This harsh and irrational method of starting the Caprice had, until that moment, achieved a one hundred percent rate of failure. This time, however, the starter managed to catch a tooth of the flywheel and start the engine.

Phoebe backed out of the spot and followed Gable Way to the two-lane road, then turned left, toward town.

"Where do you think she's going?" Glendarah asked as she watched the Caprice go past the parlor window.

"It may be nothing. Just out for a drive, perhaps." Hester considered for a moment. "Still, it's not wise to assume things." She stepped out of the room, and Glendarah followed.

The high priestess moved quickly, stepping onto the porch and to the birdcage. The bird was facing the door, as if it had been expecting the visit. Glendarah kept her distance, remaining at the front door as Hester whispered to the big black bird and took the cage from the hook. She set it on the porch and, opening the catches that kept the floor attached to the frame, lifted the cage from the base.

The raven let out a cringe worthy "Rawk!" and bounded onto the low porch wall. The bird took flight, thrusting itself into the sky at a steep climb.

Hester watched the raven turn to the southwest and slip beyond

the trees and out of sight. She became aware of Glendarah at her elbow.
"He will guide us, sister."

"So mote it be," Glendarah said with hope.

Phoebe turned onto White Lake's main drag, a two-lane street that featured the bulk of the town's shops and the police station. She parked in
between a pair of White Lake Police cruisers.

She headed inside and asked to see Detective Backstrom. She produced the card he had given her and showed it to the policewoman
behind the bulletproof glass. Phoebe was buzzed through the door and
stepped into the waiting room, a small rectangular room with windows facing the street. The walls were blue-painted cinderblock. She
sat in one of the orange plastic chairs for just a few minutes before the
detective came in from another door.

"Miss Pyncheon," he greeted.

"Hi," she said and stood. "I need your help."

"You have something on the Hillsborough case?"

Phoebe paused, looking dubious. "I thought you said that was an
animal attack."

"We're not done investigating," Backstrom said, watching her
face intently.

"Well, this isn't about that," she said. "At least I don't think so."

Backstrom said nothing, waiting her out.

"Look," Phoebe continued. She shook her hair from her eyes and
pulled the baggie from her hoodie pocket.

"You want me to look at a cookie," Clive Backstrom said without
emotion. He looked at her doubtfully.

"It's a gingerbread guy."

"Uh-huh."

Phoebe quickly told the detective about Ned Onenspek and his
apparent dependence on the gingerbread men, and her own nightmares, leaving out the sordid details.

Backstrom took the baggie and gave the gingerbread man a close look in the ceiling lights. "And you're thinking these are laced with something," he concluded.

"I suspect that, yes," Phoebe said. "Is there a way you can test it?"

"Not here," he said.

Phoebe's shoulders drooped and she crossed her arms.

Backstrom sighed and looked at her sidelong. "I can run it over to County. They have the forensic lab."

She brightened. "Can you do that?"

"I can, but I have to open a case file," he said. "You know, to make it an official investigation."

"Cool. Thanks!" she said and shook his hand. She turned to leave.

"Hey," he called after her.

"Yeah?"

"If it's positive, you realize we'll be busting the place," Backstrom said. "You may want to consider getting out of there."

"I don't have any place to go," she said. "It's why I'm here at all."

Clive nodded in understanding.

"Do you know when the tests will be done?" she asked.

"Probably day after tomorrow. Tomorrow maybe. How can I reach you?"

"I don't have a cell," she admitted. "So maybe I can sneak a phone call to you. If you call, my Aunt Hester may be tipped off."

"True enough. Give me a call tomorrow."

Phoebe left the police station and stepped out into the sun, unaware that she was being observed. She went to her car, reversed into the street, and headed back to the House of the Seven Gables under the shadow of black wings.

Hester and Glendarah sat in the deep shade of the porch upon the wooden Adirondacks, awaiting the return of Phoebe and the raven. The sighing of the screen door springs grabbed their attention.

"Excuse me, Ms. Pyncheon, Ms. D'Amitri," Ned Onenspek addressed them from the doorway. His eyes danced nervously, and he hid his shaking right hand in his pants pocket. He smiled at them with an apologetic expression laced with hope.

Hester shifted in the chair with mild annoyance. His need was theirs, however, so she braced herself to stand. "Ah, Mr. Onenspek. Is it that time already?"

Ned looked away to the dirt path that was Gable Way, as if looking for something he had lost but not remembering what it was. His breath was short and quick, and he wished that he was back in his painting. Swiping his colors, concealing himself, the white of his past, creating new the visions of old, the bloody, the lessons learned but forgotten. He needed to hide in the blood. The red of paint would suffice, but he needed the seeing of it all.

Hester's gingerbread men brought the seeing, the flashes of uniformed men clashing, cutting each other to ribbons, blasting each other apart, sending fountains of blood in every direction. When the seeing came, his hands could paint their pictures, one at a time or a few at a time, it mattered little. Ned could see his hands now, moving in a blur of activity, dotting the details, filling in with sweeps. With the scene set, the battle or torture ready, the red paint would come to the palette. With trembling fingers clamped to his brush, the blood would fly in sprinkles. A brief pressing onto the canvas made blossoms of red.

Hester touched his elbow to bring him back into the now and led him into the house. He followed like a dog at dinner time. She pushed the kitchen door out of her way, careless if it sprung back and hit him. She opened the cabinet door and pulled off the cover.

She frowned.

Ned walked up to her and he didn't like the frown. The frown was bad. "Is something wrong, Ms. Pyncheon?"

Hester's eyes peered over at him, drilling into his with deep suspicion. "Have you been in this tin, Mr. Onenspek?"

Ned's eyes jumped to his left and hung there for a second. He thought it through, unsure, as his eyes shifted right, then left again before returning to meet hers. She remained staring at him, deadly still.

"I have not touched your cookie tin, Ms. Pyncheon," he finally settled on.

"We're two gingerbread men short," she growled.

"*Two?*" Ned uttered. Panicked for an instant, he grabbed a corner of the container and, without pulling it from Hester's grasp, looked inside. "Can't be two."

"Why can't it be two, Mr. Onenspek?" she asked, catching his lie.

Ned dropped his eyes shamefully. "She was just trying to be nice."

"Who gave it to you?" Hester pushed.

"She doesn't know the arrangement."

"Who gave it to you?"

Ned shuffled his feet. "Phoebe. It was my fault. She doesn't *know* they help me, Ms. Pyncheon."

Hester snapped the cover back onto the tin and looked down her nose at the artist. "I'm not blaming her, Mr. Onenspek."

Ned's desperation rose to the surface. He began to breathe heavily and fast, looking to the tin and then to the accusing eyes of Hester Pyncheon. "Oh, please."

"Go," she demanded, still holding the tin within his reach as if to dare him to try to touch it.

After some unintelligible whines of perseveration, Onenspek turned and fled the room.

Hester hid the cookie tin in a different location and, with her fury building within her, flung the kitchen door open with only a thought. It remained open as if it waited for her to pass, then closed violently, left swinging in her wake.

"Hester," Glendarah called from the open front door. "He has returned."

The high priestess moved swiftly, joining Glendarah on the porch. The raven was perched on the porch railing, watching Hester's face steadily.

Glendarah gave a bow and stood back as Hester moved to the great black bird and conferred with it in whispers. In a moment, Hester returned to her coven sister.

"Phoebe has gone to the police," she said, seething.

Glendarah's eyes widened with concern. "Yes. Yes, the deep suspicion I felt from her as she left now fits."

Hester nodded. "Ned confessed to me that he took an extra cookie," she added. "But two are missing," she said, leading Glendarah to the logical conclusion.

Glendarah's eyes closed halfway as she tilted her head back. She sensed the approach from beyond the forest to the south. "She returns."

"Yes," Hester agreed, feeling the same. She stepped to the raven on the rail and whispered further. A moment later, it took flight in the direction that it had before, this time, with greater urgency.

"It's a shame," Hester said as Glendarah approached. "I rather liked him."

"A shame, Hester?" the blonde asked. "He will be quickly replaced."

"Yes, but the investigation should die with him," Hester assured her coven sister.

Backstrom stood from his desk and stretched. It was lunchtime and he was famished, having not eaten that morning, choosing instead to sleep until six and rely on the coffee to do its job.

Might as well get that sample to the county lab while I'm out. He retrieved the baggie with the baked suspect sealed within from a drawer and left the station. He intended to grab a sit-down lunch at his favorite truck stop along the way. It was after the peak hours of the lunch crowd, so it would be quick.

Clive angled the Ford police cruiser onto the main street and through town, joining the two-lane highway that led out of town. He gripped the steering wheel harder to guide the sedan around a familiar bend, which was, due to its sharpness and the thick forestation on both sides of the road, a blind corner.

This time, as he approached the curve, the already cloudy skies went dark and lightning flashed in his face. An intense rainfall ensued immediately after, further obscuring his vision.

"Shit," Clive muttered. The lightning was dulled by his aviator sunglasses, which, due to the sudden darkness, he had to remove, leaving one hand on the wheel.

As Backstrom looked from the road to drop the glasses onto the passenger seat, another lightning bolt turned the world a brilliant white, its bolt striking a tree ahead of him. The damp wood exploded in a shower of sparks, fire, and splinters, and the tree began to fall his way. He had not even had time to turn on the wipers.

Clive swerved, kicking out the cruiser's rear end. The smoking tree came down on the trunk. The back of the car bounced about, and Clive counter-steered. The tires screeched as they slid on the freshly rained upon blacktop.

"Fuck!" he shouted as his car slid along, this time toward a pedestrian.

The man simply stood in the middle of the road, deluge notwithstanding. Clive had time to notice that the idiot was tall and wore a long black garment with a hood. Not wishing to run him down, Clive allowed the vehicle to continue its leftward fishtail. The Ford continued sliding along the opposite lane, missing the cloaked individual by inches. The car's momentum was bleeding away, but not quickly enough.

The car went off the road, its tires throwing up gravel and grass before sailing into the thickly forested land. Rain, lightning, and branches crashed to the ground as the Ford struck several trees.

10

Gifts & Invitations

Phoebe returned to the house and went about her assigned chores. She took care of Dzolali's room first, perhaps out of curiosity, perhaps driven by her obsession. Onenspek's room was in the same unused state as it had been the day before. Then, without encountering another soul, she took care of the other rooms.

In the basement, she set the laundry machines to their tasks and went to her room to sneak in some writing. She was barely thirty minutes into it when a knock came to her door.

"Shit," she whispered, then called to the door, "Yes?"

The door opened and Phoebe knew who it was before she even looked. Water lily and vanilla came to her nose. She turned her head, unaware of the goofy grin that had planted itself on her face.

"Busy?" Dzolali asked. She stood in the doorway, wearing a simple, modern knee-length skirt and a white blouse, not buttoned to the top. Her black cherry red hair was left down to spill over her collar and shoulders.

"Nope!" Phoebe said too loudly and slapped the laptop shut.

Dzolali's face broke out in a giddy smile, and she stepped in, shutting the door behind her. A long black garment bag hung from her fingers. "I brought something for you."

"For me?"

"Yup," Dzolali said. "Cute glasses," she added, eyeing Phoebe's face until the blonde blushed.

"Oh, God," Phoebe said with irritation. She had forgotten to take them off. She swung them up onto her head.

"No. Really."

"Whatever," Phoebe said and waved her off. "What is it?" she asked, indicating the bag.

"You'll see," Dzolali said with a slanted grin. She strode to the bed and laid the bag out on it. Unzipping it, she carefully freed a dress and held it out for Phoebe to see.

Phoebe gasped. "That's beautiful," she whispered and stepped closer to touch it.

The dress was shiny emerald green from top to bottom, with a skirt that looked as if it might end just past her knees, edged with gentle ruffles and adorned with stylish buttons placed in a vertical zigzag. The bodice featured a thinly padded stitched panel, decorated with a bow at the midriff and framed on either side by more ruffles, sweeping upward into a collar. The sleeves were long and sheer.

"Try it on," Dzolali said and held it out.

"Oh, I can't."

Dzolali stepped forward, close enough for Phoebe to feel her warm breath on her face. "For me?" she begged with a purr.

Phoebe met the redhead's eyes and felt her knees wobble. "Okay," she said without thinking. She reached for the dress, but Dzolali held the hanger.

"I think you're forgetting something," she said, looking Phoebe up and down.

"Umm."

"You have to take off all that to put this on," Dzolali said and laughed.

"But, you're in here."

The next thing Phoebe knew, Dzolali had her free arm around her and their lips met. Dzolali's kiss was forward and unexpected, but as Phoebe found, most welcome. Their mouths opened and Phoebe reached up, touching Dzolali's cheek.

As quickly as it happened, the kiss ended. Phoebe was breathless, held up solely by Dzolali's arm.

"My—" Phoebe tried, but nothing further could she manage. She was dizzy and unabashedly aroused. She searched Dzolali's sultry face and knew that anything this woman said, she would do, short of, perhaps, murder.

"Get undressed," Dzolali huskily commanded. She removed her support from Phoebe and stepped back.

Phoebe took a sidestep to keep her balance. She peeled her t-shirt off, then released and kicked away her jeans. All the while, her eyes watched Dzolali's face.

Dzolali's eyes slowly covered the youngest Pyncheon's territory. Her eyes widened slightly, and an eyebrow slowly raised. She smiled approvingly and looked back up to Phoebe's face. "Verrry nice." She held out the dress.

Phoebe took it, removed it from the hanger, and slipped it on. Turning for Dzolali to zip it up, she received more than that. Dzolali's mouth landed upon the nape of her neck. Phoebe gasped again and felt faint. The zipper went up.

"Easy there," Dzolali cooed in her ear and wrapped her arms around Phoebe's midsection. She had felt Phoebe's trembling and thought she would indeed drop.

What the hell is happening to me? "I'm okay," Phoebe said and regained herself. She turned and faced Dzolali.

"That is perfect!" the Latina witch exclaimed.

Phoebe turned to look at herself in the vanity's mirror and was amazed. It did fit perfectly. Dzolali's face appeared next to her own and their eyes met once more.

"Come to my room," Dzolali commanded sweetly. "There's more."

Without a thought, Phoebe did follow, her eyes barely leaving the intoxicating shape of the woman leading her upstairs and to her room in the opposite turret.

"Sit," Dzolali directed, pointing to her larger, more elaborate vanity's bench.

Phoebe did as she was told and sat looking at herself in the mirror, entranced, while Dzolali decorated her further, trying different necklaces, bracelets, earrings, and different hairstyles.

Phoebe had never been shown such attentions, or such kindness. Her proximity to Dzolali Alameda had renewed Phoebe's notion that she loved the woman. Any reservations were discarded.

Dzolali arranged Phoebe's shoulder-length hair into a braid but left the longer, dyed blue, to lay naturally. She tenderly applied eyeliner, mascara, rouge, and lipstick to Phoebe, and when she was finished, they both stared at the transformation in the mirror. The smoky eye effect brought a shine and richness to her brown eyes that Phoebe had never been able to achieve on her own. The blue lipstick was a surprise, but as it went with the copper and midnight blue eyeshadow, it popped. The rouge was also a copper, but, finely brushed, it accentuated her cheekbones.

Phoebe could not stop grinning and blushing.

"There," proclaimed Dzolali. "Now you won't feel so left out at dinner."

Phoebe gasped. "Oh, I can't wear this! I have to help Alva in the kitchen and then set the table."

"Do you trust me?" Dzolali stepped back, forcing Phoebe to turn on the bench to look into her face. Dzolali regarded her with a thoughtful head tilt.

"Yes," Phoebe said.

"Do what you need to in the kitchen, come up here, and put on your dress."

"*My* dress?"

"Uh-huh," Dzolali answered. "A gift from me to you."

Phoebe bounced up to her feet. "I can't! I couldn't!"

Dzolali stepped into her and embraced her tightly, freezing Phoebe's protest. They stood looking at each other, saying nothing for a moment. Then, another kiss, this one deep and long.

Phoebe felt like she was floating. Her boyfriends had never made her feel so light and free, so daring, or so elated about her very being. When the kiss broke, both women gasped for air but remained in each other's clutches.

"What were you saying?" Dzolali asked playfully. "Something about you couldn't do something?"

"I'll do anything you wish," Phoebe said and gasped at her own words.

"Good girl," Dzolali said. Then a thought occurred to her. "Oh! We forgot something."

Her mind still reeling from being in her new love's arms, Phoebe said, "I can't imagine."

"Shoes!"

"Crap."

Dzolali released Phoebe and went to her closet. She looked at Phoebe's feet, told her to kick off her slip-on sneakers, and came away from the closet with a pair of ankle-high leather boots.

"Oh, my God!" Phoebe called out. "I've never worn heels!"

"Relax, they're wide and the shafts'll support your ankles. Try them."

Phoebe retook a seat on the vanity's bench and obliged. Dzolali bent and laced them up.

"There," said Dzolali and stood. "Take a walk."

Phoebe did. The fit wasn't as perfect as the dress, but they would work. She smiled in delight.

"Now those you can't keep," Dzolali said in a semi-serious tone. "I go as far as the dresses and costume jewelry. The shoes come back to me."

"Dresses?" Phoebe uttered in surprise. "How do you have dresses in my size? You're so... um... more endowed than me."

Dzolali laughed. "They're mine from a few years ago. But thank you for that."

Phoebe smiled and blushed all over again. "I just don't know what to say."

Dzolali came close again, to Phoebe's utter delight. "Say you'll come to me tonight for a visit."

Phoebe could have been bowled over with a feather. "Yes. I will."

Phoebe went back to her room to change out of the dress until dinner and resumed her chores in a profoundly giddy mood. She transferred loads of laundry from one machine to the next and folded and stacked the fresh linens on a table, not giving a huff for the noise that assaulted her ears.

A smile was plastered on her face, and had anyone been present to witness it, Phoebe would have appeared slightly off kilter. She imagined herself and Dzolali leaving the House of the Seven Gables together, off to live a life in a beach house somewhere on the coast of California, perhaps even Hawaii.

Phoebe pictured herself becoming well-known and wealthy, an author of dozens of books—all the while, giving her sweet Dzolali anything she ever wanted, cars, homes, trips, jewelry with real stones, anything at all.

As she was about to head upstairs with a stack of clean bed linens to distribute, Phoebe noticed the utility sink next to the worktable. It was where Mr. Holgrave had said he developed his film. Curious, she stepped to the worktable. She wrinkled her nose at the odor of the chemical residue.

In the corner, to the left of the sink, Holgrave had suspended a long string between two water pipes. From this string hung several long strips of developed film, apparently to dry. Looking at them under the light, she found an inordinate amount of the negatives were of the exterior of the house, taken either from some distance into the woods or close up. Many of the close-ups were of the home's many windows. All the pictures here seemed to have been taken from ground level, and none beyond those of the first floor showed any part of the inside of the rooms.

From these samples, it seemed that Holgrave was obsessed with the house, as there was nothing else present. No animals, no people, and no trees other than the ones closest to the house.

Phoebe had not seen Alec Holgrave all day. He had not been in his room when she'd stopped in to change the sheets, and she remembered his cameras were not on the table. Deciding she would ask him about his interest in the house when she caught him alone, she left the basement to distribute the clean sheets.

The nature of Holgrave's doings bothered her somewhat as she performed the rest of her chores. She kept him in the back of her mind as she entered the kitchen early to clean the microwave as Great-Aunt Hester had told her.

As she was finishing, Alva arrived.

"Oh, my," she said, "don't you look nice."

"Thank you," she answered. "Dzolali was kind enough to give me a makeover. She even gave me a dress for later."

"Oh," the cook said and smiled strangely.

Phoebe went about helping the cook, and she couldn't help but notice that Alva was a bit standoffish. Phoebe thought to ask, but she decided against it, figuring her good mood was smudging her judgment.

When it came time, Phoebe went up to the dining room, set the table, and removed the prepared dishes from the dumbwaiter. She did so hastily, wanting desperately to run and change into her dress before anyone arrived.

Finally, everything was set. Phoebe went to her room and slipped on the fancy green dress. She glided upstairs and knocked on Dzolali's door. There was no answer, so she slipped inside. Phoebe tidied up her makeup and sifted through the jewelry boxes to borrow a few items. She avoided anything with a pentagram, or a horned goat, or anything that she deemed "witchcrafty." Unfortunately, that narrowed the selections down severely. Finally, she settled on a red-gemmed necklace, a couple of rings that went with it, two matching metal bracelets, and a pair of earrings with blue gems.

Phoebe sat on Dzolali's bed to tie the boots on and checked everything one last time in the vanity mirror when she was satisfied. She was sure that Dzolali would be pleased. When she left the room, she could see Hester and Glendarah entering the dining room.

As Phoebe walked into the room, she found Dzolali and Onenspek already there, standing to the side and speaking in hushed tones. She smiled upon seeing her love, but when she saw his hand holding hers and the look in her eyes when she stared into his, Phoebe felt her blood boil.

"That dress is very becoming, Phoebe," said Glendarah, suddenly at her left.

"Thank you," Phoebe said.

Dzolali's eyes found Phoebe and her face brightened. She released Onenspek's hand and whispered something in his ear. He gave Phoebe a wave in greeting, which she returned obligingly, and he moved to stand behind his chair.

"That's Dzolali's touch, isn't it?" Glendarah went on.

"Oh, yes. She was very kind to me today," Phoebe said.

"Indeed," said Glendarah. Her deep blue eyes almost flashed with knowing as she smiled grandly.

"That is a damn sight better," put in Hester, standing behind her place at the head of the table. Onenspek moved to her and pulled the chair from the table for her to sit.

"You look amazing," said Dzolali, giving Phoebe that deliciously seductive grin.

Phoebe forgot all about Dzolali's handholding with Onenspek. Phoebe thanked her and promised she would return the jewelry and the shoes after dinner.

"My word," Holgrave said from behind Phoebe.

She turned and smiled at him. "Good evening, Mr. Holgrave. And thank you."

"Certainly," he said, taking in the sight of her respectfully.

"Good evening, Ms. D'Amitri," he said to Glendarah as he pulled out her chair, "You're looking very well this evening."

"Thank you, Mr. Holgrave," she replied and sat. "I'm feeling much improved."

Alva entered at that moment, and Phoebe assisted with the removal of the dining plate covers. That done, she took her seat.

"You do look wonderful this evening, Phoebe," complimented Ned.

"Thank you, Mr. Onenspek," she replied and gazed upon Dzolali. After a few seconds, she caught herself and looked to the plate of potatoes that was being passed.

Alva poured the wine for everyone as the small talk began. The usual topics like weather and news items were passed around much like the food itself, though for Phoebe, it was much less interesting and quite forgettable. She couldn't help but have a stomach full of anticipation over Dzolali's invitation to her room later that night. She hoped that Great-Aunt Hester would retire early enough for Phoebe to sneak past the master bedroom without detection.

Scenarios passed through her mind's eye, even the unfavorable possibilities like getting caught on the way or, she shuddered as she considered, being discovered because she and Dzolali were making too much noise.

"Are you all right?" whispered Holgrave.

Phoebe blinked and tore her eyes away from Dzolali to look at him. He had been holding the breadbasket for her, for how long, she did not know.

"Oh, sorry," she said, laughing it off. She took the basket and placed a roll on her plate, then passed the basket to her aunt. "I'm fine," she said to Holgrave. "Say, did you catch your—" she interrupted to look around, then leaned in closer to whisper, "—your little friend?"

She and Holgrave locked eyes for a moment while he worked out what Phoebe was asking him.

"Ah," he answered when he got her gist. "No, I'm afraid he's rather more intelligent than I am."

Phoebe laughed. "It's probably a 'she' then."

Holgrave grinned handsomely and chuckled. "No doubt."

Phoebe tuned in to a conversation between Glendarah and Hester.

"Rather thought it was a pack of them," said Glendarah.

"Quite possibly," said Hester. "Business was slow at the gallery to-day as a result. Until the animal or animals are captured or killed, residents will be wary. There's a better chance that out-of-towners will not be aware of the killing and will come anyway. In any case, I'm afraid I've lost Mrs. Carp as a client."

"Agreed," said Glendarah. "Poor woman."

There was a shared glance across the table between Hester and Glendarah after that statement, and Phoebe suspected Glendarah's sentiment sounded a little insincere. Emboldened by her assimilation into the group, at least in appearance, Phoebe impulsively spoke out.

"I wonder then, Auntie Hester," she started, "if it wouldn't be a good idea to halt the readings and such."

Hester's face flushed. She put her head up and looked down her nose at her grandniece. "What in the world are you chattering about?"

Oh, shit. Phoebe met her great-aunt's glower, careful to remove any attitude from her own demeanor. "I mean to say, maybe out of respect for her loss, it may look good for the community if you shut down the psychic readings part of your business."

The dining room became silent as a morgue. If insects were present on the property anywhere, as they should have been, Phoebe was convinced she would have heard the chirping of crickets.

"My dear girl," Hester addressed, letting her fork strike her plate with a resounding metal-on-china ring. "You simply do not understand what you are saying. I am a wiccan, as you should well know. That parlor is not mere folly. It is my livelihood. It supports this great house, the very same that I have granted you to stay in, for the time being, and I do not appreciate your audacious suggestion to shut it down would show respect."

Phoebe stammered, aware that all others in the room had their eyes on her. "I didn't mean that, exactly. I mean, uh, you have the gallery downtown, surely that—"

"That gallery is doing just well enough to sustain itself *only!*" Hester shouted. "Works of art do not fly from the shelves like soda pop, which is why we were able to acquire it from the Maule family to begin with. This house is sustained by the boarders that are kind enough to stay here and contribute to its support. That parlor is an essential source of additional income, not to mention a representation of the Pyncheon family legacy!"

"I'm sorry, Auntie Hester," offered Phoebe, nearing tears. Still, she did not flinch from the old woman's stare. "I meant no offense."

Hester said nothing for a moment but was unmoved. Her angst was clear, and for just a moment, Phoebe thought Hester would tell her to pack her things and get out.

"I'm sure, dear Hester, that your grandniece did not suggest it as a permanent solution, nor intend the statement as a personal attack," Glendarah said softly.

Phoebe swallowed hard, trying to push down the memories of her great-aunt's treatment of her mother and the petty argument over personal effects that she had conceded to the woman. She had wanted to knock the old bat on her bony ass that day, and that feeling was recurring.

"It's true, Auntie Hester," Phoebe said levelly. "I was suggesting that it be a temporary measure." She stopped there, not addressing Glendarah's second point on purpose. As far as she was concerned, if Hester wanted to take it that personally, she had it coming.

"Very well," Hester said finally.

At that, the guests resumed their dining, but it was a long moment before any conversation resumed. It was Hester herself that started it off.

"How are you feeling today, Mr. Onenspek?" she asked.

"Oh, very well, Ms. Pyncheon. Thank you," he responded, sounding much more coherent than the previous evening, though to Phoebe, he still appeared under the influence of something. "Well enough to have begun a new work this morning," he said with some pride. He cast his eyes over everyone at the table as he spoke.

"You're quite prolific, Mr. Onenspek," Holgrave commented. "I have to admit, I'm no expert in art, but I dare venture a guess that you're producing a new work every couple of days. Considering their . . . intricate details, it's quite astonishing."

"I have these three wonderful ladies to thank for that," Onenspek beamed. "With Ms. Pyncheon's drive and support and the inspiration I receive from Ms. Alameda and Ms. D'Amitri, I feel like I can accomplish anything."

Holgrave raised his wine glass. "To your continued success, then," he toasted. The others followed suit and took a sip.

"Thank you all," Onenspek said with honest gratitude and drank his wine.

Phoebe peeked at Holgrave from the corner of her eye, making sure she kept a smile on her lips in case she was noticed. She wondered if he was sincere in his well wishes. He noticed her glance and smiled at her.

She thought fast and spoke. "So, Mr. Holgrave, I didn't see you around today."

"We did seem to miss each other completely," he said. "I was out for a hike, taking photographs."

"Oh? Did you get any pictures of anything special?"

"Always," he answered with a grin. He said nothing more and continued with his meal.

Phoebe decided not to press him in the presence of the others, but she promised herself that she would follow up with him later. With so many pictures taken of the House of the Seven Gables, Holgrave must have some motivation for it.

The meal went on for a painfully long time from Phoebe's perspective. Watching Dzolali lean in for whispers and giggles with Ned Onenspek was torture, made all the more maddening by the occasional winks Dzolali gave her. Had the dining table been less vast, Phoebe would have tapped Dzolali's legs with her toes.

What is her deal with him, anyway? Phoebe pondered. After a while, she determined that the oddball artist, as nice of a man as he seemed to be despite his drug addiction, would not get in her way when it came to Dzolali.

"Is that séance still on for tonight, Hester?" Glendarah asked as everyone neared the end of their meals.

"I've received no information to the contrary," Hester answered. She sipped more of her red wine and cast her eyes on her grandniece. "Phoebe."

Phoebe blinked and turned to Hester. "Yes?"

"You *must* sit in tonight," Hester insisted.

In the process of taking a drink from her glass, Phoebe's eyes shifted to Dzolali, who looked back at her blankly. *No help there.* "Say what now?"

"You will join us in the parlor tonight for the séance," Hester augmented.

"I will?"

"Certainly. I can think of no better way for you to gain appreciation for the wiccan way of life and this house than to have you join us."

"Uhhh . . ." Phoebe stalled, looking into Dzolali's copper eyes. She wanted nothing to do with such a ridiculous event. As Phoebe stared, Dzolali gave a nearly imperceptible nod. "Sure," Phoebe finally said, and she downed the remaining wine.

"Excellent," Hester concluded. "You will, of course, remain dressed as you are."

"No problem," Phoebe said. She had discovered that she liked her new look very much, especially since Dzolali had created it.

"May I have your permission to attend as well?" Holgrave spoke up.

Surprised, Phoebe looked at him. Her expression must have bordered on shock, for when he noticed it, he grinned and shrugged.

Hester met this request with a surprise that was more pleasant. "Why, Mr. Holgrave, I thought the skeptic in you was more prevalent. You are, of course, most welcome to join us." She turned to the artist. "Mr. Onenspek, perhaps you can find your way clear to give yourself the night off and join the party?"

The dreamy look in Ned's eyes had returned. Onenspek snapped out of it when Hester addressed him. He cleared his throat and sat up abruptly. "Certainly."

Phoebe shot a look at Dzolali, who was wearing that sultry grin on her face again as she gazed at Ned. The green monster of jealousy grumbled in Phoebe's heart but was sated when Dzolali turned to meet her eyes once again.

"Excellent," declared Hester. "We begin at midnight, but please arrive a few minutes prior."

11

Evening Interlude

With the meal finished and the guests dispersed to the rest of the house to carry on with their evening, Phoebe took great care in clearing the dishes from the table. The last thing she wished to do was to soil the exquisite gift she wore. She decided she would wash the dishes after the farce in the parlor was concluded, but she went downstairs to let Alva know her plan.

When Phoebe entered the kitchen, she found that Alva had departed early. Carefully, she unloaded the dumbwaiter, and cleared what she dared from the plates, setting them on the counter to be washed.

Holgrave entered, this time loudly enough to not startle Phoebe. "Surely, you're not going to wash all that in that lovely dress."

"Surely not," she answered, mocking his English accent playfully.

"Care to go for a walk before the festivities?" he asked.

Phoebe laughed. "Festivities? Good one. I could use some air. Let's go."

They stepped through the screen door and were greeted by the noisy, winged sentinel. This time, Phoebe stopped and watched it for a moment. The bird eyed her calmly though steadily.

"Why in the world does Hester keep that poor thing?" Phoebe asked.

"I take it that she was not a pet person when you were a child," Holgrave supposed.

"She wasn't." Phoebe crossed her arms and stepped down to the dirt path with Mr. Holgrave remaining at her side. The air was cool but not cold. There didn't seem to be a cloud above, and the stars shone as clear as a photograph. The moon was full and cast everything in a silver glow. Even the emerald green of her dress shone metallically. "Beautiful night."

"It is," Holgrave agreed. "A perfect night for contacting the dead, wouldn't you say?"

"I wouldn't know," Phoebe said, smiling.

Holgrave began sauntering eastward, taking them past the green and red neon light of the 'Psychic' sign in the parlor window. She watched him thoughtfully as he crossed his hands behind his back. The stiff breeze sent his ponytail wagging and his suit jacket fluttering.

"Alec," she addressed, and he turned to her. "I was doing laundry today, and I couldn't help but be nosy."

"Ah. So you had a look through my latest batch of negatives," he stated.

"I did."

The pair took several slow steps before Holgrave prompted, "And?"

"And I couldn't help but notice that you seem to be in love with this old house."

"It certainly is unique, don't you think? Worthy of photographing, I'd say."

Phoebe shrugged. "I guess."

"Does my apparent obsession with the House of the Seven Gables worry you?" he asked and gave a small laugh.

"Worry? No." She shook her head and stopped walking to look at him curiously. He stopped at her prompting and waited for her next words. "But I do have to say I'm curious as to why."

Holgrave's eyes turned toward the house, now many yards behind them. "It's got character," he said.

Phoebe regarded the old Victorian along with him. She had to admit, at that moment, the place held a romantic appeal. Much of its dilapidation was hidden by the night, and the silver moonlight showcased the gray stone exterior. The windows glowed in yellow light, and the only thing that ruined the view was the neon sign.

"Have you printed any of those photos?" she asked.

Holgrave kicked a small stone from the road and looked to his feet. "I have indeed."

She had expected him to elaborate, but in what way, she didn't know. He turned his face skyward and she found herself focusing on his profile. Like the house beyond them, his face was graced with the moonlight.

"So, are you planning on keeping them to yourself?" she asked.

Holgrave looked at her briefly and took a step toward the house. "If you'd care to see them, follow me."

Follow she did. They went to the third floor without anyone seeing them, though, as they passed the master bedroom, Phoebe slowed, listening. The door was shut, but the lights within spilled out into the hall through the narrow gap at its bottom. There was some conversation within the room, but Phoebe didn't put effort into eavesdropping. They passed Onenspek's bedroom, also closed but with no trace of light. The next room, however, showed that he was in. All was quiet in his studio as they stepped through the light cast from under his door.

Phoebe followed Holgrave to his attic suite. Once inside, he bid her sit where she wished. She chose the chair near the south-facing window.

"Well, forgive me for flaunting technology in such a home," said Holgrave as he pulled a tablet from his camera bag and activated it. "I've downloaded some pictures from my digital cameras onto this so that one can view them in greater detail."

Phoebe watched him tap the screen and swipe through the pictures in the device's memory folders. He settled on one and handed the tablet to her.

She took the tablet in her hands, mindful to not touch the screen, lest the picture change or disappear. It was a nicely framed shot of the house, taken from some distance south of Gable Way. From the shadows and the orange sunlight, Phoebe deduced that it was taken shortly before twilight. The lights were on in almost all the windows, as was the vulgar 'Psychic' sign.

"Nice," she commented.

"I took that picture more than a week ago," Holgrave said. "Then, as I tend to do, I stood in the very same place and switched cameras. I had black-and-white film in the thirty-five millimeter that evening." With that, he slid an eight-by-ten print out of a manila envelope and handed it to her.

At first glance, it was a spot-on copy of the one on the tablet, though bereft of color and grainy in comparison, giving the glossy paper version a softer look. This, Phoebe knew from her experience in the newspaper business, was characteristic of film photography. She held the print and the tablet side-by-side and scrutinized them.

"Very nice," she said.

"Notice anything?" he asked, obviously hinting at some difference that he had full knowledge about.

Phoebe took her time to answer, looking at the two pictures, comparing features of the house one by one. Other than the lack of color in the photograph, she was at a loss. She looked up at him and shook her head.

Holgrave moved to the left side of the chair and crouched close to her. "Look at the raven in the cage."

Phoebe did so. "Oh, so he moved while you took the shot. Is your film a what's that called? A slow exposure?"

Holgrave shook his head. "No, I was using an eight hundred film."

"I take it that's fast," she said, teasing with his own turn of phrase.

"Relatively," he confirmed.

Phoebe brought the print closer and looked again. The raven differed between the pictures. On the tablet, the bird could be seen in his or her cage on the porch, lit by a ray of sunlight spilling onto the porch from the west. The bird's right eye reflected green, the other, still in shadow, was almost imperceptible. It was apparently quite aware of Holgrave's presence and was staring straight into the camera. If it was capable of smiling, Phoebe was sure it would have.

In the black-and-white print, however, the bird had taken on a blurred shape, as if it had brought its wing across its body, its feathers draping like a cape. The eye in the sun was white but smeared, cat-like in shape.

"So, he moved," Phoebe concluded.

"I give you my word that he did not," Holgrave said with conviction. "He never moved, the entire time I was standing there. It took a mere few seconds to take the digital picture, switch to the film camera, focus, and take this shot."

"Oh, but Alec—"

"I promise you," he affirmed.

Phoebe pursed her lips, curling her mouth to one side in an expression of doubt. From the day she'd met him, she felt that Alec Holgrave was continually holding something back from her. Now, she couldn't tell if he was putting her on or not.

Her expression must have annoyed Holgrave, for his face lost all trace of humor. He took the print and the tablet from her hands. He returned the photo to the envelope and swiped through the picture folder on the device hastily.

"Here," he said, returning the device to her grasp. "Look at that."

This next picture of the house had been taken from the east, with Holgrave apparently standing next to the old carriage house, the wall of which could be seen at the left border of the picture. The southeast turret was at the left of the shot, with the entire eastern side framed. Lights were on in the third floor of the turret, Glendarah's bedroom and the attic suite.

"Do you know what room that is, the one there," Holgrave pointed to the picture.

"Yes," she answered, thinking him silly. "It's this window here." She pointed to her right.

"At the moment I captured that picture, it was late afternoon," Holgrave explained. "The sun is kept from shining into the lens by the trees beyond the house."

"Which explains why the light is on."

"But I wasn't in there," he said, exasperated. "I had been out since late morning, taking pictures. I didn't leave the lights on."

"So, Hester was in there changing the sheets or something," Phoebe explained. Holgrave was starting to make her nervous. He was reaching for some point, as yet unfathomable to her.

Holgrave withdrew another eight-by-ten in black and white from the envelope. He laid it in her left hand, and she compared them. She gasped.

There was someone in the window of his attic suite.

"Who the hell is that?" she asked him, for the woman resembled no one in the house. The grainy quality of the print would have prevented an exact identification of the woman, or girl, but it was certain that no one in the house had shoulder-length black hair, stringy and matted, so it appeared. The woman was wearing what looked like a white nightie.

"I have no idea," Holgrave answered. "There were no boarders approaching that description here at the time. These were taken the day after I arrived."

"Alec, what do these mean?" she begged of him.

"Look here, though," Holgrave directed her, running his finger under the strange woman's image. "This dark area here."

"It's a shadow."

"Or is it a blood stain upon her nightgown?"

She pushed the photo and the tablet back to him. "Dude. You're freakin' me the hell out."

Holgrave stepped away, frustrated. He tossed the envelope back onto the table, the device on top of it.

"Hester called you a skeptic," Phoebe said. "Why are you showing me this stuff?"

"Because I *am* a skeptic and I have no explanation for it," he said. He took a breath. "Those aren't the only photographs I can't explain. Those are, in fact, the easiest to debunk, as you already have. You can say the bird moved and all I have to give you is my word. You can say some strange woman came into my room and looked out the window, and again, there's only my word to say that there wasn't."

Phoebe sighed. She knew well what it was like to not be taken seriously. Still, there was the fact that she had discovered gimmicks in Hester's parlor, so even if Holgrave had taken those pictures as he described, it was obvious that they had been tampered with during the development process.

She decided to change the subject. "Do you remember me thinking that maybe Mr. Onenspek was being drugged by Hester?"

"Of course."

"I took one of the gingerbread dudes and took it to the police."

Holgrave turned to her, surprised. At first, she couldn't tell whether it was a positive or a negative response.

"What?"

"Well, it was certainly the right thing to do," Holgrave said. "But if the police find some sort of drug, could Hester be placing traces of it in other things?"

"Maybe in the wine?" Phoebe suggested.

"Exactly."

Phoebe thought of her obsession with the ginger Latina. "I've considered that."

"You're speaking of our vivid dreams?"

Phoebe nodded and looked to the clock on his mantle. It was approaching ten. She rose from the chair. "I think I'll freshen up a bit before this farce tonight. I'll be exhausted by the time it finishes up."

"Of course," he said and opened the door for her. "See you then."

Phoebe opened her laptop and turned it on, hoping to find that the time it displayed was still close to accurate. As she recalled the time on the mantle clock in Holgrave's suite, and only a couple of minutes passed, she decided that it was.

She sat at the desk and resumed her writing. In the silence, she cursed the lack of internet access, for she would have killed for some music on her headphones. Alas, there was nothing save for the breeze beyond the window and the occasional pops and groans from the structure of the house.

Phoebe sank into the world she had created, and she quite soon settled into a fast-paced part of her story. Her heroine was in danger and, as much as Phoebe tried to avoid spending words on high-speed chase scenes, she found herself throwing her character, the biker chick, into one.

Paragraph after paragraph appeared on the laptop screen, and Phoebe was in her element, with words flowing through her, from mind to word document.

Absently, she scratched an itch near her heel. She thought nothing further of it and went back to typing. She barely got through another sentence when the spot itched again.

"Damn shoes," Phoebe muttered and reached to scratch again.

She barely touched her keys when both calves erupted in a wave of tingling. In a grunt of frustration, she pushed herself back from the writing desk and cast her eyes on her feet.

Bugs! Her borrowed boots had become covered in a deluge of ants, beetles, and what she thought were millipedes. Her chest hitched as panic overtook her, freezing her in place. She tried to sift through the reasons why these insects had come into her room, and what at that very moment had summoned them, but nothing made sense. The room was clean, free of food and anything beyond a layer of dust, yet there they were, various types of insects, working together.

And they were on their way *up*.

Phoebe screamed and leaped from the chair, knocking it across the tiny bedroom. She reeled backward, falling onto the springy but soft bed. Phoebe mindlessly swatted at her legs, feeling the bodies of the tiny villains on the tender skin of her fingers. Those that hadn't been squashed attached themselves to her hands and wriggled their way up, up over the rings she had borrowed from Dzolali and through the gaps in her bracelets.

Phoebe screamed and swatted again, rubbing her hands against the green dress, smearing insect innards all over the shiny fabric in long, thin brown and yellow streaks of goo.

Every bit of skin below her knees felt as if it were on fire. She became convinced the ants were fire ants, the beetles were surely cockroaches, and the multiple-legged, snaky things were certainly full of poison, ingrained in them over millions of years of evolution.

Phoebe rolled off the bed and tore the comforter from it, determined to wipe them off her body. She bent, sobbing, making a scrubbing motion with the comforter as a washing sponge, decimating the invading horde of creatures by the hundreds with each swipe.

Then she went after her arms, for they were still there, biting, crawling, burning her flesh as they came up. She tore at the laces of Dzolali's boots and kicked them off, sending them crashing into the far wall. She bent to wipe the insects from her burning feet once more.

As she pumped her upper body up and down, swiping the comforter over her legs she realized that the burning itching had suddenly stopped. She looked to her hands and saw the skin had reddened from the polyester comforter. Her legs and feet were similarly irritated.

No bugs were about, neither living nor dead. There was not a single detached leg, head, or body part on her or ground into the wood floor or into the fabric of the throw rug. There was not a streak of insect innards to be found, either. Relief washed over Phoebe, and she dropped onto the mattress, winded.

What the fuck just happened?

Phoebe took little time to regain herself when she thought of the dress. She rolled off the bed and checked herself over in the vanity mirror. The dress was spotless and intact. She fished through her purse, looking for her makeup brush, for some of her eyeliner had run when she'd panicked during the insect uprising.

Her eyes nervously scanned the room again. There was not a bug in sight. Phoebe looked at herself in the mirror more closely. She went as far as to duck her head under the writing desk, the place she had been sitting when it had all started, just a couple of minutes ago. Still, there was nothing.

At that moment, the sound of a manly chuckle came to her ears. It was an aged voice, not smooth, and not kind. Phoebe spun around, even though she could see in the mirror that no one was behind her. Her lack of trust in the reflection was unfounded—there was indeed no one there.

But I heard it just the same, she affirmed. Her heart was still pounding, not having the chance to recover after the hallucinated insect attack. The short laugh had happened, she was sure, but she was also sure a moment ago that there were bugs all over her, and now they were gone.

Phoebe jerked her door open and bolted out of the room. If anyone had been outside, she would have knocked them down. She flew up the stairs, hoping to find anyone, even Great-Aunt Hester. The sight of any other soul would have brought her immense joy in that moment.

So driven, she pushed open the master bedroom without knocking. There was no one inside. A corner reading lamp was on, as was a small lamp on the bedside table, leaving the great room looking almost cozy, if one ignored the candles, the Hecate altar, or the Onenspek originals on the walls.

Phoebe yanked the door shut and ran, this time to Dzolali's room. Again, she burst through the door, this time finding the one she wanted. Phoebe exploded in tears and ran to Dzolali, who had no choice but to accept the tackling embrace.

"Oh!" Dzolali called and fought to keep her balance. She had been in the middle of changing her dress and had just put her arms through the sleeves when Phoebe had burst in. Now, in her clutches, Dzolali wrapped her arms around the frightened Pyncheon girl. "What's happened?!"

In a blubbering ramble, Phoebe explained the bug attack and then tried to describe the male voice she'd heard, but by then, she could form no sounds beyond sobs. Phoebe was sleep deprived, terrified, and in hysterics.

Dzolali held her, listened, and consoled Phoebe, and the two stood in the middle of the room in each other's arms for several minutes. Dzolali was able to talk Phoebe down enough to get her to sit on the bed. Her sobs continued, however, so the redhead sat next to Phoebe and they resumed the embrace for a time.

Phoebe's left hand slipped up Dzolali's back, finding bare skin. It was then she discovered that Dzolali had not yet zipped up her dress, another Victorian era-inspired garment in satiny black. Phoebe's sobs quieted and her breathing came to her in halting fits.

Dzolali looked into her eyes and smiled. Phoebe's mascara and eye-liner were ruined, running down her cheeks and staining the blush. Dzolali kissed Phoebe, taking her face in her hands. She released a moment later and got up from the bed, retrieving tissues. She returned and began cleaning Phoebe's face.

As Dzolali sat there, wiping away the mess, Phoebe's hand dropped onto Dzolali's stockinged thigh and began a gentle caress. Their eyes met again. An urgent kiss was shared again, and this time, neither would be denied the pleasures of the other.

Without Phoebe noticing, Dzolali waved her hand and her bedroom door closed, latching quietly. She twirled her index finger, and the key spun in the lock.

12

The Séance

With little time left to spare, Phoebe hurriedly reapplied her makeup as Dzolali had done earlier that day. She was not as talented with the art as her redheaded lover, but it would have to do. In the mirror, she could see Dzolali's lovely midriff as she rearranged Phoebe's hair, so tousled had it become in the time they had taken to play.

"There. Good as new," Dzolali declared and stood back, admiring her work and watching Phoebe recreate herself.

"I'll never be new again after that," Phoebe said and giggled. "My God," she added and fanned herself.

Dzolali grunted playfully. "Just wait until we have more time." She stepped back and began brushing her own hair, equally as mistreated.

"Oh, please don't even tease right now," Phoebe purred. "We'll end up right back in bed."

"Oh, no," Dzolali corrected. "I don't dare show up late for this. Hester needs me there, and you're expected."

Phoebe rolled her eyes, deciding that Dzolali's obsession with the witchcraft thing could be overlooked, considering her other sensual talents.

Dzolali appeared behind her in the mirror again and inspected Phoebe's work. "You're good, you're good. Scoot!" she demanded.

Smiling, Phoebe launched from the vanity's bench and let Dzolali have her turn.

Quickly, and with much deftness, Dzolali wiped away the smeared work and skillfully reapplied it. In less than half the time it had taken Phoebe to fumble about her recreation, Dzolali had perfected herself.

Zipping each other's dresses, and speedily putting on jewelry, they were ready to go. Phoebe approached the bedroom door and gave the knob a turn.

"Huh," she exerted and turned the key. "I don't remember locking that."

Dzolali chuckled. "Oh, it just does that sometimes."

Phoebe stopped by her room to retrieve her boots and put them on, then the pair went down to the first floor, where, upon entering the parlor, they discovered they were the last to arrive. Phoebe was aware of Holgrave's appreciative eyes, as well as those of Onenspek, who was ogling Dzolali lustfully.

Back off, dude. She's mine now. Or am I hers?

"It's about time you two arrived," Hester admonished. "Sit."

Phoebe took the first available place, the chair in between Hester and Holgrave. Glendarah was seated on his right. A strange woman, the client, no doubt, to her right, then Onenspek. Dzolali sat to Hester's left and gave Phoebe a wink.

Phoebe's heart soared. That wink meant so much more now.

"Jennifer Bankowski, this is my grandniece, Phoebe Pyncheon," Hester said.

"Nice to meet you," said Bankowski. The woman appeared to be in her fifties, slightly plump, but not unattractive. Her hair was an obvious black dye job and cut short, its strands stylized to sweep leftward over her forehead, framing her smallish face in dagger-like wisps. Her smile was genuine, touching her eyes and revealing teeth that had either been well-maintained since the cradle or professionally installed.

"Very nice to meet you, Ms. Bankowski," Phoebe replied. It dawned on her, just as she spoke the words, that the woman was a widow. She had used 'miss' without thinking about it, feeling that it was the truth.

Three large white candles sat on the table, which, Phoebe noticed, had been altered since she had sneaked in for a peek. The crystal ball had been removed, and the tablecloth had been changed. This one was purple with gold tasseling along the edges.

Aunt Hester was in the same black dress from dinner, but she had added a necklace with a pentagram pendant, changed her rings, and arranged her hair in one long braid in the back, which accentuated her bangs, the longer of which came down in strands over her temples.

Glendarah was similarly adorned, though she had her long, blonde hair gathered in a bun that revealed her ears but left the balance spilling down her back.

Like the three witches, Onenspek and Holgrave wore black suits, though Holgrave broke up the monotony with a deep blue dress shirt and a gray ascot. Phoebe smiled, noticing that Holgrave had freed his hair from the ponytail. It was thicker and longer than she had presumed, coming down in swooping brown waves and slightly beyond shoulder length.

"Friends, we gather together here for our sister, Jennifer," Hester announced. "She has come to us to make contact with her dearly departed husband, David."

Oh, brother.

Hester took a long-nosed lighter in hand, lit it with a pull of its plastic trigger, and set the flame to the wick of the candle closest to her. She then handed it to Dzolali, who did the same, before having Onenspek pass it to Glendarah, who lit the last candle.

"Dear sister Jennifer," Hester said to her client. "Do you have a personal item of David's?"

"I do," said Bankowski. She bent to pick her purse from the floor and opened it. A moment later, she retrieved an expensive-looking watch and set it on the table.

"Very good," granted Hester. "Now, do you have something that David liked to eat?"

"I do," the client repeated, though this elicited a smile. She dug through the purse again, this time pulling a sealed package of beef jerky from within. She set it next to the watch.

At least now we know what killed him, Phoebe thought and bit her tongue to keep from smiling.

Hester gave Glendarah a nod, and the blonde wiccan turned in her seat and shut off the lights in the chandelier, then bent to the window to douse the green and red neon sign. The room around them darkened, leaving the light of the three candles to wash over the faces of those seated at the table.

In that flickering glow, Phoebe and Dzolali shared a long gaze. Phoebe was grateful for Dzolali's attentions, for the woman had calmed her. After the hallucinations in her bedroom, Phoebe was sure she could not have stayed in the house, let alone the parlor, during Hester's tricks without Dzolali's loving aid.

"Very well," continued Hester. "Let's join hands and begin."

Inwardly sighing, Phoebe took her great-aunt's cool, bony hand in hers. Holgrave's left hand, large, warm, and strong, arrived in her right. The others around her did likewise, and the circle was complete.

"Now, for those that have not participated in a séance before," Hester began, "it's important to be calm during the process. Any negative feelings will hinder the spirits and warn them away. It's also possible that the spirit may not wish to be contacted, so expect nothing. Trepidations within oneself can contribute to failure."

Phoebe watched in amusement as Hester closed her eyes and lowered her head. Her grin faded a bit when she noticed Dzolali do the same, as did Glendarah, Onenspek, and the client, Ms. Bankowski. Only she and Holgrave did not follow suit, as Phoebe confirmed with a glance to her right.

Holgrave passed his eyes over the other attendees with keen interest.

Noticing Phoebe's attention, he smiled, showing his teeth. To Phoebe, the strange photographer appeared almost giddy with excitement.

"Oh, spirits, hear us," Hester called out.

Dzolali and Glendarah repeated the demand.

"Hear our sister Jennifer's plea," Hester went on, solo this time. "Spirits, bring forth David Bankowski, dearly beloved spouse of Jennifer, who is here with us."

Phoebe watched Ms. Bankowski for a moment. The woman's brow furrowed in concentration.

"Spirits, send forth dear David," Hester bid.

Her coven sisters, with the additional voice of the widow, repeated her words. Again, Hester repeated the request verbatim, and it was echoed, with even Onenspek joining in. Phoebe had thought he had gone to sleep, so arched had his neck become since the lights had gone out.

Phoebe was smiling to herself, thinking just how much of a waste of time this debacle was, when she became aware of a vibration in the floor. She rolled her eyes, remembering the audio equipment in the little hidden room, the door to which was directly behind her.

The vibration in the floor grew, and she could hear a rumbling. *Okay, there's a subwoofer in the floor,* Phoebe thought and wondered what was next.

"Hear us, spirits!" Hester said more loudly. The others repeated her.

Phoebe, feeling the vibrations rise to a violent level at her feet, looked to Holgrave, who looked like a kid on a merry-go-round.

Phoebe was thinking this very thing when the subwoofer, or more likely, due to the increased volume, a series of subwoofers, raised from a rumbling to a thunderous roar. Her amusement turned to discomfort as the low tones seemed to reach inside her ears and shake her psyche. She clenched her jaw and suddenly felt a stiff breeze flutter through her hair. The breeze affected everyone, she could see, as the hair and clothing of every attendee twirled about and danced to its influence, as did the candles' flames.

Okay, where's the fan? Phoebe asked herself as she looked about the room. She had not noticed one when she had snooped. Certainly, with so many controls mounted on that wooden board at Hester's feet, many of which Phoebe had not been able to discover the function of, one of them must have been for the fan, wherever it was. With the thunderous roar from the audio system, the whirring of the fan motor could be easily concealed.

Holgrave's hand squeezed Phoebe's, so she looked over at him. His enjoyment had reached new heights, and she could swear she could hear him let out a giggle. She looked to the widow Bankowski and found the woman looking at the chandelier, her chin dropped in amazement.

Phoebe cast her eyes up, noting the candlelight reflecting in the tiny dancing crystals. The view was quite mesmerizing. Their twinkling was beautiful.

"David Bankowski, come to us!" the wiccans chanted in unison this time. This they repeated again and again.

With a great crash of thunder that startled all but the three witches, Ms. Bankowski herself uttered a shrill, short scream, and a flash of brilliant white light took over Phoebe's sight. Even shutting her eyelids tightly in response did little to shield her pupils from it.

A woman's scream matched the volume of the thunder coming from the floor. Phoebe dared a peek through a partially open eyelid, only to find that it was not Ms. Bankowski, nor any of the other séance attendees.

Above them all, a brilliant flare of white swirled around the room, passing just inches above their heads. Somehow, the howling woman's voice followed the flying figure and, still convinced that this was all just special effects of some kind, Phoebe marveled at the technology of the sound system that her great-aunt Hester had installed in the room. Hester's mistake, so Phoebe assumed, was that she'd pressed the wrong button, bringing forth a female voice to accompany the pyrotechnics.

Special effects or not, Phoebe's anxiety grew by the second. The sound and vision of it all was overwhelming. Aunt Hester was not unaffected, as Phoebe could tell from her tight, painful grip on her left hand. Looking to her, she saw that Hester followed the movement of the white glow, as if she didn't know what it was. If it was an act, Phoebe decided it was a damned convincing one.

Dzolali shied away from the spectacle, her facial features cloaked by her mane of black cherry hair, brightened to a pink hue under the bright light. Ned, in his perpetually drugged manner, tried feebly to follow it, but failed miserably. Glendarah, like Hester, appeared fearful but stared in one place as if trying to capture one moment of the vision as it passed the same spot on the wall. The widow had broken the circle of joined hands and had buried her face in them.

Holgrave's amusement had melted away. He, too, had become unnerved.

The streak of white light slowed its circling, and the sound of the female scream changed to a bellow. Then, the projection, or hologram, or whatever it was, halted, suspended in the air in front of Hester.

Phoebe's mouth opened in disbelief. The white glob of light resembled a woman in a long white gown. The part of it closest to Hester appeared to be a head with long black hair flowing behind and above it. The figure fluttered as if it were submerged in water.

Hester broke her grasp on Phoebe's hand and swatted at the vision. "Be gone, dark spirit!" she shouted.

The image shimmered and sent out another ear-ringing cry before leaving Hester's face and resuming its flight, a tight radius in such a small room. Phoebe watched as Hester, seeming to be legitimately riled, called again for the spirit to leave.

Phoebe was starting to get that trapped feeling and, light show or not, she wanted to bolt from the room. She must have started to move because Holgrave gave her hand a tug.

She turned her face to him, and it appeared that even he was becoming concerned.

"I'm out!" Phoebe called to him and began to get up to make her exit when the glowing projection turned on her, filling her vision. She flinched and turned away, but to her shock, something hit her, hard enough to knock her backward.

Phoebe never felt her body hit the floor.

She was flat on her back and had landed hard. The impact reminded her of falling out of bed the previous night, and Phoebe could barely move. She called out for help, but no one answered. At first, she didn't recognize the ceiling above her, so she lifted her head and looked around. It was certainly not the parlor anymore. It looked like the basement, but the laundry machines were gone, and so was the wood paneling. The light in the ceiling was nothing more than a single lamp. She focused on it as it flickered oddly. The long neon fixtures were missing, replaced by this dim one that might have been fueled by gas.

Movement against the stone wall caught her attention. It was the black-haired woman in white. Her hair hung in her face, keeping Phoebe from seeing her features. She had been walking when she caught Phoebe's eye but had stopped, standing still by the far wall, near the place where the washing machines once stood.

For a long time, Phoebe didn't try to move. She stared at the woman, afraid to do or say anything. Her head reeled, and she was convinced that Hester had slipped something to her, maybe the same junk she was using in the gingerbread dudes and feeding to Onenspek.

Phoebe squeezed her eyes shut and reopened them, but nothing changed. She worked herself into a sitting position, not taking her sight from the strange brunette.

At least I still have clothes on this time, Phoebe thought. The green dress appeared to be in good condition, and everything was accounted for, including the ankle-high boots. It was then she realized the floor was not cement, but dirt.

Slowly, painfully, Phoebe got to her feet. She brushed the dust from her back and butt. Still, the brunette said and did nothing.

Phoebe turned and saw that the stairs were still there, and she thought to back out of there and flee, but she realized that, despite the bizarre display in the parlor and the sudden switch of venue, she did not feel threatened. Any fear she had at that moment was born of the situation.

Phoebe decided to speak instead of run away. "Hello? Umm, I'm Phoebe."

The brunette took a sidestep to her left and pointed to the floor with a porcelain white finger.

"I don't know what's happening, or how I got down here," Phoebe said.

The brunette said nothing. Her finger remained pointed to the floor.

Phoebe stepped forward cautiously. As she came closer, she looked down to the spot where the woman was pointing. The dirt there appeared darker than the rest, as if it had been disturbed recently.

"So what? Something's buried there?" Phoebe asked and shrugged. She was losing patience with this hallucination, or nightmare, whatever it was.

"A key," the brunette said. She moved her finger away from the spot on the floor and lifted her hair from her face. It was a pleasant face, but a desperately sad one. Her flesh was deadly white, almost as white as the nightgown.

"A key to what?" asked Phoebe.

"A key to everything," the woman expanded. "It begins with me."

"Okay . . . what—*Jesus*!"

The brunette's chest flowered in bright red blood and it began spraying Phoebe. The fresh blood ran darker as it fountained, and in seconds, Phoebe was covered in the hot liquid, and she could see nothing beyond the red. It quickly became so thick that her vision went dark.

Phoebe tried to move, to turn and run, but something had taken hold of her, keeping her in place. Horrified, she screamed.

"Phoebe!" someone called.

She stopped screaming and called out instead, "Help me!"

"Phoebe! Come on, wake up!"

The feeling that she was falling yet again took her over, and in the dark, light could finally be seen. The voice was familiar, but it took her a moment to recognize it. It was Alec Holgrave. She opened her eyes, slightly at first. Wherever she was now, it was bright.

"What's going on?" Phoebe asked before she could even see. She blinked his face into focus. It was floating above her, and she tried to recognize her surroundings.

"To be truthful," he began, "no one's entirely sure."

"Oh, wonderful," she said dryly. After another moment, she realized that she was in the bed of the second-floor turret room. It was still dark outside, the windows were open, and Holgrave was sitting on the mattress next to her. The sheet and comforter were drawn up to her neck.

"What's the last thing you remember?" he asked.

Phoebe stared at the ceiling, trying to recall. The last thing she remembered was the dream, so the brunette with the white nightie and the spontaneously exploding chest problem didn't count. The parlor came flooding into her mind. She saw herself sitting at the round table, holding hands with Hester and Alec, then a light show.

"The séance," she said.

"Yes."

"I think I was hit with a short or something," Phoebe supposed. "That goddamned electrical nightmare Hester has wired up to her table must have zapped me."

"I suppose that's a possible explanation," Holgrave said.

"What else?" Phoebe asked with irritation and shrugged her shoulders.

"Well—"

"Hey!" she shouted. Her movement had brought the fact that she was wearing very little underneath the comforter to her attention.

"What? What the—" She passed her right hand over her body, taking inventory. She was a little light in the clothes department.

Seeing the flash of anger on Phoebe's face, Holgrave popped to his feet. "Now, wait a minute," he said, holding up his index finger. "Before you jump to conclusions—"

"What did you *do*?" she cried and buried her head under the covers.

"And there we are. Jumping to a conclusion," Holgrave commented.

Phoebe peeked over the top of the comforter. Her deep brown eyes glaring hotly at the man next to her bed.

"I'll have you know that I carried you up here, without help, I might add," Holgrave informed her, not backing down. "And then, like the gentleman that I am, I removed myself from your quarters and allowed Dzolali and Glendarah to attend to you."

Phoebe blinked. Her eyes softened, but she remained staring at him, unsure.

"Well, look," he went on and placed his hand on the doorknob, "it's after two in the morning and I'm knackered . . . from *heavy lifting*, I've no doubt." He returned her stare.

Insulted, Phoebe gasped and slapped the blanket away from her face. "No doubt, *indeed!*" she mocked, though not playfully as before.

"I'll inform your benefactors of your recently reacquired consciousness," he added and opened the door.

"Good night, *sir!*" she called after him in an offended tone.

Holgrave left and closed the door behind him. Phoebe scooted up to a sitting position and, noticing the full glass of water that had been placed on her bedside table, grabbed it and downed half.

She adjusted her strapless bra, which had gone slightly askew while she was out, and pulled the comforter back up. Her door opened and Dzolali sailed in with her kimono flailing behind her.

"Hi!" she called and sat on the mattress, sending the frame screeching. "Are you okay?"

Phoebe gladly accepted Dzolali's hug and kiss greeting and looked into her eyes dreamily. "I'm okay. I think."

"We almost called the medics on you," Dzolali said.

"Why didn't you?" Phoebe asked, a bit surprised.

"You seemed fine once the spirit was gone," she explained as if it was obvious.

"Spirit, my ass!" Phoebe shouted, for the first time becoming annoyed in Dzolali's presence. "I got zapped! That was a short circuit in Aunt Hester's crappy wiring."

Dzolali's expression turned to patient confusion. "I don't know a thing about that. But the spirit that came forward wasn't Mr. Bankowski at all. It took a liking to you, though," she finished, smiling.

Phoebe opened her mouth to speak, but Hester and Glendarah entered the room. They had not yet dressed for bed as Dzolali had.

"Ah," Hester said, "I see you are no worse for wear." She said this with a grin that, to Phoebe, appeared guardedly kind.

"She seems to think she was electrocuted," Dzolali said over her shoulder.

To Phoebe's surprise and disappointment, Hester and Glendarah laughed, and Phoebe wished for a baseball bat.

"My, oh my, no!" Hester insisted.

Phoebe narrowed her eyes at Hester. The lamp flickered.

"Ah! You see?" Glendarah blurted, gesturing to the light as if it proved something.

Dzolali giggled. "I think she doesn't."

Great-Aunt Hester folded her hands and adopted an expression of knowledge that Phoebe didn't care for. She had seen such stances before from people who thought they were about to enlighten the listener with wisdom.

Phoebe sighed. *Uh-oh, get ready for some witch-splaining.* Phoebe looked to Dzolali, but from the smile on the gorgeous Latina's face, there was going to be no help there.

"You were chosen by the spirit that erroneously, or through its own chosen will, borrowed our little doorway between the spirit world and our own," Hester lectured. Glendarah grinned knowingly.

"You don't say," said Phoebe.

Dzolali's face lit up and she nodded excitedly.

"Oh, I *do*," Hester continued. "The spirit was not the one we summoned, but it did gravitate to you, possessing you for a period of time."

"Do you remember anything?" Dzolali interjected.

Phoebe was about to tell them both about the dream, about appearing in the basement from the past, and all about the brunette and her key and the explosion of blood, but something told her to keep that to herself.

A key to everything, the woman in the nightie had said.

"Um, no. Nothing," Phoebe lied, hoping that it was convincing enough.

It begins with me.

"How odd," Glendarah commented.

"I still think I was zapped," Phoebe insisted. "It felt like an electric shock."

The blonde wiccan nodded and tilted her head in sympathy. "It often does."

Oh, my God, shut uuuup!

Hester moved to the bed and placed her hand on her grandniece's shoulder. "Phoebe, tonight, you've witnessed your wiccan powers," she said. "Your true potential is yet to be unleashed. Here, with us," Hester continued, gesturing in a wide circle, "you can embrace your heritage as a Pyncheon woman."

"Um, okay," Phoebe muttered, not knowing what else to say. Her eyes flicked from one face to the other, seeing hints of positivity on their expressions but feeling dread from all but Dzolali.

"You have your doubts," Hester stated, her smile fading. "In time, I hope you can dispose of them."

Without a word exchanged, Glendarah opened the bedroom door, and the two of them exited. Phoebe stared at the closed portal for a moment, feeling bewildered, lost.

"You look like you have a headache," said Dzolali, noticing Phoebe cringe and thinking it to be from pain and not annoyance.

"Yes, that's it exactly," agreed Phoebe.

"Come here," Dzolali said, taking Phoebe's temples in her fingertips.

Phoebe groaned pleasurably. Like Hester's back massage some twenty-or-so hours earlier, Dzolali's fingers felt magical. Her tension was lifting and, though she had exaggerated the headache, she began to feel carefree, elated, in fact, to be with her love.

"Better?"

"Hell, yesss."

"Good," said Dzolali. "Now shove over," she directed and reached up for the light, turning it off.

Phoebe didn't argue. She complied gladly and felt Dzolali get under the covers with her.

13

The Depths of Secrets

Phoebe awoke bathed in warmth, both of body and sun, soaked in the familiar scents of water lily, vanilla, and at the moment, whatever Dzolali used in her hair, as the woman's head was resting on Phoebe's right arm, which was as asleep as Dzolali.

Phoebe couldn't resist. She inhaled deeply. The motion stirred Dzolali, who turned her face up to her lover.

"Hi," she whispered.

"Hi," Phoebe returned, following it up with a kiss to Dzolali's lips.

The sun shone brightly enough that both women peered through slitted eyelids. Dzolali buried herself under the comforter, not yet ready to face it.

Phoebe, on the other hand, was more than ready to get out of the bed. She felt that she had been in it for days, and a trip to the bathroom was past due. Not seeing her clothes, again, she picked up the nearest garment.

Dzolali's black, colorfully flower-patterned kimono, fully infused with that delicious Dzolali scent, enveloped Phoebe as she quickly padded off to the bathroom.

Afterward, Phoebe took a quick but refreshing shower, then put the kimono back on. She saw herself in the mirror and froze. The no-tion that she had seen that kimono before began to settle into her mind.

Of course, silly Phoebes, she chided herself. *Dzolali wore it last night when she came in. Duh.*

Phoebe left the bathroom, took a quick look around, and dart-ed back into the bedroom. She hung the kimono over her chair and searched her dresser for fresh clothes. As she dressed, her eyes kept going back to the beautiful robe.

Phoebe went to the bed, peeled the comforter down far enough to kiss Dzolali on the cheek, and left the room. She went down to the kitchen for a quick coffee and whatever she could find to eat. Halfway through her cup, Phoebe's memory clicked.

The kimono was in the dream from the night before last. Dzolali had come in, somehow moving the chair out of the way, and in the dream, her wiccan lover had been wearing it.

No, that can't be right.

Phoebe's brow ruffled in thought as she looked out the kitchen window. She replayed the dream in her mind over and over, certain that she had seen Dzolali slip that very robe from her body before coming to her bed.

Then came the exquisite lovemaking. The restraints. The fighting with them to get at her love. Then the gargoyle came.

No. No, no. That was a dream, as was the one on that first night here. It wasn't real.

Phoebe's thoughts turned to Ned Onenspek and the gingerbread men. She wondered if it could be possible that she had been drugged. She shuddered as she further considered the possibility that she could have been somehow violated.

Phoebe shook her head and wiped her face with her hands. Was her love guilty of violating her? Had she been tricked into love with this person of her same sex, a persuasion that she had only in the slightest sense ever pondered but never seriously considered?

She needed to talk to Holgrave, but first, she needed to go about her daily chores like nothing was amiss.

Phoebe tackled the laundry first, as her own clothes and some of Onenspek's and Holgrave's were down in the great hamper, in its place under the laundry chute. She entered the basement cautiously, halting on the stairs every couple of steps to listen. The cement floor was back, as were the laundry machines and paneling. With her eyes peeled and her attention on any sound, she loaded the washing machine and set it to run. The washer rumbled and squealed, and she turned to go but was curious to have a look at the spot where the dark-haired woman from her dream, or spiritual possession, if she were to believe Glendarah, had been standing and pointing.

In the dream, Phoebe had fallen on the floor near the stairwell. She stepped to that place and faced the wall. The giant laundry machines were offset to the right, and the worktable was placed to the left. Holgrave's developing work was done on another table along the north wall to her left, and she was certain none of that was there during the confrontation.

The light. That gas light, where was it?

She looked up to the bare ceiling. To her recollection, the lamp had been mounted to the support beam just to the right of where she had "landed." The strange spirit had been standing almost in line with that same beam. Phoebe found it and followed it with her eyes. That spot, the place the woman had pointed, was under the worktable. Specifically, it was under the legs on the table's right end. There was nothing unusual on the cement surface.

The noise of the machine became unbearable once the load began tumbling. She headed to the stairs and went all the way to the third floor to strip the beds.

Phoebe found the master bedroom unoccupied, so she took care of that one first, working quickly, not wishing to run into Hester. She followed that with Glendarah's room, then Dzolali's.

Mr. Onenspek's bed, to Phoebe's relief, had finally been slept in, so she stripped it and made it fresh. She sent the linen down the chute and walked past Onenspek's second room, the studio.

A light rush of breeze pressed against her ear, entreating her to stop and pay it attention. She stilled and listened. The gentle gust happened once more, and behind it came the sound of a child's, or perhaps a woman's, call. It sounded rather far away, certainly further away than the limits of the home's walls, but at the same time, it *felt* near to Phoebe.

Disturbing the floorboards, which loudly shouted at her with creaks and cracks, she stepped to Onenspek's studio door and pressed her ear close.

The cry happened again, and Phoebe thought perhaps, instead of a child or a woman, it was Ned Onenspek, sounding as if he was suffering physical pain. Another thought occurred, and in disgust, she jumped back from the door, wondering where Dzolali was at that moment.

The small, focused wind swept to her again, this time giving the door a shake in its frame, as if the windows beyond had just been opened. Another cry, this one of obvious despair, wafted to her ears and, picturing Ned Onenspek having opened a window to jump, Phoebe tried the knob and pushed the door out of the way.

"Ned?" she called into the room. Only a stiff breeze, this one consistent, met her.

Phoebe stood for a long moment, like an actress that had been late for her cue and thrust out on stage, feeling as if she was under the scrutiny of hundreds, perhaps thousands. These eyes were indeed all around her, in the form of the characters in the paintings covering the walls. No thought was given to their straightness. They were hung to dry directly on the wallpaper, their borders nearly touching.

Phoebe stepped forward, forgetting the open door, forgetting about Ned's possible suicide dive. Her mind scrambled to decipher the paintings on the wall. It seemed impossible for her to take in one at a time. They had been suspended together in such proximity but were so distant in relevance to one another that the colors of the next one would pull her eyes away. Settling on that one, its neighbor would do the same.

Reaching the last in a row at the end of the wall, a sound of disgust slipped from Phoebe's throat as she took in the color-rich scene of an executioner dropping a guillotine blade on a prisoner, most likely of the French Revolution, while an attendant carried away a wooden basket full of heads, two of which threatened to tumble out, much to the bearer's indifference to the situation. The blank look on his blood-speckled face told her he had seen much worse, and a few more bouncing skulls were nothing new.

The overwhelming blue and purple of the one below it was of an exploding volcano, its lava flowing between short buildings and com- ing up the street in the foreground, toward the viewer. The bright red and orange lava had gathered up many victims, both human and some animal, many dead but some alive, their flesh charring as the hot mess flowed. People in the foreground, as yet untouched, sprinted in horror, their faces frozen in desperate fear. One man had turned to the danger, his shoulders sloped in surrender.

Another was of a woman being stalked in a dark room. A single ray of light revealed the danger of the room: a man in black tattered rags, armed with a sword. In the gloom, the mutilated body of a man lay in a bloody mass on the floor. The woman was a redhead, her hair set in a wavy, old-fashioned arrangement. Her clothes, and those of the deceased male victim, were decades out of fashion, though elegant. In moments, the beastly killer would be on her, and Phoebe saw no way for the woman to escape her doom.

Phoebe turned to the wall on her right and found that decapi- tation was a theme for many of Ned's works. Dismemberment and the arrangement of separated limbs as prizes was the theme of still more. More and more paintings, with horrors of Mother Nature, mur- der, trauma of vehicles both of land and of sky, war, and war, and still more war.

The horror of death was everywhere, even at her feet, as many paintings were not hung because either Ned had run out of room or hooks, or the will to elevate them. These paintings were on the floor, leaning against the walls on either side of her, even blocking the closet door at her right. Paint splatters were all over the wood floor and crushed into the burgundy runner under her feet. She could see paint on the wallpaper. In between the works were splashes and even the outlines of some paint that had dried there but that was now long gone.

Phoebe carefully stepped further inside, noting the cool air filtering through the stale room. Once past the entryway, she looked around the corner. The bed had been removed, and in its place, two large easels had been set upon drop cloths that had once been white. On the easels were more Onenspek nightmares, neither complete. Beyond and all around the easels was more paint on the walls, border-to-border, floor-to-ceiling. Phoebe could not bear to look directly upon them, for her peripheral vision was gathering enough horror in reds and blacks to last a lifetime.

The windows had been opened. The curtains, long ruined in the process of Ned's creations, sailed gently in and out. At first hidden by this dream scene of an artist's prolific period was the figure of Ned Onenspek himself, draped in drapery, looking out upon the dead forest.

Phoebe gasped when her eyes found his ghostly figure in the fluttering fabric, for he was slight of figure and had been unmoving. "Ned?" she tried.

She heard the cry again, faintly and from behind. She turned to see nothing more than the walls covered in nightmares. A shadow passed over the wall, and before she could scream, Phoebe was in the clutches of a madman.

"Where?!" Onenspek demanded shrilly with his arms around Phoebe, one around her midsection, the other around her neck.

Phoebe's scream was cut short by the pressure of the crook of an arm. She grasped at it with both hands, her nostrils filling with his foul odor, a mixture of excrement, urine, and sweat. How he had come to be in this condition since just the previous night, she barely had time to contemplate.

"Where?" he repeated and tightened his hold. "I need it. You fuckin' gave me one, so you should know!"

Phoebe's ear rang, overwhelmed by his bellowing directly into it. She couldn't have answered if she'd wanted to, as there was no airflow.

"You see, we have a *fucking* problem!" he shrilled. "I can't continue my work if it all stops. It all stops when I can't continue my work."

"Ack!" Phoebe attempted.

"It's kind of a symbiotic relationship. Do you know what symbiosis is?"

Phoebe nodded, though it brought pain.

Ned laughed and she could feel him shake his head. "Possibly, possibly. But in case that's a bluff, I'll explain. It's a *relationship*—"

He squeezed every time he emphasized a word. Phoebe choked in response and her world began to dim.

"—between two *entities . . .* where *one* helps the *other* for a mutually bene-*fucking*-ficial outcome!"

Phoebe coughed and her throat flared painfully.

"I think yer getting it. So," Ned said between breaths, "tell me where you've moved the fucking cookies."

He had lessened the pressure, perhaps by accident, perhaps to allow her to talk. She forced air in and out in a furious pace, pushing away the darkness that had encroached upon her vision. She took the opportunity and stomped her left heel upon Ned's foot.

Onenspek screamed and let his grip slip. Phoebe lifted her left arm and twisted that way, elbowing Ned in the beak. He stumbled back on his heels, eyes shut to the pain, his arms pinwheeled to keep from falling.

Phoebe, seething with the rage that had built up with interest over the last few months of personal and professional failure, compounded with the lack of sleep, the previous night's séance, and the jealousy and confusion over her need for Dzolali, turned her defense offensive.

She closed on Ned, who had recovered his balance. She clocked him with an uppercut from her right, which knocked his head back. His eyes seemed to gain appreciation in his paint splatterings on the ceiling.

"Phoebe!" a masculine voice called from behind her.

Not to be distracted, she sent her left fist in for good measure, catching Onenspek's right cheek. Ned spun around, falling through the unfinished painting on the right. He crashed to the floor with a crunch, the easel and the painting ruined.

Her name was called again, louder this time and from much nearer. Phoebe raised both fists and danced around on the balls of her feet to face whoever was the next contender. She wheezed and coughed, her throat still burning.

"Easy now!" called Holgrave. His eyes were wide with concern, darting between her and the fallen artist. He had his hands up once again in surrender, a stance he was becoming accustomed to taking in the presence of the youngest Pyncheon woman.

Eyes burning with tears of anger and fear, Phoebe took a moment to recognize the newcomer to the room. She settled from her defensive stance and dropped her fists. She stood there, panting for breath as she stared into Holgrave's face. "What are *you* doing here?"

"Apparently, aborting a rescue," Holgrave said, disarming her with a smile. His hair was down, strands falling in his face.

Holgrave went to Onenspek, kneeling at his side, being careful not to put his knee into the wet, ruined, or perhaps improved Onenspek original, which now bore the artist's blood as well as his paint. The man was breathing.

Holgrave looked to Phoebe in amazement.

"Fucker attacked me," she said between wheezes. Her voice was gravelly and uneven, and sounded not in the least bit apologetic.

"It appears, fortunately for him, that he shall live to regret it," Holgrave said and stood.

Phoebe nodded curtly, unable to conjure a kind word of relief.

Holgrave stepped to her, his caution discarded. "Are you all right?"

"I dunno. I think, yeah." She felt tears streaming down her cheeks. She sensed her great-aunt approaching, and she was not alone. Phoebe faced the open doorway expectantly.

Holgrave followed her eyes. A moment later, he heard the floor creaking and bumping to the rhythm of rushing footsteps.

Hester wafted in, her feet unseen beneath her long dress. Glendarah and Dzolali appeared right behind.

"What the devil is happening in my house?" Hester demanded. Her eyes were abundant with outrage, becoming more intense when she saw Onenspek's fallen form. "What have you done?!" she thundered at Holgrave.

Before he could muster a thought to word his defense, he found himself pointing at Phoebe.

"Yeah. Thanks, dude," Phoebe said and shot him a hard look.

Holgrave shrugged apologetically.

"*You?*" Hester roared, turning on her grandniece.

"He attacked *me*," Phoebe fired back and coughed from the strain. "He's strung out and came after me for one of your goddamned ginger-bread whatevers!"

Hester blinked, and for a lightning-quick moment, there might have been compassion. Her eyes passed over Phoebe's form, as if looking for injury.

Phoebe pushed on in the silence. "He grabbed me from behind. Tried to choke me out."

Hester snapped her fingers and pointed to Onenspek. Glendarah moved to the unconscious man's side. With Holgrave's assistance, they turned him over. Ned's eyes remained shut, but he coughed, spewing droplets of blood that had streamed down from his nose.

"Sit him up," Glendarah said, and together, they brought him up into a sitting position. "Ned," she said quietly.

Phoebe closed the distance between herself and Hester, turning her head up to the old woman's face. "I don't know what you're giving him," she whispered, "but it's making him crazy. Maybe even killing him. You disgust me, Auntie Hester." With a glance to Dzolali, who wore an expression of shock, Phoebe stormed out.

Phoebe went to her room and threw herself onto the spongy bed, face down, and cried. Her throat hurt from Ned's grip, and the strain of the emotion added to her discomfort. She felt like a child, crying into a pillow, something she hadn't done since her high school days.

She forced herself to stop blubbering and rolled out of the bed. She felt angry, violated, and confused. She stared out the windows for a time, sitting on the cushioned bench. Someone knocked on the door. She ignored it.

Phoebe spent the next several hours in her bedroom, distracting her mind by working on her novel with her earbuds in. Without internet access, her variety of music was limited to what she had downloaded onto the laptop, so when the first song she chose that afternoon repeated, she stopped the music and pulled the tiny speakers out of her ears.

Almost on cue, there was a knock on the door. Phoebe saved her work and grumbled a "Who is it?" even though her psychic gift had already told her. Out of spite, she ignored it.

"Dzolali," came the answer.

Phoebe was about to say that it wasn't a good time, but the questions in her mind were nagging, debilitating. She rose quickly, bumping the office chair with the backs of her knees and sending it sliding across the floor. She unlocked the door and pulled it open.

"Are you all right?" Dzolali asked, her concern obvious and sounding sincere.

Phoebe repressed the urge to embrace Dzolali but said nothing as she moved out of the doorway to allow her entry. She kept her expression carefully neutral.

Dzolali stepped inside and closed the door behind her. She stared into Phoebe's face questioningly, which somehow, to Phoebe, felt indignant and insulting.

"I need to know something," Phoebe said.

"Okay," Dzolali answered dubiously.

"I've been having dreams about you since I got here," Phoebe exuded in a rush, needing to get the words out and to have her questions answered once and for all. "Vivid dreams, too. And then, it just so happens that you liked me, and we ended up spending the night together and this morning, I find that kimono, the same one from the dream. You have to tell me if you somehow got in my head to fuck with me. That shit my Aunt Hester is feeding to Ned, is it a drug?"

"Wait a minute—" Dzolali stepped forward, her arms wide.

"Stand the *fuck* back!" Phoebe shouted and held out her hand. "Have I been dosed with whatever Ned's on?"

Unexpectedly, Dzolali's face lit up in amusement and she laughed. "I don't need drugs for you, Phoebe." She took another step, then another. With her copper eyes meeting Phoebe's, Dzolali stepped past her protesting hand and held her prey still with a mere thought.

Phoebe could not move, not even to look away. She felt Dzolali's presence in her mind, blatant and bold. Without physical contact, Phoebe's will was stripped away, along with any doubt that psychic abilities existed.

Dzolali pushed further, and Phoebe was reminded of her undying love, her need, for Dzolali. Phoebe no longer wanted to flee or fight. Locked in her sultry gaze, even her clash with Onenspek was forgotten.

Dzolali planted a kiss, and Phoebe reciprocated.

Phoebe blinked, and she realized that the kiss had ended. Somehow, in the second that passed, Dzolali had stepped away and opened the door.

Oh, no! She's leaving!

"Hester wanted me to tell you to get back to the laundry," Dzolali said over her shoulder as she went out. "I left a dress for you to wear tonight. Check your closet."

With that, Dzolali was gone, and the door swung shut, clanging like jail cell bars. It was a few moments before Phoebe broke the staring contest with the closed door.

She shook her head clear, backed up her story onto her thumb drive, and shut down the laptop. There was a lot of work to do before she had to help Alva in the kitchen. No time to waste.

Dzolali entered the parlor with the shadow of concern on her face. Hester was preparing for a client scheduled for a palm reading.

"Did she speak?" Hester asked without looking up from her tarot cards.

"She did," Dzolali answered.

"But there's a problem," Hester concluded.

"There is. She confronted me with the knowledge that I had visited her in her dreams. She's under the impression that she's been drugged, like Ned."

"And what did you tell her?" Hester left her tarot cards on the round table and stood, facing her coven sister.

"I had to renew my spell over her once again," Dzolali said. "She fought me a little, but I told her that you wanted her to resume her chores."

Hester smiled, though it was without humor. "Good. Was there any trace of the spirit that entered her last night?"

"There was something," Dzolali answered. "I just can't be sure. Phoebe's just so strong, I don't think she knows she's fighting me."

"I'm *sure* she isn't," Hester said. "If she was, she'd be quite formidable."

"I can't read her," Dzolali admitted. "I can't tell if the spirit possessed her or just passed through."

"Or if it remains?" Hester asked.

"Not even that, High Priestess."

"She will come into our coven," Hester Pyncheon said thickly. "And when I'm gone, she will make a powerful high priestess."

14

Acquiescence

Phoebe went on with her chores, her mind distracted with the image of Dzolali and the memories of the previous night's excursion. She transferred items from the washer to the dryer, added more to the washer, and set both to run.

A whisper at her ear halted her retreat from the basement.

Even over the screeches and droning thrum from the laundry machines, she heard it, as if someone had been matching her walking pace and spoken directly in her ear. Phoebe felt a brief pang of fear, settling to a resigned level of anxiousness. The fight-or-flight response was soothed like a blanket on cold feet. Phoebe looked about the room and even stepped to the dumbwaiter door, opening it to listen.

It was no use. The room was filled with noise. Thinking herself utterly insane, Phoebe shook her head and again, more quickly, headed for the stairs.

The vision of the black-haired woman in the nightgown infiltrated her sight, obscuring all that had been real just a heartbeat before. Phoebe cried out in terror and stopped, just as she was about to put her foot on the first step.

Phoebe blinked, but there the image stayed, just as Phoebe had discovered her in the dream. *My God, who are you?*

Alice.

The reply came to Phoebe as if she had thought the word. The name meant nothing to her, but for certain, she knew that it was the very same entity that had possessed her during Hester's séance.

"I can't see," Phoebe said aloud. She reached out with both hands. She could not see them, but she did catch the railing of the basement stairwell in the palm of her right hand. She gripped it tightly, unsure of her ability to remain fully in her own reality.

You do.

"You're not real."

But I am.

Phoebe felt like she might fall. She gripped the railing tighter and stepped forward until her left foot struck the bottom step. Still, the vision of Alice stood before her. The wall behind the woman was stone, not wood panels, and the floor beneath her feet was dirt, not cement.

"Get out of my head," Phoebe commanded.

In time.

With her other hand, Phoebe felt for the stairs. Her right foot stepped onto the first, followed by her left, which found the next one. Her aim was to find the first floor and put distance between herself and the House of the Seven Gables.

Tears flowed freely down Phoebe's face, and she sobbed like a little girl drowning at the beach. After a moment, Phoebe realized that she was not crying simply from her own panic. She was feeling Alice's emotions. Phoebe stopped trying to climb away, fascinated by this development. Instead, she opened her mind to accept Alice's feelings.

There was a terribly powerful melancholy coming from the ghost. The emotion felt ancient, though not as antiquated as the house itself. It was certain now, that the house bore deep, dark secrets. Phoebe felt it on her being, broadcast to her by Alice.

As Phoebe acquiesced to her situation, her eyesight compromised.

Grasping onto the reality of the basement staircase, the vision of Alice and the basement from the past gave way to another scene. Alice again starred in this movie, though now she was somewhere else in the house, surrounded by four people, each wearing masks. Three of them were women, one a man.

Alice was bound by ropes at her ankles and wrists, and her midsection was completely wrapped by another long coil of rope that looped through a hook in the ceiling. Phoebe recognized the room. It was the attic suite, where Alec Holgrave now made his temporary home.

The room was quite different in the vision. There was no bed, no end table, and the walls were unfinished panels of wood, where now there was plasterboard and paint.

The masked people were witches, bound together into a coven. Their masks were hideous distortions of humanity, mixed with animalistic traits. The man, Panas, who stood behind the bound and suspended form of Alice, wore a goat's face mask with horns.

The tallest woman among them was on Alice's right, Ceridwen, the High Priestess of the coven. Her mask covered the upper half of her face and swept upward as it went back into what looked like a curled-up hand fan. Her eyes shone through two small, almond-shaped holes.

The witch with the long-nosed mask, Lornabeth, held a bowl in front of Alice's throat. The shortest one with the wicked grin, Hepzibah, held a knife.

That's my mom's bowl! Hepzibah's my great-aunt Hester's aunt!

Hepzibah placed the long, curved blade against Alice's throat and dragged it. Blood flowed into the bowl and soaked deep into Alice's nightgown.

Phoebe screamed, unable to pause the movie or change the channel. She thought her eyes shut and felt the lids close and her brow tighten, but the horrifying vision went on.

And on.

Phoebe collapsed onto the stairs. She felt the cool wood on her face, chest, and legs. She felt the rail post in her grip, but her eyes and ears remained back in time, out of her control.

She watched as the coven drained Alice of blood, leaving her to dangle by the thick rope. When the bowl was full, Lornabeth took the bowl away, careful not to spill any more. The light went out of Alice's eyes, and as it did, Phoebe's vision then faded to black. It was a moment before she realized that she could again see her reality and that she had shut her eyelids tightly.

Phoebe lifted herself up and turned to sit on a step to gather her nerves.

Instead of finding the basement as she had left it moments ago, the walls and ceiling had disappeared. Other than the stairwell on which she sat, any trace of the House of the Seven Gables was gone.

Before Phoebe was the forest, its trees decrepit, and the ground, mostly barren of grass, was in a state between dirt and mud. The air was damp and carried a chill, with wisps of fog stirring about the black limbs of the trees surrounding her.

Phoebe felt a wave of panic strike her. "Oh, my God. Hello?" she called.

At that moment, as if in answer to her call, movement in the field ahead of her drew her attention. It took a moment for her to comprehend the shapes that were sprouting from the moonlit soil. Human forms took shape as one after another rose through the dirt, and oddly, none of the muck clung to them.

Phoebe could not count them, but in her transfixed state, rooting her to the last bastion of her reality, the wood surface of the stairs, she found that the gathering crowd was translucent.

There were men and women, even a couple of children, all looking upon her with silent regard. Some were eyeless, others steadily gazing, but all in some stage of decomposition, some manner of decay. The worst of them were skeletal, wearing antique fashions, stained and in strands, hanging like drapes upon their frail frames. The more recently deceased were contemporary in their clothing, but they differed not in their apparent intent.

They stood, bound together, facing Phoebe as if they were meeting together in a common cause, though in life, certainly, they could not have met. This Phoebe not only deduced from the anachronistic clues they wore upon their bodies, but from the thoughts and feelings broadcast en masse.

Their journey to the surface complete, Phoebe found that she was no longer afraid. The realization that she was calm struck her odd, and she squeezed the skin of her left forearm with her right hand, hard, to take stock of her level of consciousness. The skin ached in response.

Wordlessly, Phoebe cast her eyes over the impossible crowd, each of them still as the moai statues of Easter Island on a blue-tinged, star-lit night. Without her addressing the gathering, her mind heard their proclamation.

It must all end.

Phoebe blinked and withdrew a step, drawing herself up and gaining a different perspective of the crowd, which was many bodies deeper than it had at first appeared. Their collective voice, as her mind categorized it, spoke to her at once, in chorus. Though not afraid, Phoebe was uncomfortable, like an infant with young, untested ears at a concert. She heard, yet felt them all, at the same time.

It must all end, they repeated.

"What must end?"

The house. The coven. The tyranny of the Pyncheons.

"But I, I *am* a Pyncheon."

On this, the dead were silent, regarding her as they had before.

She had no problem with the idea that the House of the Seven Gables should cease to exist. The place had lost its nostalgic value, what little there had been to begin with, as many of her memories were of sour times, and she would need little prodding to take a match to it.

The word 'coven' now grew plainly defined to her. They meant Great-Aunt Hester, Glendarah D'Amitri, and Dzolali Alameda. The

congress before her did not intend their meaning to end at a disband-
ment but a total annihilation of the union, without regard for pre-
serving life.

Phoebe's heart sank at the thought of murder, for she knew that
she was no killer. The prospect of her carrying out such acts seemed to
her impossible, as the very act of climbing Mount Everest might be to
a quadriplegic. Further, the thought of losing Dzolali when so much
was yet to be shared brought her to tears.

"There's no way I can do it," Phoebe said, though the intended
audience was herself.

It must all end, they repeated just the same.

Phoebe looked away, only to find Alice standing next to her, looking eye-to-ruined-eye. "How?" Phoebe asked.

You are of Pyncheon blood. Few beyond a Pyncheon have the power, Alice replied.

The vision of Alice streaked with blood emerged once again
from the wound Hepzibah had inflicted upon the young chambermaid's throat.

Phoebe covered her face in her hands and begged for the horror to
stop. Her voice was shrill and near panic as she shouted through her
fingers, her body shaking from the effort.

Having received nothing in reply, Phoebe lifted her face to beseech
the gathering for relief from their charge.

The basement was again what it had been minutes before. The
roar and whine of the laundry machines resumed, as if they had never
paused. The light was white, the floor concrete, the walls paneled and
near, the ceiling low and wooden.

How can you help us if you can't accept who you are?

Alice's question hung thickly in the air, like cigar smoke in a vault.
It reverberated, repeated, and floated in her mind. Phoebe could sense
the closeness of Alice but saw nothing of the ghost in her reality.

Overwhelmed in the residual emotion of the moment, Phoebe
used the handrail to get to her feet. She ascended to the first floor,

where she stood in the doorway for a moment before reaching back to shut the door.

The dress Dzolali had left for her was satiny black, with a high lace collar and a plunging neckline. As the skirt was knee length, Phoebe added dark stockings and shiny black high heels.

Phoebe had put her hair up with an ornate metal hair clip, revealing her birthmark clearly. She had blackened her eyelids with a smoky eye effect that rendered her brown eyes vibrant in comparison. Her lips were black, and her rouge a deep amber that faded into her jawline. Her earrings were long, dangling upside-down crosses. The charm on the necklace was a bronze-colored pentagram, and she wore a ring on almost every finger. They were quite elaborate, featuring skulls, more pentagrams, and gemstones.

As she set the table, she heard someone walk into the dining room and then come to an abrupt halt. Eyes were upon her, and she turned.

"Good evening, Mr. Holgrave," Phoebe greeted him with a cold tone. Her eyes held his for a moment, almost daring him to comment on her appearance.

"Good evening, Ms. Pyncheon," he returned and gave a bow. "You're looking well."

"Thank you," she said flatly, with an expression that invited nothing further. She turned back to the table, continuing to dress it with silverware.

"In case you were wondering," Holgrave dared go on, "Mr. Onenspek will be fine."

"That's marvelous," Phoebe said stonily.

Holgrave attempted to lighten the mood by smiling humorously. "I was certain that you had broken his nose. When I walked in—"

Phoebe turned to him, stepping closely. "Mr. Holgrave, if you don't mind, I'd rather not go over the unpleasantness. I'd prefer to put it behind me."

"I'm sure Ned Onenspek would like to do the same," Holgrave added, his smile unfettered.

To this, Phoebe said nothing. She turned away from him and began to unload the dumbwaiter.

"May I help?"

"That's not necessary," she answered.

"Right," he said. "I'll just stand here, then. Shall I?"

This time, she said nothing. She returned to the dumbwaiter, sent it down, and closed the door. She stepped to the window overlooking the backwoods and stared into it.

"Good evening," Glendarah greeted them as she stepped into the dining room, followed by Hester.

Holgrave returned the greeting, giving both ladies a slight bow and a smile. Phoebe turned from the window. With surprising confidence, considering how upset she had made her great-aunt by decking her artist friend, Phoebe welcomed the witches with grace and a friendly grin.

Hester and Glendarah smiled guardedly at first and looked to one another. Phoebe took no notice of the curious glance they shared but went about unloading the last of the evening's meal from the dumbwaiter, placing it on the table with a spring in her step and a renewed poise to her spine.

Holgrave pulled the chair for Glendarah, and Phoebe moved quickly to do the same for her great-aunt. Hester arched an eyebrow as she watched Glendarah's surprised, pleased face.

"Thank you, Mr. Holgrave," Glendarah said.

Dzolali entered lastly, and Holgrave noted a shared warm glance between herself and Phoebe. Both ladies beamed upon seeing the other, and when Holgrave made a move to seat Dzolali, Phoebe got there first. Holgrave aborted the act and took his own seat.

Alva arrived to serve, and Phoebe sat at her place.

"I'm almost afraid to ask, but," Phoebe began softly, and nodded to the empty chair.

"He'll be fine," Dzolali assured her. "His pride is as wounded as his face, but it will heal more quickly." She finished with a giggle.

Phoebe returned Dzolali's humorous grin, and the two stared for a few heartbeats.

"What are you smiling about?" Hester suddenly fired.

Oops. "Apologies for appearances, Auntie Hester," Phoebe answered immediately. "I am glad that I didn't hurt him and . . . I guess, Dzolali's comment made me smile. I've been terribly worried since it happened."

"Oh?" Hester followed in a tone that clearly expected Phoebe to continue. Her expression of doubt was deep and sincere. The words that Phoebe had said before storming out of Onenspek's studio had stung, true or not.

Phoebe cleared her throat and looked down at the napkin in her hands. "Um, additionally, I am aware that I said some hurtful things—"

"Indeed," Hester interjected and straightened in her chair.

"—and I beg for your forgiveness, Great-Aunt Hester." She quieted and studied Hester's eyes, fashioning a contrite expression.

The two women looked upon one another for a long moment. Holgrave sat motionless, silently looking from Phoebe, to Hester, to Dzolali, and back. Hester appeared doubtful, Dzolali prideful, and from what he could see of Phoebe, her right eye as it held Hester's left, she appeared calm and sincere.

"Apology accepted, dear," Hester said. "Mr. Onenspek has been working very hard and was most likely dehydrated. Not thinking clearly."

"I understand, of course," Phoebe said.

The meal continued with no more mention of the incident, nor of Onenspek's injuries. Phoebe bore the pain in her knuckles as she grasped her utensils, aware of the bruising and swelling that made them ache.

When dinner was finished, everyone filed out, though Phoebe

wished Dzolali had remained behind to keep her company as she cleared the table and sent everything to the kitchen.

Phoebe changed out of the dress and removed the jewelry to finish the laundry and the dishes. She put on a t-shirt and jeans, then went to the bathroom up the hall to remove the makeup, which, after a moment, she decided she liked enough to leave alone.

She went to the basement and went about folding the dry and transferring the wet loads of laundry. As she thought about it, she realized that the entities, or ghosts, had not harmed her in any way. She remembered the feeling of calm that had washed over her, even in the full view of the apparitions. She wondered if it had been a dream, for the details of her time with Dzolali, even those of the first night, seemed clearer.

With the stack of folded bedding draped across her arms, Phoebe returned to the first floor without incident. She went to the third floor, placed the clean sheets in the linen closet, and then went back down to the kitchen to do her dishes.

Phoebe was pleased to see that Alva had done most of the cleaning before she left. Phoebe dried what dishes were in the rack, put them away, and turned on the faucet to finish.

She heard the door swing inward and turned to see Holgrave peering through the opening, smiling sheepishly.

"Come on in, Mr. Holgrave."

"I was wondering if I could be of assistance."

"That's becoming a habit with you," she said pleasantly.

"I don't mind the least bit," he said with sincerity as he stepped in.

"I do appreciate it."

He took his place at the sink and began scrubbing a plate. Phoebe watched him a moment, which Holgrave noticed.

"What is it?" he asked.

Phoebe eyed the cabinet across from them. "I was just thinking of Ned," she said and wandered to it. "Was he out long?"

"He came to after you stormed out," Holgrave stated thoughtfully. He turned to watch her search the cabinet. "He was quite ashamed of his behavior, I should mention."

"Huh," Phoebe uttered with curiosity. The gingerbread man tin was gone.

Holgrave followed her stare. "I'm sure Hester moved it," he said.

Phoebe agreed and began opening other cabinets. "Is Hester working in her parlor?"

"Yes. All three of them are, actually."

She opened another. No luck there. Crackers and giant cans of soup were stuffed in that one. The next one had much of the same, but something shiny caught her eye.

"A-ha," she said.

"Find it?" he asked over his shoulder.

Phoebe grabbed the stool and climbed on it. "Nope. Somethin' better."

Holgrave, noticing what she was doing, shut off the water and quickly dried his hands. He moved toward her to assist if she needed it.

Phoebe moved some items out of the way and pulled a bottle of whiskey from within. She showed it to him, an impish grin on her face.

Holgrave smiled and accepted the bottle from her hand, which he then took in his own to help her down. It was a soft hand, and warm. For a fleeting moment, their eyes met.

"Are we supposed to have this?" he asked.

"It's the good stuff," she said and shrugged. "Not the cheap crap you've been sneaking from the credenza in the living room."

Holgrave was shocked. "You *knew?*"

Phoebe giggled and hunted for tumblers. Finding a pair, she set them on the kitchen island. She looked at him expectantly.

"No ice for you?" He poured one.

"Nope," she said. "I like things neat."

"Duly noted," Holgrave said as he poured hers. He set the bottle down and they clinked the glasses together. "To your very good health, Ms. Pyncheon."

"Right back atcha," she said and drank with him.

Holgrave's eyebrows rose as she emptied it.

Noticing his expression, she said, "Don't be judgy. It's been a trying day. Another, please." She turned from him and began drying the dishes he had washed.

"I assure you I am not . . . er . . . being judgy."

"Thank you."

"As for Ned, I dare say he will be looking to make his apologies to you at some point."

"I should think so," she said, imitating his accent.

Holgrave finished his glass and poured more. He left the glasses on the island and returned to the sink. He turned the water on and continued his scrubbing. They were nearly finished.

"I must say, Ms. Pyncheon, you looked, still look, actually, quite different this evening at dinner."

"Like it? Dzolali's been very generous sharing her old clothes so I'm not standing out so much."

"Yes. Quite," he said.

She could tell there was something more on his mind. "What?"

"Well, forgive me, but you've rather, in the most superficial of ways, I must add, accepted your great-aunt Hester's way of life."

"The wiccan thing?" she asked with a slanted grin and had another sip of whiskey.

"Exactly."

"Just trying to not get kicked out," she said, then quickly added, "Can't beat 'em, join 'em."

"I understand," he said. "I was shocked at your transformation. It seemed complete," he explained. "Not being, as you say, judgy."

"Sorry, if I was a bit cold at dinner," she offered.

"Think nothing of it." He returned to the sink to wash the remaining dishes.

Phoebe wanted to tell him about the possession, as she had come to understand it, with the spirit of Alice. She wanted to tell him about the occurrence in the basement, the ghosts of people that were somehow attached to the property, and the vision of Alice's murder that she had been forced to watch. She remembered the use of the bowl in the vision, the same one that, at that very moment, was lying in the trunk of her car.

Instead of thinking of that any further, she chose the very next thing on her mind. "I was going to call Detective Backstrom to see if anything came out of that gingerbread thing, but . . . things took a turn."

"I understand," he said and handed her the plate to be dried.

"And I think they know I took one," she added in a whisper. "But instead of blaming me, they took it out on Ned and cut him off."

"So, it was withdrawal," Holgrave surmised. "Withdrawal drove him to attack you."

"He was demanding a gingerbread," she confided. "That's when he had me around the throat."

"Of course," he said as if he had discovered a clue.

"When I made the mistake of calling Hester out in front of everyone . . ." she trailed off and thought back to the one visitor that Phoebe had let into her room afterward.

"What is it?"

The thoughts and doubts crept back into Phoebe's mind. As she thought through the events of the day, and had spent time away from Dzolali, her feelings of love and devotion to the Latina subsided just enough to allow her to examine things.

Is she bewitching me or seducing me?

"Phoebe," Holgrave tried again. "Are you all right?"

She shook her head clear and looked to him. "Yeah, sure."

Holgrave was sure that wasn't exactly true, but considering what she had been through that day, he let it go. "Well, if there's nothing else I can assist you with, I think I'll go watch telly for a short bit."

Phoebe gave him a half-smile. "Just be sure to go easy on the credenza bar. That dime-store-grade shit in there will mess you up."

"Right," he said. "Good night, then."

"Good night," she replied and watched him leave the kitchen.

She stood in silent contemplation for a short time before pouring another glass of the high-grade whiskey. Before drinking it, she put the cap on the bottle and returned it to the cabinet. She put the stool back in its place next to the island and became aware of a breeze at her neck. Before thinking another thought, Phoebe knocked back the entire contents of the tumbler.

She placed her hand on the smooth wooden surface of the island, and her body went rigid. She coughed. The breeze was there again, and it was warm. With the house so quiet, she could hear the movement of the small bursts of wind that were striking her neck. Behind that airy noise was a faint, returning thump, as if someone were rhythmically double-tapping on a door while wearing winter gloves.

As the phenomena continued in synchronicity, Phoebe realized the resemblance to human breathing and a beating heart. That thought, together with the warmth on her neck, broke her fear-born paralysis. She bolted for the kitchen door.

I don't believe in haunted fuckin' houses. I don't believe in ghosts, sorry, Alice, but fuck you very much!

Phoebe went up the hall toward the front of the house, intending to visit Holgrave in the living room. The parlor across the hall from Holgrave was busy that night, however. As Phoebe approached, the parlor doors opened and a client stepped out, and turned back to whomever it was she was speaking to.

Phoebe stopped abruptly, grabbing onto the round post cap of the staircase handrail. She heard Glendarah's voice through the open door, and there were cars still driving up. Through the open screen door, Phoebe could see their headlights cast a white glow into the night.

The idea of running into any of the coven, even Dzolali, was suddenly an abhorrent idea. Worse still, she didn't even wish to take the chance of being introduced to one of Hester's clients. She didn't want to be associated with Hester's fraudulent psychic readings or have someone think she was part of the coven.

Phoebe launched herself up the stairs, not caring if someone heard the pounding of her footfalls or the creaking of the steps. On the second floor, she rushed into her room. There would be no writing this night, she knew, for her exhaustion was clouding her mind, and her body was weak. The pain in her knuckles rang through her hands anew from the washing of the dishes, and shame settled in. It was not for defending herself against Ned, but for having donned Dzolali's dress and embraced the antiquated fashion so willingly.

Phoebe shut the light off and crawled into bed, fully clothed save for the sneakers. Thinking on it a bit, she sat upright, turned the lamp on, and got back out of bed. She stepped to the bedroom door, thoughtfully staring at the key in the lock.

She recalled confronting Dzolali about the drugs in the gingerbread men. Phoebe had accused Dzolali of drugging her, but what Dzolali's reply had been, Phoebe could not remember. The fugue that covered those moments spurred a decision.

Phoebe pulled the key from the lock and went to the center window, opening it. She reached her hand outside and was about to drop the key to the ground when reason returned.

What if I have to pee? Never mind that, how will I get out of here in the morning?

Phoebe sighed, pulled her hand back in, and closed the window. She walked to the door, not knowing what else to do but take her chances.

Wait!

Phoebe went back to the bed, key in hand, and shut off the light. Then, into the darkness, she threw the key. Just to be certain her mind couldn't contemplate where it landed, Phoebe shouted curses into the pillow, muffling the metal clanking of the key when it struck whatever it struck on its way down.

Ha! Now, I honestly don't know where the key is. Plausible deniability!
Drunken and exhausted, Phoebe's consciousness soon left her.

15

Relentless

Phoebe dreamt of someone at her door, turning the knob with a jiggle. Then there was a knock. Her corner room had transformed into a vast library, and the knock echoed up and down the rows of dusty books. Her bed was tucked in between them, though she could see her tiny door in the distance.

"Phoebe, dear," Dzolali called through the door. "Come open the door, baby."

"No," came Phoebe's answer. "Ga'way. S'eepin'."

"Darling, girl. Open up," she called again. "Get the key and open the damn door," Dzolali growled.

Phoebe raised her middle finger to the bedroom door, and the knocking stopped. She sighed in relief and raised the blanket to cover the lower half of her face. In a moment, however, she realized she was not alone.

Phoebe opened her eyes and found Alice, once more standing in the basement and pointing to the space against the wall. Phoebe was becoming angry, not knowing what it was that Alice was trying to say, and apparently failing in her attempts at forewarning her of the danger yet to come from Hepzibah and friends, who, as the knowledge of the nightmare granted Phoebe, were not far, and looking for them both.

Phoebe tried to form the words of warning, but whatever came out of her mouth was scrambled, unintelligible. Still Alice remained, stubbornly pointing to the disturbed section of the dirt floor.

The frustration built until Phoebe snapped awake. "Goddamnit, Alice!" she called out. She sat up, expecting to find herself on the basement floor. Instead, she was sunken into the depths of the mattress and in the confines of the corner bedroom as she had left it.

Phoebe lay back down and tried to relax, but several minutes of rolling this way were not successful, so she got up. She went to the desk and opened her laptop, thinking she would do some writing to get her mind on something else.

The time was closing on 3:00 a.m., so said the clock in the corner of her screen. She sat in the chair and picked up her story where it left off, but after fifteen minutes, she realized that she had been chipping away on the same paragraph, writing it, then revising it, only to revise it again.

Finally, Phoebe grunted in frustration, saved the file without backing it up, and powered down the computer. She realized she needed the bathroom, so she went to her door. It was locked.

"Shit," she muttered, just then remembering what she had done with the key. "Oh, this is just *peachy*."

Phoebe turned the overhead light on and scrutinized the room. She stepped to the bed, thinking through her position at the time when she'd thrown the key across the room.

She scanned the floor, not seeing it. She went all over the bedroom, working out many scenarios featuring the flying key bouncing off this, ricocheting off that, ending up on the floor, even a couple of scenarios where it landed on the window seat cushions.

Phoebe pulled up the cushions and searched around. Nothing.

The urge to urinate cared not for her predicament and built within her as she bent over furniture and pulled out the writing desk, even lifting the laptop and searching underneath.

"Oh, my God, Phoebe," she groaned. "You are such a stupid bitch!"

She leaned on the dresser, then realized it was the one piece of furniture she had not checked. Her excitement renewed, she looked underneath it, then behind it, with no results. She put her body between it and the wall, forcing it forward. Once it was a foot from the wall, Phoebe got down and checked for it.

Not there. Fuck!

She began to pace, fully in the throes of bladder discomfort. Incensed, she gave the dresser a shove. It teetered and came back, and its front feet thonked on the floor and gave out a rattle.

The metallic sound was unexpected from a wooden piece of furniture, so Phoebe stared at it. The Air Castle fan stood on top, as it had since she moved in, so it was certainly that. She took it by the cage surrounding the wooden blades and gave it a shake. The rattle occurred again, and something fell out, landing on the dresser's wooden top with a clink.

It was the key.

Squealing delightfully as relief without lifelong embarrassment was in her future, Phoebe snatched up the key, unlocked the bedroom door, and floated to the bathroom.

She finished and watched her face in the mirror as she washed her hands. Her eyes were lacking any trace of tiredness, though she had been asleep only for a little more than two hours until the dreams of Dzolali at her door and of Alice had occurred.

Damn you, Alice, she thought, then wondered if she had truly repelled Dzolali's advance or if she had been mistaken about it all.

Phoebe stepped into the hallway, dimly lit as it was by the low-wattage lights. She returned to her bedroom and grabbed her sweater. She went downstairs and stepped outside through the front door, leaving the inner door open.

The night was chilly, so she zipped the sweater and put up her hood.

With thoughts of Alice rattling around, Phoebe stepped off the porch. Her exhalations drew chutes of steam into the air, lit by the waning moon and the stars. The neon sign in the parlor window was off, so it couldn't spoil her eyes' adjustment to the change. She wondered if the caged raven, kept in the parlor at night, would squawk at her.

Her restless legs carried her in the direction of the old carriage house. Once there, she gave the big door a tug. It opened and she went inside. The lights had been installed more recently than those inside the house, so she flipped the switch up, waking the neon tubes above.

The Cadillac shone in the white glow, its deep shade of red still brilliant in places, despite the age and dust. She walked along its considerable length. For a two-door, it was giant, being longer and wider than her Caprice four-door. Despite the mixed memories of her childhood at the House of the Seven Gables, the Coupe De Ville was a magnificent beast. The tinted windows and the black vinyl top completed the elegant design. Phoebe knew very little of cars, but the Cadillac just made her want to drive.

The thought of her stealing the car keys and taking it for a ride made Phoebe giggle, knowing how incensed her great-aunt Hester would become.

Phoebe sauntered to the back of the car, taking in the view of the trunk and bumper. In the corner of her eye, she saw the handles of yard tools leaning against the far wall, inside what used to be a horse stall.

She moved closer and saw shovels, a pickaxe, a wood axe, and a collection of snow shovels.

The image of Alice came to her again. Impulsively, Phoebe grabbed two of the tools from the wall and stormed back to the house.

She closed the inner front door softly, aware that the screen door's screeching springs had made too much noise already. Phoebe stood for a moment, listening to the house.

The familiar breezy sound came to her ears yet again. Shortly after that, the faraway thumping could be heard. Both sounds were so soft that Phoebe was half-convinced she was simply insane.

I don't believe in haunted houses! she reminded herself and purposely stepped to the basement door. She pulled it open and raised her hand to press the button for the lights, but they were already on. *Must have left them on.*

She stepped down and turned to close the door, careful to not knock the tools against the wall or railing. With her eyes cast to the far wall, working out that she had to drag the table away from the washing machine, she didn't catch movement from her left.

As Phoebe stepped onto the cement, a dark figure lunged at her from the shady corner. A glinting of metal revealed a knife held waist high and being drawn back.

Phoebe screamed and jumped to her right, dropping the pickaxe to the floor with an ear-shattering clatter. With her weight on her right foot, she swung the remaining tool in a large sweeping arch, dropping back from her attacker.

The shovel missed, clanging like a broadsword against the wooden railing of the staircase.

"Phoebe!" the knife-wielder shouted. It was Holgrave, standing with mad eyes staring at her, the knife pointed to the ceiling, gripped in his gloved hand.

Phoebe's mind broke at the apparent betrayal. She thrust the shovel at him, forcing loose his grip on his weapon, which tumbled to the floor. He caught the shovel in both hands to save his face, but having flinched, he missed her sprint up the stairs.

Holgrave dropped the shovel and pursued her.

Phoebe burst through the front doors and fled for her car. From the parlor, the raven responded to the ruckus with a short flurry of squawks. Driven from fear, Phoebe concentrated on making tracks, legs and arms pumping along at a pace she didn't think was possible.

Her sneakers slid along the loose dirt when she tried to stop, and she collided with her car door, the rebound almost sending her to the ground. She reached for her keys, yanked them free from her front pocket, and began fishing for the keyhole. She couldn't see it in the dark, but she could feel for it.

"Phoebe," Holgrave called from somewhere behind, trying to ride the balance between shouting and whispering.

"Oh, God. Oh, God," she mumbled frantically. Finally, the key went into the lock and she turned it. Yanking the door out of her way, she got in and slammed it behind her just as fleeting footsteps were catching up to her. She smacked the lock button down.

"Phoebe, wait," Holgrave said, slapping the glass of her driver's door.

"Get away from me!" she yelled as she sent the ignition key into the slot.

"Phoebe, I didn't know it was you," he said through the glass. "Honest, please wait. I thought it was one of them."

Phoebe turned the key. The starter was in a good mood. The engine caught. She eyed Holgrave as her foot feathered the pedal to achieve idle. She reached for the gearshift.

"Wait, please," he pleaded with his hands up, showing that he had dropped the knife. "I'm so sorry. I thought they'd caught me." He was trying hard to keep his voice down. He looked back at the house, excitement in his face.

Phoebe realized at that moment that no matter how much she suppressed her psychic ability, it never failed to read people, at least to give her warning that they were near, or hints to their emotional state. But Alec Holgrave was different and had been since they'd met in the living room of the House of the Seven Gables. She couldn't read him at all, which is why he kept startling her by his sudden presence.

Why? she asked as she searched his face. *Why can't I read you, weirdo?*

"I'm terribly sorry," Holgrave continued. "The knife's the only thing I have. I left it in the basement. Please don't be frightened of me."

"Why the *fuck* were you in the basement?" she shouted through the glass.

Holgrave lowered his hands and appeared to clear his throat. "It takes a bit of explaining."

"No shit, asshole!"

"All I can do is apologize," he replied. Dejected, he stepped back, assuming that she intended to drive off.

Phoebe put her foot on the brake and the transmission into reverse. Taking this as proof of her intent, Holgrave turned back to the house and began walking. Phoebe sighed and watched him a moment. He stopped by the house to look over his shoulder, but in the darkness, his face was hidden.

Fine, stupid psychic bullshit, don't help me, she thought. *Leave me to my own devices then.* She slapped the gear lever up to park and shut off the car. Slowly, with her eyes on the still figure of Holgrave, she left the relative safety of her car and shut the door behind her.

Holgrave took a sidestep away from the house and into the moonlight, knowing that she would be more comfortable if she could see him, if only slightly better.

"Let me see your hands," she called to him, pointing. She was walking, but watching, and had left her car unlocked just in case.

Holgrave held them up. There was nothing in them. For the first time, she gave notice to what he was wearing: jeans and a denim shirt with the top few buttons undone. There was white dust on both and sweat stains at his pits.

Warily, she approached with her hands free to defend herself if need be. She had done all right with Onenspek, but Holgrave was certainly stronger.

The two of them stared at one another for a long moment.

"May I put my hands down, now?" Holgrave asked gently.

"Yeah," she answered. "Why were you down there, and why're you all filthy?"

"As I said, it will take some explaining," Holgrave said and lowered his hands to his sides.

"So, explain."

Holgrave glanced at the house. "I'd rather do that in a few hours."

"Oh, really?" she said with deep doubt. She eyed her route to the Chevy.

"We may have awakened someone," he added quickly. "I'd hate to disturb their sleep further." He watched her face carefully and gave an almost imperceptible nod.

Phoebe took the hint. They were standing near the house, not far from the open windows of the parlor. Other windows may very well have been open, and voices carry far in the silence of a forest clearing. She kept her eyes on Holgrave, intent on not making the first move.

"I promise you. Everything will be explained," he whispered. "At the moment, I need to return to the cellar to—wait a bloody minute." He frowned and lifted his chin, regarding her with a sideways stare. "What exactly were *you* doing down there?"

"Me?"

"Indeed. You."

"I don't need to answer that," Phoebe said indignantly. "You were the one lunging at me with a knife."

"I didn't lunge," he defended. "You threw a shovel at me." Holgrave placed his hands on his hips and leaned forward. "*And* you had a pick-axe, which, fortunately for me, you let slip."

"So?"

"So? *So?*" Holgrave interrogated, sounding offended. His mouth dropped agape, and he waited for an answer.

"So it seems we both have some explaining to do," Phoebe said finally.

"Right," he said, making his way to the house. "I shall straighten out our little mess and head to bed. I recommend you do the same."

Phoebe followed, closing the inner door behind them. She watched as Holgrave walked up the hall to the basement door, which had been left wide open enough to block the hallway.

He turned before going down. "Be silent on your return to bed. I shall talk to you in a few hours." He hesitated, then added, "Good night."

"Pfft!" returned Phoebe as the basement door closed. "Good night, my ass."

16

Excursion

Phoebe returned to bed. With the faint lightening of the sky outside her bedroom windows, she knew she would want to be asleep long after dawn. She pulled the shades and prepared to sleep in. She also took the precaution of locking the bedroom door, though this time she didn't bother with throwing the key. She kept it on the side table instead.

Some hours later, her great-aunt Hester knocked and knocked loudly.

"What?" Phoebe croaked.

"Why is this door locked?" Hester demanded.

"'Cause I felt like it!"

"Young lady, it's nearly half past ten, and you have chores to do!"

Shit, that's later than I thought. "All right. Getting up."

"You'd better," Hester warned.

"Bite me," Phoebe mumbled and tossed the cover off her still-clothed body.

Rising, she realized that for the first time in days, she felt like she'd had real sleep. She stretched, picked out her clothes, and went to the bathroom to shower, only then to remember in a flash what had transpired the night before.

Phoebe showered and took time to put on only sparse makeup, as the remnants of the smoky eye effect had startled her when she'd caught a glimpse of herself in the bathroom mirror, and dressed in a simple jeans and t-shirt outfit with her slip-on sneakers. She had a feeling the day would be long, and comfort was required. She took her hoodie and car keys with her, having decided an errand into town was likely.

Phoebe went to the kitchen, poured herself the last of the coffee in the pot, microwaved it, and walked through to the front of the house. She could hear Glendarah's voice through the parlor door, and a strange red car was parked in front of the house. The psychic readings had started early that day.

She stepped out onto the porch to enjoy the cool air. The loud greeting from the shiny black-feathered raven didn't startle her. She was looking his direction when she came through the door, expecting it to announce her arrival.

The coffee wasn't fresh, but it wasn't bad. She sipped it and stepped off the porch. Looking to the carriage house, she could see from the partially opened door that the Coupe De Ville was gone. At the very least, one of the three witches, most likely Hester, was out.

Phoebe walked past the parlor, intentionally ignoring any words coming through the open window. The 'Psychic' sign was lit, and she knew that she could be seen through the sheer white curtains. She didn't care. She wasn't hiding anything. Around the corner, she saw her car and the blue Mercedes.

I wonder where Alec is this morning.

She returned to the kitchen and washed the morning dishes. With still no sign of Holgrave, she decided to call Detective Backstrom for an update on the allegedly drug-laced gingerbread man caper.

She punched Backstrom's number into the wall phone's keypad and waited. After a few rings, the automated voicemail recording greeted her in Backstrom's voice. She left a message and hung up the phone.

Phoebe considered the possibility that the detective was on a case, away from his desk. She tried the cellphone number listed. It, too, went to voicemail, only this was a direct route, no ringing. The phone was either off or beyond cell coverage.

Strange time to not have your phone on if you're a detective.

Phoebe went to the basement, both to check for Mr. Holgrave, and to retrieve a load of laundry from the dryer. Holgrave wasn't there, and neither were the pick and shovel she had abandoned. She assumed Holgrave had moved them.

She took the fresh linens to the third-floor closet, then went about her rounds, sending the soiled laundry down the chute and making everyone's beds. It was nearly noon by the time she was done, and she hadn't encountered a soul, which was refreshing.

Phoebe returned to the kitchen and tried her phone calls again with the same results. It had been two days, more than enough time to test a lousy cookie, in her admittedly uninformed opinion of the efficiency of police crime labs.

Concerned and anxious, Phoebe decided to head downtown herself. A conversation with Holgrave could happen whenever it happened.

Phoebe stepped through the screen door, flipped off the noisy caged raven that had announced her exit, and strode to her Caprice.

She shut the car door and placed the key in the cylinder. Turning it, the starter whined. The engine didn't get the clue it was supposed to start.

Phoebe spewed a short but well-practiced string of profanity and gave the steering wheel several poundings with the heel of her hand. She tried several more times, but the car refused to cooperate.

Phoebe flipped her hood over her eyes and rested her forehead on the steering wheel. Sometimes, the finicky starter would need to be waited out.

A few moments later, she sat back and looked through the windshield in thought. Her eyes cast to her left, and that's when she noticed

Holgrave watching her. He was leaning on the pretty blue Mercedes, all but confirming the sedan belonged to him. He smiled and waved. She removed her key and got out of the car.

"I think you could use some time away from this house," said Holgrave.

"That's kinda what I was out here trying to accomplish, genius." She smiled, despite her sarcastic tone.

Holgrave chuckled. He turned, opened the car door, and stood to the side.

Screw it, let's go. She accepted the invitation and folded herself into the vehicle.

Holgrave shut the door after her and came around to the driver's side. He got in and turned to her, regarding her closely. "We have some things to discuss, but it appears you have something on your mind already."

"I tried calling the detective about the gingerbread dude," she huffed and folded her arms. "I can't get him on the phone."

"Interesting," Holgrave said gently. "Time for an unannounced visitation?"

"That was my intent," she said and looked to her old rusted, white heap. "But my car has decided to take the day."

Holgrave grinned and started the Mercedes. The engine immediately settled to a refined thrum. "Right. Off we go." He backed onto Gable Way and turned left onto the paved road. Without much prodding, the Mercedes propelled itself to a healthy rumbling tune, pressing them into the seats.

"This thing's quick," she commented. "How fast does it go?"

"I imagine quite a bit faster than I shall ever become comfortable with."

Holgrave drove into downtown White Lake, keeping the car reined in down the side streets. They rode together in silence for a time, cruising aimlessly.

Phoebe thought it felt good to be out, away from the House of the Seven Gables. As she watched the world go by, her heart lightened. Even gentle, romantic thoughts of Dzolali seemed tainted, though her love remained. At least Phoebe thought it did.

Holgrave made a left turn down the main street and parked in front of the police station. He shut off the motor and said, "Would you mind company?"

"I would not," she answered and opened the door.

"Are you going to register a complaint with the police about Mr. Onenspek?"

Phoebe sighed and stared at the station's front doors. "I have a feeling he's suffered enough."

He opened his door. "As you wish. Right, then. Let's go see this Detective Backstrom."

They walked into the station and Phoebe strode up to the reception desk as she had the other day. She was greeted by a different officer at the desk.

"Can I help you two?" asked the sergeant. The man was broad shouldered, shaved bald, and had intensely deep brown eyes that matched the color of his skin.

"Yes, I was here the day before yesterday talking to Detective Backstrom," Phoebe began.

"Oh, yeah?" the sergeant said curiously. He eyed them both intently.

"Um, yes," she said. "I brought in something for the forensics lab to test. I suspected that the item was laced with a drug."

The sergeant just watched her as she spoke, gave her a thoughtful frown, and said, "You say this was the day before yesterday."

"Yes, sir . . . Sergeant Ranier," she said, having read his nametag.

"What time did you come in?"

What's with the twenty questions, dude? Phoebe blinked and thought about it before answering, regretting the fact she didn't own a watch or a cellphone. "I believe it was late morning. Maybe eleven-ish."

The sergeant nodded. "That's about right."

"I'm sorry?" Phoebe said. She glanced at Holgrave, who shrugged and shook his head.

"Detective Backstrom was involved in an automobile accident that day," Ranier explained.

Phoebe covered her mouth in her hands. "Oh, my God. Is he okay?"

Ranier's eyes shifted from Phoebe to Holgrave and back. "It's bad, but he's in intensive care. He suffered some broken ribs and a head trauma. He's in a coma at this time."

Phoebe's eyes reddened, and she stifled her emotions. She didn't wish to break down. "That's horrible. Is there something that can be done, I mean for his wife, family?"

"That's very kind of you," Sergeant Ranier said. "Detective Backstrom is divorced and has no children."

"I understand, okay," Phoebe choked out. "I hate to ask this next thing. It seems so trivial."

"You're wondering if he sent your item to the lab," Ranier presumed correctly.

Phoebe nodded.

"Considering the timeline, I doubt it. It sounds like you were here just before he left for lunch. Whether he was planning to head to the County Forensics Lab, no one'll know until he wakes up."

Phoebe waved it off. "It's no issue, I'm sure. I just hope he'll be okay."

The sergeant stood up. He was as tall as Holgrave. "I tell you what," he said, pulling a notepad from his pants pocket, a pen from the one on his shirt. "Let me get your name, the description of the item you brought in, and your number."

Phoebe told Ranier her name and explained her situation, having to rely on Hester's home and office number for communication, and suspecting Hester of being behind the drugged cookie.

"Okay," Ranier said and wrote it down, including the phone number. "Gingerbread, huh?" He wore a crooked grin. "I've seen all kinds of things being laced—never a gingerbread man."

"It takes all kinds, I guess," said Phoebe. "I'm not entirely sure about that, anyway."

"I understand," said Ranier. "I'll look into it. I can check his desk and have someone look through the wreck. Be sure to stay in touch, Ms. Pyncheon."

"I will, Sergeant Ranier," she said and turned from the window. "Thank you."

Phoebe and Holgrave left the police station. For a moment, Phoebe just stood there on the sidewalk, not knowing what to do next.

"I can't believe it," she said, thinking about Clive Backstrom. She searched the sky. It was a bright blue, sunny day, and Backstrom was missing it, maybe never to awaken. It didn't seem fair, and she felt certain that such an accident couldn't have been a coincidence.

"I don't like it," Holgrave said, to her silent approval. "Say, have you ever seen your great-aunt Hester's art shop?"

Phoebe shook her head, saying nothing. As she thought about it, a perusal in an art shop, even if it did belong to Hester Pyncheon, was better than heading back to the house so soon.

"Let's go for a walk," he suggested. "It's right up here, around the corner."

White Lake was a touristy town, and as such, the sidewalks were moderately busy. Phoebe and Holgrave zigzagged through the out-of-towners and a few locals and, after a few minutes, arrived at the corner.

Phoebe went right around, only to stop short. Holgrave bumped into her.

"Shit," she said glumly, her eyes staring ahead.

"Terribly sorry," he offered, then saw what she was seeing.

Dzolali and Hester had come out of the gallery and were casually making their way to the Coupe De Ville, which was parked in front.

Phoebe ducked back around the wall of the corner pub, staying mostly out of sight. Dzolali boarded the car on the passenger side, while Hester got behind the wheel. A moment later, the Cadillac backed out of the space and headed up the street.

Phoebe relaxed once the car turned left at the next street and went out of sight. "All clear," she said.

They walked up to the storefront, an older-style, red brick two-story building with large windows that went nearly to the ceiling of the first floor. One couldn't see inside, however, as the windows had been covered on the inside by a reflective shade. The sign above the entryway, hand-painted in red on black, read simply, 'Pyncheon Art.' The door was set back from the sidewalk. Holgrave opened it for Phoebe, and she went in.

The shop was not what Phoebe was expecting. The carpet was a deep, perfectly clean and uniform light gray. The middle of the store was taken up by a center wall that ended in a point that faced the door straight-on, tapering to the back of the establishment. Along this wall and the outer walls were paintings, large and small. Larger ones, with their own easels, sat at the front of the store, on either side of Phoebe and Holgrave, with their backs facing the tinted windows.

From what Phoebe could see, every one of the pieces on display were Onenspek's ghastly creations. Reluctantly, Phoebe took a closer look at the one on the easel at her left. It was Ned's, alright: a landscape of a battle that took place somewhere over some ridiculous thing at some time in the past. The combatants wore white, loose-fitting outfits, had long, dark beards, wore red turbans, and were fighting people in tan uniforms and white turbans. There were elephants, camels, horses, and people, all being hacked to pieces and bleeding red all over the canvas. Meanwhile, hovering above the scenes of the dead and the dying were what Phoebe could only guess were demons, giving their grotesque, distorted forms, blending human traits with those of animals and birds. They were feasting on the innards of the defeated.

"Blech," she declared and looked at the bottom, noting the price tag. "Jesus *wept!*"

"What?" Holgrave asked. He assumed Phoebe had found a new level of disgust, though when he followed her pointing a finger to the number written on the small yellow square stuck to the frame, his jaw dropped. "My word."

"Pardon me," someone from behind them said. The voice was male, quite refined, so it could be surmised, from the elongation of the word, 'me.' The man's wide eyes, partially hidden behind the little round-lensed glasses on his nose, made him appear mad. The maroon sport coat, electric blue slacks, and tie with swirly pinks and purples didn't help, either. He was bald on top, well-trimmed all around, and appeared by the little wrinkles and white hair running along the top of his ears to be in his sixties. He was healthily thin and appeared to have missed no appointments at the tanning salon up the street.

"I see you have found our premiere artist," he observed with a creepy enthusiasm. "Ned Onenspek, very much a genius at painting the darkest moments of humanity. Is he not?"

"Yes, he is not," Phoebe said. "Four grand, dude? Really?"

The art retailer's eyes went from fervent to suspicious as he pushed his glasses up the ridge of his considerable nose. He measured Phoebe from top to bottom, wearing a smarmy grin that told her he was making all sorts of judgments about her character.

The salesman glanced at Phoebe's companion as well. The taller, younger Holgrave returned the look with his arched eyebrow.

"Yes, well," the salesman said, "if you take your time about it, you'll note his brushstrokes are rushed but precise, giving the characters the appearance of haste, which augments their expressions of horror."

Phoebe looked over her shoulder at Holgrave, who gave her the briefest of nods. She shrugged and turned her attention back to the proprietor, who went on and on about the artist she had knocked out.

"At the moment, Mr. Onenspek is staying at a boarding house right here in White Lake—"

"Oh, we know," Phoebe interjected. "We're staying there, too."

The salesman brightened, his smile revealing his well-maintained teeth. "Oh, so you've actually *met* him."

"I have," Phoebe said and rubbed her bruised knuckles. "I'm Phoebe Pyncheon. Hester is my great-aunt."

Somehow, it was possible for the art dealer to become even more excited. He snatched up Phoebe's hand in both of his and gave it, not a shake, put a brief pressing. "It's wonderful to meet you, Ms. Pyncheon. I'm Gordon Knoff. That's with a 'k' and two 'f's."

"Nice to meet you," she said, trying to mean it.

"No doubt you've seen Mr. Onenspek at work," Knoff surmised.

"You could say that," she answered.

Knoff made an airy noise of great delight as he let go of her hand and clapped his own together. "It would be a wondrous delight to watch such a man at work. Your aunt speaks highly of him, and apparently, he's capable of creating nearly a painting per week. Astoundingly prolific when one considers the detail in his art."

One a week? Huh? Phoebe thought. She looked to Holgrave, who stood just over her right shoulder. She saw confusion on his face.

"Oh, forgive me," Knoff uttered and stepped forward, putting out his hands in greeting toward Holgrave. "Gordon Knoff, I'm the manager."

"Alec Holgrave," he introduced himself, and shook hands.

"Well, then," said Knoff, clapping his hands together again. "Please do browse at your leisure. Ms. Pyncheon and Mr. Holgrave, if there's anything you need, I'm at your service."

"Thank you, Mr. Knoff," Phoebe said.

The art dealer stepped away, leaving his two visitors to themselves.

"*One* a week?" Phoebe whispered.

"Indeed not," Holgrave agreed. "Considering the great number of them here and on the walls of your great-aunt's home, he's doing at least thrice that number. Come. Let's peruse."

Holgrave sauntered to the artwork on the south wall, with Phoebe reluctantly following. These were much smaller paintings that could be grouped together. Their prices were relatively lower than the one on the easel, but they still caused cringes.

Each one of them was a horror, and no matter how impressive Onenspek's talents, Phoebe detested his work. After a moment, all she could stand to look at were the price tags. She left Holgrave behind and arrived at the end of the wall, then turned to the one behind that partitioned the shop. The next painting her eyes landed upon rooted her shoes to the gray carpet.

"Holy shit," she murmured.

Holgrave, who was still gazing at the work on the first wall, turned around to the sound of her voice. His eyes found what Phoebe had noticed.

"My word," he whispered.

The painting depicted a woman with white and blue hair, white only because it was under an intense attack from a bright ball of yellow light, thrust at her head by what Phoebe interpreted as a witch. The victim, wearing an elegant black dress, much like the one that Dzolali had given Phoebe, was suspended from the ground, apparently by the beam of light. The woman's spine arched, and her arms were thrown wide, her face contorted in pain and fear.

"That's me," Phoebe whispered, pointing to the woman under attack.

Holgrave had noticed the resemblance, too, but decided to minimize it for Phoebe's sake. "Oh, I don't know—"

"Shut up," she shot back. "*Look.*"

"I am," he assured her. He leaned forward, taking in the facial features of the black-haired witch casting the yellow blast of energy. He sighed and stepped back.

"What?" she asked him.

"Nothing. Perhaps we'd better go," he said and turned to face the door.

Phoebe grabbed his left forearm. "Tell me."

Holgrave looked again at the painting. Beyond the action in the foreground, there were homes and buildings. "The town in the background appears to be White Lake. Here, the main street. There, the farmland just south."

"I see that," she replied impatiently. "There's something else. Tell me."

"Yes, I will," he said, not taking his eyes from the painting. There were intricacies and subtleties that Phoebe was not seeing, as she was searching his face, either trying to read intent, which he knew that she could not, or just giving herself something else to look at besides the image of the suffering of a woman who resembled her in painting form. "But not here."

"Fine, let's get the hell out of here," she whispered. She turned and headed for the door.

Holgrave stared at the painting for a moment longer. Behind the image of the woman with the white and blue hair, and painted masterfully in a ghostly transparency, was a staircase. To the woman's right, equally transparent, for a dark forest lay behind the foreground battle, was a wall of stone. Beneath the feet of the black-haired witch, whose beauty he knew well, and the woman patterned after the youngest Pyncheon, was what appeared to be a dirt floor. Throughout that dirt floor were apparitions of faces and, as he peered closely, some of the faces were skulls, while others still had traces of flesh upon them.

"That is one of my favorites, sir," Knoff spoke, suddenly at Holgrave's left side.

Holgrave hid his surprise well. "Yes, splendid. When, if I may ask, did Mr. Onenspek paint this intense scene?"

Knoff tilted his head to the left in thought. "That one arrived here, I believe, a little over a month ago. Perhaps the first week of August. His paintings usually sell quite quickly. This one might be the oldest in the gallery."

Holgrave nodded and passed his eyes over the establishment. "And does this gallery feature any other artists?"

"Not at the moment, sir," Knoff said, elaborating not a bit.

"I see," Holgrave said. He struggled to think of an appropriate exit, then decided to use Phoebe as an excuse. "I seem to have misplaced Ms. Pyncheon. If you'll excuse me. Thank you."

17

Revelation

Holgrave stepped out into the sunny day, looking for Phoebe. Instinctively, he walked to his left, retracing their steps. He found Phoebe, standing around the corner, her hood up and hands in her pockets.

"Come with me," she ordered and walked past him, leading him across the street.

Holgrave saw no reason not to acquiesce, so he followed, lengthening his stride to catch up to her. Soon, he fell in step alongside, but it was brief. Phoebe maintained a brisk pace, weaving through the traffic of tourists and leaving him to walk behind. He could not tell if she was frightened, angry, or both, but he decided to keep what Knoff said about the painting featuring the Phoebe lookalike to himself.

When they arrived at the White Lake Public Library, Phoebe bounded up the stairs and went inside without waiting for Holgrave. The library was busy, but in comparison to the tourists outside, the pace of the patrons here was sloth-like, pleasant, and as quiet as a tomb. Phoebe went to the media area, found an unused computer, and sat down. It was not until then that she looked to make sure Holgrave had followed.

"I need to look something up," she said lowly.

"Apparently," he agreed.

She logged onto the internet and found a search engine, then entered "Ned Onenspek" on the line and tapped the magnifying glass icon next to it. To their surprise, a great number of results came through.

Phoebe paged up and down, her mouth open in wonder as she took in the titles of the many, many articles written about the man and his art. She chose one and it opened. Holgrave bent his knees and read over Phoebe's shoulder.

The article, written by an art critic for an online magazine, described the style of Ned Onenspek in positive notes, praising the artist for his multi-layered talents of creating a realistic, almost three-dimensional scene with his use of light and shadow. The critic was, apparently, a fan of terrifyingly convincing battle scenes and horror. His only complaint, though it was written as praise, was that the critic could not afford the 'rising star's' works, as each one rose 'meteorically' in value.

Phoebe backed out and found another article, which mirrored the first in sentiment and praise. A third, then a fourth, echoed them. Paging through results, Phoebe found a website written in German. Onenspek was big in Europe as well.

"Son of a bitch," Phoebe said breathily.

"My word," Holgrave agreed.

There were a few sites that were handling the resale of Onenspeks in auction form, and the numbers associated with both bids and price were staggering. Of course, Hester Pyncheon could not profit from these, but the fact that 'Pyncheon Art Gallery' of White Lake, Michigan, was the exclusive seller of new Onenspek work was plain.

Phoebe logged off, stood, and motioned Holgrave to follow once more. She found a vacant row of books and walked down its length, looking through the collections for people on the other side.

"What the hell?" she whispered. "Knoff said that they get one a week. Do you remember how many are just in his room?"

Holgrave nodded. "At one per week arriving at the gallery, he could halt production now and go for a long vacation."

"Onenspek should be filthy rich," she said. "He could go anywhere in the world."

"Well, perhaps," Holgrave said with reservation. "Surely Hester is taking her cut from the sales. Knoff told me that there are no other artists featured in the gallery."

"She's taking advantage of him," Phoebe said. "I can feel it."

"I don't doubt it at all," he replied.

Phoebe stared into Holgrave's eyes. "Okay, so spill."

Holgrave looked around briefly. "Sorry?"

"You recognized the witch in that painting," she accused.

Holgrave sighed. He knew that he had to be truthful and saw no way out of it. Phoebe's stare was demanding. "Yes. I did. It's quite a resemblance to the woman in a dream I had."

"I knew it!" she said too loudly.

Holgrave put his finger to his lips. "To be honest, it was several dreams."

"And?"

"And what?"

"Who is she, you dork?" Her whisper was rising again.

"I've no idea."

Phoebe checked for eavesdroppers again. "Were they sexy dreams?"

Holgrave rolled his eyes and began to blush.

"Thought so." She said this definitively, and the look in her eyes was telling.

"You? You've dreamt of her, too?" he asked.

"No. Dzolali."

"Ah," he replied. "That makes sense."

Phoebe appeared offended. "What?"

"Well, you two have hit it off, as you Yanks say."

"Is it that obvious?"

Holgrave nodded but quickly added, "I'm not being judgy. You are both consenting adults."

Phoebe crossed her arms and took a step closer to him. "She appeared to me in a dream the first night I got here."

"Really?"

"Yeah, well, it was nice at first," Phoebe admitted and turned red. "Great, actually."

"I see."

"And the next night, the same thing." Phoebe lowered to a whisper he could barely hear as she said, "When I awoke, I was convinced that I was in love with her. I think she was getting into my room. Her scent, that water lily and vanilla, was all over everything."

"Indeed!" Holgrave was intrigued. "The woman that visited me on both occasions had the same effect. The scent was more musky, with lavender," he recalled with a pleasant smile that quickly disappeared when he noticed Phoebe could see it. "I was convinced I was mad."

"But that woman, the brunette, doesn't exist," Phoebe said, though at that moment, she recalled the morning two days prior, when she'd walked into the kitchen and sworn that she had seen a tall, dark-haired woman at the kitchen window.

"What?" Holgrave asked, noting the expression on Phoebe's face.

"Um, nothing," she said, but went on. "But you didn't wake up feeling like you were in love with this visitor," she concluded.

"Not at all."

Phoebe shook her head, both in disgust and dismay. "It's too much of a coincidence that we both had similar dreams."

"Perhaps," he said guardedly. "I think we should run along."

On the ride back, Phoebe sat watching the trees go by, intending to be silent, but the previous night's encounter with Holgrave came to mind. "Hey, you weren't developing film in the basement last night," she said definitively.

"I was not," he confirmed.

"What *were* you doing down there?"

"Tell you what," he said. "I'll tell you what I was doing down there, if you tell me what you were going to do down there at half past three in the morning with a pick and a shovel."

"Deal," she agreed. "You first."

"Right," he said and pulled the Mercedes to the side of the road. He put it in park and turned to her. "My name is *not* Alec Holgrave."

Phoebe stared at him, and although her psychic abilities, which now would be welcome, continued to fail her, she could see truth in his brown eyes. "Oh, *that's* just stellar," she said. Panic flashed through her and she glanced out the window, planning an escape route.

"My name *is* Holgrave, however," he added, seeing that Phoebe had grown uncomfortable. "It just so happens that it's my Christian name. My surname is Maule."

"Why does that name keep popping up in conversation?" she asked.

"The Maule family was once quite prevalent in this area," he explained. "In fact, we used to own the art gallery that is now in the hands of your great-aunt."

"Really," Phoebe said with a trace of doubt, although she felt she had no real reason to doubt him.

"My English ancestors settled here in the late seventeen hundreds. The Maules were teachers, blacksmiths, woodsmen, hunters, and even a few lawyers and doctors."

Phoebe said nothing. She just watched his face as he spoke.

"My great-great-grandfather made the error of crossing the Pyncheons in a business deal," he explained, looking beyond the windshield. "I'm not sure of the specifics of that initial incident, but since then, members of the Pyncheon family worked to take away everything that belonged to anyone by the name of Maule."

"And, so, you're what? Here for revenge on my great-aunt Hester?"

"Perhaps," he said, though he grinned crookedly. "Over the years, the Pyncheon family took over White Lake, either by attempting to own everything or becoming an elected official, judge, and so on."

"What does this have to do with you being in the basement?" Phoebe asked, anxiously curious.

"Your great-aunt Hester's father arranged to, shall we say, swindle my great-grandfather, Horace Maule, out of his shares of the Butterfield Overland Mail Company."

"Never heard of it."

"Indeed," he said, and quickly added, "Few have because the company was purchased nearly a century ago by Wells Fargo."

"Okay," she said, looking at him blankly.

"When a company is sold, the stockholders of that company either have their stocks transferred into the purchasing company, or the purchasing company buys out the stockholders' shares. While I was going through my father's business files, I found documents from Wells Fargo that indicated they had transferred them into their portfolio. Unfortunately, since the Butterfield stocks were acquired long before an internet, they needed the certificates in hand to verify the ownership."

"Why didn't your father do something about this?" Phoebe asked.

"I'm not sure," Holgrave answered. "He can't now, anyway. He passed away some months ago."

"Oh! I'm sorry," Phoebe offered.

"Thank you," he said and sighed. "Anyway, I did peruse my grandfather's will, and there's specific mention of the certificates and the fact that they're missing. In case they were recovered, my father could have redeemed them. However, since my father didn't include any information on them in his will, it tells me that he had no luck locating them."

"They must be worth quite a lot," Phoebe commented.

"They are."

"Well, how do you know they're here?"

Holgrave looked into her eyes intently, as if pondering one more time whether he could trust the youngest Pyncheon. "My great-grandfather had a diary, in which he describes being *bewitched*, into freely giving them over to a Hepzibah Pyncheon, who was your great-great-aunt."

"Do you believe it?"

Holgrave's eyes turned hard as he looked upon her. "I didn't until I came to stay at the house. The trickery in the parlor, though I didn't investigate as deeply as you, was ludicrous on the surface. However, as you've come to know, there are odd happenings there."

Phoebe turned away, looking into the polarized world beyond the safety glass. She crossed her arms and feet. "I don't know what I believe anymore."

"Your dreams sound remarkably similar to mine," he said.

"So?"

"And you bore the full brunt of the spirit the other night—"

"That was an electrical shock!" she retorted, her voice filling the cabin of the Mercedes.

"—and it knocked you on your arse for a few hours," he went on, not raising his voice. "I watched you for those hours. You dreamt."

"Again, so?"

"What did you dream about?"

"What difference does it make to you?" she asked, exasperatedly raising her hands up, then letting them drop to her legs with a slap.

"I don't wish to see anything happen to you," he said.

"Same question."

"Pardon me for saying so, Ms. Pyncheon," he said, quite riled himself, "but you are not protected against your great-aunt's power."

"I don't even know what that's supposed to mean," Phoebe said.

Holgrave reached to his neck, unfastened the highest button, and reached in. "This is a protection stone against black magic." He withdrew a pendant on the end of a thick silver chain. It was a circular piece of black rock with designs carved upon it.

"You're a crazy person," she said hotly.

Holgrave pushed on as if she had not said a word. "On the front of the charm here, is a Feng Shui symbol."

Phoebe laughed harshly. "I don't need help rearranging the fuckin' furniture."

"Typical Yank!" Holgrave returned with equal fire. "All you people do is glean your culture from the rest of the world, commercialize it, re-define and defile it, all the while stubbornly ignorant of any meaning!"

Phoebe, stunned, had no retort.

Holgrave leaned closer so she could see the charm. The outer edges of the medallion featured writing in a language that Phoebe did not recognize. The center was taken up by what resembled a steering wheel of a ship.

"Each point of the wheel represents a type of black magic," Holgrave explained. He turned the charm around, revealing the design carved into it. To Phoebe, it looked like two capital As, with one flipped upside-down and laid upon the other, the points of which touched the outer circle. "This side is basically the same thing, but the design is Pagan."

"So?" Phoebe ventured to ask, though she kept her voice quiet.

"According to my great-grandfather's diary, the charm was made by a Pagan priest of white magic and blessed by his wife, a white witch."

"Dude," Phoebe said in a tone of disbelief. She leaned against the door and crossed her arms, thinking about bolting from the car again.

Holgrave removed the necklace and held it in his hand. "Ms. Pyncheon, if you can honestly tell me that you can rationally explain everything you've seen and experienced while you've been at the House of the Seven Gables, then by all means, don't allow me to lend this to you for a night."

Phoebe's first reaction was to take it in her fingers for a closer inspection.

"Even if all you wish to do is humor me, then wear it around your neck for a day," he said and put the Mercedes in gear. He pulled out into the narrow road, continuing their short journey back to the house. "If you don't see any difference in your dreams tonight, or perhaps if you come to realize that your love for Dzolali is true, then you may throw that charm at my skull at breakfast."

Phoebe, realizing they would come into view of the house, quickly placed it around her neck and stuffed the charm under her t-shirt. Around the last bend, they could see a strange car in front. One of the coven had another client in the parlor. As they drove by, they could see both Hester and Glendarah sitting on the porch. Their expressionless faces turned as the Mercedes rolled past.

"What should we tell them?" Phoebe asked.

"It's likely that they will soon discover our gallery visit," Holgrave said. "I recommend that we simply say that we were out for a drive and admit to stopping in for a look. Nothing more."

Phoebe thought of something else. "Should we mention the prices we saw on that stuff to Ned? He might want to know he's getting ripped off."

"I would say keep that under your bonnet for a bit longer," he suggested.

Holgrave parked the Mercedes, and he and Phoebe walked to the house. The raven greeted them in its usual manner, while Hester and Glendarah continued to stare in their direction with unreadable faces.

"Good afternoon, ladies," Holgrave greeted them.

Both returned it politely enough. To Phoebe, however, Hester was not as gracious.

"Phoebe, I don't wish to suggest that you aren't free to leave the premises," Hester said, "but do not allow your work to suffer. Alva is awaiting your presence in the kitchen."

"Uh, okay," Phoebe answered and followed Holgrave through the front door. "On it," she called over her shoulder.

Holgrave turned to Phoebe as they arrived at the staircase. "Remember to call me Alec."

"Yes, Mr. Holgrave," Phoebe replied sweetly.

"I think I shall retrieve my cameras and make myself scarce until dinner," he said with a wary grin.

Phoebe nodded and went to the kitchen. Alva was indeed well into the task of preparing that evening's dinner, so Phoebe took up her role as assistant, though there was much on her mind.

18

The Charmed

With the dining room table prepared, Phoebe returned to her bedroom and contemplated her dress for the evening. She sifted through the extravagant collection that Dzolali had given her, trying to decide, though it had occurred to her that, out of protest, she should present herself at the table 'as is,' in the jeans and t-shirt she had been wearing all day.

Not much of a protest if Dzolali has no idea what I'm protesting, she thought.

After everything she and Holgrave Maule had discovered and talked about that day, Phoebe had felt her desire and feelings for Dzolali weaken. Holgrave's words had rattled around in her mind since their return to the house, and Phoebe found herself worrying about her reaction to seeing the woman.

She was just about to go with the 'as is' idea when she found a dress that would work. It was a light salmon color with a narrow skirt that went to her shins and a white lace collar that encompassed her neck. She put it on, forewent the visit to Dzolali's room for jewelry, and handled her own makeup. It was already five to seven.

Phoebe slipped on the pumps that Dzolali thought would go

with everything and quickly went upstairs. As she suspected, Dzolali, Onenspek, and Holgrave were already seated. Dzolali's face brightened when she laid eyes on Phoebe, but Phoebe kept her own smile restrained.

"Pardon me, everyone," Phoebe greeted as she walked in.

"Ah, there you are," replied Hester.

Phoebe just smiled, trying not to meet Dzolali's eyes, or anyone's for that matter. She did catch a glimpse of Ned Onenspek's face and bit her lip to stifle a gasp. His chin was bright red and purple from her uppercut, and his right eye was similarly colored, and heavily swollen. The assaulted eyelid was twice its usual size, and Phoebe doubted if the man could open it beyond halfway.

Good, Phoebe thought, remembering what he had done to earn those bruises. She had covered the marks at her throat with foundation. As casual conversation went on around her, Phoebe ate in silence. At one point, Onenspek's eye met hers. Phoebe did not look away. Ned gave a smile which might have been interpreted by anyone else at the table as apologetic. Not receiving anything from Phoebe but a cool stare, Ned turned his attention back to his food.

Dzolali noticed this interaction and caught Phoebe's eyes. The two women looked at each other for several breaths. Phoebe realized that she was not overcome with the feeling of adoration that she'd had the previous day. Attractiveness, certainly, but the insane need to be with her was gone. Equally surprising to Phoebe was the knowledge that she was happy about this development. A sense of freedom had returned to her. She smiled at the Latina triumphantly and gave her a wink.

Dzolali returned the smile, though Phoebe thought it appeared to be mocking her.

Dinner concluded as per usual, just after the stroke of eight, and Phoebe began to clear the table, again attempting to avoid everyone's eyes, except Holgrave's. As she bid him a good evening and picked up his plate, she felt a gentle tap on the shoulder.

"Pardon me, Ms. Pyncheon." It was Ned Onenspek.

Phoebe looked at him, her face carefully free of expression, though her fingers did clench around a steak knife.

"I cannot say how terribly sorry I am for my behavior yesterday," he said with a lisp, brought on by the swelling of his mouth on the right side.

A torrent of expletives rained through Phoebe's mind, though from his being, she could read that he was genuinely sorry. Additionally, Dzolali had just stepped to Onenspek's left and was watching Phoebe's face intently, apparently curious about Phoebe's response. But there was something else in Dzolali's face, something new and suspicious.

"I understand, Mr. Onenspek," Phoebe settled on, and turned to her work, loading another pile of dishes into the dumbwaiter. For a long moment, she was convinced that Dzolali was going to send Ned on his way and stop to talk with Phoebe.

When Phoebe turned around, she found herself alone. She surprised herself by breathing a sigh of relief. She reached toward her chest to take hold of the amulet Holgrave had lent her, but Phoebe found that it was already out, having slipped out of the bodice when she leaned over as she served dinner, no doubt.

So that's what Dzolali was looking at. Could she even know what it is?

"Of course she knows what it is," Phoebe answered herself. She finished her tasks in the dining room and hesitated before leaving. She tucked the charm inside her dress and walked briskly to her bedroom.

When she opened the door, Dzolali was there. Her back was to the door, and she was staring out the window.

Phoebe, though startled, attempted to act casual. "Hi!" she greeted her.

Dzolali turned and stepped around the bed. Her form-fitting black dress accentuated her attributes, and Phoebe felt her heart flutter as the Latina approached.

"Haven't seen you all day, dear," Dzolali greeted. Without halting, she reached out and pulled Phoebe to her, then planted a kiss on her lips.

Phoebe's breath left her lungs. Dzolali's grip was tight, folding around her body at the bottom of her rib cage. Her lips were warm, her scent as strong as her passion.

Phoebe realized in that moment that her body was not reacting to the redhead as it had before. There was no powerful rush of lust this time, no feeling of need, and no passion. *Oh, my God. This amulet works!* She broke the kiss and smiled as she pressed her hands on Dzolali's shoulders and gently applied pressure.

The hint was taken, and Dzolali loosened her grip and backed away. She arched her eyebrow and stared into Phoebe's face. "What's wrong?" Dzolali asked.

Phoebe knew from Dzolali's flat tone that she already suspected the answer was around Phoebe's neck. The fact that the charm had an effect at all was a great breakthrough for Phoebe, but the anger within her rose to the top. The realization that Dzolali had invaded her dreams, had tortured her and tricked her into feeling love for her, and then had swooped in to take full advantage, was all too much.

"Get out," Phoebe ordered and stepped to the side, pointing out into the hallway.

Dzolali tipped her head back and put on a condescending grin as she looked down her nose at Phoebe. "What's this all about, little one?"

Phoebe took Dzolali by surprise by striding right up to her, placing her nose just inches from the taller Latina's. She kept her voice low, but it trembled with rage. "I can't prove it, but you've been in my head since I got here. You *made* me dream about you, tortured me in the night with some sicko fuckin' nightmare you probably think was some romantic fuckin' gesture. Well, it wasn't. What you think of as a spell, I consider a curse."

Dzolali was not intimidated. She was physically stronger than Phoebe, and had Phoebe been anyone other than a Pyncheon, she would have knocked her teeth out. Instead, she smiled. "You really want me to leave?"

"Yes," Phoebe said, though the remnants of Dzolali's bewitching made her regret the words. She stepped to the side and fought hard to keep from eyeing her longingly. Having been so close to the woman, Phoebe had taken in her scent, which Phoebe had formed an almost Pavlovian response to in a short time.

Phoebe reached back and slapped the door shut. Her knees were weakened by the encounter, but she smiled at herself. She had won out over her desires, fueled by nefarious means or not.

She touched the medallion that Holgrave had lent her. *It's all true. Witches, spells, all of it. They're all true.* To Phoebe's reckoning, this was the only answer to it all. Hester's enslavement of the artist, her own attachment to Dzolali, the encounter with the ghost of Alice, and all the strange happenings in White Lake that were thought to be coincidence, all of these things and more were quite real.

Twice now, the simple-looking, decorative amulet had come to her rescue, saving her from more of Dzolali's seduction.

"I've got to get the hell out of here," she whispered to herself as she began to extricate herself from Dzolali's dress, which suddenly disgusted her. After removing it, however, Phoebe put it on the hanger carefully and put it in the closet. Despite her outrage with the garment's owner, there was no reason to subject the inanimate object to her angst.

Phoebe slipped on her t-shirt and jeans and stuffed any items of clean clothing into her garbage bags. There were two outfits of hers that were in the laundry at that moment, and with her only having a little over fifty dollars to her name, Phoebe knew she needed every stitch.

Looking out into the night through her borrowed room's three windows, Phoebe decided her departure would have to be put off at least until the morning. She may have to go through the motions of stripping beds and laundering bath towels to reclaim her clothes, but it would be worth it.

But where do I go? she asked herself as she sat at the writing desk.

She opened the laptop and logged on before remembering there was no Wi-Fi. Phoebe sighed.

She considered simply going to bed, but instead, since she had the laptop open and was far from tired, it was the perfect time to do some writing. She settled into the chair and continued the story.

Phoebe found it difficult to get her mind off the goings on at the House of the Seven Gables, but in time, she caught her stride, and the words began pouring out of her, appearing on the screen, it seemed, even before she felt her fingers tapping the keys.

Page after page went by, and Phoebe, stopping every once in a while to read back a paragraph here and there, felt pride in her work. She had missed her long, late-night writing binges. The long-unchecked clock of her laptop read a few minutes past midnight.

The house was quiet, and for the longest time, all Phoebe heard was her fingers clicking on the keyboard and a gentle breeze against the windows. As she continued her work, Phoebe didn't notice that the breeze had increased to a stout wind. Soon after, rain began pattering on the glass.

Phoebe glanced up at the windows, her fingers still tapping away. This was the first time it had rained during this visit, and hearing rain strike the house took her back to her childhood, when she would rush into the house after school to get out of the rain, but once she was sheltered from the weather, all little Phoebe could think of was leaving.

The rainy days were the longest, she thought. Phoebe took a break from typing and stood. She stretched out her stiff back and stepped to the windows, which, being so old, allowed the smell of the rain into the room, even closed.

The sounds and smells of the weather sent a pleasant chill through her body, and Phoebe closed her eyes to it. In the distance, beyond the trees, thunder rumbled, and she reopened them. A reflection in the glass sent her screaming. She spun around so fast, she twirled to the floor, landing hard on her backside, with her spine pressing into the window bench.

There was no one there. The door was shut, and she was quite alone. Phoebe peeled herself from the floor and realized what had happened. She took the place where she had just been standing and peered again into the window.

The reflection was that of a wrought-iron lamp, set upon a hutch next to the door. The dark brown lamp shade made quite the image in a reflection upon glass with water cascading down the outside.

It looked like a man, Phoebe thought in relief. *The tall skeleton in the dark hood.*

She laughed at herself and returned to her computer. It was late, but she wanted to get more work in before she went to bed.

Phoebe fell deeply into her creativity, typing at what might have been a hundred words a minute. The story was flying along like never before. Phoebe stopped and reread often to make sure she was making sense, and she was. Her prose was well-sculpted, and the story flowed right along. After a time, she realized that it was going along so well because she had freed her mind from Dzolali's influence with the help of Holgrave's amulet.

It was either the charm or my determination, I can't tell which.

A flash of lightning caught her eye and she turned to it, cringing as she did so. The thunderbolt came to earth just beyond the glass, or so it sounded. The crack was a shock to her ears and powerful enough to rattle the windows. Phoebe covered her ears and let out a small cry of discomfort as she watched the world light up. The white glow of the electrical strike gave way to a lingering yellow. One of the dead trees was hit and caught fire. The rain was falling hard enough that it was extinguished almost immediately.

Another lightning strike, this one further off, knocked out the power. Her room was lit only by her laptop screen. Phoebe uncovered her ears and turned her attention to the laptop, tapping the save button out of habit-formed paranoia.

When the lights came on, a hooded figure was standing at her left.

Phoebe screamed once again and left the chair, knocking it over as she backed away. By the time she hit the floor and spun around, he was gone. The closet door was open, as she had left it, and the colorful dresses that Dzolali had given her were within.

What the hell? Phoebe took a deep breath. She reasoned that there had been no man at all, but the light returning to her eyes had caused an optical illusion.

Still, real or not, the damage to her nerves had been done. There was no hope to get to sleep anytime soon, she felt certain of that. She stood, backed up her work on her thumb drives, and powered the computer down.

Phoebe slipped it into her backpack and zipped it shut. At the first hint of sunlight, she would be out the door. The rhythm of the rain soothed her nerves, but not enough for her to stop pacing the room.

She wondered if Holgrave was awake. Before she made a conscious decision to do it, she left her bedroom and climbed the stairs to the third floor.

Dzolali, with her mind's eye, followed Phoebe Pyncheon out of her room and to the stairs. "It's working."

"Very good," commended Hester. She released Dzolali's hand from her left and Glendarah's at her right and stepped away from them. Hester was in her youthful form, hair black as night, her skin tight and flawless, and her posture youthfully straight as she took a seat in her great high-backed chair.

Dzolali wore a smile of triumph and turned to face the door, waiting for Phoebe's knock. She was confident that her methods of seduction had worked as they always had.

Glendarah, not convinced but hopeful, stood behind the cushioned chair near the fireplace. She had also transformed herself, shaving decades from her appearance and turning her hair a golden blonde. She watched both Hester and Dzolali in silence.

Phoebe stepped lightly along the hallway, though not nearly as carefully as she would have a day or so before. Now, she didn't really care if
she was discovered heading to Holgrave's attic suite.

She noted the ray of light passing beneath the master bedroom's
door and couldn't help but tiptoe past it. Phoebe halted at the end of
the hall, however, and turned to watch the door.

Phoebe felt an energy focused on the heavy wooden portal and
frowned in confusion. It was as if someone inside, and more than one
person from the feel of it, was expecting her arrival.

She looked down to Dzolali's bedroom door. There was no light
and no energy coming from it. *The coven's having a meeting in Hester's
room*, she surmised. She moved on, quickly but quietly, past Onenspek's
rooms, where the studio lights were on and the bedroom's off.

Phoebe got the chills as she approached the next turn. She put her
hand to the back of her neck and sped up, suddenly convinced that
someone was watching her—and from quite close by.

By the time she got to the attic staircase, her imagination was fired
up, and she looked all around the corridor. She was expecting to find
something: a bird, a bat, some winged creature stalking her. But there
was nothing.

Phoebe opened the door and went in. Closing it behind her, she felt
as if she had shut something out. She climbed the stairs and knocked
on the door.

Dzolali let out a cry of frustration through her teeth. She had followed
Phoebe through the hall, her mind's eye remaining close to her ear as
Dzolali tried calling to her in that fine plane of existence, where the
voice could not be heard by an ear, but the suggestion may be received
by the subconscious.

Instead, Phoebe simply moved faster, covering her neck as if she
were cold. Once she reached the door to the attic, however, it was

over. For some reason, Dzolali could not make her mind's eye slip beyond the door.

"What's happened?" Hester asked, a trace of impatience in her voice.

Dzolali returned her full consciousness to the moment and turned to face her high priestess. "It hasn't worked, Hester," she said, bewildered.

"You said she was on her way here," Hester reminded her harshly and left the chair. Her watery blue eyes were wide and angry.

"I'm sorry, High Priestess," Dzolali offered. "But she went to see Mr. Holgrave."

"Holgrave? Whatever for? What are they doing?" Hester drilled as she came closer to the Latina witch.

"I can't see, Hester, my High Priestess," she answered quietly, though her eyes did not look away.

"How is this possible?" Hester pressed.

Glendarah answered for their youngest coven member. "We've all sensed the man's strength since the day he arrived. You've felt it yourself, Hester, my love."

Hester turned to Glendarah. "So, you're saying he's protected himself?"

"It would seem so."

Hester looked to Dzolali and softened her anger. "Do not worry, dear Dzolali. You've done what you could. We will have to confront Phoebe together. Soon, she will be one of us."

"Thank you, High Priestess," Dzolali answered, clearly relieved.

19

The Search

Phoebe didn't wait for Holgrave to answer the knock before sailing through the door. She closed it behind her and said simply, "Hi."

Holgrave looked upon her, intently confused, so it appeared. "Good evening, Ms. Pyncheon." He came closer, inspecting her face oddly.

"Yeah, hi," she repeated. "Why are you looking at me like that?"

Holgrave blinked and stepped back. "Oh, no reason."

"Uh-huh," Phoebe said, not believing him. "Anyway, it's been a spook-fest in my room tonight, which is too bad, because I was working, and on a roll, I think. And then I just had to get the hell out of there, and I didn't know where else to go."

"Indeed."

"Yeah." She nodded vigorously. "And then I started packing, because, like, as soon as the sun comes up, I'm all ass, sneakers, and smoke, let me tell ya."

"Oh," he allowed. His eyes shifted as he tried to translate her words. "Does that mean you're planning on leaving?"

"Betcher ass, buddy."

"Ah."

Phoebe became aware that she had been rambling, so she took a deep breath to calm herself before continuing. "Sorry. It's just this storm was bad, and then the lights went out. And, like, twice, I could swear some guy was in my room. Once in the reflection in the window when I was looking out and then when the lights popped back on. But it was just the closet."

"I see."

"Don't look at me like that."

"Like what?"

"Like I'm a crazy person," she said and crossed her arms. "I'm not Looney Tunes. No one was there, but it freaked me out."

"I understand."

Phoebe looked around the suite. In shifting her feet, she noticed the sweeping sound from her sneaker's sole. "Hey! Is that salt?"

"Indeed, it is," he answered. "Salt protects against evil spirits."

She bent down and touched her finger to a large granule. "This is the Himalayan stuff, man. Not cheap!" she scolded and stood, showing the pink crystal to him. "Will Himalayan even work?"

Holgrave blinked, taken aback at the question. "I hadn't thought of that. I hope so."

She noticed for the first time that he had a candle lit and a bundle of some sticks perched on a deep plate set upon the table. The bundle was smoking.

"What's that?"

"Sage," he answered. "I'm burning it as part of a protection spell."

Phoebe turned to look at the door. "Oh!" A white pentagram was drawn upon it.

"Don't worry, it's only white grease pencil," Holgrave said. "It will come off."

"I don't care," Phoebe assured him. "Like I said, I'm outta here in a few hours. What's the spell for?"

Holgrave stepped to the fireplace but kept his eyes on Phoebe as he explained. "It wards against black magic. I had to have something since I lent you my charm."

"If you're worried so much, why don't you just leave?"

"I'm still searching for the stock certificates."

At that moment, Phoebe recalled the encounter in the basement. "You think Hester's keeping them in the basement? There's a safe in the master bedroom you know."

"I know," Holgrave answered with a sly look about him.

"You cracked it? Searched there already?"

Holgrave nodded.

"Talented man," Phoebe granted. "What *is* in there?"

"Papers. Deeds. Some properties I recognize as being once owned by my family," he explained. He walked to the window and watched the rain as he spoke. Phoebe followed him. "A great amount of cash, and—" He turned to her and looked down into her face. "—some ancient paper with what I believe to be spells written upon them."

"Did you take any of it?"

"No."

"My gosh! Why not?" Phoebe exclaimed and shrugged. "Sounds like they owe you and your family big time."

"I'm only after what was taken," Holgrave answered.

"Okay, Mr. Honorable."

Phoebe wandered to the table where Holgrave kept his cameras and photo albums. Apparently, he had been inserting the pictures he had taken of the House of the Seven Gables. Many were strewn about the table, the largest of which was the black-and-white photograph of the east side of the house. She picked it up with care and looked to the strange figure in the window of Holgrave's attic suite.

"Holy shit."

"What?" asked Holgrave, at her side in a second.

Phoebe swallowed hard. There seemed no point in denying anything anymore. Simply claiming coincidence would not suffice. "This woman in the window." She pointed to the figure. "I think that's Alice."

"Alice?" Holgrave uttered with a gasp. He leaned forward to get a closer look.

Phoebe nodded and gave a surrendering sigh. "Yes, the spirit from the séance. Her name's Alice." Phoebe noticed Holgrave's expression of shock. It was more than just the sudden knowledge that Phoebe had acknowledged the ghost's existence, it was recognition. "You know her?"

Holgrave looked up from the picture. "Are you certain of this? *This* is Alice?"

Phoebe cast her eyes to the ceiling. "I can't believe I'm going to say this, but, that's what the ghost said her name was."

"My God."

"Oh, for the love of drama, just tell me already," Phoebe demanded.

"In my great-grandfather's diary there is mention of an Alice Pyncheon. Cousin of Hepzibah, bearer of the mark of witches."

"What's that?" she asked.

Holgrave arched an eyebrow. "Have you seen the birthmark on the back of your great-aunt Hester's neck?"

"Yeah. It kinda looks like a shamrock with a samurai sword stuck through it," she said with a grin.

"Are you also aware that you bear the same mark?"

"I've seen some mark there, usually when getting my hair done," she admitted. "I've never taken a close look."

Holgrave went to the dresser, opened the top drawer, and pulled out a hand mirror. "Come here," he directed, motioning her over to the full-length mirror next to the dresser.

Phoebe did, though her feet felt heavy. Her steps were more of a shuffle. She faced the mirror and watched Holgrave's reflection as he moved behind her.

"Pardon me," he said, and lifted her hair from her neck. He moved the handheld mirror into position.

Phoebe gasped, for in the center of the reflection's reflection, a twin of the slashed shamrock was on her neck. "Oh, my God. What does this mean?"

Holgrave let her hair down and replaced the mirror to the draw-er. "From what I gather, the Pyncheon family has an apparent genetic predisposition for psychic energy." He returned to her and continued speaking gently. "Pyncheon women who bear such a mark are the most powerful."

"Alice, when she knocked me on my ass," Phoebe recounted, "I was in the basement, but it was all wrong."

"How so?"

"The laundry machines were gone. The walls were stone. The floor was dirt. It was lit by a gas lamp, at least I think it was gas, mounted on the support beam."

Holgrave grew thoughtful. "A vision of the house from the past."

Phoebe nodded. "And Alice was there. Standing against the far wall, pointing to the floor."

"Indeed," Holgrave inserted. "Was there anything on the floor?"

"Nothing. Well, it was darker, as if it'd been dug up recently."

Holgrave's eyes widened. "Come with me," he said and went through the door, leaving it open behind him.

"Why not?" she murmured, certain he was too far away to hear. "Not like I had any plans."

The pair walked through the hallway, slowing as they arrived at Onenspek's studio, which was still lit. They could hear no activ-ity inside.

Phoebe continued to follow Holgrave, who tried to tiptoe to the satisfaction of the floorboards beneath them. The storm outside droned along, assaulting the gables and roof tiles of the house. Holgrave and Phoebe creaked and popped along, through the quiet house, past the master bedroom where neither could hear if anyone was within.

Down the stairs they went, proceeding cautiously, as if they could be discovered any moment. For Holgrave, he assumed nothing, as the chills on his spine convinced him they were being watched. He looked back at Phoebe and found a nervous expression on her face, and she was rubbing the back of her neck. Plainly, she was experiencing the same feeling.

Once on the first floor, Holgrave stopped and listened. Phoebe did the same. Nothing could be heard over the rain and thunder. Holgrave moved to the basement door, opened it, and turned the lights on. He ventured down the steps and Phoebe followed, closing the door behind her.

"Here," Holgrave bid her follow. He went behind the curtain he had put up to shield his developing work from the ceiling lights. Phoebe moved around it as he did.

"What are you doing?" she asked, watching him remove the screws from a section of wall paneling.

"Showing you what I've been doing down here," he explained.

Holgrave deftly worked the screwdriver and pulled the white-painted wood from the wall and leaned it nearby. Phoebe could see that Holgrave had been busy digging his way through the drywall and the original stone wall. A hole large enough for her to get through in a crouch was there, but the darkness within was uninviting.

Phoebe crossed her arms and tilted her head to the side. "There's no way you're getting your security deposit back."

Holgrave grinned. "I rather thought I'd get away with it."

Phoebe leaned down to look inside but could see nothing. "All right, what makes you think the stock certificates are in there?"

"Well," he began and cleared his throat. "I, um, it was the last wall left to try."

Phoebe straightened and stared at him, her mouth open. "You mean—"

"Yes, I've tunneled everywhere," he admitted, looking sheepish.

Phoebe chuckled and shook her head. "Did you find *anything?*"

"Actually, yes," Holgrave said. He grabbed a flashlight from the worktable next to them, turned it on, and squeezed through the hole he had made.

"Um, dude," Phoebe said, again crouching so she could keep her eyes on him. "I'm not going in there."

His face reappeared from the hole. "Come on, be sporting. I did all the work, after all."

Phoebe cussed under her breath and placed her foot beyond the remnants of the thick stone wall. The earth there was soft and damp, giving way gently to her weight. She stepped in the place where Holgrave shined the light and remained crouched as he was. Looking up, she saw the ceiling was low. Thick wooden support beams stretched from east to west, and all around them were stone pillars, set a few yards apart, upon which the weight of the house rested. Cobwebs were everywhere.

"Ew," she mumbled.

"That's the spirit," he offered with a drip of sarcasm.

"Bite me. I hate spiders."

"In that case, I promise you won't care for this," Holgrave said, panning the light to a pile of objects at her right.

Phoebe bent her knees, coming to rest on her heels, and peered closely. Collected there were items of jewelry, strips of cloth, remnants of leather goods that may have once been belts, a small women's handbag, and a shoe. Among these items was a metal box and a stack of papers. Everything there was thickly covered in dirt, while the box showed rust, and the papers mold.

"So, whose stuff is this?" she asked in a whisper. The personal belongings were quite old and certainly had been buried beneath the house for such a long time that the owners must have been long gone.

"It's mostly newspaper, but I've found some letters, both personal and business. Hardly any of it legible. There are pocket watches . . . very, very old. As is the jewelry. That shoe," he said, thrusting his thumb toward the hole behind him, "is a woman's ankle boot. When I handled it, it nearly disintegrated. The other leather goods are in similar shape. It takes many decades to reach that point of decay."

"And the other places you've dug?"

"Similar items," Holgrave stated with a nod. "They're everywhere down here."

Phoebe was silent for a moment. She walked away, around his curtain. Holgrave turned off the flashlight and followed.

"Where did you say Alice was standing?" he asked.

"There," Phoebe answered, pointing toward the washing machine. "The place on the floor was just under the table there. That beam," she said and traced the wood support beam above them, "leads right to where she was pointing."

Holgrave walked up to the table and verified it with a glance to Phoebe, who nodded. He went to the other end of the table and dragged it to the side. "Do you have a load of laundry to run?"

"Sure. Why?"

"It may help to cover the noise I'm about to make," he said and returned to the hole in the wall, within which he had hidden the tools she had brought down.

"Ah," she said and began loading the washer with items in the laundry bin.

Holgrave returned with the tools as Phoebe prepared the load. She turned it on once it was ready, and the basement filled with the groaning, screechy sounds of the antique machine.

He handed Phoebe the shovel and took a hold of the pickaxe in both hands. "Right. Are you certain this is the spot Alice pointed to?"

Phoebe nodded, wide-eyed.

Holgrave brought the pick upward, as high as he could without hitting the low ceiling, and swung it down. Its tip struck the cement floor near the wall. Phoebe jumped at the sound of metal clanging against the hard surface.

Holgrave struck again and again, chipping away at the floor. At first, pieces the size of pebbles came free, but as he went, the damage became pronounced. A whole section came loose upon his next strike, and he paused to pull it clear.

Phoebe nervously looked back at the basement door, certain that the noise he was making could be heard by anyone on the first floor. Anyone on the second or third that happened to wander near the dumbwaiter or the laundry chute would be able to hear it, though the sound would be masked by the washing machine.

Holgrave worked up a sweat as he smashed the pickaxe into the floor over and over again. Phoebe watched silently, anxious to get things over with. She considered tapping Holgrave on the shoulder and saying goodbye, but she shunned the idea.

As Holgrave chipped away at the floor, Phoebe thought about where she could possibly go on the half tank of gas and sixty bucks. Anxiety welled up within her, bringing a sting to her eyes. She pictured herself sleeping in the back of the Caprice, parked on the street somewhere in some tiny town, out of gas and out of options.

Something will work out.

"Ah-ha!" Holgrave announced eventually. He leaned the pickaxe against the wall and took the shovel from Phoebe's hand. He thrust it into the hard earth and stomped on it, pushing it in further.

Phoebe moved around him to watch his work. Holgrave dumped the dirt on top of the broken chunks of cement. As he went deeper, the dirt became dark with moisture. This made the job harder for Holgrave, who doubled his efforts, grunting with every shovelful. His shirt became soaked with sweat, and it dripped freely from his brow.

The pile of muddy earth and cement grew higher, and Holgrave was required to step into the very hole he had created to continue digging. He stopped a moment and looked up at Phoebe.

"Are you quite certain that Alice was pointing here?" he asked and again wiped his brow with his sleeve.

Phoebe was at a loss for an answer. Doubt filled the space left over from her suddenly misplaced certainty. She tried to picture Alice standing and pointing at the floor, but she could not.

"Phoebe?" Holgrave tried again.

Phoebe put her hand to her forehead. She had become lightheaded, and her knees weakened. In the very spot she stood, she sat hard and crossed her legs.

Holgrave launched himself from the hole he had made and went to her side. Crouching, he took her hands in his. "Are you all right?"

Phoebe looked up into his face and smiled. *What a handsome fellow. Fellow? What a word to use*, she mused. The face of Dzolali entered her mind at that moment, taking the place of Holgrave's. Phoebe squeezed her eyes shut and yanked one hand away. She tried to retreat, scooting along the cement floor. The groans and squeals of the washing machine grew painful, and she felt as if she were losing her mind.

Phoebe opened her eyes, and the smiling face of Dzolali remained. Phoebe looked left and right while still trying to pull back, but Dzolali's grip tightened. Phoebe grabbed the medallion that Holgrave had given her. She shut her eyes again, and suddenly, a dark-haired woman came to her.

It was Alice. Be calm, Alice said. The voice came not to Phoebe's ears but to her mind. It is a ruse.

"Please, make her go away," Phoebe pleaded.

"Make whom go away?" Holgrave asked her.

Phoebe opened her eyes and saw him there, her hand still in both of his. Dzolali had gone. "What the hell is happening?"

"What? What did you see?" he pressed.

She told him.

"Dzolali?" He looked to the basement door, knowing he wouldn't find her there. The glance was instinctive. "She might be looking for you," he proposed.

Maule is correct, said the voice of Alice. Phoebe's eyes looked for the voice before she realized that Alice Pyncheon was in her mind, and only she could hear the ghost's words.

"Is he?" Phoebe asked.

Confused and concerned, Holgrave gave Phoebe's hand a tug. "Phoebe? Are you with me?"

"Yeah."

"Am I digging in the right place?"

Yes! Tell him yes! He is almost here! Alice's voice screamed.

"Yes, she says yes," Phoebe said to Holgrave.

He must hurry!

Holgrave stared into Phoebe's face, doubt mixed with worry.

"Hurry, Holgrave," Phoebe begged of him.

Holgrave let her go and returned to the hole.

Phoebe felt Alice's presence, plainly and powerfully. She thought the question, *What do you mean 'almost here'?*

Alice Pyncheon's spirit did not answer.

Holgrave dug feverishly, and the dirt flew from the shovel, scattering across the floor. Pebbles and rocks in the dirt clicked along the cement and bounced off the north wall of the basement.

The shovel clinked.

Holgrave froze and set the shovel to the side. He bent low, and only the top of his head could Phoebe see.

"What is it?" she asked him.

Holgrave was too busy scooping damp earth away from his find. In a moment, it was clear. Against his instinct to leave it alone, and in fact, to flee from the House of the Seven Gables forever, he reached his hands around the object and lifted it for Phoebe to see.

It was a skull, darkened with the permeation of earth and age. The jawbone had detached and was still somewhere at Holgrave's feet.

"Oh, my God," Phoebe groaned.

He's there! Alice rejoiced in Phoebe's mind.

Holgrave reverently set the skull on the undisturbed section of floor and dug further with his hands. Phoebe wished to look away from the skull, but the empty eye sockets held her in place, unable to move.

A moment later, Holgrave lifted the remains of a garment. Holding it to the light, he gently swiped away clumps of clay-like earth.

"That's Alice's gown!" Phoebe called out. She covered her face in her hands, and the tears flowed freely. Hot and quick, the drops slid through her fingers and down her cheeks.

Holgrave sighed. Without question, he took Phoebe's words as fact. He lifted the garment further, gave it a shake, and more dirt came free. He felt something strike his feet. When he looked, he found bones on and around his shoes.

"Dear Lord," he murmured.

Phoebe grimaced as she took a long look at the gown. From her memory of the first possession by Alice, Phoebe recalled the image of Alice's own sister, Hepzibah, drawing the knife across Alice's throat and the blood flowing. As Holgrave held the gown in its decayed state, Phoebe could discern blood from earth.

She forced herself to look away and dried her tears.

Holgrave bent down and swiped at the dirt and bones further. A glint of gold caught his eye. "There's something else here," he called over his shoulder.

Phoebe brought herself to her feet and, with her eyes avoiding the skull's empty stare, approached the edge of the broken floor. She watched as Holgrave carefully extracted a gold chain from the dark, stony ground.

"Almost have it," he grunted as he dug further. "It's attached to something . . . rather substantial."

His dirt-stained fingers pulled the object free. He held it in both hands, his thumbs rubbing the excess from its surface. Quite soon, it was clear enough to decipher. It was a pendant, and a fairly large one. The centerpiece was a circle with a raised pentagram, and mounted on either side were slivers of moon, their points set outward.

Holgrave moved his hand up and down, feeling its weight. "I think this is solid gold."

Take it, Phoebe, Alice commanded. It's yours now.

Phoebe reached around her neck and took Holgrave's borrowed charm from it, passing it over her head. Holgrave watched her do it and took her meaning. He had no qualms over the unspoken transaction. He handed the heavy necklace to the young Pyncheon and accepted his in return.

Phoebe took the heavier chain and continued wiping it free of mud. She stared at the charm in awe and realized that the pentagram, as a symbol, no longer inflicted feelings of taboo within her.

Quickly, put it on.

Phoebe did so, paying no mind to the item's condition or its previous resting place, around the neck of a decaying body. She stood and stepped back from the hole, clasping the pendant in her palm.

Holgrave draped his necklace over his head and climbed out of the hole. "Well, it's a certainty that my stock certificates aren't to be found here."

Phoebe turned to him. "Is that all you were after all this time, Holgrave?"

"Certainly not," he assured her, though his hopes had been high.

At that moment, the washing machine silenced. It was finished washing the load of bed linens inside. Phoebe and Holgrave cast their eyes to the ear-menacing machine.

"Ah," Holgrave said. "That's better."

"Is it indeed?" a strange female voice called from the stairwell.

20

Discovery

Phoebe spun around so quickly she lost her balance and fell into Holgrave, who instinctively grabbed her and held her up.

Three women had arrived at the foot of the steps, unheard. The two on the left were unknown but familiar to Phoebe, while Dzolali stood smiling at her from her place on their right.

"Who the hell are you people?" Phoebe shouted. Her hands were on her chest, and she could feel the newly recovered pendant beneath her t-shirt.

"That woman in the middle," Holgrave whispered, though all could hear him, "is from my dream."

"What's wrong, Phoebe, dear?" the brunette said. "Don't you just love my facelift?" With that, all three of the women laughed.

There was something in the voice, the manner of speech, the way the woman grinned and placed her hands on her hips in a stance of arrogance, that made her familiar. But the eyes, clear blue, like unpolluted water at a beach somewhere, these clinched it.

The woman *was* her great-aunt Hester. The woman at her right, the blonde, was certainly Glendarah, shed of close to four decades from the look of her tight skin and vibrant yellow hair.

The three witches, dressed in their black Victorian-era gowns, tittered gleefully. To Phoebe, Dzolali appeared to be the most menacing. Her glare was venomous, so satisfied she must have felt from her brilliant manipulation of Phoebe's heart and mind.

At that moment, Phoebe felt nothing but hatred for the redheaded Latina and disgust for herself for the time she'd spent with her, no matter how pleasurable it had been.

"So, what have we been busy digging up, Mr. Holgrave?" the transformed Hester dripped as she approached him. Her pale blues scanned his blushing face and then dropped to the skull on the floor. "Oh, now, I wonder who *that* could be."

Oh, my God. I'm so stupid! Phoebe thought as the rest of Alice's possession came to her. She remembered the impossible happening, when the room disappeared and a field of the dead stood before her in the bluish-silver moonlight. *We're standing on a burial ground. These witches, maybe the whole Pyncheon family, are nothing but serial killers!*

Hester came within a few inches of Holgrave's face. She smiled seductively. "Well, Mr. Holgrave. Now that you can see me in person, don't you wish you had given yourself to me?"

"I don't, actu—"

"Too late!" Hester bellowed in his face and, despite her youthful beauty, she turned ugly, snarling and hateful. "Dzolali!"

"Yes, High Priestess."

"Summon Mr. Onenspek," she ordered. "I think it's time for a household meeting."

Dzolali's smile seemed molded in plastic. Her pronounced canines glinted under the neon bulbs above. Her eyes closed and her chin lifted, apparently in concentration. "He's on his way, High Priestess."

"Good," Hester granted as she studied Holgrave's face. "I have to wonder, Mr. Holgrave, just how you were able to withstand me for lack of a better word."

"It wasn't difficult," he said in a matter-of-fact tone.

Hester's smile faltered and her eyebrow crept up her wrinkle-less forehead.

"We'll see how long that smugness of yours lasts," Hester said threateningly.

In a blur of motion, Holgrave released Phoebe, reached back for the pickaxe with his right hand, and twisted his body to the left, bringing the large hand tool flying forward in a whipping motion.

Phoebe jumped back, convinced that Holgrave would pierce her with it instead of Hester. She need not have worried, however, as the pickaxe never completed the journey.

Hester raised her left hand in a gesture that resembled someone signaling for the waiter. Without a sound, the pickaxe's movement stilled so abruptly that it appeared to have impacted something.

Holgrave stared at the motionless tool in surprise. To him, it felt like it was stuck, as if he had pierced a mountainside. He could not free it from the nothingness that seized it.

Glendarah and Dzolali laughed lightly.

Hester dropped her hand to her side and appeared mildly amused. She tilted her head in sympathy and pouted her lips. "Aw," she uttered. "Aren't you just the cutest?"

Hester's companions laughed harder, Glendarah so much so that she dabbed a tear from her eye.

Phoebe watched the exchange from her crouched position in front of the washing machine. The outrage she felt over Holgrave attacking her great-aunt Hester was but a fleeting emotion, as the young brunette before her bore no resemblance to the woman she knew as Hester Pyncheon, except perhaps from old black-and-white photographs taken when the woman was young.

Holgrave looked past the annoyingly amused Hester Pyncheon and saw Ned Onenspek come down the steps. As Holgrave looked away, the pickaxe was torn from his grip and given flight. It crashed into the wall at his right, breaking the wood panel before falling to the floor.

Looking to Hester, Holgrave found her hand raised again. This time, her fingers were curled, and both arms were stretched in the direction of the fallen pickaxe. An expression of arrogance was plastered on her face. She chuckled harshly, showing her teeth in glorious self-satisfaction.

Hester turned to the sound of Ned's footsteps. "Ah, here's your artist, Dzolali."

Dzolali smiled predatorily, though she took Ned by the arm as if they were about to take a walk down the aisle. Ned appeared oblivious to anything odd going on. Instead, he gazed into Dzolali's face like a lovesick teenager.

Holgrave and Phoebe exchanged glances, neither knowing what to do. Hester's unconventional disarming of Holgrave astounded them both, and at the moment, neither could think of anything but escape, though the witches and now Ned blocked their way.

Phoebe shrugged, not knowing what to do or say. She grabbed hold of the freshly unearthed medallion and curled the material of her cotton shirt around it. *What do we do?*

"Hester," Holgrave said in a calm tone. "I'm not sure what the idea is here, but you have to—"

With a wave akin to swatting away a winged insect, Hester sent Holgrave reeling back, where he collided with the wall, inches away from tumbling into the hole he had dug.

"Holgrave!" Phoebe shouted, afraid for him as he struck the wall with a crack. He slid to the floor, rolled onto his side, and covered his head with his hands.

Hester looked upon her grandniece, that look of triumph worn stiffly, masklike. The expression infuriated Phoebe, and without thinking, she launched herself from the floor, pushing off the washing machine. With arms reaching for Hester's throat, the youngest Pyncheon lunged. Surprised, Hester slipped away in a cloud of dark smoke, leaving Phoebe to land on the floor, knees and elbows first, until she slid to a stop not far from Dzolali.

The Latina witch laughed gleefully, covering her mouth with her free hand. Ned looked down upon the fallen Phoebe, who was shaken by the impact with the floor. He made a move to lend her a hand, but Dzolali held firm to his arm.

"Hey, are you all—?"

"Shhh!" interrupted Dzolali. "Never mind, Ned darling."

Ned straightened and turned back to stare into Dzolali's face, forgetting Phoebe altogether.

Phoebe looked back and found Hester standing right where she had been, though she had turned to face her grandniece. The victorious evil grin had returned.

But it slipped, thought Phoebe, recalling Hester's faltering expression as she lunged. *She can't read my intent.*

She saw Holgrave climb to his feet, resting much of his weight against the wall. He seemed dazed, but there was no blood. Phoebe pushed herself up to her feet, aware that Dzolali was staring into her face challengingly. She did not return the gaze. Instead she went to Holgrave.

"Are you all right?" she asked.

He nodded, though not convincingly. He winced as he felt the back of his head.

A sharp clattering of metal startled them both. Phoebe looked to the floor to find a sledgehammer and two of the largest nails she had ever seen.

"Very carefully, Mr. Holgrave," Hester spoke in a tone of warning. "You will do us the honor of driving those railroad spikes into the side of that support beam." Hester pointed to the ceiling, the second to last beam before the southern wall.

"And this seems the apropos time to inquire as to why I should do such a thing," Holgrave said.

With a hand gesture from Hester, the sledgehammer and one spike left the floor and moved through the air with no visible means of propulsion. "You'll do what I command, or I'll drive one into your skull myself," she said sweetly, as if offering a child a choice of ice creams.

Holgrave slowly reached for the floating items and took the railroad spike in his left hand. He felt no resistance as it came into his hand. The sledgehammer was likewise released into his grip. The skeptic in him searched the items and the ceiling for tricks—some sort of wire system came to his mind first. He found nothing.

Phoebe watched as Holgrave held the spike's pointed end to a place on the thick wooden beam, taking direction from Hester on just how and where she wanted the spike to be driven. After five hefty strikes on the head of the spike, Hester called out to him.

"That's enough." The other spike lifted from the floor, obeying Hester's hand gesture. With a flicking motion of her index and middle fingers, the spike suddenly flew, point first, into the same beam some six feet to the right of the first one.

"Now tap that one in, Mr. Holgrave," Hester ordered as the other two witches laughed at Holgrave's expression.

Holgrave did as commanded, and when he was finished, the sledgehammer was taken from his grip.

He turned to Hester and shrugged questioningly. "Why didn't you just do that yourself?"

"Because watching you do it brought me joy, you stupid little man!" Hester roared.

Phoebe watched Holgrave's face as anger washed over his features. For a moment, she was sure he would try to rush Hester again, but whatever forces were at her command were unknown to him, so he held his ground.

"Glendarah."

"Yes, High Priestess," the blonde witch answered and stepped to Hester's side.

"Bind his hands and feet," Hester ordered.

As if it had always been there, a length of thick rope appeared in Glendarah's demure hands. She stared daringly into the face of Holgrave as she moved closer, hoping he'd try to resist her orders.

Instead of fighting her, Holgrave kept his hands to his sides and returned the woman's stare. He kept his emotions blank, but the message was clear.

Glendarah pulled his hand, and he resisted. It was Glendarah's time to appear angry. She snapped her fingers, and the shovel at the back wall took to the air, narrowly missing Phoebe as it slid past.

The shovel turned on its axis and brought the flat side up and back. As if the tool were in the hands of an invisible man, it swung like a baseball bat. The flat of the tool collided with Holgrave's midsection with a fleshy clap. He folded in two as the air was forced out of his lungs. Holgrave dropped to the dusty cement floor and was left trying to suck oxygen back into himself.

"Stop it!" Phoebe shouted and rushed Glendarah. Her legs, stretched in a long running stride, simply stopped moving forward. She almost toppled to the floor, but fortunately both feet kept some contact. It felt as if her ankles were being gripped tightly by large, powerful hands.

"Do that again and I'll stuff you in that machine and put it on spin!" Hester screamed, pointing at the washing machine behind Phoebe. To Ned, she said, suddenly calm and sweet once more, "Ned, be a dear and give Mr. Holgrave a hand to his feet."

"I would be most happy to," answered Onenspek.

Holgrave let his arm be taken by Ned, who asked softly, "Are you all right, Mr. Holgrave?"

The Brit looked Ned in the face, thinking he was hearing a conspiratorial tone from the man. Instead, Onenspek's eyes were free of focus, utterly blank as they passed over Holgrave's features, as if he were standing a football field away.

In any case, Holgrave responded, "Yes, I think so. Thank you, Mr. Onenspek."

"Anytime," Ned said. He patted Holgrave on the shoulder, and with a child-like grin, he rejoined Dzolali.

Phoebe knew Holgrave was hurting. He was slightly bent forward and labored to breathe. His face was reddened, and his eyes were droopy, as if he could have just lay down right on the spot and fallen asleep. He folded his arms over his chest, hugging himself, and noticed the strange manner in which Phoebe stood.

Phoebe felt like an action figure posed as a marathon runner. The picture was spoiled by her arms, which were left free to dangle at her sides.

Glendarah grabbed Holgrave's wrists and expertly looped the rope around them. She then ran the rope under his arms, over his shoulders, and paused to push him in the direction of the spikes he had been made to drive. Glendarah wrapped him from ankle to shin, then around his arms and midsection. Magically, the endless rope seemed to originate from Glendarah's sleeve, and there was enough to be looped over the spike. With that done, the blonde witch tied off the end around the door handle to the boiler room, just off the south wall.

So bound, Holgrave could not move and could not so much as hop away from the south wall. He tested the limits and quickly found he had no options.

Phoebe watched all of this helplessly. She did not even grasp the odd twin-moon and pentagram charm around her neck for fear that she would call attention to it. Something told her it would be a bad idea to let it be seen. She wondered about that, realizing, even though Holgrave's Feng Shui and Pagan decorated charm had seemed to help her resist Dzolali, it was not doing a thing for him now.

In her mind's panic, Phoebe sent out a plea for help. *Alice! Alice Pyncheon! Help us! Please!*

For a heartbeat, Phoebe thought it worked. The pressure holding her in place by the ankles lessened but did not let go. Glendarah took a step back, watching Phoebe as if she were waiting for something.

Phoebe's right foot, the one behind her, slid forward and lifted from the cement. The foot was planted ahead of her, and then her left foot was brought ahead in the same fashion.

Her proximity to Glendarah was soon ideal. In an act of desperation, Phoebe swung her open right palm out and ahead. Her palm contacted Glendarah's cheek, sending out a cracking slap that reverberated from the cellar walls.

Glendarah dropped back a step, off balance and holding her bright red left cheek. Her eyes were surprised, angry, and a little frightened.

What the hell? Fear? Phoebe marveled, thinking it odd that fear would ever appear on one of their faces.

Glendarah seethed, letting out a long hiss of rage. Her closed right fist flashed out, catching Phoebe's left temple and rocking her head back and to the right. Had the sinister force holding and guiding her legs not been there, she would have fallen. Everything went dark for a few seconds, and Phoebe fought to regain consciousness. She breathed through her nose, quickly and rhythmically.

Phoebe's eyesight returned, and she realized that she was staring at the ceiling. Her legs still bound, her upper body had leaned way back, giving her a dancer's pose. Coming around, she straightened.

"Enough of that," Hester quipped. "Glendarah, wrap this up."

Phoebe was guided to the place under the second railroad spike and turned to face the coven. Holgrave was to her right. Glendarah produced another endless spool of rope, binding Phoebe in identical fashion and anchoring the rope in the same door handle behind Phoebe and Holgrave.

"Very good," Hester commended Glendarah, who bowed and stepped back enough to view her handiwork.

"Now what, *Auntie* Hester?" Phoebe asked hotly. Her cheek was stiffening from Glendarah's punch. Soon, it would be swollen, but in considering everything else, Phoebe thought a puffy black-and-blue cheek might turn out to be her most minor problem that day.

"Well, Phoebe, dear. We tried to be nice," Hester explained and stepped closely to her grandniece. "Dzolali gave you every kindness—"

"Kindness! I was violated while I slept!" Phoebe shouted.

Hester laughed heartily. "Violated? My, oh my. No one that Dzolali has ever shown interest in has considered themselves violated."

"What else do you call having my dreams invaded while I'm asleep in my room?"

"*My* room!" Hester howled. "The House of the Seven Gables is my home, you ungrateful, ignorant little shit!"

"I was violated while I slept!" Phoebe insisted, spittle flying from her mouth. "I was bewitched, or drugged, or whatever you freaks call it!"

It was clear that they'd never see it that way. Phoebe suspected as much before she ever brought it up. Tied in this way, however, Phoebe knew that she had little time left. She remembered the vision of Alice, tied and suspended the same way until her throat was cut.

"You are a Pyncheon woman," Hester said more calmly. The tears in her eyes over the mention of the name insulted Phoebe, however. "And you bear the witch's mark on your neck."

"Yeah, so I've noticed," Phoebe said with disgust.

"And you don't even appreciate your power—your status!" Hester said in disbelief. "You have such great potential."

"And yet I was violated."

"Oh, Goddess Hecate!" Hester called to the ceiling. "You're so two-dimensional, Phoebe! So very short-sighted. You could one day have your own coven."

Sensing a dead end on that argument, Phoebe changed tactics. "Why don't you tell Ned about how much money you're making from his paintings?"

Hester turned to look at Ned and Dzolali, both smiling, Ned nodding as if he were simply listening to a Sunday sermon. "Go ahead," Hester bid as she stepped back.

"Ned," Phoebe began, speaking quickly, "there are paintings of yours at Pyncheon Art, priced in the thousands of dollars. They're taking advantage of you!"

Ned giggled and looked into Dzolali's eyes. Then he turned to Hester. Both women remained silent and just stared back at the artist.

"It's true, Ned," Holgrave took up. "I saw them. The whole gallery is full of your work. Your name is famous—known all over the world."

Ned met Holgrave's eyes. His smile faded slowly. "Hester. No. Hester, you said they were going okay, but you said the market was strained. My best sale was a couple hundred dollars. Just enough for rent and supplies."

Hester said nothing. Her grin was crooked, her brow arched as if to say 'I told you so.' Dzolali shared the expression, and when the three witches exchanged glances, their giggles quickly expanded to laughter.

Ned, thinking he was being put on by someone, but unsure of just whom, smiled and let out a chuckle. With his arm around Dzolali, he hugged her tightly to him. She embraced him right back, but there was something sinister in her eyes that Phoebe didn't like.

"That's a good one, guys! Real funny!" Ned shook his finger at Holgrave and Phoebe.

"Ned," Phoebe tried again. "You are making these people rich off your work. I searched your name on the internet when we were in town."

"People are clamoring for your paintings, Ned," Holgrave said. "Sold even for second-hand profits. The gallery is charging *thousands*, not hundreds."

"And they *are* selling," Phoebe assured him.

Ned was no longer smiling. "What? *What?*" He looked to Dzolali, confused and pleading. But there was something else.

Is he about to crack or did it work? Will he help us?

Onenspek's facial muscles relaxed and he seemed to collapse onto Dzolali, who was quite strong enough to hold him upright. Her smile never faltered as she let the man slide down her body. Ned's limp form fell to the cement with a skull-cracking smack.

In Dzolali's left hand was a long, curved blade, covered in dark red blood, as was her right hand. Dzolali's eyes settled on Onenspek with dispassion.

"Well, now," Hester said to Phoebe. "Don't you feel better now that you got all that off your chest?"

Phoebe whimpered, too disgusted, too frightened, too guilty to look away from the dead artist, whose life's blood was collecting in a rough circle around him. He had fallen facing away from the captives, but Phoebe saw his sides expand and contract with breath.

"Ned? *Ned!*" Holgrave called out.

"You're a fucking monster, Hester," Phoebe cursed through sobs. "*You're all fucking monsters!*"

Furthering Phoebe's rage, the witches roiled with amusement, their laughter surpassing her sobs in volume. Phoebe fought the ropes, pointlessly twisting and pulling, contorting and pushing, but with no result. She soon exhausted herself, much to the delight of the witches.

Wishing to switch Hester's attention from Phoebe, Holgrave said, "So, what was the purpose in killing him? He would have willingly continued painting for you."

Hester sidestepped and faced Holgrave, coming close enough that they could smell each other. Hester knew the Brit was familiar with it and used her proximity to her advantage. "And now, with Mr. Onenspek gone, his works, of which we have a small truckload, will double, perhaps triple in value for a time before the market gets saturated and prices drop. Best not have too many works of genius around the house."

"You still didn't have to kill him," Holgrave insisted. "I doubt he would have said anything. He seemed happy enough."

"Bah!" Dzolali spat as she wiped the blood from her blade. "Good riddance. I won't be able to get his filthy stench off me for months. Sick little pervert."

"You see?" Hester said to Holgrave as if Dzolali had proved a point. "We're happier he's gone. And if we're happy, well, honestly, that's all that matters."

"And I'm next. Is that right?" Holgrave asked challengingly.

Hester gave him a quick scan from feet to face. "I don't see any reason to keep you. You're quite more valuable to us as a sacrifice."

"And what about her?" he asked with a tilt of his head toward Phoebe.

Hester turned to Phoebe and put her hands on her hips. "She had her chance."

"Chance to what, Aunt Hester?" Phoebe retorted. "Join your sick little group? Why?"

"Oh, you would have been a priceless addition, dear," Hester said and stepped close to her grandniece. "You have no idea of your power. You could have been the best of us . . . in time."

"Why? So I can con some poor artist into painting for me? What's it all for, Hester?"

"The house needs to survive," Hester answered. "However powerful the coven becomes, the House of the Seven Gables still has earthly needs."

Dzolali came closer, watching Phoebe's face intently, hungrily.

Hester continued. "I could have taught you so much about what you are and what you can do."

As her great-aunt spoke, Phoebe felt Hester move into her thoughts. It was a harsh invasion, a sickening surrender of her mind's control. Hester's very being walked into Phoebe's with ease, imposing images of things that were and what could have been. The basement all but disappeared, replaced by whatever Hester wanted Phoebe to experience.

Phoebe saw the gargoyle that appeared in her nightmare, the one that had picked Phoebe from her bed and dropped her that impossible distance. Its black flesh, the deep gray teeth and long black shiny claws shimmered in her mind's eye. Phoebe relived the drop to the bedroom floor and let out a long cry of terror.

"What are you doing to her?" Holgrave shouted. "Stop!"

Phoebe heard Holgrave's voice and grasped onto it, seeing the image of her hands reaching out to his, appearing from the darkness as she remained in freefall. Holgrave sounded as if he had moved quite some distance from her, though his hands were right in front of her, disembodied and matching her rate of fall.

Phoebe reaffirmed her vision of taking a hold of his hands, and the sensation of falling slowed, then ceased. The gargoyle snarled from quite close by, just above her, from the sound.

Hester's defeat was not permanent, and her assault flowed in a different direction. The venue shifted to the master bedroom's balcony. Here Phoebe stood, unbound and clothed in a gloriously elegant black gown, with the hands of Dzolali and Hester on her shoulders. Wordlessly, they smiled upon her as if Phoebe were their pupil.

The sound of canvas, or perhaps something made of burlap, came to her ears. Phoebe thought of a tent coming loose in a high wind. Looking up, however, she saw the gargoyle return in flight. It landed upon the stone-tiled balcony hard and sent vibrations through Phoebe's feet.

Phoebe stared up into the beast's horrifying face. It was dripping water onto the balcony, but it was not water alone. Phoebe looked down and saw the twirls of red within the clear water and knew it was blood. The fact came to her by Hester's unspoken narration, the story told in pictures and feelings rather than words.

It was the blood of Kenneth Hillsborough, the son-in-law of Darla Carp and president of the White Lake City Council. The man that had wanted to appropriate the land upon which the House of the Seven Gables sat had been killed by this black beast that towered over Phoebe and the two witches.

Phoebe wanted to back away, but Dzolali and Hester held her in place. The gargoyle bent to bring its face closer, and in the reflection of the eyes of onyx stone was the reflection of Glendarah, her arms spread in mockery of the gargoyle.

But it was not a mockery, Phoebe found, for the beast receded to nothingness and the demure figure of Glendarah filled its place. She was soaked through, her blonde hair had darkened and had become plastered to her head. Glendarah's black dress was wrinkled with moisture, the maxi skirt clinging to her legs as water and blood seeped onto the balcony's surface.

Glendarah was the gargoyle. She had killed Hillsborough. She had tormented Phoebe in the night, coming to the aid of Dzolali, whose passion could not contain Phoebe's will.

The scene of Hillsborough's death was brought to Phoebe's mind as seen from the eyes of the gargoyle. Phoebe cried out in horror, but what came to her ears was the creature's terrifying howl. Entrapped in the gargoyle's point-of-view, Phoebe watched the man be torn into by the claws and then the mouth biting down into the defenseless human's throat.

Phoebe could taste the blood just as if she had been the creature herself. It was Glendarah's memory of the attack, Phoebe tried to remind herself, but the vibrant color of the night and the flowing blood was just as vivid as the hours she had spent in Dzolali's company.

Phoebe yearned for Dzolali at that moment. She wanted away from the gargoyle, away from the awful blood and gore of the dying Hillsborough, and into the arms of Dzolali. Water lily and vanilla needed to cover the wretched, wet iron smell of blood, and so it did.

Phoebe tasted Dzolali on her lips and felt the Latina witch's heat once again. The gargoyle was gone, pleasantly gone, and in place of it, Phoebe received the gift of her love's attentions.

Phoebe opened her eyes and found the copper eyes of Dzolali staring into her face, half-closed in passion. Dzolali needed Phoebe, wanted her forever, if only, if only . . .

Phoebe saw herself and Dzolali standing together, joined in unholy matrimony, as the High Priestess Hester Pyncheon and her own love, Glendarah D'Amitri, looked on. The future Phoebe was grandly dressed, somehow taller, more voluptuous, adorned fully in her black Victorian gown and high-heeled boots, her fingers lavishly festooned with rings of power, her neck bearing charms of black magic, and her eyes hard and cruel. Her blonde hair was done up high and voluminous, decorated with a tiara of silver and gold. Tiny metal skulls hung from her ears, and decorative piercings had been pressed through the flesh of her nose and blackened lips.

Phoebe focused on the vision of the woman she could be, a wiccan so powerful that her energy glowed in red and blue orbs in her palms. No one could touch her, no one could stand against her and the House of the Seven Gables. Those that dared would be destroyed.

A scene of the town of White Lake came to Phoebe's mind. It was burning, and the dark witch, the future Phoebe Pyncheon, floated above it, leveling the buildings with her glowing missiles of supernatural power.

She watched as her future self set the town, then the state, then the world, on fire. Repulsed, Phoebe screamed, fighting against her restraints, thinking of nothing but pushing herself away from Dzolali and Hester, who tormented her while Glendarah watched with a smile. Phoebe screamed again and again to make it all stop.

"No!" Phoebe bellowed, and Dzolali was sent reeling back. Her hands pinwheeled as the young witch tried to recover her balance, and she would have had she not been so disarmed by the surprising rush of power from her would-be victim.

Dzolali tripped on the body of Ned Onenspek and landed hard on her back, the bottoms of her shoes slick with the man's blood. She avoided hitting her head on the cement by tucking her chin to her chest. She came to rest having not taken her shocked and angry eyes from Phoebe's face.

Hester was also pushed back a step or two. She shot her grandniece a look of surprise and quickly shelved it, turning her expression passive. She caught movement from her left and turned in time to see Dzolali charging Phoebe, the small dagger in her hand.

"Wait!" Hester demanded and flung her arm up. Her fingers curled, not into a fist, but close, as if she were catching a ball.

Dzolali froze mid-step with the blade raised. Her long, black cherry hair streamed behind her, like she was trapped in a windstorm.

Hester stepped to Dzolali and removed the knife from her grip. "Not just yet," she said. "Her power is ours to absorb, through the sacrifice to Panas."

"Yes, High Priestess," Dzolali said resignedly. Her teeth were clenched and her eyes hot with rage, but she relaxed as Hester wished. Slowly, she was released from Hester's power and left to stand on her own.

Hester moved to Phoebe, getting close enough to whisper. "You have little time left, and all the powers you're capable of will never be realized, never be implemented. When the witching hour comes, your blood is ours."

Phoebe was too frightened to speak. The horrific images that Hester had planted in her mind echoed, and so much more became evident in those echoes. Like the beach erodes with every passing crash of the waves, more and more of the coven's misdeeds became exposed.

The image of Darla Carp slipped into Phoebe's mind. The woman was hanging from a rope in her garage at that very moment. Phoebe watched Hester walk to the stairs, and as she did, the short mental image of Hester showing up to the Carp residence followed, like a superimposed image over an old movie.

Phoebe watched helplessly as the scene unfolded in her mind's eye like it was a page from Phoebe's own memory, as if she had tagged along. Phoebe saw Hester enter the Carp home, unexpected and un-wanted. She bewitched Darla Carp into tying her own noose, slow-ly, methodically, as if in a trance. Phoebe watched the woman put her head through it and maneuver a short stepstool into place under-neath a support beam. Darla's eyes were empty, staring at nothing but the closed garage door. Hester tied the other end of the rope around a hook on the wall meant for a gardening tool. Without a second thought or hesitation, Hester kicked the stool out from under Carp and exited the garage.

Carp's neck snapped when she reached the end of the rope. Her end followed within seconds, her complexion deepened to blue and her eyes strained against the lids, nearly bursting beyond their sockets.

Phoebe wept. It could no longer be prevented or restrained. It was all too much.

"Phoebe," Holgrave called to her gently.

Phoebe could only muster a shake of her head. The crying would not be stopped so easily.

Holgrave let it go. There was no reason to not let Phoebe weep. The coven left them to the basement with only the body of Ned Onenspek to keep them company. Holgrave was grateful for the small favor of them leaving Ned facing away, though the dark red blood seeping from the body was a slowly widening pool. The footprint left from Dzolali's trip had already filled in and she had tracked it onto the floor and up the stairs.

With her hands bound, Phoebe could not wipe away the streaks of tears. She blinked her eyesight clear and turned to see Holgrave straining against the ropes, fruitlessly trying to free himself.

Giving her own rope another tug with feet and hands, she noted they didn't give, or even slide along her flesh when she moved.

For a long moment, Phoebe and Holgrave looked to one another in silence. The ropes were tight and made breathing difficult. Phoebe found that struggling against it was exhausting.

"Save your strength," she said.

"For what, exactly?" he asked, exasperated.

To this, she had no answer. She sighed and looked away. Finding only Ned's corpse again, she closed her eyes.

21

Sacrifice

Even tied uncomfortably tight, Phoebe's and Holgrave's exhaustion won out. Both had drifted to an uneven, fragile sleep, broken when their bodies relaxed enough to pull the rope more tightly around their ribs.

Phoebe had no idea how much time had gone by, but it seemed like more than an hour, maybe two.

"Holgrave?"

"Yes?"

"What's the witching hour?" she asked.

Holgrave turned to her. "It's between three a.m. and four."

"Is that central time or what?" she asked and gave him a weak smile that did nothing to cover her fear.

Holgrave returned it. "That is a very good question."

Shortly afterward, they could hear footsteps on the floor above. The basement door opened, and heavily heeled footsteps announced their company. A pair of black ankle-high boots appeared first, followed by the long skirt of Hester's dress. She reached the floor, her water blue eyes inspecting her captives, including Ned, as if making sure he was dead.

Glendarah and Dzolali followed right behind Hester, deliberately descending the stairs, carrying the birdcage from either side.

Oh, great. What the hell is this? Phoebe thought. Visions of the raven pecking Ned's dead eyes out of his head came to her, and she nearly wretched.

Hester and Glendarah kept their youthful appearance in place. Phoebe wondered just how powerful a witch had to be to create such an illusion.

"Thank you for your patience," Hester said and chuckled. She stepped past Onenspek, carefully avoiding the pool of blood that had expanded greatly since the coven had left.

Dzolali and Glendarah set the birdcage on the floor. The fabric cover was over it, so the only clue Phoebe had of the bird's presence within was a brief rustling of wings.

Phoebe looked to Hester's hands and found her mother's bowl, taken from her Caprice's trunk.

Hester noticed Phoebe's eyes land on the heirloom. "I remember you mentioning that you brought it with you. I thought it appropriate that we use it during the proceedings."

Phoebe didn't have to ask what for. She remembered what Alice Pyncheon's ghost had revealed to her. She felt faint, knowing that she and Holgrave were to meet the same fate.

Oh, God. Help us, she thought. She gave her wrists a twist, but the rope held firm, giving her no indication that it had any weakness whatsoever. Phoebe was certain that if the coven decided to leave them alone, the rope itself could serve as the sole instrument of their deaths. It would just take time. Somehow, that was worse than the sacrifice she knew was coming.

Hester strode up to Phoebe. "I don't suppose you've come to change your mind about joining my coven."

Phoebe decided to lie. "I'd never," she said, her voice shaky. The truth was, Phoebe was well beyond panic and had considered acquiescing. But she thought of how Onenspek had been used then discarded, and then how Darla Carp had been manipulated to get to Kenneth Hillsborough, who had wanted to see the House of the Seven Gables destroyed to develop the land.

And the police don't intimidate them, Phoebe thought as she recalled Detective Backstrom. Phoebe knew that, even if she joined her great-aunt Hester with the intent of betraying her later to make her escape, there would be no true escape.

Phoebe faced her great-aunt Hester, reading her eyes. Since childhood, Phoebe had associated that clear water blue with hardness, self-centeredness, and a dark mysterious strength. In front of her now, that same woman, transmogrified and empowered by witchcraft, had turned icy cold.

In the tight bounds of Glendarah's rope, and the gaze of her great-aunt, Phoebe could feel the emotions in the room. Her psychic abilities began to flood her with information in the form of sensations.

From Hester, Phoebe felt jealousy, narcissism, and even a little fear. The fear surprised Phoebe, but she gave it little thought. Curious about the information she was receiving, Phoebe looked to Dzolali.

In Dzolali, Phoebe felt adoration, masked by the duty to her coven, and a faint trace of hope. She held Dzolali's gaze for a little longer, thinking herself into the Latina witch's mind. It took little more than wishing it so to be welcomed inside, and beyond the surface lay a myriad of mixed and conflicting emotions and thoughts. Phoebe felt Dzolali's feelings for her, earnest and powerful, not just a conjuring by Hester or Glendarah's doing. She also felt a deep, insatiable drive in the woman. Flashes of Dzolali's torrid past flooded in. The scenes featured Dzolali with many men and women, and no two partners were the same.

Phoebe forced herself to separate from the Latina's mind. The scenes of her exploits were intense, and they interfered with her read of the woman. The overriding feeling from Dzolali was that she didn't want Phoebe to die.

Phoebe then focused on Glendarah. Contempt was a main

contributor to the woman's outlook of the youngest Pyncheon. There was fear of change mixed with devout faith in Hester and in the house. Glendarah was supremely confident in herself, and the most fearless of the three.

"Well, what is it?" Hester pressed, eyeing Phoebe suspiciously.

Did she feel my communication with her? Maybe she sensed me reading the others. "I've no intention of joining you, Hester," Phoebe voiced quietly.

Phoebe sensed relief from Glendarah and distinct disappointment from Dzolali. Most distressing to Phoebe was that her great-aunt Hester was pleased. Hester thought time had no meaning, that she could maintain her youthful appearance indefinitely.

More images sprang from Hester's mind and flooded Phoebe's, triggered perhaps by the relief she felt over Phoebe's decision. The pictures were of Hester visiting her niece, Harriet, Phoebe's mother. Harriet was ill in these images and becoming more so as they went on. But there was more to it. Phoebe could see Hester moving about Harriet's bed while the sick woman was asleep, replacing the prescribed medications with lookalikes that she had created.

Phoebe gasped and stared at Hester in shock and renewed hatred. "You killed my mother!" she shouted.

Hester's confident demeanor faltered, though it was from surprise rather than guilt or denial. She narrowed her icy blue eyes and came closer, whispering, "She denied her heritage, too."

Phoebe spat, wetting Hester's altered face. In response, Hester slapped Phoebe's cheek, following through with her arm. Phoebe shrieked from the pain but did not flinch from her great-aunt. Her anger was too strong. The memories of her mother's suffering flooded her, blinded her to any danger. Thoughts of murdering Hester came to the surface, primarily those of strangulation.

"Stop! Hester, please stop this and let us go," Holgrave shouted. "No purpose can be served by keeping us or killing us."

Hester turned to Holgrave and tried to tell him to be silent, but pressure against her throat prevented it. Hester forced a cough, cleared her throat, and tried again. Her voice failed her, and it felt like thumbs were digging into her neck. She found Phoebe's eyes, hateful, wide, and intensely focused on her throat, and knew what to do.

Hester lifted her left hand, sweeping it in a backhanded slapping motion.

Phoebe cried out in surprise as her head was struck. She had seen and comprehended the motion Hester had made, but she was standing too far away to have made contact.

In that moment, Phoebe put it together. Hester's cough coincided with her visions of strangling the miserable old hag, and she had struck back to break her concentration. In a heartbeat, Phoebe regained her will and brought an even more violent image to mind.

Hester turned to Glendarah. "We must get started qui—" She was struck in the side, hard, and the impact of the attack interrupted her speech. It was big, like a man's fist, and for Phoebe's second attempt on her, it was surprisingly well delivered.

Glendarah surmised what had happened and summoned her power, focusing it into her right hand. A white glow appeared there, erupting from the tips of her fingers and culminating into fiery tendrils of white. She then raised her hand and thrust it out, looking like a baseball player throwing a ball.

The brilliant white light flew from Glendarah's palm and struck Phoebe's bound body, encapsulating it briefly. Phoebe cried out once again, though this time the assault was much more intense. Her entire body felt like it had taken an impact and an electrical shock at the same time. The shock lasted a few moments, leaving behind a metallic taste in her mouth so strong she became nauseated.

The feeling was intense enough to ruin Phoebe's concentration on Hester, and her assault ended for the time being. She was certain that she was going to lose her dinner, not that it would matter soon. If anything, she wanted it over with and tried to let herself regurgitate, but nothing came up, and she couldn't make the feeling pass.

What was I just doing? Something about Hester and mom.

"Phoebe! Are you all right?" Holgrave called to her.

Bleary-eyed, Phoebe put great effort into lifting her head and turning it toward the familiar voice. A handsome man with dark hair and a well-trimmed beard was there next to her, bound as she was.

"Oh, hi," Phoebe said. At least, she thought she said it. The attempt was made, but she didn't hear herself speak. *What the hell happened here?*

Glendarah, having dealt with Phoebe, turned to Hester. "Are you all right, my love?"

Hester nodded and put her hand on the place Phoebe had struck, her ribs on the left side. "Good thing she doesn't realize what she's capable of," she whispered.

"Let's finish this before she does," Glendarah urged. "The witching hour passes soon."

Hester gave her another nod. "Release the raven, and call forth our High Priest."

Glendarah moved swiftly, her heels clicking along the cement as she went to the birdcage. She pulled off the black fabric cover, revealing the big raven, who eyed Glendarah not with animal-like trepidation but with expectation.

"Dzolali," said Glendarah, who noticed her standing motionless. She felt a storm of emotions in the young witch's mind and saw that she was staring at Phoebe. "Dzolali! Help me with the cage! Now!"

Dzolali snapped out of it and joined Glendarah at the cage, releasing the clamps that kept the floor connected to the wire top. Together, they pulled the top of the cage over the raven's head, freeing him.

"Ugly-ass bird," Phoebe mumbled. Slowly, her memory was returning. She stared at Hester, remembering that she was angry at her for something.

"Phoebe," the man at her right, Holgrave was his name, called again.

She looked at him, noting his expression of concern. Phoebe blinked and turned to the witches. She focused on the redhead, and more memories poured back into place. The memories of passion, muddled by her bewitching, stirred more feelings and visions. As they did, Phoebe's anger accompanied them.

"I'm all right, Holgrave," she said firmly.

Hester gestured to the body of Ned Onenspek, using both hands. His corpse was dragged along by her unseen grasp, leaving his blood upon the concrete in streaks. The limp body slid along as it gained momentum and tumbled into the hole Holgrave dug. Onenspek's feet were left visible, sticking out above the surface of the floor. His black shoes were shiny loafers and his socks argyle. His trouser legs had slid up with the help of gravity, revealing his hairy, pasty white legs.

Phoebe, who normally would find this sight funny if it were not for the circumstances, looked away.

Hester put her hands together, palms out, thumbs and forefingers touching at the tips, and gave a pushing motion. The blood bubbled and moved toward Holgrave's hole, now Onenspek's tomb. As if the foundation of the House of the Seven Gables itself had tilted, the blood ran into the hole. Much of it was coagulated, and fully staining the off-white cement, but it would have to do.

Hester spread the large round black rug over the area, its white pentagram design face up. Dzolali and Glendarah moved to the rear of the basement staircase and returned with a large version of the statue of Ba'al that Phoebe had seen in the living room on the mantle. It was identical other than its size. The two witches placed it near the pentagram rug and retrieved candles from the area behind the stairs. They set them all around Ba'al, who had been placed facing the captives, and lit them.

"Ladies," Hester called and stepped to the edge of the rug, their captives to her right and in her view. Glendarah took Hester's left hand, Dzolali her right. Glendarah took Dzolali's hand, completing the circle. They bowed their heads in the direction of the statue. "Spirit of Ba'al, pray thee watch over our coven this hour."

"So mote it be," Glendarah and Dzolali said in unison.

Phoebe noticed a trail of black smoke gathering around the raven, who had not left his perch though the cage had been freed from the base. The cloud first encircled the bird's feet, then curled around them like a long snake, which continued coiling around and around, working its way up.

The circle of witches watched as the blackness formed from nowhere and maintained its proximity to the raven's perch.

Phoebe stole a glance at Holgrave, who watched tight-lipped and grim. Though the man had eluded her powers of perception, she had not attributed it to anything other than her own inexperience with the gift. Now, however, having flexed the muscles, she decided that there was much more to this Holgrave Maule.

Phoebe and Holgrave watched as the black envelope of smoke thickened to the appearance of a heavy curtain. It stretched from the floor to the ceiling and simply stayed there, strangely in motion but contained.

The three witches shared glances, clearly gleeful in anticipation of what was to happen next. Phoebe, though no fan of birds, felt a touch of concern for the creature, for the blackness that had appeared around it was so thick that she felt that it would surely die from inhaling it. Even though the black smoke remained on the other end of the basement, Phoebe took in the aroma of a multitude of things burning.

Phoebe coughed and felt her nausea return. Oddly, the witches had no trouble breathing. Hester laughed with a sort of triumph and clapped as the smoke bent into another form, that of a very tall man wearing a black robe with a hood covering his head. The bird was gone, the perch pinned beneath the newcomer's bare feet.

"Hail, High Priest Panas!" Hester called and bowed. The others did the same.

What in the hell just happened? Phoebe thought and found from Holgrave's expression that his thoughts were on a similar path.

The hooded man stepped from the birdcage's base and into the pentagram. All in the coven had their eyes on him as he came forward, as if waiting for acknowledgement.

Phoebe stared into the shadow cast by the hood. What she could see of the face was covered in black hair, kept short but unkempt. The whiskers skewed in every direction, and the lips set beneath the mustache were thick and pink, and what she could see of the nose was plank-like along the bone. The nostrils were flared and round. The man the witches called Panas stepped up to Phoebe in three strides. He stood before her, paying no attention to Holgrave.

Phoebe cranked her chin up to meet his eyes, though all she could perceive was a faint glimmer beneath the hood. He seemed to see right through her, and Phoebe could feel the presence, feel it as sure as one could sense a passing pedestrian by the faint breeze felt on the skin.

"She meets my gaze," said Panas. His voice, deep and effortlessly penetrating, vibrated the air in Phoebe's proximity. His exhale was unpleasantly warm, and the scent upon it was foul.

"Dude. *Mint*," Phoebe commented through a grimace, though she did not look away.

Hester arrived at Panas's right, her expression stern. "Do not look upon Panas, and watch your tongue."

"Oh, bite me, Auntie Hester," Phoebe spat back. She shifted her eyes to Hester just long enough to say her piece, then returned to the stare down with Panas.

Panas grinned, revealing rotting teeth. There was little whiteness to be seen in between the stains of red, brown, and black.

Hester rose her tightly clenched fist and shook it. Phoebe felt a tightening in her stomach, powerful and painful. She let out a brief cry, and her partially digested dinner did finally erupt, flowing weakly over her lips and down her chin.

Holgrave was about to protest, but Panas raised his index finger. Holgrave's mouth worked, but no sound came out. Holgrave was silenced, left in awe of the coven's high priest, whose eyes could not perceive his bound figure with the hood so far forward over his head.

Phoebe coughed and gagged, writhing against the tight restraints.

"Cease," Panas commanded, and Hester unclenched her fingers.

Phoebe sucked in oxygen with a harsh rasp and shot her great-aunt an intensely hateful glare. Hester smiled and flicked two fingers, which resulted in a twinge of pain in Phoebe's innards. The younger Pyncheon gasped but did not look away.

"Enough!" shouted Panas.

Hester dropped her hand immediately and the grin died on her lips.

Panas reached to his hood with both hands. The flesh among them was wrinkled like dried tobacco leaves. The nails were long, discolored, and appeared sharp. He pushed his hood back, revealing his face to all.

"Matthew," uttered Holgrave, shocked. "*Matthew* Maule!"

22

Panas

Panas shifted his golden eyes to Holgrave for the first time. The eyes, like two embers amongst earthen ash, were sunken into the grayish brown flesh. His eyebrows were thick, long, and as black as the rest of his facial hair. Together with his pronounced brow, they remained shaded from the lights overhead.

"Do *not* speak that name!" protested Hester, becoming shrill. She thought a moment. "How do you even come to know it?"

Panas answered for their captive. "He should, Hester. He is *Holgrave* Maule."

Hester turned to the high priest of her coven, appalled. "And you knew this? You knew this and never spoke of it?"

Panas turned his glimmering eyes upon Hester. The gesture shut down any further conversation. She cast her eyes to the floor and stepped back.

Phoebe recovered her breath and much of her composure. She took in the features of the man Holgrave had called Matthew Maule and compared the two men. There was no resemblance whatsoever.

Panas stepped slowly around Phoebe, looking her up and down. "Short for a Pyncheon," he commented.

Ugly for a Maule, Phoebe wisely chose to keep in thought.

Panas laughed. The sound was animal-like, thunderous, and painful to the eardrum. It was his response to her thought, and there was no doubt.

Fuck. Phoebe rolled her eyes, wondering how she could keep a thought to herself.

"My niece chose her mate poorly," Hester offered as some excuse.

Panas smiled. The high priest was in her head, reading her as clearly as headlines on a newspaper. His hand reached for Phoebe's mane and lifted it away from her neck. She grimaced in disgust at his cold, slimy touch.

"She does bear the mark," Panas commented. "I thought as much."

Phoebe passed her eyes over the coven. Their eyes showed intense interest, though Dzolali's gaze held a hint of sorrow. Phoebe looked away quickly, not wanting to form a thought that could be read.

Panas returned to Phoebe's view and looked into her face. "And there's no way, young one, that you can be persuaded to join my Hester's coven? To take your rightful place as a Pyncheon woman?"

Phoebe thought to scramble her words, filling her mind with images of her past life. The apartment, her job, former boyfriends, her stupid car, places she had wanted to visit before she died. Anything at all.

"Try as one might," Panas replied to Phoebe's attempt, "your answer is given. And it is a shame to waste one with so much potential. So it was with your mother."

His statement cemented the visions Phoebe had gleaned from Hester, and her rage built ever more.

"She's not our last chance," Hester said reverently.

What? What the fuck does she mean by that? Phoebe's mind screamed clearly.

Panas smiled. It was an ugly sight. "True enough, High Priestess."

Phoebe shifted her eyes back and forth between Hester and Panas. There was no answer to her question coming.

"Do not fear, Phoebe Pyncheon," Panas said instead, though not in a way that would prevent that very emotion. "You will not be completely wasted." He turned to Hester. "It was the spirit of Alice Pyncheon that joined with this one on the night of your séance. It is time we disposed of her with finality."

To Phoebe, Hester appeared to go whiter around the cheeks. "As you wish it, High Priest."

Panas bent to pick up the skull Holgrave had retrieved from the hole that Ned Onenspek now occupied. He held it high, as if admiring Alice's bone structure, and set it down in the middle of the pentagram. The coven again formed a circle and joined hands.

It was Panas that led the chant, "Ba'al, hear my plea. We call upon the spirit of Alice Pyncheon. Bring her forth, Ba'al, to stand bound in our circle." He repeated this twice while the rest of the coven remained quiet, bowed.

Phoebe gasped as the floor of the basement changed. The off-white, chalky surface of the cement faded away, darkening to a blue that was almost black. Strewn throughout the surface, she could see faint shapes that she at first could not identify. Slowly, they came into focus, and if she had not been so bound, she would have leaped from the floor. All around them were the ghostly forms of the dead, the buried victims of the Pyncheon family, as they had been interred.

Phoebe and Holgrave were transfixed as the dead squirmed and writhed in their graves, as if trying to dig their way to the surface. A white glow above the ground came into view, and they saw, standing in the pentagram, the ghost of Alice Pyncheon, her feet hovering over her own skull. She appeared as she had during her possession of Phoebe, prior to her throat slashing: alive, sad, but otherwise in health. Her long black hair draped around her face, and her white gown was clean and flowing. She stood staring at nothingness in the distance beyond Phoebe and Holgrave, utterly still.

"Alice Pyncheon," Panas addressed in a full authoritarian voice, "I release your spirit from your servitude of this coven. Ba'al, I pray thee make it so and dismiss this spirit from our house!"

"So mote it be," the witches chanted.

Alice Pyncheon's ghost grew faint, and her figure drooped as if doused with a deluge.

"No," whispered Phoebe.

"Be gone from here forever, Alice Pyncheon!" Panas commanded.

At that, Alice disappeared from the circle. The blueish black ground where the wraiths churned and wriggled faded away as well, leaving only the cement floor.

"It is done," declared Panas. He and the coven released one another's hands and left the circle. His face was passive, even bordering on boredom as he stepped past Phoebe without meeting her eyes. Once alongside her, he turned and bid Dzolali to come forward. "The blade," he said and pointed to Hester.

Dzolali bit her lip and hesitated. Her watery-eyed gaze searched Phoebe's face.

"Please, no," Phoebe whispered as tears tumbled down her face.

Dzolali sniffed and mouthed the words, "I'm sorry. I love you."

"Dzolali!" Panas shouted. His powerfully deep voice pained the ears as he turned to the young witch.

Dzolali nodded briefly and drew the long, curved knife, the one she had used to dispatch Onenspek. Stepping forward, she presented it to Hester, who took it in hand. Hester, in trade, gave Dzolali the bowl of Harriet Pyncheon.

Phoebe's eyes settled on the bronze bowl, seeing once again the familiar symbol upon its side. The same symbol she now wore around her neck that formally belonged to Alice.

Oh, Alice. I'm so sorry. Alice, I wish you could help us now! Phoebe cried out in thought.

Panas gave a chuckle.

Phoebe stared at the high priest. Sheer terror covered her being in that moment, and she thought of pleading for mercy, begging to join the coven, but the image of herself came again, that image of Phoebe, the high priestess witch of the House of the Seven Gables, flying over

White Lake and reigning fire and death upon its buildings and people. She shut her eyes tight and tears streamed again.

Holgrave said something, but Phoebe did not turn her focus to him other than to acknowledge his words as pleas for her salvation, not his own.

Phoebe, Alice called to her, sounding far away. Phoebe you must summon us forth!

With her vision distorted with tears, Phoebe peered at Panas. He did not hear Alice. She looked to Hester, then Dzolali, who had come near, holding the bowl close to Phoebe's right breast. Phoebe saw Panas move behind her and out of sight.

How? Phoebe thought to Alice Pyncheon.

With all your will. All your might, was Alice's answer. Only together can we fight the power of the coven.

I thought Panas destroyed you!

One cannot kill what is already dead. Call us, now, Phoebe! Alice urged.

Hester, blade in hand, moved around Dzolali. Glendarah came closer, watching Phoebe's face with a delight that made Phoebe envision her bludgeoning.

Phoebe's mind raced, trying to decipher what Alice had meant, then with panic boiling over into sheer terror, she took a deep inhale and cried, "Alice Pyncheon! I call upon your spirit! Alice Pyn—"

Panas yanked Phoebe's hair, thrusting her head back and exposing her throat.

"No! Please!" Holgrave screamed.

"Alice Pyncheon! I call upon you!" Phoebe yelled, close to emptying her lungs. "I call upon you, spirit of Alice Pyncheon! Spirits of this house, I call upon you all!"

The cold blade touched her skin as a great rumbling at her feet began. The vibrations of it traveled up her legs and through her entrapped body.

"What?" Hester said from behind her, but it was quickly squelched.

The rumbling became a roar, and the basement floor and walls shook with a sudden violence.

Phoebe strained against the grip of Panas to look about. Glendarah's smugness was gone. She looked about the walls and floor, her arms out to her sides as if to keep balance. Dzolali struggled to keep the bowl level, and she, too, scanned the walls for an answer.

The light fixtures began to vibrate. One bulb burst, showering the floor with white shards. The roar increased to an ear-piercing thrum, and Phoebe shut her eyes.

Dzolali screamed. A chorus of voices then joined the earthquake's rumble. The thin wood panels cracked, and some of them fell away to the floor. The industrial-grade washing machines swayed, cracking the cement as their feet crashed back to the surface. The door of the washing machine swung open, then slammed shut again.

The floor once again turned dark, like a field of dirt in the dead of night. The spirits wrestled with the trappings of their graves, but they sprung free, and like passengers aboard an elevator, they surfaced in pairs, trios, and quadruples. Transparent figures began to walk the floors among the living, menace on their decayed faces. Others floated above her, flying like angels with their arms spread wide and their mouths open as they bellowed.

The walls and ceiling of the basement evaporated into nothingness, revealing a vast, dead land. Dead trees of bare branches and the brown dirt of the land stretched beyond the house's structure. It was again that land of the dead, the land that had appeared to Phoebe when Alice had possessed her that second time. The light above was no longer electric neon but of the stars and the moon.

The spirits swooped all around Glendarah, and she shrieked, warding them off with her clawed hands. In her right, a ball of energy formed, but quickly fizzled. Two on foot attacked her directly, decayed men in the ancient suits they were wearing when they were murdered. Glendarah howled madly and was thrust into the air. When she landed a short distance away, a group of angry spirits descended upon her.

Dzolali swung the bowl in her defense, but it had no effect on the ghostly figure that dove onto her. Its long, flowing white hair and gown identified the wraith as a female, and it took Dzolali's throat in its skeletal grip. Spinning violently, it took Dzolali with it, flinging the defenseless young witch in another direction.

The earthquake shook on with Phoebe and Holgrave in their places, the ropes held to the now invisible beam and spikes.

From behind Phoebe, Hester screamed, a long, high-pitched wail of torturous terror. Phoebe shut her eyes, even though there was no chance for her to see the horrors unfolding. She listened for the voice of Panas, but he said nothing. Instead, his grip on Phoebe's hair simply ceased.

Phoebe kept her eyelids clenched and hung her head, wishing to see no more. Holgrave was quiet, and despite her concern for him, she knew the vengeful ghosts would do him no harm.

All about her, the spirits called and bellowed, chilling her blood and sending her body atremble. A call reminiscent of a rebel yell sounded directly in front of her, and Phoebe snapped her head up, eyes open.

It was Glendarah, bloodied, beaten, and in her current, aged form. Her dress was in shreds and her gray-blonde hair in shambles. She produced a blade of her own, a small but wide dagger, and had it raised above her head as she charged Phoebe. Her face twisted into a murderous grimace.

"Alice!" Phoebe screamed. "Guys! A little help!" She twisted and bucked in her entrapment, but the rope, though now weakened, held firm.

Glendarah's pace was not what it once was. Her embattlement had done injury to her right leg. Nonetheless, she was almost upon Phoebe when she was descended upon by a fast-moving, glowing spirit. Perhaps it was Alice Pyncheon herself, but the attack was too swift to see. Glendarah's clothes and hair flailed about in the brief struggle, and when it was done, the witch dropped to the ground, covered in blood and unmoving.

Her dagger had found a home in her own chest.

An image of Glendarah, almost like one of Holgrave's negatives from his black-and-white film, left the body and rose into the air. Glendarah was looking up, her hair flowing to a strong wind, her face expressionless. Her arms were out to her sides, palms up, as if checking for rain. Her rise halted abruptly, and the specter of Glendarah turned her face downward to see what was wrong.

Phoebe found that Glendarah's form had been seized by the feet by two great hands. Larger than life and looking big enough to have grabbed her by the waist, they held on. A head, shoulders, and arms belonging to the hands came from the ghostly ground. Phoebe presumed it to be a demon, with a hideously gnarled face, tightened into a stern frown. On top of its bald head were two horns, much like the goat-horn charm she had seen around the witches' necks.

The demon snarled deeply, loud enough to be heard over the cries and howls of the freed spirits and the earthquake's thunderous crashing. Glendarah screamed, higher in pitch than seemed humanly possible, as the horned monstrosity pulled her downward. In a flash, Glendarah's spirit was taken from their sight, sinking into the ground from which the Pyncheon victims had arisen.

Phoebe blinked hard, trying to comprehend all she was seeing. *Was that the devil? Just a demon? Did he just take Glendarah to hell?*

Movement to Phoebe's left caught her eyes, and there Dzolali crawled weakly in her direction, a trio of ghosts ripping into her back and legs with their claws or skeletonized fingers. Another tore at her head, ripping away her once beautiful hair. Dzolali looked to Phoebe and reached out her hand, as if pleading for mercy. She collapsed, dropped her face to the ground, and became still. The spirits moved on from their task. Those on foot sauntered away, aimlessly, perhaps cheerfully, as they might have in life on a casual stroll through the woods. Others, airborne, floated away, upward, and soon headed out of sight.

Just as with Glendarah, the ghost of Dzolali left her earthly flesh.

She did not expect to rise, however. Her hair stretched into a fan of strands to the unseen wind, and she kept her hands to her sides. Her form left the dirt but steadied seemingly by itself, and in the demon's grip, Dzolali cranked up her leg and made a stomping motion. Dzolali became a demon of her own, her face contorted into a hateful, monstrous mass of frown and fangs, and as her future caretaker came up to insist on her capture she fought with her claws out.

She kicked and swatted, but her strikes were ineffective. The demon took her ghostly form in both hands and flung her down through the dirt. She was gone, and he, the demon or the devil, followed.

Alice herself flew into Phoebe's view, radiant with light and warmth. She came close to her and reached above her. Phoebe cast her eyes where the ceiling had returned and saw the railroad spike that kept her in place slide out of the beam. It fell away to the cement floor with a clang. Alice moved to Holgrave and did the same.

The ropes binding them undid themselves, dissolving into the nothingness from which Glendarah had conjured them. They were free.

The vision of Alice Pyncheon smiled and winked out of existence. The trembling at Phoebe's feet ebbed away, and the rumbling silenced. The dead lands faded away, allowing the walls of the House of the Seven Gables to return. Many of the light fixtures had failed, with a few more of the tubular bulbs having come free to shatter upon the floor. More of the wood panels had broken and lay in splinters.

Phoebe whispered, "Thank you, thank you, thank you." Phoebe turned to Holgrave and saw his eyes cast downward. From his expression, she knew that he had found her great-aunt Hester lying on the floor.

Dzolali was lying sprawled in front of the staircase, face down and covered in blood. Glendarah's remains were upon the pentagram rug, staining the black-and-white fabrics with red. Phoebe turned and found Hester, quite dead and in a sitting position against the wall, bearing many scrapes and cuts along her face and body. Her black dress was mostly missing, torn away in strips. The sacrificial blade that she had intended to use on Phoebe had been plunged into her chest. Hester had returned to her aged self, and her eyes had been gouged out.

"Oh, my God," Phoebe groaned and looked away, covering her mouth with her hands.

Holgrave rubbed his wrists and stared about the room, wide-eyed. He had never seen so much gore and death in his life, and it struck him dumb.

Phoebe had had enough of the basement, and though she wanted to sprint up the steps, hop in her car and never stop, she could not. Dzolali's corpse was in the way.

Dzolali's arm was outstretched, pointing to where Phoebe had been bound. Phoebe closed her eyes but kept seeing Dzolali's agonized face begging for help—or perhaps bidding a goodbye, she'd never know.

Phoebe tore her eyes away from Dzolali's remains and stepped over the body, onto the first step and upward, concentrating on one step at a time. She heard Holgrave following.

Phoebe didn't stop walking until she was through the front door and down the porch steps. The soft dirt of Gable Way was a comfort, as was the cool air of predawn. The continued silence of the area was no comfort, however. She expected more change to come from such an impossible scene.

Phoebe turned around and found Holgrave standing close, a look of concern on his face. She looked past him at the house. The lights were on throughout the hallways, she knew well from experience, but in the growing dawn, the only visible evidence of the practice was on the first floor. The windows of the living room glowed faintly yellow. It was brighter through the screen door.

Nonetheless, Phoebe's world had completely changed, and for all time. Hester was gone. The lovely and dangerous Dzolali was gone. As was the witch, Glendarah, and the poor artist, Onenspek.

"Oh, my God," she said to Holgrave, returning to the verge of tears. "Panas. Where did that freakshow go?"

"I've no idea."

"Wait," Phoebe said, recalling the encounter. "You knew him. Called him 'Maule.'"

"Yes," Holgrave answered. "Matthew, to be exact. But it cannot be. Matthew Maule was my great-great-grandfather. I know him only from old daguerreotype pictures of him. Long dead."

"So, whoever that is, he's still in there," she surmised and looked to the house's windows once again.

"Perhaps," Holgrave said. "But I don't think so."

"What'll we do now?"

Holgrave thought this over for a moment, then took her by the shoulders and looked her in the eye. "I have an idea, but we need to be 'on the same page,' as you Yanks say."

23

Erasing the Night

It was Holgrave who volunteered to go inside and call the police, using the phone in the parlor. He watched Phoebe from the window and kept his concentration on the sounds in the house. The conversation was short, and he was assured that units were on the way.

Holgrave hung up the phone and was still for a moment, listening before he ventured out of the room. He turned to the front door, and as he pushed through the screen door, a squawk sounded, and from quite near.

Holgrave froze, and he felt the blood run from his face, leaving it cold in the dewy morning air. He spun around, and as he did, the squawk rang out again just before the screen door clacked shut.

There was no one there.

Holgrave took a deep breath and rolled his eyes as he exhaled in a cheek-puffing whoosh. He turned back to the door with an eyebrow arched. Beyond it, he could see Phoebe, who shrugged and put her palms out to her sides as if to ask, 'What?'

With his index finger, Holgrave pressed against the screen door again, slowly. The springs screeched and creaked. "Idiot," he admonished himself and left the porch.

By the time he rejoined Phoebe, they could hear the roar of motors in the distance. At such an hour, the night sky gave only a hint of the coming sunrise. A blip of a siren sounded in the distance, signaling a cruiser crossing a major intersection, and then only the call of winding motors remained as the cars came closer.

Phoebe and Holgrave watched the red and blue lights dance through the trees. Tires ruffled over the dirt of Gable Way, and the first of the police cruisers slid around the last bend, bathing them in lights.

"All right," Holgrave said to her. "Steady on."

Phoebe didn't react, though she heard him. *We'll see how this goes.*

"Miss Pyncheon," Detective Sergeant Arman Khalid said, "I know this is going to be a frustrating process, but it is a necessary one. I need to go through your activities of this morning once again."

Phoebe, Holgrave, the detective, and two uniformed White Lake officers were with them in the kitchen. Khalid, Phoebe, and Holgrave were perched on the stools around the wood-topped island, and the two uniforms stood near the kitchen door, which they had propped open. The house was the focus of the White Lake Police Department, and officers and detectives, forensic men and women, trafficked in and out of the home.

Phoebe looked into the man's mahogany eyes. "I understand. Whatever you need." She wiped her tears, still flowing, honest ones, born of the stress, fright, and the loss of a family member, though not a loved one.

"You say you awoke, and it was still quite dark. Why is it you opened your laptop again?" The detective spoke reverently but succinctly, his eyes never wavering from her face.

"I didn't get around to buying a clock from town. I haven't even been here a week," Phoebe explained, adding that small detail this time around. "No cellphone, either. My laptop's time was close to accurate, so I use that to check the time."

"And that time was?" Khalid led. He had written it down from her previous answer.

"About four forty-five," she said and shrugged.

"And then you dressed and went to the first floor, here to the kitchen," he led on.

Phoebe nodded and sniffled. "I was going to make coffee."

"Then you heard the sound from the basement," Khalid continued.

"I opened the door and the lights were on," she went on. "And that's when I went down a few steps and found Dzolali."

"And you say you went no further," Detective Khalid went on after checking his notes.

"I freaked and ran back upstairs. I couldn't find Auntie Hester, or Glendarah, or Mr. Onenspek," Phoebe repeated the story, but this time her voice cracked. She thought of Ned Onenspek as just another victim of the Pyncheon family, and as a Pyncheon, she was ashamed and felt pity for the exploited artist.

Khalid pressed on. "And that's when you ran up to waken Mr. Maule."

"Yes." She picked up her coffee, now cold, but took a long drink anyway.

Detective Khalid shifted his eyes to Holgrave, a signal for him to tell his story once more.

"I dressed quickly and followed Miss Pyncheon downstairs," said Holgrave. "As she said, the lights were on, and I found Miss Alameda at the bottom of the stairs. I looked about and found the whole horrible scene. I came right up and phoned for help."

"And you heard nothing at all," the detective said, almost hinting that Holgrave should have.

"Nothing at all," Holgrave assured him. "The attic suite is quite isolated."

Detective Khalid nodded, keeping his face passive.

Another uniformed officer, this one with sergeant stripes on his

sleeves, stepped into the kitchen. "Detective Khalid, Baker needs
to see you."

"Okay," Khalid said and stepped from the stool. "Sit tight. Be right
back," he said to Pyncheon and Maule.

Phoebe gave a curt bob of her head. She peered at Holgrave, who
gave a weak, sympathetic smile and patted her shoulder.

*I wonder if the cop suspects us somehow, though how could they think
it was us?* Phoebe pondered and sighed deeply. *What if we're arrested?
Do I even care? Am I the Pyncheon that pays for the crimes of the family?*

Khalid arrived at the basement door just as the coroner's people were
carting up the first body, zipped up in the shiny black plastic bag
strapped to the medical gurney. He watched them arrive on the first
floor, drop and lock the gurney's wheels, and cart Dzolali Alameda's
body through the front door.

Khalid checked his shoe covers and was about to head down the
stairs when he saw Baker coming up. She removed her facemask and
held up her hand. Knowing her well, Arman knew not to proceed below.

"It's a horror show down there," Baker said. The petite, curly-haired
blonde removed her gloves and shook her head.

"What's it look like?" asked Khalid.

"Each victim died a little differently." Baker jerked her thumb in
the direction of the front door. "Alameda was beaten before being
clawed to death."

"Like the Hillsborough attack?"

Patty Baker wiped her sweaty forehead with the back of her bare
hand. "Hard to say until I get some chunks of her under the micro-
scope, but it could have been an animal. Onenspek was stabbed in the
back. We have the murder weapon—"

"Great," Arman Khalid interjected.

"—found in the chest of victim number two, the D'Amitri woman,"
Baker finished and grinned crookedly.

Khalid frowned and crossed his arms. "Okay."

"D'Amitri's body showed a lot of slices and dices, too, similar to those on Alameda," Patty continued as she leaned against the doorjamb. "The owner of the place, Hester Pyncheon, was the worst of it. Her eyes were scooped out. Looks like a rough tool was used, maybe more claws, dunno yet. She was stabbed in the chest like D'Amitri."

"Did you find them?"

"Nope." Baker grinned darkly and put her fists on her hips.

"Here's the crucial bit," the detective sergeant said. "What's the time of death?"

"They're all still pretty damn warm," Baker explained. "No more than an hour to an hour and a half ago. They all died within moments of each other."

"And these two," Khalid indicated the pair he was questioning in the kitchen, "would still be scrubbing the evidence away."

"Oh, yeah," confirmed Baker. "We'll have fingerprints processed pretty quick. DNA'll take a few days, but I'd say there's no way in hell your two suspects had anything to do with it. They'd be covered in people-goo."

"Nice," Khalid said and chuckled. "Did I hear someone say there's a laundry chute leading to a bin down there?"

"I sifted through it myself. There's no blood on any article I can find," she said.

"Okay. Thanks, Baker."

Arman Khalid thought a moment and decided to check a few things. He found the staircase and made his way to the second floor, where Phoebe Pyncheon had said her room was located, the southeastern turret. He found it quickly and went in after pulling on his latex gloves.

The detective pulled out his cellphone and began to take pictures of the room. He saw no evidence of blood on the furniture or the doorknob. He opened the drawers of the dresser and saw that she owned few clothes, other than a handful of ancient-looking costumes in the closet. All were clean.

Pyncheon's car keys were in the pocket of her hoodie, draped over the wooden chair. He found her laptop, opened it, and turned it on. It was not even protected by a password. He opened her email, but as there was no link to the outside world, all he could see were old messages from a week before. The computer's history showed only access to a novel she was writing.

Khalid closed the laptop and left the room. He walked to the bathroom two doors up from the turret and looked around. There was no blood anywhere. Not in the drain of the shower or in the sink. The hand towels were damp from use, but otherwise spotless.

The detective went up to the third floor and explored. He found the master bedroom that Phoebe Pyncheon had mentioned. Other than it being oddly decorated, with strange statues and candles lying everywhere, there seemed nothing particularly out of place. The bed had not been slept in.

He wandered by the rooms that Phoebe had indicated had been occupied by the artist, Onenspek. He opened the first door, the bedroom, and stepped in. That bed appeared to have not been used, either.

Khalid went next door, into the studio. The images that the man had painted were disturbing, but very well done, in his uneducated opinion. The detail was nicely depicted, and the scenes truly horrifying. Stepping further inside, Khalid took a mass of pictures with his phone, then left.

Finding Holgrave's attic suite was a little more difficult, but when he poked his head inside, he found nothing unusual. He backed out and shut the door, then something occurred to him. Khalid turned and went back into Holgrave's room.

The bed was made.

Like the rooms of the other victims, Hester Pyncheon and Ned Onenspek, Maule's bed had not been slept in. Phoebe Pyncheon's bed was made as well, as he recalled.

Arman Khalid went from door to door at that point, checking to see which rooms had been occupied by D'Amitri and Alameda. He came to the conclusion that they, Alameda and D'Amitri, had occupied the third-floor bedrooms of both turrets of 666 Gable Way, and like everyone else's, the beds had the appearance of not being slept in.

The detective headed back down to the first floor, noting to himself how loud the steps creaked, as did the floorboards, for that matter. He walked back into the kitchen as another of the deceased was rolled through the front door.

Saying nothing, Khalid gave Holgrave and Pyncheon a long look, remaining expressionless. He sat upon the stool and took a moment before speaking.

Holgrave lifted an eyebrow, and he looked to Phoebe and back. "Something amiss, Detective?" he asked.

"I just came down from upstairs, and everyone's beds are made," Khalid said flatly.

Holgrave didn't hesitate in answering. "I made mine this morning."

Khalid looked to Phoebe, cueing her turn.

"I made mine, too," she said. "I do that every morning when I get up."

Arman Khalid pointed to Holgrave. "You said Miss Pyncheon came running into your room this morning to get you."

Holgrave shrugged and adopted a confused expression. "Yes. She did."

"He was already awake, Detective Khalid," Phoebe inserted before the man had a chance to follow up. "I never said I woke him up. I said I went up to wake him."

"I had just finished making my bed and was about to dress when Miss Pyncheon came in," Holgrave filled in.

Khalid nodded. Something wasn't right, but he didn't know what. In any case, considering what the forensic detective had told him, these two people hadn't had a hand in the actual crime. Khalid suspected, and strongly so, that they were involved somehow, but the investigation was young.

The detective smiled and slapped his palms on the kitchen island. "Okay!" He stood from the stool and wandered to the door to see the coroner's people coming back. There was at least one more stiff to haul away.

"The basement is a crime scene," he told them. "It's off limits to you. In fact, I'd recommend getting a room in town."

"Sure. Can I go up and get my stuff?" asked Phoebe

Khalid caught the eye of the uniform next to him. "Officer Matheson will go with you."

Phoebe got up and headed out, and the officer followed.

"I'll go with you, Mr. Maule," Khalid said and dismissed the remaining policeman.

Holgrave headed up, with Khalid just behind. Once they arrived on the third floor, Khalid called for Holgrave to stop. They were right outside the master bedroom, and Khalid opened the door.

"What was going on in this house, Mr. Maule?" the detective asked. He waved his arm over the room. It settled upon the statue of Hecate, another of Ba'al, and all the candles strewn throughout the room. "What were you people into?"

"Oh, no!" Holgrave protested. "I'm just a boarder, Detective. Ms. Pyncheon, Hester, that is, was an eccentric and fancied herself a wiccan. The same can be said for Ms. Alameda and Ms. D'Amitri. They were nothing more than self-proclaimed psychics and fortune tellers. I'm sure they have a reputation in town. They had clients visiting every day while I've been here."

Khalid grunted and pulled the door shut. "Let's go."

Holgrave went up to his room, leaving the door open for the detective. He began packing his clothes, emptying the chest of drawers first. He turned and noticed Detective Khalid inspecting the table, upon which sat his photographs and cameras. Khalid did this without touching, leaning over the table with his hands behind his back.

"I see you've got a thing for this place," said Khalid.

"It is a truly remarkable house, Detective." Holgrave continued packing, though he kept his eye on the policeman.

"Why three cameras, Mr. Maule?" asked the detective.

"I find that traditional film, black-and-white or color, tends to see things that a digital camera cannot. And vice-versa," Holgrave explained. He stepped to the detective's side and sifted through the stack of printed photographs. "I like to take long walks about the property and the forest surrounding it. I take the cameras with me and snap a few as I go. The house, quite naturally, becomes the focal point."

"I see," said Arman Khalid. "Leave those for now. Just take what you need."

"The cameras as well?" Holgrave asked.

"Yes, please," said the detective. "You never know what details might be found on a camera."

Holgrave looked at the detective for a moment, but met only a passive stare that told him nothing. "Certainly," Holgrave reluctantly agreed and went back to packing his clothes.

Phoebe took very little time packing her things. She picked up her backpack and reached for her laptop.

"You'll have to leave that, Ms. Pyncheon," said Officer Matheson.

"Seriously?"

"I'm afraid so. I'm sure it'll be released to you once the detective has it cleared."

Phoebe rolled her eyes but protested no further. She was exhausted, and all she wanted to do was sleep and forget about the horrors she had witnessed in the basement. She wanted to forget it all, though she knew that was too much to ask of her brain. She couldn't even talk about it, for to do so was to deviate from the story, and then she and Holgrave would be suspects for sure.

"It's best to say we weren't down there to begin with," Holgrave had told her when the police were on their way. "How would we explain any of it?"

Phoebe was not a liar, at least not a good one. She was not comfortable in keeping the attempted sacrifice from the police, but Holgrave had been right. They were lucky they hadn't been arrested on the spot and interrogated in isolation, like they do in the movies.

Phoebe sighed and shook her head, clearing the image of herself in a black-and-white movie, with Detective Khalid in a tan overcoat and a black fedora.

"Are you all right, Miss?" asked Matheson. He was a tall, slightly pudgy fellow, balding but still good looking, with sympathetic eyes that she had not noticed before.

"Yes, fine," Phoebe answered. "Just . . . this is all just a nightmare."

"I understand," said Matheson. "Do you have everything?"

"Yeah," answered Phoebe. She had managed to get her belongings into one of the garbage bags. The rest of her clothes were in the laundry bin in the basement, or crime scene, as the police now considered it.

Matheson stood to one side and let her out of the bedroom. Phoebe led him back down to the first floor and out onto the porch. Holgrave was there with his two suitcases, as was Detective Khalid.

"All right," began the detective. "This is the part where I tell you to not leave town." He smiled, but it was lightning quick, gone in a heartbeat. "You're people of interest, not suspects," he told them as he looked from Phoebe to Holgrave and back. "If I thought either of you were capable of having a hand in this, I'd be taking you in for interrogation."

"I understand," said Holgrave.

Phoebe remained quiet but nodded her acquiescence.

"All right," said Khalid. "Get settled at the inn, and I'll be in touch. Expect a call or visit from me or another detective later today."

With that, Phoebe and Holgrave were allowed to leave. Phoebe, too shaken to drive, let alone put up with any of her car's issues, rode into town with Holgrave in his Mercedes. A White Lake Police cruiser followed them.

They checked into separate rooms at the White Lake Inn, a motel near the main route out of town. The inn was old and had been around since Phoebe was a child. Since Phoebe had no money, Holgrave Maule was kind enough to pay for her room, a favor she was most grateful for. She took her key, an actual metal shard with teeth cut into the blade, and unlocked her room's door. She pushed it open and looked inside before stepping in.

The room had a queen-sized bed, a small flat-screen television on top of the dresser, a chair, and a small table with an attached lamp. The main lights were mounted on the wall behind the bed. The walls were white textured stucco.

"Will you be all right?" asked Maule from her left.

She was too exhausted to react from being startled. "Yeah. Just need rest."

"I'll be right here," he said, indicating the room next door.

Phoebe nodded and went inside. She dropped the garbage bag of clothes onto the rose-colored carpet, dragged the thick purple comforter to one side and collapsed onto the bed. She sank into the mattress and the pillow, noting that at least they were a little more comfortable than those at the House of the Seven Gables.

A triangularly folded card sitting on the side table claimed that the White Lake Inn had free Wi-Fi.

"Great, and the cops have my laptop," Phoebe muttered with irony into the pillow. The vision of Dzolali came to her mind, and despair for her lost love, though it had still been new, struck her hard. She wept hard into the pillow until, exhausted, she fell asleep.

Epilogue

Phoebe nervously stepped onto the porch of the House of the Seven Gables. The police had locked it up, and much of their yellow crime scene tape was still fluttering about. Detective Lieutenant Clive Backstrom, who had recovered from his automobile incident, though he depended on a cane to walk, had taken over the still-unsolved murder case from Arman Khalid. Phoebe and Holgrave had been cleared of any crime, but the details of the case had largely been kept from them, and for the most part, out of the media.

Backstrom had shared the opinions from the forensics team with Phoebe and Holgrave: that the murders were a mixture of ingroup conflict. Fingerprints on the weapons belonged to Hester, Glendarah, and Dzolali, with not a trace from Onenspek, Holgrave, or Phoebe. The other wounds, primarily those resembling claws or bites, were theorized as belonging to a bird of prey of some kind, substantiated by the presence of a large birdcage at the scene.

Backstrom had opined that it appeared to be a case of fraud over the profits of Ned Onenspek's artwork. Onenspek had very little money in the bank and just a small amount in cash, while 'Pyncheon Art' registered sales in the hundreds of thousands. An argument had ensued, apparently, resulting in the deaths of the three women and the artist.

Hester Pyncheon had left no will, so it was determined that Phoebe had no motive to be involved with the massacre. Onenspek's family claimed the artwork that was left in the house and the gallery, which was now closed.

Phoebe pondered these things as she looked to the place where Great-Aunt Hester had once kept that awful raven. She stared at the hook from which the cage had been suspended. She recalled the metamorphosis of the ugly black bird into the monstrous man the witches had called Panas and that he had disappeared somehow from the basement. The police had not found anyone in the house, and Phoebe had talked with Holgrave about the possibility that he had been mistaken about the man he had called Matthew Maule. Holgrave insisted that the man, at the very least, bore a strong resemblance to his great-great-grandfather but could not have been Matthew Maule, as he had long been deceased.

Neither the bird nor the man had resurfaced.

Technically, with their possessions returned to them in the weeks following the investigation, Phoebe had no legal rights to be on the property. The house was in probate court, and Phoebe had no intention of claiming the place for herself. If she could get away with it, she'd burn it to the ground.

Holgrave stepped onto the porch. "Are you all right?"

Phoebe snapped herself out of her trance. "Yeah," she said and pulled open the screen door. She unlocked the inner door and they went inside.

The door to the parlor, where Hester, Glendarah, and Dzolali had once committed their fraudulent acts of fortune telling, stood wide open. Phoebe looked inside and noted that someone had discovered the hidden door, for it was open, too. The carpet around the round table was pulled up, so she knew that Hester's electronic tricks had been discovered. The crystal ball was clouded with a fine layer of dust.

With Holgrave standing behind her, reverently, Phoebe moved from the parlor door. Looking up the hallway, she noted that the basement door was not only shut but shut with finality. It was sealed with a clear plastic sheet, and crime scene tape crisscrossed its midsection.

Phoebe turned to see Holgrave saunter into the living room. She followed. While the furniture appeared to have been moved about, everything was there, even the statue of Ba'al on the mantle. The very sight of it brought back memories of the coven's last moments, and she could almost feel the tight bindings of Glendarah's rope on her skin. Phoebe turned from the statue and took a deep breath, to find Holgrave standing near the window, considering the piano set against the east wall. She rubbed her forearms with her hands as if curing a chill.

Phoebe stepped next to him and gave the Price & Teeple upright a long look. Phoebe remembered her mother being so proud of the family heirloom, and she had been quite adept at playing it. Carved from quarter sawn oak, the legs and case of the instrument featured swirls of darker wood within the lighter, creating a tiger stripe effect throughout. Upon the forward legs at each side, an old man's face was carved. They could have been twins, exquisitely shaped into matching expressions of joy or heartfelt contentment. In a direct line above the faces, on the upper half of the antique, gargoyles had been shaped into the front pillars. Their expressions were intimidating, no matter what emotion the artist had been trying to portray. Their wings were spread, though stubby in order to remain sturdy. The upper cover of the piano, the part her mother would swing out partway to hear the hammer strikes and tone more clearly, was decorated with what Phoebe had always thought of as curling grapevines.

Holgrave opened the keyboard cover, revealing the genuine ivory keys. Gently, he tapped a few of them, releasing rich tones of hammer upon strings.

"Needs a bit of a tuning," he commented.

"Never mind that," Phoebe said dismissively. The house was giving her bad vibes too dark to be called 'the creeps.' "Alice said that what you seek is here."

Holgrave arched his eyebrow. In any other circumstances, Phoebe would have considered the gesture endearing. At that moment, however, she just wanted to smack it off his face. Alice Pyncheon had come to her in a dream and given her the message for Holgrave. Now, it was up to him and she hoped he hurried things along.

Reading Phoebe's anxious expression, Holgrave began by opening the top cover and looking inside, using a small penlight to illuminate it. He pulled open the front cover, raising it up high and running the light over the hammers and strings.

"I don't see anything," he said. He lowered the front cover and dropped onto his knees so he could remove the lower cover, which guarded the pedal mechanisms. He passed the light over the area and found nothing that didn't belong there.

Phoebe noted this, too, as she was looking over his shoulder. She sighed and took a step back, crossing her arms in thought.

Holgrave replaced the covers of the piano and stood back. "Are you sure this is where—?"

"Dude," Phoebe said breathily. "Yes, I'm sure."

"All right, all right," Holgrave came back soothingly.

"Sorry," she offered. "This place . . ." She shrugged and looked into his eyes.

"I know."

"She stood right where you are and pointed," Phoebe explained once more and mimicked the gesture as she recalled it. "She said, 'What he seeks is there.'"

Holgrave watched her hand and followed it. He grunted in thought and moved closely to the wall, lighting the area behind the great instrument. "There's a vent!" he declared.

He rose, placed the tiny flashlight in his mouth, and pulled at the corner of the piano. It was immensely heavy, but its wheels did give, and it rolled partly, until the front of it contacted the credenza with a knock.

"Damn." He pushed it back into place and looked over the situation. The credenza couldn't be moved, for the couch was in the way, and the couch needed the coffee table's space.

Without speaking, the two of them worked out the puzzle. Phoebe and Holgrave each took an end to the rectangular table and moved it out into the doorway. Setting it down, they scooted the throw rug to the side, then slid the couch forward. They turned the credenza, making way for the Price & Teeple.

Holgrave pulled again at the piano, turning it to face the windows. The vent was a vertical metal cage, like the others throughout the house, large and meant to exude as much heat from the furnace as possible. Being such, Holgrave had no trouble seeing the area within once he lowered himself to the floor and shined his light in.

"There's something here!" he called in surprise. He lifted himself onto his haunches, gave the vent further scrutiny, and asked, "I don't suppose you have a flathead screwdriver?"

Phoebe twisted her lips at him, an obvious "no." "Wait, I think there's one in a kitchen drawer."

Neither one of them moved. There had been no thought given to wandering further into the house.

Holgrave stood. "Let's stay together," he said and took her hand.

Phoebe, despite her anxiety of having to walk past the basement door, sealed by tape and plastic or not, smiled over his chivalry. She grasped his hand, and briskly, they walked through the hallway to the back of the house, into the kitchen.

It took a mere moment to locate a screwdriver, and they returned to the living room in like fashion. Holgrave went to the floor and began loosening screws.

Phoebe's anxiety swelled and she desperately wished Maule to hurry. Other than the metal-on-metal scrapings Holgrave was making, the house was silent.

But not quite. Phoebe kept utterly still while Holgrave worked, and she could hear it. She swore she could. The house was making that gentle whoosh of air, though this time, she knew the house's windows were shut, at least the ones in the rooms they had been in.

Though the coven's dead, the house lives on, Phoebe thought. A chill traveled throughout her body, and she shivered violently. She wanted to shout at Holgrave, tell him to hurry up, but she bit her tongue. Lashing out would do no good.

She turned to keep her eye on the open door, convinced for a moment that Panas, or Matthew Maule, or someone would come striding in.

"Damn," Holgrave muttered and sat up.

"What?" Phoebe squeaked.

"I peeled the wallpaper away to get at the blasted vent, but the paint underneath is not willing to let go."

"But you're sure you see something in there?" she pressed.

Holgrave nodded and wiped sweat from his brow and forehead. "It looks like a wooden box, as described in my great-grandfather's diary."

Phoebe, driven by the need to separate herself from the House of the Seven Gables once and for all, reached for the heavy lamp on an end table and picked it up. She unscrewed the fastener from the frosted crystal shade and tossed it onto the couch, where it bounced violently enough that it nearly crashed to the floor. She spun the bulb out and chucked it there, too.

"What in the world are you doing?" Holgrave asked, still seated upon the floor.

"Look out," she warned and strode forward, pulling the power plug from the wall behind her.

Phoebe raised the heavy metal lamp over her right shoulder. Holgrave pushed away from the wall, ducking out of the way. The heavy base of the lamp came down, crashing into the wall. The lamp left a crescent-shaped divot, and pieces of plaster tumbled to the floor.

Phoebe raised the lamp again and gave it a lumberjack downswing. The divot became a dent, then on the next strike, the dent became a hole. She took a step forward and swung again, lower. The lamp, now bent, began destroying the wall on the far side of the vent.

Holgrave held up his hand to shield his face from flying debris, or possibly the lamp if Phoebe let it slip. Miscalculating on a downswing, Phoebe struck the heavy oak piano, giving the oak a gash on the back corner. The diverted lamp struck the vent square, denting it severely and bringing a corner of it away from the wall.

"That's it! Phoebe, stop!" Holgrave called.

Phoebe aborted her next swing, lowered the destroyed lamp to her side, and let it drop to the floor with a clang.

Holgrave went to the wrecked vent and pulled at the corner Phoebe had forced away. It came away without much further effort. He took his penlight and shined it into the hole, reached in with his other hand and pulled out the hidden object.

The item, a thin wooden box covered in dust, flipped open in his hand, letting dust and bits of paper fly. The box had once been latched closed, but rust had erased the mechanism from existence.

Holgrave grasped a handful of the tattered, flimsy paper, focusing his small light upon one of the largest remaining. He sighed heavily, and his shoulders slumped.

Phoebe looked from behind him. "Hey is that—?"

"It is," Holgrave confirmed frustratingly. "This debris appears to be what is left of the missing stock certificates of the Butterfield Overland Mail Company."

"Is that *all* of them?" she asked, though she kept her eyes on the door.

Hearing the urgency in Phoebe's voice, Holgrave sifted through the mess. He grimaced when he discovered mice feces rolling about the bottom of the box. He pulled a notepad from his sport coat pocket and flipped to a page.

Phoebe could see a list of a dozen or so numbers written on the notepaper and quickly deduced that he was checking serial numbers against the scraps they had uncovered. After a few moments, Holgrave shook his head despairingly.

"Are those the ones?" she asked.

"Sadly, yes," he answered and dropped the box to the floor. He stood and gave the oak piano a shove back into place.

"I'm sorry," Phoebe said. The breathing sound was becoming clearer to her, and she fought against the urge to sprint out of the house. She felt her car keys in her hoodie pocket.

Holgrave shrugged as he moved the credenza back into place. Together, they quickly put the couch and coffee table back where they had found them.

Phoebe stepped onto the porch with Holgrave just behind. He paused at the door, his hand on the knob as he gave the place a long look.

"To think I came all this way, spent all this time here," Holgrave said lowly, just loud enough for her to hear. "Just to find them turned to dust." With that, he pulled it shut and let the screen door spring back into place. The creaks sounded like laughter.

"Well, I'm getting the hell out of here," Phoebe said. She'd had enough. She bounded down the steps and went to his car, parked right outside the front door, where she pulled her bags and backpack from his back seat.

Holgrave joined her, taking a bag from her hand. She smiled and thanked him but spared no time making tracks to her Caprice. It was alongside the house, right where she had left it. She hadn't bothered locking it, so she pulled open the back door and tossed her things inside. Holgrave added her second plastic bag to the seat.

Phoebe shut the door. "Well, that's it, I guess," she said as she took one last look at the House of the Seven Gables.

"Indeed," said Holgrave, looking only at her. "I do find it a shame that we couldn't have met under more pleasant circumstances."

Phoebe met his eyes. "Indeed," she mocked playfully. She reached back and opened her door.

"Where are you off to next?" he asked.

"I don't know," she answered truthfully. "But I promise I'll pay you back."

Holgrave waved it off. "It was the least I could do. You've lost everything."

"I'm paying you back," she insisted and got behind the wheel. She rolled the window down and closed the door.

"You have my information," Holgrave said and offered his hand. She took it and smiled.

"Take care," she wished.

"You too," he said and stepped back.

With her car's starter problems in mind, she turned the key, half-expecting to hear the whining of the starter. There was not even that. A short series of clicks reported from beyond the dashboard, and then the lights went out.

"You have *got* to be fuckin' kidding me!" she shouted angrily. She punched the wheel and turned the key again. There was silence. Even the cry of the barely functioning starter would have been welcome, but it was not to be.

"Phoebe—" Holgrave began.

"*Rawk!*" came a familiar cry.

Holgrave and Phoebe frantically looked for the source of the sound, but they couldn't locate it. It was the call of the raven, both were sure of it.

Phoebe, near panic, cranked the key uselessly over and over but only received the same nonresponse from the Caprice. It was done.

"There!" Holgrave shouted.

Phoebe poked her head through the open window to follow his outstretched arm. Holgrave was pointing up to a gable of the attic suite.

The raven was there, staring down at them. Phoebe's first thought was that it was much larger than she remembered. Comparing the bird's height to the window beneath its perching place, it was close. The bird was immense, unless there was some sort of optical illusion happening. Phoebe discarded that thought. She no longer disbelieved in witchcraft, ghosts, and haunted houses.

"Come on," Holgrave blurted and pulled open her door.

Phoebe, having been leaning on it, nearly spilled out, but Holgrave steadied her. She got to her feet, staring at the impossibly enlarged black bird.

"*Rawk! Raaawk!*" it cried and spread its wings.

"Holy shit," she choked out.

"Get in my car. Go!" Holgrave ordered her. He pushed her shoulder to get her moving.

Phoebe took a look back at the dead Chevy, and seeing Holgrave yank out her belongings, she reached out in time to catch the bag he had launched at her. She sprinted to the Mercedes, not daring to give the raven another glance.

She heard footsteps behind her, thudding out a mad pace and passing her on the right. *Holgrave Maule's a track star!* she thought and pushed her legs harder.

Phoebe got into the car on the passenger side, keeping the bag pressed to her chest. Holgrave shoved her other bag over his driver's seat, following it up with her backpack, and dropped himself behind the wheel.

The raven landed on the open driver's door. Phoebe screamed, her eyes glued to the massive claws clenching it.

"Oh!" Holgrave uttered and tried to reach for the door handle. The bird's massive black beak plunged down and clamped onto his jacket sleeve, tearing a piece of it away. "Blasted bird!" Holgrave shouted.

Thinking quickly, Holgrave took his left leg and thrust it outside, giving the door panel a hard kick. The door swung out to its full extension and bounded back, slamming shut just as Holgrave brought his foot back inside. The raven leaped into the air to keep from getting its feet jammed.

Madly, Holgrave laughed as he turned the key and started the engine. He pulled the gear lever into reverse and punched the accelerator.

"Whoa!" Phoebe shouted and slid onto the floor. Her garbage bag of clothes mashed her in the face, saving it from the dashboard.

"Sorraaay!" Holgrave called as he craned his neck behind him to see where he was going. He spun the steering wheel to the left and let off the gas pedal, allowing the front end of the car to slide around. Its front wheels passed over the dirt and wisps of grass as Holgrave's right hand pulled the gear lever from reverse to neutral. Then, as the front of the car came back onto Gable Way, pointing west, he put the car in drive and sped away down the dirt pathway.

Phoebe climbed back into the seat, steadying herself against the door as the car went around the first turn. Immediately following was the right bend, so she grabbed on to keep from tumbling over the center console.

"Dude!" she called, watching as Holgrave took the right, fishtailing the back end of the Mercedes around it. The tires kicked fans of dirt into the air as they went.

"Sorray!"

Holgrave reached the main road and braked hard. Quickly looking right and left, he urged the car to the right, toward the main highway out of town. The tires, wet with dirt, spun the filth away until they screeched hotly against pavement. Holgrave let off the accelerator once it reached highway speed.

"Are you all right?" he asked once he found the interstate on-ramp.

"Yeah," she answered between breaths.

The pair remained silent for a long time, just driving west at speeds beyond the limit, but not so much as to gather attention from the police.

The hours passed with little conversation. Phoebe drifted to an uneven and light sleep. When she awoke, the sun was in her eyes. It was after five in the evening.

"Where are we?" she asked and rubbed her eyes.

"Almost into Chicago," he said.

A few more moments passed before she asked, "What do we do now?" It was something that had been on her mind since they hurried out of White Lake. She was a most unexpected passenger, and she knew not whether Holgrave regarded her as a burden or as a welcomed guest in his life. She swallowed as she waited upon his answer.

"I don't know," he said glumly, looking over at her. "Pizza?"

Phoebe's worry fell away in an instant, and she burst out laughing.

Holgrave joined in as he angled the Mercedes to the exit ramp leading downtown.

The raven perched on the porch of 666 Gable Way, biding its time. Perhaps contemplating his next meal. With the sun having marked the passing of most of the day, it leaped from the porch rail and settled upon the dirt road. It pecked at a worm and walked eastward, casually, lazily, until its gait lengthened into a stride.

Ahead, the carriage house lay, and its doors, unlatched, were swung open at the behest of a stiff breeze. Their hinges creaked and popped, but the doors did spread.

The form of the raven fell away in a dark cloud and stretched vertically, carried forward by legs that lengthened. Its steps became heavy footfalls as it approached the maroon Coupe De Ville.

The old Cadillac's engine turned over, clumsily at first, but with a feathering of the accelerator, its idle smoothed into a gentle rumble.

The raven was no more, and a hand settled upon the old car's door handle. Panas slid behind the wheel and sat a moment before bringing his legs in and pulling the door shut. He concentrated on his path, the road to take him away from the place he hoped one day to return to.

The Coupe De Ville rolled out of the carriage house and along Gable Way. Without pausing, the car turned right onto the black-topped road heading out of town.

Dani Lamia Collection

(Elevated Horror and Supernatural Thrillers)

ISBN: 978-1-933769-70-7

In a world where dreams and reality overlap, when a dream world stalker begins killing her tormentors, a bullied high schooler must stop The Raven's deadly attacks on her behalf.

ISBN: 978-1-933769-68-4

When an idealistic priest learns, in the confessional, that a psychopath is murdering locals, he must find a way to stop her, without giving up everything he believes in.

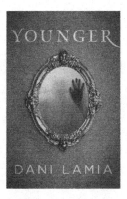

ISBN: 978-1-933769-64-6

When the spirit of a vampire is unleashed during a séance, a resident finds herself growing more youthful even as her friends rapidly age. She must find a way to stop the process before everyone she loves is dead.

ISBN: 978-1-933769-60-8

When a struggling film director chooses a haunted bed and breakfast for the location of his next film, the darkness within him turns the otherwise peaceful spirits into a nightmarish reckoning for him and his crew.

ISBN: 978-1-64630-004-4

In a world of wealth and power, siblings feuding over the estate of their recently deceased father are sent on a scavenger hunt with the family fortune as the prize. But things turn deadly as long-buried secrets are revealed and it becomes clear that only the winner will survive.